The Age of Goodbyes

LI ZI SHU

Translated by YZ CHIN

THE FEMINIST PRESS
AT THE CITY UNIVERSITY OF NEW YORK
NEW YORK CITY

Published in 2022 by the Feminist Press
at the City University of New York
The Graduate Center
365 Fifth Avenue, Suite 5406
New York, NY 10016

feministpress.org

First Feminist Press edition 2022

告別的年代 copyright © 2010 by Li Zi Shu
English translation copyright © 2022 by YZ Chin

Originally published in Taiwan in 2010 by Linking Publishing Co.

First printing November 2022

Cover design by Dana Li
Text design by Frances Ross

Library of Congress Cataloging-in-Publication Data
Names: Li, Zishu, 1971- author. | Chin, YZ, translator.
Title: The age of goodbyes / Li Zi Shu ; translated by YZ Chin.
Other titles: Gao bie de nian dai. English
Description: First Feminist Press edition. | New York, NY : Feminist Press,
    2022.
Identifiers: LCCN 2022026329 (print) | LCCN 2022026330 (ebook) | ISBN
    9781952177699 (paperback) | ISBN 9781952177712 (ebook)
Subjects: LCGFT: Novels.
Classification: LCC PL2946.Z47 G3613 2022 (print) | LCC PL2946.Z47
    (ebook) | DDC 895.13/52--dc23/eng/20220603
LC record available at https://lccn.loc.gov/2022026329
LC ebook record available at https://lccn.loc.gov/2022026330

PRINTED IN THE UNITED STATES OF AMERICA

Praise for *The Age of Goodbyes*

"*The Age of Goodbyes* is a sprawling Southeast Asian epic featuring kopitiams, mosquito coils, and serialized television dramas; a sequence of not-quite-love stories that ache with longing; and an utterly self-conscious commentary on the limits of narratives. Centering the lives of women often relegated to the margins of history, Li Zi Shu has written a trancelike, poetic meditation on intergenerational trauma, rooted in the literary tradition of Chinese-language novels but infused with a García Márquez–like magical realism. It takes a master to pull off a work this ambitious, and Li does so without any of the seams showing. I love this book both as a reader and writer."

— KAREN CHEUNG, author of
The Impossible City: A Hong Kong Memoir

"Weaving together magical realism, surrealism, and political realism, *The Age of Goodbyes* narrates a history with no name, silenced memories of racial violence, social injustice, and civil rights repressions. Li Zi Shu—brilliantly translated by YZ Chin—shines the light of justice for minority communities pressed into erasure with her fabulist, agonistic, and ever-playful vision."

— SHIRLEY GEOK-LIN LIM, author of
Among the White Moon Faces:
An Asian-American Memoir of Homelands

"A multidimensional hall of mirrors that demands to be explored more than once, *The Age of Goodbyes* packs an emotional punch that you won't see coming. YZ Chin's vivacious translation perfectly complements Li Zi Shu's heightened sensibility."

— JEREMY TIANG, author of *State of Emergency*

"*The Age of Goodbyes* is a colossal feat of storytelling. Like stones thrown into a pond, its many narratives unsettle the surface. The pleasure in reading the novel is in waiting for them to touch bottom and stir up all that's resting there."

— JEANNIE VANASCO, author of *Things We*
Didn't Talk about When I Was a Girl: A Memoir

You're reading this book, which is a novel. The author brings up "writing such a magnum opus" in the afterword. "Magnum opus" is a word choice worth scrutinizing, since you've rarely seen any novelist describe their own work with such a term. The term rightfully belongs to the domain of literary critics, and is more suited for a foreword or introduction. Coming from the author, it produces an impression of arrogance bordering on a faux pas.

If you had to guess, you'd say the writer of this book is either a small-time hack with delusions of grandeur or else a bookish academic with not insignificant accomplishments under their belt. Both types would tend toward self-aggrandizement and be a little in thrall to themselves. At the very least they would cling closely to their own opinions.

But you have no idea how to verify your hypothesis, because this is an incomplete book. Maybe it's also an incomplete novel. It was already in this partial state when you stumbled upon it—hardcover, with nothing amiss at first glance, its rust-green cover bearing only the characters "The Age of Goodbyes" stamped in gold. Though the book looks ancient, its pages damp and yellowed, there is almost no sign it has ever been flipped through. Furthermore, the book releases a pungent inky smell when opened, as if it had been placed there hot off the press, causing it to retain that fresh scent unique to new books.

This book has no title page. You are a little skeptical of your own eyes, and so you turn the pages back and forth in search of it. But there really isn't a title page, and what's more, there is no copyright page, and no publisher is indicated. Not even the author's name can be found. Most curiously, its page numbers start at 513, as if this book's first page is actually the novel's five hundred and thirteenth page . . .

This is so odd that it attracts your attention. A book that starts from page 513. You can't help but squat down and start reading:

In 1969, Chan Kam Hoi suffered a sudden heart attack while viewing the film Floozy's Allures. *Although at the time Old Majestic Cinema was packed to the rafters, the audience was captivated by the film, and as a result no one was aware of Mister Chan's condition. Due to lack of timely medical attention, Mister Chan ultimately perished on the scene. This development became well known around town and caused rather a sensation.*

These are the first sentences in *The Age of Goodbyes*. The description is exceedingly bland. You think it fits the bill of an opening paragraph, yet it could also very well be a random passage lifted from something much longer.

At that time, you hadn't yet realized that this is a novel. Those damn bland words, they read almost like a snippet from some obscure column in the discontinued *Southern Screen* magazine. You recognize this particular writing style and effect. The language has a rotten tinge of days gone by, being thoroughly saturated with the tropical flavors of Nanyang as well as the salacious scandals of its migrants. This style of writing still appears occasionally in some weekly or other, since it's especially well equipped to relay the old tales of a mining town and reminisce about long-dead public figures. It is also used to relate sensational tales of yore, or subtly implicate town residents for old entanglements and love affairs.

You'd always assumed this was a disappearing language, one suited to the biographies of those from your grandfather's generation. Therefore when you first read this ambiguous "introduction," you very naturally chalk this book up as one of those annals self-published many years ago by some clan association (it could be the Chen Clan Association, or the Hakka Guild). Very possibly it was done to commemorate one of its leaders' prominent family, penned by an association member who wore black-framed glasses and had a way with words (and who happened to be a veteran newspaper reporter). They spun a grandiose yarn, starting with "Chan Kam Hoi, of Dabu county in Canton province, born 1930, died 1969 . . ."

If it were really that kind of commemorative journal, then the identity of the author has no investigative value. You can just imagine this man, now well in his twilight years. If he didn't have Alzheimer's, then he'd very likely still be a correspondent at some tabloid, or maybe he'd have his own column, tasked with writing risqué gossip surrounding former government officials or with capturing plain old nostalgia.

That said, a book that starts on page 513 still seems bizarre. Could it be a technical printing error? You can't help but flip to the book's very last page.

 . . . *After overcoming diverse obstacles, Du Li An finally found success in securing an eatery. The remodeled restaurant was launched after the Mid-Autumn*

Festival. The next year Du Li An's sister-in-law was blessed with her eldest daughter, Emily, whose one-month birthday was celebrated with a reception at the afore-mentioned restaurant. Eighty-eight tables were set out for the dinner reception, which was attended by numer-ous exalted guests and celebrity figures.

What a baffling way to end a book. The narrative, still bland, could pass as an ending, but also leaves room for more. The phrase "eldest daughter, Emily" has the effect of "to be continued." You feel as if the author suddenly became bored and fed up with the never-ending narra-tive, abruptly tossed their pen aside, and allowed their generation-spanning family story to screech to a halt. Although they also hint at the ongoing personal rela-tionships and plot development still to come through the phrase "eldest daughter, Emily."

This is a book you found in the library. It sat heavy like a brick, left on a bookshelf in some corner of the building. That shelf, labeled "Other," is wedged next to one dedicated to "History/Biography."

The categorization of books in the library is very precise. This, in combination with the librarians' atten-tion to detail and commitment to their mission, means that an appropriate spot can be found for almost every book. Within such a place, to be categorized as "Other" is to be exiled. You believe the books on that shelf went through many attempts at identification. Maybe the librarians even held meetings to discuss these books, but in the end they came to the conclusion that their contents were too ambiguous, impossible to pin down. After that, they unanimously agreed to let the books languish on this five-level metal bookshelf.

Then again, this is clearly a book that has never been read. The ink used during printing has almost glued the pages together, evidence that the book has long been sealed shut. Its fate of exile was decided before it was ever opened.

The shelf housing "Other" books is in the most remote room at one end of the library. The tiny room is a refuge for old and damaged volumes, as well as a repository for quite a number of titles that haven't been checked out or requested in many years. In contrast, there aren't that many books on the "Other" shelf. The one titled *The Age of Goodbyes* in your grasp is placed not only on the lowest shelf but also closest to the wall, as if buried deep in the folds of time. For genera tions, spiders bred there, thriving, then dying; a wasp defended the spot with its stinger until its very last breath, its body long since gnawed hollow. That particular corner attracts the most dust and is also the easiest to forget or overlook.

But now you feel that it has silently held its position all this time, perhaps so that it would one day be discovered by you.

CHAPTER ONE

—1—

Du Li An knew from the start that this is a novel. Yes, a novel and not an annal. That was why she didn't take it as seriously as you have. Not to mention that when she laid her hands on this book, it hadn't yet seemed so hefty. She put down the book when she got to the third paragraph of page 513 and said to her mother, who was keeping up a stream of complaints about the tropical weather, "All right already, stop fussing, I'm reading a novel." She was referencing this very book, *The Age of Goodbyes*.

This is the first Du Li An to appear in the novel. Then again, it might not be entirely accurate to say so, as you have after all picked up a book that starts on page 513. We do know that the anonymous author has a particular penchant for the name "Du Li An," having created various versions of Du Li An across different ages and having used other names of similar meaning. But we have no sure method of determining whether any Du Li Ans appeared, unbeknownst to us, in the previous missing 512 pages.

In fact, we have no way of verifying the existence of those 512 pages.

If this is a novel, beginning the book on page 513 might be an odd writing technique to convey certain information. Being a born-and-bred local, you have some inkling of the possible meanings and implications behind the number 513, despite your youth. Years ago, during the nation's general elections, the National Front coalition that had always dominated Malaysian politics lost its two-thirds parliament seat advantage. On May Thirteenth, the opposition alliance held celebratory parades in major cities, which led to unexpected riots, arson, and bloodshed. The government announced a state of emergency and implemented nationwide curfews for four days.

You remember the number 513 used to be taboo. Even many years after the incident, people habitually lowered their voices when bringing up this sequence of digits. They used a kind of sound hemmed in the throat, advancing no farther than the nose, to "speak" these numbers. They were always accompanied by mysterious glances and meaningful gestures that you found disconcerting. So much so that your heart races every time you open this book and see the number on the first page's bottom-right corner. You think the missing 512 pages hint at a void, the prohibited, and carry within them a quality of challenge, accusation, or the unspeakable.

On the very day of May Thirteenth, Du Li An sat at her mother's noodle cart reading a novel. Her mother, name unknown, traced her roots back to Guilin in Guangxi. Everyone in the neighborhood called her either Sou Gei or Fried Noodle Lady.

Sunlight permed the hair of trees lined up on the equator. Steam rose from the asphalt roads. A dog that was run over last night grilled on the road like a laobing.

Chan Kam Hoi had died just two days before. On the third day that *Floozy's Allures* played in this mining town, a life was lost inside the cinema. Crowds stood under telephone poles plastered with election ads and spread the news. And Chan Kam Hoi himself smiled from the posters on the telephone poles, as if denying with practiced charm a little gossip that reflected poorly on him.

So it was that the boss of Kam Hoi Hardware Store died in the front row seat of the cinema's balcony, right on the eve of elections. It was a swell seat. From it, the blond floozy's red lips and buxom chest filled one's eyes, took one's breath away. Maybe Chan Kam Hoi did die that way, of asphyxiation. *Floozy's Allures*, which a mere few days ago had drawn a large audience, was immediately branded a lethal program. The bumbling cinema management invited a Taoist priest into the cinema, clad in yellow robes, to chant nonsense, rattle bells, wave swords, fast, and perform rituals. Naturally, rumors of the cinema being haunted spread like wildfire. The Old Majestic's box office clerks twiddled their thumbs at their counters for a good long while after that.

Every afternoon Du Li An went to work at Old Majestic, selling tickets for the 5:00, 7:00, 9:00, and weekend midnight shows. During the day she had to help Sou Gei prepare various fried noodles, tong sui, yam cakes, fried yam dumplings, fried dough patties, etc. Then they'd load up a tricycle that had been modded to fit a cart and an awning. They biked the cart to Main Street before noon, in time to catch the employees from the shops on both sides of the street on their lunch breaks.

Scrawny Sou Gei would arch her back, mustering the strength to pedal her tricycle. All along the street she'd squeeze the little trumpet installed on the handlebars, making it go "bo bo, bo bo." In time to that rhythm she'd yell out, "Fried noodles——, tong sui——" Her voice was familiar to everyone. Even though it'd been many years since she'd moved to town, her Cantonese still had a Guangxi accent, inherited at birth and infused with the native whiff of rubber plantations. Along with her buck teeth, her accent was her hallmark, always reminding you of her humble beginnings.

People would soon forget Sou Gei. After all, during that time women like her were a dime a dozen—clad in matching floral-print tops and pants, broad-brimmed straw hats on their heads. They had washboard bosoms and broomstick waists, their entire bodies hard as rocks. As they worked, they complained in accented Cantonese about extreme weather, compulsive gambler husbands, unmarried daughters, or good-for-nothing sons.

The novelist, too, clearly forgot about Sou Gei very quickly. Their eyes were glued on Du Li An, just then in her prime. Of course Du Li An was aware of the gaze. Her expression was lively as she aimed a smile at the camera lenses perched in her consciousness. Hoo boy, this was as captivating as Li Li-hua in the movie magazines. *Stare to your heart's content, dork.* Du Li An produced an even more enchanting smile, and the novelist couldn't help but describe it as "arousing." Too bad that Sou Gei's bellyaching was so disruptive, her whining spewing forth without end like the greedy flies that hovered above the yam cakes, or like the punctuation marks rampant among the text, lingering between the words.

"All right already, stop fussing, I'm reading a novel," Du Li An huffed in exasperation, putting down the book in her hands.

It was the very first novel she had ever read in her life. The book was very heavy, its pages packed with words like a million ants lined up in neat formation. Before this she'd perused only idol magazines and comic books illustrating folk tales from China. That's why reading this "magnum opus" was so laborious to her. She closed the book and raised her head to stare at the election ads on a telephone pole. Look, Chan Kam Hoi was smiling at her. His likeness, printed over the hulking characters "In Service of the People," seemed to politely refute his own death. In Du Li An's opinion, the man's eyes were dishonest, as if even in death he let them dawdle on her breasts. Scoundrel.

Speaking of Chan Kam Hoi, he had very little hair and very many years behind him. Perhaps due to his nightly dose of medicinal wine or his regular diet of game meat, his face was always glowing. He loved to turn a semi-amused, half-drunk expression on others. Du Li An shuddered under his gaze, but Guen Hou, the woman who used to peddle snacks and packaged Western drinks by the cinema entrance, found her stomach swell up when he leered at her. In the end it was arranged for her to move into one of the innumerable houses in Mi Shan New Village, "new village" being of course a euphemism for a former detention camp. Thus began a break from her life making ends meet on the streets.

It was said that when Chan Kam Hoi was lifted into the black hearse a few days ago, Du Li An snuck glances from the advantageous height of the counter at which she sat. Audiences from two showings of *Floozy's Allures* packed the cinema's foyer like sardines, everyone making a fuss and shrieking, Oh, it's him, it's Chan Kam Hoi.

"But look what day it is, isn't he a candidate for state assemblyman? What's he doing watching a movie here instead of canvassing out there?"

None of your business now, what do you all know? Lying on the stretcher, Chan Kam Hoi fixed his eyelids at half-mast, his lips slightly curled at the corners in his usual semi-amused, inscrutable expression. As if he had the utmost confidence in the election outcomes the following day, or as if his abrupt death while watching *Floozy's Allures*, on election eve was part of his campaign strategy. Or maybe he was following orders passed down by party leaders, to affect a kind of opinion poll.

Du Li An could scarcely believe that merely an hour ago the man had been grinning and saying to her, Ah Li, you're so pretty, you're even more beautiful than Fanny Fan Lai.

Fanny Fan? Pshaw! Du Li An subconsciously looked down at her chest, checking to see whether she had popped a button. Men, dirty men! They all flocked to the big-titted. She remembered that when *Summons to Death* and *The Golden Buddha* were showing, the cinema became filthy with smoke and grime, filled with miners, construction workers, draymen, cooks, and funeral home workers rubbing shoulders with bosses from all kinds of industries as well as various politicians. Even her own dad asked her to set aside a few tickets so he could swagger in for a bit of the action with some of his gambling buddies.

What was so special about Fanny Fan? All she had going for her was a bit more meat on her chest and a bit less fabric on her body. Men lost control when they saw her exposed flesh. They got going like wound-up gears. She remembered her dad rushed home after the midnight showing to embrace his wife. In the next room, Du Li An and her brother could feel the floor quaking, could hear Sou Gei's mutterings, sounding out a teeth-chattering string of cusses.

"Don't you damn well dare, oh, you. Don't you damn well dare."

Overhead, a dim moon hung in the tin mining town's sky like an oil lamp with a soot-darkened shade. By the weak light coming through the window, Du Li An glanced at her younger brother lying on the floor. All around her, the air was suffused with the musk of mosquito coil. Sou Gei ground her teeth and the floorboards shuddered. Out on the street, someone trundled past pushing a tricycle selling glass noodle soup.

Du Li An's brother was fourteen or fifteen. He'd done poorly at school and had dropped out early. Since then, he'd worked odd jobs at a restaurant called Wa Zai, where he had recently been promoted to kitchen helper. *The Age of Goodbyes* does not mention his name. Du Li An and her parents simply called him Ah Sai.

After looking into it later on, you discover that by the tail end of the twentieth century, the name Ah Sai had taken on a whole new meaning within the distinctive Cantonese that had evolved in isolation within the small town. In the tin mining town's dictionary, the moniker means "boss," deployed strictly in face-to-face situations. At the turn of the century, Ah Sai had almost entirely replaced other equivalent naming conventions popular in town, such as "boss," "proprietor," or "shopkeeper." Henceforth, people would hear frequent cries of Ah Sai all over town, especially in coffee shops otherwise known as kopitiams.

On the day of May Thirteenth, Du Li An saw Ah Sai head toward the bridge on Old Street. He was on the back seat of someone's bicycle, and he waved at her. Du Li An knew from the way he was dressed and from the racquet hanging off his back that he was going to play badminton yet again. To represent the country as a badminton player had always been Ah Sai's dream, though he wasn't quite sure what it took to become a national athlete. He and Du Li An both thought that as long as he played at the badminton court every day, he would one day be discovered by a talent scout like one of those diamond-in-the-rough movie stars.

Watching her brother's figure blur with sunlight and disappear over the bridge, Du Li An had no inkling that the day would become so unusual. For the past few days, the small town's streets had bustled with a liveliness akin to holiday celebrations. The elections had just happened, and the town's men were still immersed in the heightened excitement brought on by the results, candidate Chan Kam Hoi's sudden death, and the end of *Floozy's Allures'* run. They sat grinning in kopitiams, their voices extra loud and their gestures especially exaggerated. People handed each other cigarettes and fought among themselves to serve tea. From time to time they erupted into boisterous laughter, or else they ran their mouths and spewed filthy swear words, though their attitudes remained friendly.

Later, whenever Du Li An's mind flashed back to that day, she thought the scene was so joyous it seemed P. Ramlee would hop out at any moment a la Charlie Chaplin. That image, so cinematic, in reality carried a premonition of disaster.

Du Li An helped Sou Gei move her cart after it had been parked for two hours on Main Street. They pushed the stall to a lane populated with dry goods stores that sat near the old plaza, hurrying so that they could make the 3:15 p.m. afternoon tea break. All day long the salty scent of dried shrimp and the sweet fragrance of coffee floated through the lane, which was full of various upscale and established businesses. Chan Kam Hoi's hardware store was located right on the corner, three shopfronts merged into one. That day the hardware store's shutters were drawn. On the shutters, the deceased Chan Kam Hoi's campaign posters formed a neat line, though most of them were torn, leaving all of the Chan Kam Hois bruised and broken. Sidestepping propriety, a speaker from the Western goods store next door blasted an upbeat, obscene tune.

Handsome guy of the finest kind,
handsome guy you've triggered my mind . . .
Oh so handsome, oh so fine . . .
My entire soul is hooked on you . . .

The lane bustled as trucks were unloaded. The workers' sweat left light-red stains like candle wax on the bulging hemp bags. Those receiving stock issued commands on the five-foot way, while a trishaw driver exerted himself against his pedals, exposing a mouthful of nicotine-stained teeth. The trishaw moved at a snail's pace. An opulent-looking hand extended from under the grayish-black canopy, fluttering a folding fan.

Like all other days, the hot air carried a faint odor of animal corpses being grilled.

The lane backed onto Pei Hwa Primary School. Every afternoon between three and four, the teachers who didn't have class scheduled flocked out. They emerged from a fire lane set among a row of shops, in search of a plate of noodles or a bowl of red bean paste. Du Li An kept her eyes fixed on the people coming out of the school. Every time she glimpsed a lanky figure dressed in shirt and slacks, she either nervously turned around to fuss over something, or she opened that hefty book in a hurry, pretending to examine the army of ants in the book with focused diligence.

After a long wait, the beanstalk named Yip Lin Sang finally emerged from the narrow lane's slanted shadows. Du Li An's heart leapt with joy. It was like a mouse-deer was thumping erratically in her chest, putting her at a loss. For some reason Du Li An was most timid in front of scholars. These bespectacled, polite people spoke like hosts on the radio, every sentence glittering with five-dollar words. That, combined with the earnest expressions on their faces, made her nod along even though she couldn't understand a word. Du Li An was passably eloquent, since she interacted with a fair number of people daily. Even when silver-tongued men like Chan Kam Hoi tried to take advantage of her, she was able to handle them with ease. Yet for some reason, every time she saw Yip Lin Sang she became tongue-tied and at a loss for words.

You jot down the name "Yip Lin Sang" in a notebook. In the novel, his ancestors are from Panyu of Guangdong province. About six months ago, he was transferred from Batu Gajah to the tin mining town's Pei Hwa Primary School. His skin is slightly dark, and he has a mouth of good teeth. He is not nearsighted despite being an ivory-tower type, and even has a very intimate way of looking at people, as if he's looking at children. His brows are especially eye-catching, like two swords. No wonder Du Li An fancies this person. You have a good feeling about him too. Yip Lin Sang, what a strange name. His twin brother, named Yip Mong Sang, won't be revealed until later. You like him as well.

—2—

You hug the hefty book to your chest and bring it back to Mayflower. On your way upstairs you run into Uncle Sai, who is heading out the door. As he lights a cigarette, he tells you that a friend has died. He has to attend the wake and might be back late. You mumble an acknowledgment and slide sideways past him, paying no attention to who exactly has died. The third floor of Mayflower is saturated with the smell of cigarettes.

Every room seems to be occupied by lingering ghosts and filled with otherworldly noises and odors. As if possessed, the stair's wooden steps moan before a foot is even placed on them. All the doors have rusty hinges and protest whenever they are pushed or pulled. The taps in the bathrooms can never be turned quite tight enough and produce drips like Time's unceasing dance. The air is so damp that clothes have to be put out on the balcony to dry.

You can still vaguely hear Uncle Sai's footsteps even after you close the door of room 301. He walks to the bottom of the stairs, pushes open the iron gate, then pulls it shut. You turn on the lights and open your book at the desk. The fluorescent lamp starts up as if it's housing a lonely cicada. Ever since your return it's been clamoring in a monotone, making sounds that are first like agonized complaints, then like Buddhist prayers chanted for eternity. The lamp has acted up ever since Mother died. But you're so used to it now that you haven't noticed the lamp's longstanding fantasy concerning cicadas.

Under the lamp's cold, pale light, you spread open the book and read closely, taking notes as you go. The book's inky scent, thick and fresh, disperses slowly in room 301. You think it must be similar in taste to opium or some other numbing drug. The scent twirls graceful as a snake, tunnels slowly into your nose. Once it hits your bloodstream, it makes you hallucinate. You see the ants on the pages move and change formation. Or maybe they're stealthily trading positions. You feel your eyelids sink heavier and heavier. In that last moment before you finally flop down on the book, you almost make out Du Li An, Ah Sai, and Yip Lin Sang.

When you awake, you find yourself on the bed. It is where Mother swallowed her last breath. Although you discarded her mattress for a brand-new one, you can still feel, on the bed under you, the shape hollowed out by Mother while she lay dying. You lie supine in this trench of death. It's like reclining in a giant wok that was used to cook someone to death. Right before she passed, Mother kept saying she wanted very much to eat some meat. So you went to the Indian restaurant at the end of the street and bought some mutton curry. The stench of it still permeates the room. She devoured it in a sloppy hurry. Bits of curry dripped from the corners of her mouth, stained her thighs. Once satiated, she sat up on the bed with her legs stuck straight out, the whites of her eyes showing slightly. But you knew she was looking at you, gazing upon you tenderly like a spirit peering through a medium. You could not see the eyes within her eyes, but you intuited a sense of goodbye. I've been satisfied with my life on earth, and I have no more asks. What about you? Um, did you go to the library today? Did you find your father?

That stench still persists, standing in as a kind of teasing. "Find your father?" As if she's hidden him, and all of this is simply a prank she designed when she opened her legs and went into labor. You were destined since birth to play this game. Mother always loved enticing you with the various toys that she bought for you and then immediately hid. But even at a young age you vaguely understood that there was something fishy going on, that sometimes the toys Mother mentioned did not actually exist. She said, Stop bothering me, I bought a laser gun for you this morning. Go find it.

"What kind of laser gun?" You let go of her sleeve.
"A blue gun that shoots flashing red lights."
"Does it make sounds?"
"Sure does. A rat-tat-tat like a machine gun."
That gun was among the objects you could never

find, even after you thoroughly ransacked all three floors of Mayflower. The kitchen and counter on the bottom floor, including that locked drawer, plus the rattan chair and footrest in the little hall; the five rooms and bathroom on the second floor; rooms 301 and 305 on the third floor. You moved aside the calendar and paintings on the walls, opened the wardrobes that smelled of mothballs, and even knelt on the floor to peer under the bed. You opened the suitcase Mother placed there and dug out everything inside. There was a shimmering blue gown and a chipped trophy that you'd won, but no laser gun. For a whole week you kept searching for the gun Mother mentioned, until you had no choice but to doubt its existence. When you sought confirmation from her, she lifted her chin and raised her brows, peered at you out of the corner of her eye with a victor's expression. Ahaha, so you can't find it.

The laser gun wasn't the only thing you never found. From that day on, Mother kept describing numerous things you'd never seen. A watch with a round face featuring a circle of roman numerals; a pair of tennis shoes with silver laces; an English-Chinese dictionary said by teachers to be a "must-have." If it wasn't for the fact that you often really did find the presents she'd told you about—a whole box of marbles, a Power Rangers pencil case, a pair of new canvas shoes and two pairs of white socks, a Rubik's cube, a two-thousand-piece jigsaw puzzle, a new book bag, a cell phone—you might have long gotten sick of these treasure hunts. You've turned Mayflower inside out countless times. You became familiar with its every corner, and you know better than anyone where everything is located. Mother, in her shrewdness, never hid something in the same place twice. You even discovered her penchant for secretly alternating the position of objects, such as moving a nail clipper from the dresser on the left side of the bed to the dresser on the right. Or she might take a pocket radio from the first drawer and put it into the drawer directly underneath.

You suspect Mother did all these things for no reason other than to disrupt your mind and muddy your memories, thereby making it harder for you to find anything. Mayflower started with ten rooms that were decked out in almost identical fashion. The patrons left behind various odors that blended well together, such as nicotine, sweat, the lubricant from condoms, and the occasional alcohol or vomit. These smells make it so every room seems to be fashioned from the same template, like ten old downtrodden sex workers, so amazingly similar to each other that they are hard to tell apart. You have seen such sex workers. The swollen bags under their eyes lift up empty stares; their cheeks sag precariously, dragging the corners of their mouths downward. When you walk near them, you catch a whiff of mold emanating from their deepest, most private parts.

But Mother never provided an explanation for her behavior. She's dead, what more is there to say. At the end all she uttered was directed at the ceiling: "All the days of my life, forever." The line sounded almost like song lyrics. She left behind so much uncertainty. Her habit of hiding things and sneakily altering the environment turned Mayflower into a motel of perplexing mystery. So much so that, long after her death, you still suspect Mayflower is pettily swapping assorted things around. As if Mother is still alive and has returned, only this time she has hidden herself, playing a different kind of hide-and-seek with you.

Of course Mother would never let this kind of game come to an end. She never tired of it, such that whenever you go on a hunt you cannot help thinking about her. Sometimes you curse her: Mama. On her death bed, she described to you the "thing" she'd kept hidden the longest in her entire life. She knew you knew of its existence but were too afraid to ask.

"Haven't you always wanted to know about your father?"

You turned around to face her. She lay on the bed, smugly jiggling her leg, looking as she always did when she crossed her legs and threw you yet another riddle.

Father. Where could she be hiding him? You both understood that this would be your last battle of wits. You stared at her for a long time, hoping to see the eyes sunken within her eyes, eyes like marbles that have rolled into the depths of murky waters. *Oh, Mother, you thought of everything.* She expanded the search area, which led you to sweep the library. You were in a mild state of disbelief that Mother would ever utter such a word as *library*. She said you must first locate the oldest library in this city, which can be found in one of its most remote corners.

"He used to spend all day holed up in there, researching and writing a book."

"What kind of book?"

"No clue." Mother closed her eyes as if trying to remember, or as if doing her very best to come up with a good lie. "He said it was an exceptional masterpiece."

"He's an author?" The word felt clumsy in your mouth. Only when the word tumbled out did you get the sense that it must be a profession that could not possibly exist. Or maybe the feeling arose from the fact that the word brought to mind an outdated phrase in a written language lost to time. Exactly like the word *father*—you didn't realize the word was taboo until you uttered it out loud.

Mother made no reply at the time. You let it go. You

had to carefully protect this willingness to talk, which was as fragile as spider silk. She was someone whose enthusiasm quickly fizzled out. On the flip side, she was easy to please. She also liked teasing others to get their attention, though at the same time she seemed afraid of entanglement. She simply left as she pleased. You remember that at the very last she merely let out a burp, giving back to this world a room full of the smell of mutton curry.

She fulfilled her cherished wish. Human lives are after all long and dragged out; she was able to die at a moment of satiation and no regrets, maybe even of minor victory. Her eyelids were not all the way shut, just like they never were when she slept. It was as if she were spying on your reaction after mocking you. *Hey, I'm dead, what of it?* You exhibited the utmost calmness in response. Slowly, you turned around and continued burying yourself in that day's homework. In the evening Uncle Sai returned with dinner. You put down your pen to listen. Downstairs, the sound of the iron gate being pushed open, then pulled shut. The footsteps followed reliably, from faint to loud. You counted in your head. In about forty-three steps, he would arrive in front of room 301. Knock knock.

This is what you like about Uncle Sai. He comprehends the kind of dignified distance concealed within the sound of knocking. Mother usually never knocked. When she did, it was to throw you off by mimicking Uncle Sai. This simple trick never fooled you, of course. What she didn't know was that before the two raps on the door, there had to be forty-three male footfalls. Even if she knew, it wasn't something that she could mimic.

You opened the door and told Uncle Sai that Mother "seems to have" died. To your astonishment, he did not appear surprised. He unhurriedly handed the takeout boxes to you. "Well, see if you can finish both of those." Then he walked to the bed and stood over it with both hands crossed behind his back. He never reached out to touch her, as if he were standing in an exhibition hall checking out an off-limits mummy. He shouted for her, shouted her name. Then he waited in silence for a while, like he was waiting for his own voice to drift back from the underworld. "Yup, your ma is dead," he said while nodding, sounding very firm. You noticed that he said, "your ma" and not "she," like he wanted to cut off all ties; this was no longer a woman you both shared. He'd returned her to you.

Uncle Sai tiptoed out as if worried he would wake Mother up. Standing just outside the room, he dug out a cell phone and made a few calls. While he haggled with people over the phone, you sat down to eat dinner. When you were almost through with your portion, Uncle Sai swiveled his head to say, It's done, 5,500 ringgit; they'll be here tomorrow morning.

Mother's wake lasted one night at the funeral home. There was no fasting, and no one shed a tear. Uncle Sai found a bunch of folks from the Buddhist Association to say some hasty prayers. The few old sex workers who pop in and out of Mayflower came for a spell too. You followed Uncle Sai's instructions and patiently fed the paper money in your hands to the fire, one by one. When someone from the funeral home asked whether you had anything you wanted buried with the deceased, you shook your head, but Uncle Sai took out an unopened carton of cigarettes from his shirt pocket. "This is for her."

The funeral home worker placed the cigarettes between mother's hands. When the sex workers saw this, they too produced the cigarettes they carried. Half a pack or a few sticks, they all got tossed into the coffin.

Time passed in a blink because you had a task that kept you busy. It wasn't until the entire mountain of paper money was burned to ash, and not till those who came to pay their respects left for supper in the dead of night, that you slowly descended into the depths of loneliness. Mother was gone, and that was it. You walked to the coffin. Through the viewing window, you looked at the way she seemed to be holding her breath. Her eyes remained a little open, as if to say, Shh, don't tell the others I'm here. Go now, go find that laser gun.

She was a strange mother, one who had always treated you like a playmate. You thought it might be because she never wanted to grow old, and so she intentionally ignored your maturation. Ma. You wanted to caress her, but what you touched was only a piece of framed glass. From that unfathomable distance, a vague smile seemed to surface on Mother's face, still smug and unspeakably mysterious, like a queen on a poker card.

The next day, after all the ceremonies were completed, you took a trip to the other end of the city by bus, transferring once. Just as you had a few years ago, you walked a short distance after getting off the bus to reach an all-boys English school. There you stood at an inconspicuous corner and waited for the students to flock out of the gates after school. The sun beat fiercely down, and the last bell didn't ring. The many parents waiting for their kids kept checking their watches. Unlike them, you had unparalleled patience. You were no longer prey to the restlessness that had seized you when you straddled childhood and teenagehood. Even though a lot of time had passed, you still believed that you could pick him out with one glance. Him, your J. In truth, you had already caught sight of his mother, that plump, rich-looking woman, sitting in a brand-new car that looked like it had been driven there straight from the factory. Maybe she was listening to music. Her face was gentle, bearing light traces of a smile.

—3—

Another Du Li An appears in the second half of the novel. From a quick scan, you grasp that the writer's intention is to prop up this particular Du Li An as the author of *The Age of Goodbyes*. This confuses you. The feeling that arises is akin to wandering down a winding hallway and opening all its doors, none of which look like the others. And in the end you find yourself back where you started, or at least it's a place that greatly resembles where you started.

Perhaps to distinguish herself from the previous Du Li An, the later Du Li An gives herself a pen name, "Shaozi," an obscure reference to the *nephelium chryseum* plant, a close relative of the rambutan. In the book, Shaozi is an amateur writer *who devotes her life to composing the myths of womanhood.*[1] When it comes to this Du Li An's life story, the author does an about-face on the preceding writing tone and style, intermingling novelistic narration with descriptive traits of biography, while also throwing some essayist qualities into the mix. The word choices are odd as well, half-academic and half-colloquial. You almost wonder if there's more than one writer involved.

Even from a hasty flip through, you are shocked by much of the book. To you, the book is either a jumbled pastiche or very likely a deep, difficult, and complex

1. Excerpted from "The Immortal Du Li An—Myths of Womanhood Woven by Shaozi" (author's name anonymized as "The Fourth Person"), published in 2003 in *Of the Same Roots Monthly.*

masterpiece that you may never be able to comprehend. But at least now you know why this book was exiled to the "Other" shelf in the library. It really is hard to pin down. Its internal logic is a mess and it often contradicts itself. Maybe it's exactly as the literary critic in the book says. To "The Fourth Person," this is a "discordant book."[2]

2. See "Victim of Multiple Personality Disorder—Dissecting Shaozi's *The Age of Goodbyes*"—"Under the guise of capturing history, *The Age of Goodbyes* actually reveals the author's traumatic memories and her long-untreated mental illness, namely multiple personality disorder, from which she irrefutably suffers. Along these lines, *The Age of Goodbyes*, being mainly a reflection of her illness, is a discordant book."

CHAPTER TWO

—1—

The Fourth Person says *The Age of Goodbyes* does not technically qualify as a novel. This Fourth Person is obviously a rigorous critic. Motivated by his lifelong, unwavering focus on Shaozi's body of work, he carried out extensive research into the historical background and even the geographical aspects of said book. According to him, the tin mining town described by Shaozi is not fictional. Certain occurrences and characters in the book, too, have their basis in reality. But due to the novelist's lack of knowledge and literary prowess, she bungled the handling of History with a capital H. Under her pen, factual events appear as mere gossip. He goes so far as to cast aspersion on Shaozi's stance toward history in general; in his opinion, all she did was perch in Old Street kopitiams and listen to some old folks' anecdotes about the tin mining town of a bygone era.

These old folks retained a deep impression of the character she's most interested in. They refer to him as "Steely Bo," once a small-time triad ringleader whose direct boss, Elder Zong, was a secret society don of much renown. Back in those days the triads demarcated their territories with the old river as a border. The most profitable stretch was the north shore, spanning Old Street to the train station, which covered an area of Chinese businesses and Indian markets. This was precisely the area controlled by Elder Zong of Toa Pek Kong Society. With his intimidating, stout build, Steely Bo was once Elder Zong's right-hand man back in his prime. His neck, which sported a solid gold chain as thick as his little finger, was broader than one of his thighs. He had an arrogant swagger about him, and people greeted him by the respectful moniker "Brother Bo of Kien Tek Hall."

By the time you are reading this novel, Kien Tek Hall no longer exists, according to research by The Fourth Person. But the Toa Pek Kong shrine remains standing by the Old River, still rubbing shoulders with Pei Hwa Primary School. When The Fourth Person visited, he saw a small temple sooty with a hundred years' worth of incense, slowly and silently melting into the background like a ninja. In front of the temple, a pair of stone lions held bouquets of ancient incense bits in their mouths full of smoke-stained teeth.

Steely Bo witnessed his fair share of things in that temple. As a teenager, he attended classes at the old shrine for a few years and loitered in the area during his free time. After Elder Zong became his godfather, Steely Bo made a name for himself and rose to prominence as the leader of Kien Tek Hall. In his new position, he often accompanied Elder Zong to conduct business in the temple, which saw someone sacrificing chickens and making blood vows every other day. Later on, Elder Zong almost lost his life there, right under the watchful eyes of Toa Pek Kong. Many a triad member held their wedding ceremonies there too, sometimes with their wives, other times with their mistresses. Naturally Steely Bo's own wedding was also conducted at the Toa Pek Kong shrine. There was quite a sizeable turnout in his honor. The gang members caused a ruckus, exclaiming: What luck, Steely Bo, your wife is such a catch!

His wife was indeed beautiful, with a figure more alluring than that actress Fanny Fan Lai's. The bride couldn't help but furrow her brows. *Fan Lai?* She risked a glance, taking in the room. There wasn't a single man who wasn't winking and wiggling his eyebrows, a suggestive smile on his lips. She looked down at her breasts, self-conscious. Had she popped a button? A wave of bashfulness crested within her and her ears began to grow hot, followed immediately by a burning at her cheeks. She averted her eyes and looked upon Sou Gei's miserable long face. Meanwhile her younger brother Ah Sai never let his gaze wander from the tips of his shoes, his face screwed up tight like sorrowful Wong Fei-hung on TV. Du Li An suddenly felt her heart seize.

Ah Sai had practically stopped talking to anyone at home for the past two months, all because of her impending marriage to Steely Bo. She knew her brother was angry about the twenty-year age gap between Steely Bo and her, not to mention his brashness stemming from his wealth. There was the sight of his arms and back too, every inch covered by dragons, tigers, and other tattoos. Even more preposterous was that he already had a wife and children back in the fishing village that was his childhood home. On top of that, there was constant gossip, whether true or exaggerated, linking him to numerous women in this small town.

Even Guen Hou, who used to peddle packaged Western drinks in front of the cinema, came to talk her down. "I'm the cautionary tale. See?" Guen Hou struck a pose, which was mimicked by the three-year-old girl in her arms with a turn of her head, the two of them wearing the same pathetic expression. Pity came over Du Li An. The little girl's face was shaped like an eggplant, slightly crooked. All over her face were traces of last night's tears and snot, while remains of her last meal lingered at the corners of her mouth, all of which told a story about the state of their lives. Rumor had it that after Chan Kam Hoi died, Guen Hou received nothing but a tiny row house in Mi Shan New Village. With her resources dwindling, she had no choice but to cart her daughter around begging for help from various parties. Better start peddling again, or else it's washing dishes at food stalls for you.

Guen Hou barely made it through a few sentences before self-pity made her bawl; the one who came to dispense advice ended up requiring coaxing instead. Flustered, Du Li An was totally ineffectual, and in the end it was the little girl who lifted a tiny, dirty hand to wipe away her mother's tears. This scene often replayed itself in Du Li An's mind. It was like a cork stopper floating on water—no matter how hard she pushed, she couldn't sink it to the bottom. It was also because of this scene that the eggplant-faced little girl began to grow on Du Li An. Ah Sai used to wipe away her tears like that too, when he was little. Who knew there would come a day when he'd kick away the pillow she'd gifted him and turn his back on her from then on.

It was real hot that night. Their armpits oozed sweat. Even the mosquitoes were extra thirsty; ignoring the mosquito coil's counsel, they acted like guests at a generous banquet. In this scenario, the Du siblings were two red jumbo-sized packaged drinks that the insects kept sticking their straws into.

Du Li An spent all night smacking mosquitoes, wiping away sweat, scratching itchy bites, and turning over thoughts she didn't have time to entertain during the day. After a round of carpet-bombing the mosquitoes took a break, waiting to ride again when the mosque's call to prayer would sound at dawn. By then Du Li An was too tired to resist. Groggily she watched as Ah Sai struck a match, then knelt to light a new mosquito coil in a corner of the room. The soporific smell affected her and the mosquitoes alike. As her consciousness gradually faded, she heard herself mumbling an explanation about what went on between her and Steely Bo to her brother. But Ah Sai, squatting in the corner, did not respond. Du Li An swallowed some saliva with difficulty. She had more to say, but she sank slowly into recitations of the Quran that stretched out as endlessly as a river.

Not long after that night, Du Li An was rushed to the hospital with a fever. Sou Gei needed to mind her stall, so she asked Ah Sai to deliver meals that she'd prepared for Du Li An. Ah Sai didn't refuse, but at the hospital the siblings had nothing to say to each other. Ah Sai was bothered by the fact that the ward was full of women, so he waited outside on the balcony as soon as he put down the boxed meals. Once, arriving late, he ran into Steely Bo making oatmeal for his sister. Bursting with muscles, veins popping from the backs of his hands, which sported ostentatious gold accessories, Steely Bo looked particularly clumsy maneuvering a tiny teaspoon. Ah Sai stared at the back of Steely Bo's head, which showed signs of balding. His hairline was receding in front, too, but he still used a good half can of wax to create a pompadour. He really was the picture of a lowlife criminal.

Since then, whenever Sou Gei recalled that bout of illness she would say to anyone and everyone, Ah, fate, it has long predetermined everything.

"She had her pick of men and ended up with a total

loser. You can't outrun fate." That was her refrain for a good half of her life.

Ah Sai kept his eye on Steely Bo. Though only a few years younger than Sou Gei, the total loser followed Du Li An's lead and called Sou Gei "Ma."

Ma, have some seafood, have some dessert.

These are the best durian on the market. Here are a couple bolts of fabric that Ah Li picked out for you; here are two little gold chains and a pair of jade bracelets.

Here, for Ah Sai, leather belts and trousers. For you, Dad, a gold watch.

These are just small gestures, there's no need to thank me.

After all, we are family now.

Don't worry, Ma.

I'll take good care of Ah Li.

A big mug in hand, the total loser wandered around in search of hot water. He grabbed hold of a passing Indian cleaning lady and asked in his limited Malay, voice booming: Eh, where's water? Hot water? Everyone's ears rang in the fourth-floor sick ward, assaulted by his cacophonous voice. Du Li An hung her head, slightly uncomfortable. But in the next moment she couldn't resist sneaking a glance at him.

The total loser kept sounding his discordant demand. Where's water? Where's hot water?

The next day when Ah Sai returned, he saw that a jumbo-sized thermos had appeared by his sister's bedside. Du Li An peeked at the stainless steel thermos while she ate, a complicated look in her eyes. Ah Sai, too, was wrapped up in mixed feelings. Both of them were thinking of that period, years ago, when their dad had racked up gambling debts. Now and again he went through the house for things he could take to the pawnshop, and like clockwork Sou Gei fought him each time.

She flung herself like a macaque onto him, gibbering, pounding, slapping, and swearing to snatch back her gold chain or jade pendant or radio or electric fan or thermos. These items changed hands frequently at the pawnshop, especially the jewelry. Doubtless the thermos was the first to break down.

Back then, was it not precisely Steely Bo who'd led the gang of men to collect the debt? The siblings remembered the front door being kicked down and several thugs pinning the old man to the floor. Smacks resounded. The old man let out unearthly yells. One of his front teeth was punched out. Steely Bo lifted a thermos from a table and pounded it heartily into the old man's left hand. The thermos's cap wasn't screwed on tight and hot water sprayed everywhere, scalding the old man's hand into a steamy mess.

Ah Sai recalled the scene clearly. He was nestled in Sou Gei's arms. Sou Gei was so thin that her chest was concave, forming a cavity just the right size for him. His sister trembled behind Sou Gei, her fingers tugging incessantly at Sou Gei's sleeve. Both of them heard Sou Gei grinding her teeth as she mumbled repeatedly:

Lord in heaven, they're gonna kill him.

Steely Bo's figure at that time was lean and muscular. He didn't yet have a bald spot, and his arm was adorned only by a strange green bird with a long tail. There was overall a slight resemblance to Bruce Lee in *Fist of Fury*. With savage force, Steely Bo pitched the thermos at a wall, breaking it and spilling more hot water everywhere. He wiped his hand on the old man's singlet and followed that up by spitting on the floor. Ah Sai remembered the look Steely Bo gave over his shoulder right before he left. It was violent and brutal, like he meant to slaughter the entire family.

Yet now Steely Bo said he wanted to marry Du Li An,

and moreover promised to take good care of her. Ah Sai would rather die before he believed a promise of this sort. But his sister was hard to read. To say that she was a willing participant would be to disregard how awkwardly she behaved in his presence. On the other hand, she didn't exactly push him away either. Ah Sai felt that his sister became indecipherable under Steely Bo's waves of expensive presents. And even Sou Gei's attitude was opaque to him, difficult to parse.

At dawn, when he clambered up from sleep to light a mosquito coil, he heard his sister muttering in her dreams. I'm twenty-six, Ah Sai, just let me be, I promise I won't blame anyone for my choices. He remained squatting for a long time, hesitating over what to say. He wasn't sure either if he could possibly project his response into his sister's dream.

—

The teacher surnamed Yip appeared the day before Du Li An's wedding. Through the Venetian blinds, Ah Sai saw him pacing back and forth downstairs. Ah Sai has seen him before; Du Li An once arranged for them to play badminton together. And so Ah Sai recognized him from his lanky figure alone. Mr. Yip. Ah Sai opened the window.

Yip Lin Sang lifted his head. To him, from that angle, Ah Sai looked exactly like an older student at Pei Hwa Primary School. Yip Lin Sang raised a hand to shield the clean morning sunlight. Swiftly Ah Sai came downstairs carrying a tome with both hands. Yip Lin Sang began to form a basic understanding of things as they stood. He accepted the book.

"Your sister isn't around?"

"She said to give this back to you if you came."

Yip Lin Sang nodded. "She doesn't have a message for me?"

Ah Sai scratched the back of his neck and dug the Japanese slipper on his right foot vigorously into the sandy earth. "She said she can't make sense of this book. She couldn't finish it."

Yip Lin Sang nodded again. After a while, he stared at Ah Sai like he was his own child. Ah Sai thought the man was waiting for him to finish talking, so he scratched behind his ear and said, "She said thank you."

Finally, Yip Lin Sang grasped the meaning of that particular goodbye. Smiling bitterly, he glanced down at the book in his arms. The gold-stamped words on the hardcover twinkled in the sunlight. "Tell your sister to take care of herself. You tell her I hope she has a good life." After saying this, he stretched out a hand and gave Ah Sai's crown a quick ruffle.

"And you too. It's time for a haircut."

Under his palm, Ah Sai lifted his head like a young boy. Yip Lin Sang had been released from jail that very day. He was disheveled after an entire month in there. His face sported a hangdog expression and an uneven beard. Ah Sai remembered watching him being dragged away by authorities on the street. Uniformed police clad in helmets poured out from an armored car and quickly broke through the people's ranks as if they were playing a schoolyard game. As the crowd scattered, a few who were more stubborn rushed the police car, facing down the armed officers by waving sticks that had previously held up banners. Mr. Yip was one of those few, but his opponents held thick shields in one hand and batons in the other. In mere moments they beat him down and forcefully dragged him into the car.

Du Li An did not sprint forward to help. She even held back Ah Sai, saying, There's no point. Let him be locked up for a few days, and he'll be released when the time is right. Ah Sai himself never had a real impulse to rush forth. He turned to look first at his sister, swallowed into shadows cast by a veranda, then at Mr. Yip doggedly struggling in front of the armored car. So tall, and so skinny, he twisted like a willow branch. The long stick in his hands had been confiscated, yet the banner that read Something Something Economic Policy was still tangled around his waist.

Just as Yip Lin Sang walked away, the old man came downstairs whistling a tune. He looked at the lanky figure and asked Ah Sai, That him again, Mr. Parti Rakyat Malaysia? Ah Sai did not reply. It wasn't until Yip Lin Sang's back disappeared around the street corner ahead that Ah Sai angled his head to observe the upstairs window. There, his sister's face hung like an ominous mask, devoid of expression. He couldn't tell what she was looking at. Was it almost noon? Ah Sai lifted a hand to shield the sun; its light settled quietly on the back of his hand.

—2—

You go to see J. Just as before, you maintain a spy's distance. Even so, you recognize him at first glance. You spot him before his own mother does amid the avalanche of students released from school. He looks practically unchanged, almost like the reflection you see in the mirror daily. He's decked out in snowy white, sparkling like a pearl under the sun, whereas a cloak of shadows gnaws at you in your mourning clothes. You feel as though you can see through him. His slightness, fragility, and gentleness; his stomach prone to indigestion, his agitation triggered by teenage hormones. The gaping emptiness this morning that followed last night's masturbation.

Smiling, he enters that new car. A classmate waves goodbye to him when they walk past. Another makes a "call me" gesture with their fingers. His mother talks at him and hands him two tissues. He wipes his face with the tissues and responds to her with a clownish expression. Gradually the car glides forward, parting the crowd slowly. You see mother and son in profile, both bearing slight smiles. Like the prince and queen on poker cards. The car windows reflect light and their faces fade away.

J is still here. You're content with this knowledge. On your return trip, you nod off on the bus. A different person is seated next to you each time you wake up. Indian girl, pregnant Malay woman, Chinese crone. This makes you feel like Time is performing magic tricks onboard. You've taken this bus home before. One of those times, you wore a victorious smile on your face, your book bag squeezed tight against your chest, the same way you'd hug a new toy that you'd found when you were little.

That afternoon you returned to Mayflower and pushed open the creaky door of 301, just like you are doing now. Mother wasn't inside, but you could hear her moans coming from 302 next door. You dropped your book bag and rummaged in the drawers until you found the mini radio. You turned the volume up, beating back with angsty rock the sounds breaching the walls. But instead of holding back, Mother let her groans grow louder as if in protest. You started on your homework. Math was the most effective, since in theory there was an answer that already existed. A truth hidden in a void. The more you focused, the calmer you felt. The music sunk alongside dust motes visible in slanting sunlight, and with them the lewd sounds from next door stopped. Afterward, when Mother entered the room humming, you didn't spare her a single glance.

You didn't respond either, when she asked what you wanted for dinner.

She approached and placed the radio on your desk, her fingers twisting the volume knob back and forth as she yammered on about something trivial. Anything to prevent you from concentrating on your homework. You put down your pen and crossed your arms. A great idea crossed your mind. You turned off the radio.

"I found something you couldn't. But I'll never tell you where it is."

"What is it?" She didn't catch on.

"You'll eventually remember what you lost. I'll never tell you." You lifted your chin and repeated your words with a faint smile. "I'll never tell you."

Since then you have kept J hidden. Occasionally you take two different buses to that all-boys school to wait for him. As long as he is safe and thriving in a sun-saturated place, you are at ease. On every return trip, you imagine that one day Mother will remember what she lost; she will slyly entice you to seek out your J, misplaced who knows where. She'll cross her legs and, flip-flop dangling from her toes, she'll suddenly say, Oh, by the way, did you know you have an older brother?

Or maybe a younger brother.

Lin Sang, or is it Mong Sang? You're almost convinced it's Yip Lin Sang. That man sat within a scene painted by Mother, lifting his head from several stacks of books and documents to glance at you. Time, rusted amber, frozen in that moment. He is the likeliest candidate for someone who sits in the library and writes a "magnum opus." Yip Lin Sang, birthdate unknown, of Guangdong Panyu stock, born in Batu Gajah, Perak. A leftist scholar in the Labour Party. Marched in numerous protests, made countless trips in and out of jail. Naturally, he was unable to keep his teaching job. Later he spent a few decades on Jerejak Island, Penang, thanks to the hospitality extended under the Internal Security Act.

You write down Yip Lin Sang's words in your notebook: *I hope she has a good life.* Whereas Steely Bo said, *Don't worry, I'll take good care of her.*

The sun has moved on to patrol other rooms, plunging 301 into dimness. You press a light switch. You've become accustomed to turning on the light instead of opening the window, just like you've grown used to the cicadas squatting in the lamp, as well as Mayflower's surly silence. You and Mother have never lived anywhere else for as long as you have lived in this motel. The two of you drifted across cities and towns, pausing at many similarly humble places. At each one you entered through side doors to ascend a flight of stairs into rooms that were sparsely furnished, manned by desk fans slowly shaking their heads. There was only ever one shared bathroom per floor. At dusk, there were always several sex workers chatting and smoking in the hallways, holding washbasins and wearing flip-flops.

If you walked down the narrow hallways at those times, they would very likely reach out their hands to tousle your hair. They'd jostle to touch the crown of your head like believers praying in temples, or like tourists fondling some huge penis-shaped stone molded by nature. They'd call after you, but they never used your name. At each and every motel, your name was known only to Mother, and even she never used it. She called you Kid just like everyone else did, or Hey, Handsome when you grew older. As if by doing so you'd be unable to identify her amid the throng of pajamas-wearing, washbasin-bearing sex workers.

You were too young back then, and those stays too brief. There was no need for either of you to remember the names of any of the streets or motels. You knew that no matter where you went, each room would have only a single window, and outside each window there would run a lone alley. Mayflower was no exception, yet after moving in Mother never again left. How many years ago was that? The cicadas bred in isolation, housed within the lights. Room 301 became your home, free of all kinds of men that would enter and leave. Enter and leave.

Uncle Sai installed used AC units in all the rooms on the third floor. It didn't take long for the majority of them to malfunction in various ways. The most common defect was water leakage, making the third floor especially humid. Moist air swelled in the rooms. Winter fog saturated dreams. Mother complained often about joint pain, prompting Uncle Sai to take her for acupuncture treatments. He brought her to other traditional Chinese medicine practitioners as well, who applied warm, mashed-up herbs secured tight with plastic cloth and topped off with bandages. All wrapped up like this, Mother's knee resembled a zongzi. She had to lean on Uncle Sai when she walked. You saw the way the sex workers sniggered, half covering their mouths, and you formed a groping understanding as to why Mother had stopped relocating, and why she'd started designing the unending treasure hunts for you that spanned the entirety of Mayflower.

Over the course of a decade, Mayflower had degraded to its current rundown state. The sex workers it once housed were either old or dead. Every room was fitted with a ceiling fan; all the AC units sat quietly like antiques, untouched. The johns dwindled by the day. Uncle Sai hired an old man to look after the place, which freed him to venture out and pool his resources with a few others to invest in some paltry businesses.

Come evening, he'd buy dinner and ascend the forty-three steps to your door. Knock knock.

In the absence of Uncle Sai and the johns, the vastness of Mayflower became your little universe. You walked on all the floors and opened all the doors, exploring spaces large and small, after which you carefully covered them up once more. Even now you nudge pictures hanging on walls out of habit, suspecting it might reveal some secret entrance to a hidden room. And you still half believe that an undiscovered cellar lurks underneath the kitchen or front desk, piled full of all those items you never did find. The ghost of Mother, complete with engorged knee. The truth within the illusion.

After Mother's death, the space inside Mayflower gradually lost its meaning. You can no longer summon any interest in rooms other than 301. But this old building produces sounds to emphasize its desolate loneliness. Or maybe loneliness itself is a converse mirror that can reflect sounds. The dripping of water. Forty-three footsteps. The peculiar creaking of a door being opened or shut. The broken springs in mattresses. The flushing of toilets. Flip-flops. The blowing of noses. Snatches of conversation. Mahjong tiles knocking together. Coughs. TV. Mosquitoes. Women moaning. Knock knock. The broken fan in 202. Hawks and spits. Cockroaches on brisk journeys. Geckos in heat. Upturned washbasins hitting the floor.

Uncle Sai still buys you dinner. And every Monday morning, you still find your allowance sitting on top of the wardrobe in the room next door. The wrinkled bills make you feel as if Mother has been to visit, dragging her limp, rotting leg, tidying up all of your things, and then hiding herself in some unknown spot inside Mayflower. Go find it, why don't you. Go find it.

In the novel, Shaozi is a wunderkind. At age twenty-one she published the novella *The Lefty Who Lost Her Right Brain*, which secured her fame when it won a prize overseas. During her time, bagging such a prize was a big deal, especially because Shaozi never went to college. Furthermore, when the prize was announced she was still working as a small-time vendor selling underwear in night markets. The lauded novella very obviously referenced this country's historical events. After much consideration, local newspapers and publishers declined to publish it in its "birthplace" because it could be said to touch upon sensitive topics like race and politics. Not to mention the timing; Operation Lalang had just been carried out, and the Communist Party of Malaya was on the verge of surrender.

Because of this, *The Lefty Who Lost Her Right Brain* is a "hollow" book to the vast majority of local readers, who may have heard of it but never encountered the thing itself. In the many years following the announcement of the prize, the publishing world still never quite found the right time to publish the novella, and the author herself didn't feel too strongly about seeing it in print. Then one night a fire broke out in Shaozi's residence, torching all of her handwritten manuscript drafts. Thus it came to be that *The Lefty Who Lost Her Right Brain* was virtually lost to humankind. After Shaozi's premature death, this legendary work, her breakthrough debut, grew ever more mysterious. A scant few people in this country can claim to have read the novella in its entirety.

The Fourth Person is one of that handful. According to him, the novella is volume 1 of Shaozi's "Myths of

Womanhood/The Du Li An Saga."[1] The Fourth Person's research characterizes all of Shaozi's historical fiction as "myths of womanhood under the guise of history." He furthermore concludes that she has an incurable penchant for fabricating historical details.[2] From the choice of words in his discourse, it is obvious that this particular critic views the "overhyped" Shaozi with derision.

Setting aside her creations for a moment—Shaozi herself was perhaps a more colorful character than any of the mythical women she wrote into her works. She was a wunderkind, she made her name early in life, she died young. On top of that, she maintained a low profile in literary circles, and rarely attended any events. Even when she did show up, she was reliably late to arrive and early to leave, always alone. In the entirety of her life she formed relationships with only a few writers, and she never accepted any media interviews. Yet when she traversed her hometown streets as "Du Li An," she was vivacious and expressive. Not only that, but she was known to be unselfconsciously forthright, honest, and bold, cutting a gallant figure. To top it all off, she was filial to her mother. All of these qualities earned her the honorific of "Sister Li," which was what the triad members and other night market vendors called her, even though she was rather young.

At age thirty-five, Sister Li succumbed to a genetic heart condition. Because she was survived only by her mother, who had no one else in the world, a few vendor associations in town pooled their resources to hold an elaborate funeral on her behalf. The event lasted

1. See "The Immortal Du Li An."
2. See "The Fabricator of History—A Brief Analysis of Shaozi's Fiction," published in 2003 in *Of the Same Roots Monthly*.

three days, drawing not only many businesspeople in town but also mafiosos who appeared in person to pay their respects. Attendees streamed forth unceasingly; many hands held up the coffin during the procession, which was graced by countless wreaths and trailed by long, snaking lines of cars. It was a spectacular sight. Chinese newspapers in circulation at the time each received several inquiries to take out full-page obituaries and condolences, so it was only natural that they sent reporters to cover the funeral. All told, the scale of it was impressive enough to rival the death of an elected representative.

According to newspaper reports gathered by The Fourth Person after the fact, there was a sea of white chrysanthemums at Sister Li's wake, surrounded on all sides by many calligraphy scrolls. The one framed in the center was taken from a Li Yu poem: "Not a trace now, the lush beauty of yore, all things stripped like leaves into nothingness; nowhere to turn amidst the world's vastness, millennia to bid the east wind goodbye."

Almost everyone Chinese in town heard about Sister Li's grand funeral, yet few of them knew about her alter ego. Thus it was that Shaozi's death was not discovered until fully half a year after Du Li An's passing, which coincided with the publication of her short story "Last Words from Last Night" in the arts section of a newspaper. After multiple fruitless attempts to contact her, the newspaper editor finally found out about her death.

Shaozi's "unremarkable death" was in such contrast to her sudden fame years ago that it caused quite a stir in the world of letters at the time. Many in literary circles condemned the Chinese media for being so oblivious. There was much lamenting among local literati over the fact that the vendor "Sister Li" was elevated above the writer Shaozi. For the most part, the media responded by downplaying the discovery as much as they could. Coincidentally, the old prime minister who'd been in power for many years was stepping down, and the people were optimistic about his successor, who was lauded as a moderate. In addition, the global hike in paper prices was forcing newspapers to be parsimonious with their column inches. As far as Shaozi went, the dead are dead. They do not long remain top of mind.

Waves of fresh talent emerged in the local literary scene after Shaozi's death. Many were awarded international prizes, thus injecting vigor into the local landscape, which looked to be on the cusp of taking off. And yet it was precisely during this period that The Fourth Person, whose presence used to dominate the world of literary criticism, began to fade from the front lines. Eventually it seemed he retired from literary circles, and almost never published articles of any sort.

In the novel, the critic "The Fourth Person" made his debut only after Shaozi had established herself with two major literary prizes. His first review of Shaozi can be traced to a collection published by a local literature association in 1990. After that, he became Shaozi's most devoted and yet most hostile follower. His teaching career and academic research focused on Shaozi, revolved entirely around her. He dissected every one of Shaozi's works and went so far as to introduce himself as Shaozi's "tapeworm burrowed deep within her bowels" in front of his students.

The Age of Goodbyes explains that The Fourth Person took an early retirement, after which he spent his days hiding in his study, piled high with books weighed down by thick layers of dust and shadows. There he reread Shaozi's work time and again. After he lost use of his lower body due to a stroke, he spent several years in a wheelchair compiling an edition of Shaozi's unpublished work. And when his application for funds to publish the collection fell through, he financed it himself.

He declared in the book's afterword that Shaozi's death made him feel "uneasy and rudderless, like a shadow suddenly losing sight of its physical body in broad daylight."

It strikes you as curious that the author of *The Age of Goodbyes* never bothered to give this critic a "humanizing" name, and moreover never explained his background or origins in earnest. Unlike Shaozi with her multiplying aliases and nicknames, The Fourth Person treads the earth without a name, like a shadow with no need of a body, or a soul without a resting place. In the novel, he resolved to put together a six-volume *Collected Works of Shaozi*, yet his plan was repeatedly postponed because he simply couldn't raise enough funds, despite multiple attempts to persuade Chinese businesses and regional associations. This dragged on until the eighth of August, when the whole world had its eyes on an Olympic opening ceremony. The Fourth Person, exhausted down to his last atom, keeled over in his study like a shawl tossed by wind.

When his family pried away the sheaf of papers clenched in his cold hands, they discovered it was a review of Shaozi's unpublished work. The manuscript was titled "Victim of Multiple Personality Disorder— Dissecting Shaozi's *The Age of Goodbyes*." This last work made its way into a collection alongside the majority of the critical articles he had written while he was alive, and the collection became a must-read for any scholars of Shaozi. The novel mentions that, of these scholars, many had read only The Fourth Person's criticism without ever once coming into contact with Shaozi's work.

CHAPTER THREE

—1—

Ah Sai rarely showed his face in the tin mining town after he moved to the capital. After all, it was always the same old, same old with his family. On the occasions he telephoned for them, he had to rely on the good graces of others to walk to his family home and shout up to the window, Sou Gei, Sou Gei, Fried Noodle Lady. Once she heard this, Sou Gei rushed down, her wooden clogs clacking on the stairs. Not that she had anything important to say; her greetings were none other than the commonplace: Have you eaten? Which was followed by regurgitated complaints against her husband, or rehashes of how things stood between Du Li An and Steely Bo.

Du Li An's home had a telephone installed, so Sou Gei often encouraged Ah Sai to call his sister and ask after his brother-in-law. But Ah Sai never obeyed. It ended up the other way around; one day Du Li An called the Chinese restaurant and summoned him from the kitchen to give him news of Sou Gei's death.

Business was booming at the restaurant in the capital. Ah Sai stood by the cashier's counter, the phone in his hand. The boss lady at the cash register asked him, Did something happen? Why are you holding the receiver and not saying anything? He said, My mom died. Auntie Fong, my mom died.

Auntie Fong gave Ah Sai seven days off and even sent someone to buy a bus ticket for him so he could make it back to the tin mining town that very evening for the viewing. Ah Sai boarded the bus with his limp duffel bag. He couldn't sleep a wink the entire ride. Instead he leaned his head against the window and watched as the bus traversed villages and towns, wondering whether the phone call had been a prank. That was the first time he'd ever heard his sister through a phone, and her voice had sounded unfamiliar. She'd choked out, "Ah Ma is no more," reminding him of that Hokkien lady who lived on their street. One morning, after she went to a hair salon to take a call, she ran through the streets in her pajamas crying, Ah Ba is no more! Her daughter, skinny as a bamboo pole, chased after her. Suddenly the girl followed suit and clamored as if to notify the entire street, Ah Ba is no more!

He arrived in the small town to find Sou Gei already in her casket, which seemed not only too large but also too lavish. This made her appear somewhat reserved, as if she'd been seated in an ostentatious car that didn't suit her and was worried about breaking something. Her cheeks were flushed and she was doing her best to press her lips together, looking just as embarrassed as she'd been when Steely Bo bowed and called her "Dear mother-in-law" when he came to ask for Du Li An's hand. Ah Sai's old man seemed without a care in the world. He crossed his legs and shelled peanuts alongside those who came to offer their condolences, acting exactly as he would if it'd been a wedding instead.

Ah Sai met Steely Bo's pair of children for the first time at the funeral hall. They were about his age, and yet they called him "Brother Sai" because of the perceived generational hierarchy. The male child was tanned and robust. He'd inherited Steely Bo's squat figure, and like him also had an air of pent-up energy waiting to be released. The daughter, on the other hand, was thin and pale and sickly, as if sunlight had not touched her for a long time. Sou Gei had previously brought them up over the phone: Your brother-in-law's children have moved in. They said they want to acquire some employable skills here.

Du Li An had changed. She was plumper and her skin glowed. When Ah Sai sat with her burning offerings of paper clothes, he felt as if she'd been swapped with another woman. She gave off an entirely different aura as she kept an eye on Steely Bo's children, and occasionally turned to them to assign them various tasks. The siblings called her "Auntie Li," reminding Ah Sai of the boss lady at the restaurant. Yes, that was it. Just like Auntie Fong, his sister was acquiring the attitude and posture of a boss lady.

"Those two are peculiar. They keep their mouths shut like blood cockles. You'll have a hell of a time prying them open." Du Li An relegated them to a corner, where they sat folding paper yuanbao ingots. But she didn't seem to entirely trust them. She turned her head from time to time to inspect the pair. "Ah, it's not easy for me."

Ah Sai kept quiet.

Du Li An snuck a glance from the corner of her eye. On his face was a rigid expression, as if he was bothered by something. So she changed the topic to the resurgence of dengue fever due to recent weather, saying, You can get mosquito coils where you live, can't you. There's a wedding coming up at Uncle's, but poor Mom won't be taking part in the festivities. Elections, right, aren't there going to be elections this year? Do you think the Queen of England will come this year? Ah, it's time for another election, how time flies.

Ah Sai understood the meaning behind this last lament. His heart softened as he gave his sister a look. Hadn't that candidate died in the cinema during the last election? His sister was still selling tickets at Old Majestic cinema at the time. After that the rumors about it being haunted started to circulate. Supposedly that man's ghost lingered in the women's bathroom. And then when *The Big Boss* was showing, his sister invited him to the movie. Her treat. When he arrived, he discovered a man with a pompadour standing behind her.

"You don't recognize Brother Bo? Go on, greet him." Du Li An nudged Ah Sai's elbow.

He remained silent, his eyes bulging at the man's hand perched on his sister's shoulder. Du Li An turned her face to the hand sporting two gold-encrusted jade rings and said, Ignore him. My brother keeps his mouth shut like a blood cockle.

That whole afternoon, Steely Bo's children sat in their corner folding yuanbao. The son had a distracted air about him; when he wasn't lazily stretching his arms, he was turning his gaze every which way. The daughter, on the other hand, seemed preternaturally quiet and focused, as if she meant to transform the paper ingots in her hands into works of art. After observing them for a whole afternoon, Ah Sai remarked that the siblings were indeed odd. They never spoke to each other. Having made this observation, he couldn't help but be amused. He exchanged a look with Du Li An. They started sniggering, holding in their laughter.

The humble Sou Gei, who spent her whole life unnoticed, was thus celebrated for quite a few days after her death. This was all due to Steely Bo's many friends from the seedier side of town. Elder Zong of Toa Pek Kong Society paid his respects in the flesh, trailed by an entourage of triad members. Their appearance caused a stir in the funeral hall, forming a "climax" of sorts during the viewing. This greatly excited the old man, who became more proactive at serving guests, and as a result more infelicitous phrases came out of his mouth. Du Li An, on the other hand, was the picture of calm. Just before Elder Zong departed, he made a point of turning around and saying, Ah Li, you've arranged everything so well. It must have been tough.

That night Du Li An rested in the funeral hall's back room, eyes open and wide awake on the canvas bed. Steely Bo and Ah Sai entered one after the other, both asking why she wasn't napping. It wasn't like she could admit she was happy, so she massaged her temples and told them she had a headache. Ah Sai asked, Does it hurt a lot? Why don't I find you a couple of painkillers. She was just about to refuse when Steely Bo pushed open the door holding water and pills.

The day before the funeral, the restaurant in the capital dispatched via bus an old uncle who worked as a cashier. He arrived with cash meant for condolences, pooled from the boss and his coworkers. This caught Ah Sai by surprise, and Du Li An seemed even happier than when she was greeting Elder Zong. When the old uncle insisted on making his return trip that very same day, she used all her persuasive powers to keep him for dinner, and even had Steely Bo send someone out to buy him local specialties such as pomelos and gai zai beng. These were then sent on the bus with the old uncle, so that he could share the fruit and cookies with his colleagues back in the capital. Du Li An even hand-picked two larger pomelos and made identifying marks on their raffia encasing, before asking the old uncle to make sure the boss lady received them.

"The boss lady is called Auntie Fong, right?" Du Li An

looked at her brother. Without waiting for him to answer, she turned to the old uncle and said, "We're very grateful that Auntie Fong is so understanding. We hope to continue relying on her care in the future."

The old uncle wasn't the only visitor that day; Guen Hou from Mi Shan New Village arrived around the same time, bringing along her eggplant-faced daughter. Guen Hou was working as hired help in someone's household at that point, and it hadn't been easy for her to get a half day off. Eggplant Face ran and skipped about, but never made a fuss or bothered anyone for attention. Wearing shoes that bore the hollow imprint of butterfly bows that had long fallen off, she entertained herself by strolling around the funeral hall. Du Li An asked them to stay for dinner as well. Presented with a tableful of rich dishes catered from Wa Zai Restaurant, Guen Hou began to eat sloppily. It fell on Eggplant Face to be vigilant. From her mother's pocket she drew out a handkerchief and patted first her own mouth, then the corners of her mother's.

Because she was seeing the old uncle off, Du Li An could not extend her hospitality to mother and daughter as much as she wanted to. Instead she tasked Steely Bo's son with accompanying them on their short walk to the bus station. The sickly sister mutely tagged along without uttering so much as a single "hi." After one backward glance, Eggplant Face unexpectedly paused and waited for her to catch up, then reached for her so that they were walking hand in hand.

Odd to say, but even though Sou Gei's death initially caught everyone by surprise and put them at a loss, they recovered quickly. Her death was accepted as reality, and the atmosphere in the funeral hall wasn't one of much grief. There was a lot of busywork on the day of the funeral procession, due to the high number of attendees and the quirky nature of the officiating Hakka Taoist priest. Not to mention the procession clashed with horse racing day, and so Du Li An's old man couldn't help but feel torn. Instead of helping, he kept making excuses to venture out for betting-related reasons. The busier everyone got, the more it felt like a holiday. Sou Gei was in the ground before anyone had time to mourn. Ah Sai managed to squeeze in a last look—it had been no more than a few days, and already she seemed to have shrunk even more in the coffin. And so it was that such a miniature person was ferried away in her mismatching, luxurious coffin, accompanied all the way by mournful music, and entombed in the unfathomable depths of the vast cemetery.

Ah Sai stayed home for two days and one night after Sou Gei was buried. On the eve of his return trip to the capital, Du Li An arranged for a lavish dinner at Bai Li Lai Restaurant. When they arrived, Ah Sai and the old man were greeted by the sight of Steely Bo's children. The son seemed preoccupied as ever, constantly shifting in his seat while wearing an infinitely bored expression. The daughter remained as silent as a person who didn't exist. Most of the time she kept her head down and shoveled tiny bites of rice into her mouth, ignoring the main dishes. Du Li An put some meat into her bowl, saying, Come on, eat more; you're so skinny. Thank you, Auntie Li, the girl said in a voice barely perceptible to others.

Ah Sai observed and thought, *Strange, the siblings really have nothing to say to each other this whole time.* In contrast, the old man and Steely Bo had opened three large bottles of beer and kept filling each other's cups until they overflowed. They talked about betting and made election predictions, unconscious of how their voices rose higher as alcohol coursed through them.

Steely Bo wagged his head again and again to issue corrections against the old man. Occasionally he cast his eyes left and right before adopting a tone of mystery as he "leaked" some confidential information he'd heard from Elder Zong. This piqued the son's interest, but the daughter's head hung ever lower.

"Look at her," Du Li An said, and lightly bumped her elbow against Ah Sai, her glance slanting across the cups and plates on the table to rest upon the girl's utensils. Ah Sai saw that the bowl had been emptied of rice, but the meat remained. "You see that? It's so difficult for me." Du Li An leaned close to him, barely moved her lips, and spoke with the voice of a spy.

"Your brother-in-law says Elder Zong wants him to start a business." Du Li An lowered her voice. "He wants me to help him."

"You know very well that you must find someone you trust when starting a business." She paused, her expression earnest. "Ah Sai, I trust no one more than you."

Ah Sai did not reply. Du Li An's reference to "your brother-in-law" reminded him of Sou Gei. It was at that moment he finally felt, keenly, that Sou Gei no longer existed in this world. No more of her nagging kvetches over the phone. No more nudges for him to call his sister. Why would I call, there's nothing much to say.

Aiya, you could ask after your brother-in-law.

Remembering Sou Gei made Ah Sai sad. He turned suddenly quiet and looked sorrowfully at Du Li An with an expression she could not comprehend. She froze for a moment, then said, It's okay, not a problem if you don't come back. From what I see you're doing rather well for yourself there. The boss lady treats you well.

"Plus, it's a big city over there. You'll pick up more experience." She patted Ah Sai on his shoulder as if comforting a child who had picked himself up after a tumble.

The bus seemed to shoot forward with great speed on the trip back to the capital. The driver maneuvered the bus along winding roads as if it were a dragon to be tamed. Ah Sai sat at the back of the fuming bus, tossed about until he almost threw up the multitude of dishes mingling in his stomach. He thought back to the scene after dinner. The old man said he was off to gamble and headed alone in the direction of the club. Ah Sai and his sister, along with the teenaged siblings, all squeezed into Steely Bo's car. When they rounded a corner they saw the old man stumbling along on the five-foot way. Du Li An rolled down a window, letting in the strains of the old man singing Cantonese opera at the top of his lungs:

> Oh a light boat skims off like a leaf;
> now we're separated by mountain peaks.
> The birds fly south, the birds fly south,
> and when will those birds in pairs return?
> Ah poor me, how lonely I am.
> Ah poor me, how lonely I am!

—2—

Mother wanted you to call him "Uncle Sai." Because "Sai" literally means "small," to you the moniker implies the existence of another person, of an older generation or even beyond, worthy of being called "Uncle Dai." But after all these years, such an older uncle never materialized. Sometimes you're stopped on the stairs of Mayflower and questioned, Have you seen your Uncle Sai? Where has he disappeared to? Through this you vaguely intuit that he is "your" Uncle Sai. When you mull it over, it seems to carry a taste of the familial.

Mother asked you to call him that. You did. Uncle Sai stepped forward from a mound of backlit figures, his grin exposing a mouth of crooked, yellowing teeth. He said, This is a good kid, he listens. You turn around to step on the floorboards, making them creak.

Mother asked you to call him. You stood on the third-floor stairway and leaned against the handrail for support, shouting down. Uncle Sai. Uncle Sai. Your voice, breaking, changing, croaked out unfamiliar sounds. Low and coarse, the sounds followed the stairs' curvature and spun to the bottom. Some time passed before his response could be made out. What is it?

My ma wants you. You and your shadow on the wall spoke into the immense, gaping emptiness.

Mother called you. You turned back. Her legs were puffy, veins showing like green earthworms tunneling their way out of her skin. When you looked upon her left kneecap, swollen as large as a basketball, you experienced a hazy premonition that Mother was not long for the world. And she indeed became confused, uttering a bunch of head-scratchers with her eyes rolled back. She asked whether you remembered living on a street with many shops that sold coffins. She said she went back there last night and saw an old man playing erhu while someone tossed paper cars and paper people into a raging fire.

Uncle Sai said it was a precursor to death. You've heard of it too. In fact, when you lived on the street lined with many coffin shops, it was the old man who sat outside the shops who described this to you, your mother, and the other sex workers. You used to peer across the thresholds while they chatted. The shops were uniformly dim, their floors coated with ashes like light snow. There must have been a shrine farther in the recesses. You couldn't make out what was being worshipped. The only things visible were blooms of fire from candles or oil lamps, the flames motionless.

But why did that precursor to death drag on for so long. Mother lived for a long while, lugging around her rotten leg, suffering pain from which you were unable to relieve her. It was only after her sudden craving for meat and the lamb curry you brought back that she died in contentment, clasping her engorged belly. You were almost convinced the lamb was poisoned, but Uncle Sai said no, it was the period of lucidity before the final journey. His face was blank when he told you this, as if he'd grown numb to matters of life and death, just like the old man who whiled away the rest of his life sitting outside coffin shops.

But what you were reminded of was a death row inmate's last meal. You thought of the fried noodle lady who choked to death on durian in *The Age of Goodbyes*. Of people wishing for nothing more than to die in a moment of contentment.

Mother called. You woke from one dream to discover her trapped in another. In that dream, her calls surprisingly resembled her cries of passion you once heard from the room next door. Who? What man was in there? She lay dead in the room. Uncle Sai told you to find another one in which to sleep. You shook your head, sitting by the bed all night to be with your slumbering queen. At midnight Uncle Sai knocked on the door and said, Try turning on the AC, why don't you. It's hot, she might start to smell. You did as told. The AC unit released violent coughs, as if spewing up all of its ancient innards.

So you turned it off and continued to sit by the bed. In truth, you believed she had long started stinking from inside out. You recalled the seaside motel you lived in for two weeks. Even the sunshine gave off the smell of salted fish. Scores of touristy people, cameras dangling against their chests, walked past two little shops selling seafood products on the same street. Mother said, Well, time to go, I'm no match for the young little tarts here. So the two of you left that place where you could listen to the sea breeze, trading it for the street of mourning and burials. In your memory that was a place on the cusp of the living world, an alternate dimension unknown to humankind during the day. It was only after nightfall that its gates were thrown open, welcoming people to its banquets of the dead. But all said, motels were identical everywhere. Desiccated pillows, mattresses repeatedly soaked through by sweat, railings that threatened to collapse at any moment, and sticky handrails lining the stairs.

Mother said, No matter where it goes, the snail carries its own shell on its back.

Before the sun rose, you dreamed of a maze with endless doors and infinite corridors. A few of the doors were opened a crack, their hinges squeaking. Someone peered through one such crack with cold, sinister eyes. It was all very realistic. And then it was day. You rubbed your eyes. Like soft gossamer silk, sunlight smoothed Mother's stiff, cold face. You almost believed she would wake up.

They arrived. Afterward Uncle Sai did a count and said the condolence money was more than two thousand ringgit. You very much wanted to tell him that someday you would pay back what was owed, but you hesitated for a long while, never managing to spit it out.

—

You stop going to school after taking the public exams. You find the library Mother spoke of, the oldest one in the city. There, you stick your hand into depths forgotten by time, seeking the book in your imagination. It all goes smoother than you'd imagined, nothing like the needle in the haystack Mother made it out to be. She'd been to that library but was never again able to find the way. But you, you're far better than her at the art of finding. She forgot that her own expertise lay in hiding and forgetting.

In the end, what she remembered was the street of mourning and burial, and the scrumptiousness of lamb. She couldn't even recall J. When you pressed her, she turned toward the ceiling those clear eyes shining out from within her muddled ones; she gazed at the deep pits found inside Time that were invisible to you. She said, No, of course not, why would you have a twin brother?

Uncle Sai never heard Mother talk about him either. He stood in front of Mother's coffin, flicking off cigarette ashes. He said, If it were true, it's not like she would forget, and there's no way she would keep something like that from you with her very last breath.

This devastated you. The self she had long lost might not have been able to remember.

Mayflower is empty during the day. The old sex workers smoke outside in the shade of the trees, while the old man responsible for the motel's maintenance sits lost in thought in the broken rattan chair by the front desk. Everyone is limp and sapped of energy, like candles burned down to stubs on altars, merely counting down the remainder of their days. Mayflower is like a convalescent home. Yet no matter how long they have stayed in this place, the sex workers counting down their lives here still consider themselves mere passersby. They know nothing of each other's pasts. Maybe there's too much overlap among their experiences, and there's nothing particularly of note. On the other hand, they know quite a bit about Uncle Sai's history.

"Your Uncle Sai, there's a bit of story there." The old sex worker exhales a cloud of smoke. Through the resulting fog you watch her adopt the posture of an informer, already harboring an idea of what she'll say. It's as you've seen; after you called out to him, a diminutive man emerged from a mound of backlit figures. A strange worm is tattooed across his left arm, a clumsy version of the blue and white pattern on porcelain. He said to Mother, with his mouthful of crooked teeth, Your son's a good kid.

"Your Uncle Sai used to mess around with the mafia when he was young. Later he did drugs too. Took a whole lot for him to finally get straight."

She blows another puff of smoke in your direction after her big reveal. You lift your eyes to look at the branching trees, which makes you feel like a colossus is towering above you, holding open an enormous umbrella littered with holes. The sun is blinding. All you mean to do is yawn, but instead you awake to find yourself curled up in the hollow space left by death. It's very late at night. Uncle Sai is sitting up with a friend at a funeral viewing. You get up and distractedly flip through the masterpiece spread open on the desk. On a whim, you jot down this sentence:

He enables prostitution and gambling, plus has unclean relations with the old madam.

Not long after Mother died, the sex workers told you that a very young Thai girl moved into Mayflower. "It's true," they exclaimed in unison. "Your ma wasn't dead yet when the girl moved in." They described her as being very skinny with narrow hips and a wide face the color of copper. Also a huge mouth and pearly white teeth. They said her name is Mana. Yes, Mana. We call her "the golden rattan cane" in secret. Have you really not seen her?

Mana may be a sex worker, or she may be Uncle

Sai's other lover. She may even be a ghost. You haven't detected her presence at all in Mayflower, even though she lives here. In this old building, even a single drip from the kitchen tap downstairs sends shockwaves up to the third floor. Drip drop. Could it be that Mana is a tiptoeing Siamese cat? You find this hard to believe. Everyone has seen Mana; you alone have not detected her existence in the slightest. They say your Uncle Sai has hidden her because he doesn't want you and your ma to see her.

Go on then, go find Mana.

You think about the cellar and the hidden room you used to yearn for in your fantasies. The location of treasures. Mother is in there guarding the watch and laser gun meant for you. And Mana, Mana is a doll that resembles a Siamese cat, all skin and bones with pale green eyes shaped like almonds.

During the long school break, while you wait for your exam results, you open your notebook and add a task to your to-do list: "Find Mana."

—3—

Because an abrupt shift in style happens in the novel's second half, you can't help but suspect that *The Age of Goodbyes* is a kind of perverse, jumbled biography. Therefore you go online and enter "Shaozi" and "The Lefty Who Lost Her Right Brain" into the search bar. But there are no relevant results. With that, you have no choice but to accept the text as pure invention. *If it cannot be said to constitute a novel, then it can only be a made-up biography.*[1]

"A made-up biography" are The Fourth Person's exact words. Later, students who referenced this explanation

1. See "The Fabricator of History."

of his often made the same careless mistake. They kept misquoting him as "If it cannot be said to constitute a factual novel, then it can only be a made-up biography." If The Fourth Person were alive and well, he would naturally be incensed by the lack of rigor evident in the attitude of these supposed scholars. He was such a scrupulous person! He went through numerous rounds of edits when he worked on Shaozi's collection of unpublished work for publication; it was said that not a single error could be found among its 300,000 words. In contrast, because Shaozi had never been properly and systematically instructed in linguistics, grammatical mistakes proliferated in her writing despite her exceptional literary style. Typos in her manuscripts abounded like ticks on a dog, causing editors untold headaches. To survey Shaozi's twelve books published prior to her death was to admit that "an error-free book" featuring her work would be the first of its kind.

Either way, Shaozi paid no attention to such criticisms. In truth, Shaozi's lack of reaction and distant attitude were confounding, considering the overwhelming passion that The Fourth Person directed at both her and her work. She remained the "Sister Li" who managed a business selling cheap underwear, plus a few night market stalls hawking pirated DVDs on the side. She bet on sports and drank like a fish. While she never married, rumors had it that she tore through a slew of lovers. They were of course no better than the average citizen, or else they were some small-timers associated with the triads. Naturally Shaozi's exemplary body of work[2] far outshone her roster of lovers.

Throughout *The Age of Goodbyes*, the author takes an exceedingly odd, bisected approach to explicate the

2. Setting aside *The Age of Goodbyes*, Shaozi published twelve books in her lifetime, including eight short story collections, three novellas, and one volume of essays.

relationship between Shaozi and The Fourth Person. In the book, the two never cross paths. In fact, Shaozi seems not to be aware of The Fourth Person's presence. She and The Fourth Person appear to exist in overlapping dimensions within the same time-space. Or they are separated by a one-way mirror into two parallel universes. Through the window, The Fourth Person examines Shaozi and his own faint figure cast upon the glass. On the other side, Shaozi goes about fully unaware of the world behind the mirror.

You start to wonder whether "Sister Li" is even conscious of the existence of "Shaozi."

When you go on Internet forums and bring up these features of the book, some netizens say they are reminded of Narcissus from Greek myths. He who was enamored with his own reflection in the water. Some other netizens bring up the Cypriot king Pygmalion, who fell in love with his own stone sculpture. These opinions are of course borne out of thin air, seemingly fitting and yet ultimately falling flat due to their illogic. Yet the trope of "a sculptor who falls in love with his sculpture" also appears in the novel. It takes place after The Fourth Person's death, which more or less revived sales of Shaozi's posthumously published work. Collectors everywhere understood that Shaozi's oeuvre must be paired with The Fourth Person's critical analyses for their collections to be considered "complete." This was especially true because The Fourth Person was found clutching his review of *The Age of Goodbyes* in his dead hands, and this after pouring body and soul into self-financing the publication of that very book. This caused shockwaves no advertising could achieve, resulting in a rush on both *The Age of Goodbyes* and the collected critical work of The Fourth Person, titled *Always by Your Side* (five volumes). This rush was a rare phenomenon in the usually barren literary market. *Always by Your Side* went through reprint after reprint, which ushered in numerous successive rounds of editing. With the third print edition, the many mistakes that slipped in because of the haste to publish the first edition were finally fully corrected.

Questions began to arise after the third edition's release—was *The Age of Goodbyes* really by Shaozi's hand? These suspicions may have surfaced because of *Always by Your Side*'s unusually robust sales record, since the book fell more into the category of academic criticism and thus by all expectations should have been ignored by the market.

At first, such misgivings were only topics of conversation at small literary gatherings over tea or drinks. But somehow the doubt spread, snowballed into a gossipy hot issue among the literati, and eventually morphed into something worthy of serious literary discussions. As far as literary phenomena went, the wide-roving attention dedicated to the topic was on par with the previous "scorched-earth" controversy initiated by Chinese Malaysian writers and scholars living in Taiwan. All of this was followed by various eminent authors and academics expounding their opinions upon the topic, which then prompted lawsuits by The Fourth Person's surviving family members. One can well imagine the multitude of falsehoods flying about, all mixed up with the truth.

No doubt Pygmalion's name was brought up during the cacophonic waves of discussion at the time. In the Greek myth, this Cypriot king poured all his passion and energy into completing a statue of a young girl, which he named Galatea and which he subsequently fell in love with. Some literati, either experts in psychology or those who dabbled in it, did not rule out the possibility that The Fourth Person had a "Pygmalion condition." They came to this conclusion after researching his extremely unusual approach to Shaozi during the second half of his life, as well as the unique conditions by which *The Age of Goodbyes* and *Always by Your Side* were created, not to mention the complicated referential relationship between those two books.

In truth, before the full manuscript of *The Age of Goodbyes* was unearthed, Shaozi had not published a single novel, nor does there exist any record that she intended to write one. On the other hand, because of his many years of deep research into Shaozi's work, The Fourth Person was believed by most to be able to imitate Shaozi's writing style in order to construct the "Shaozi novel" of his imagination.

Although suspicions had been raised and the vast majority of local thinkers had thrown themselves into the raging hot debate, the whole controversy nevertheless remained "unresolved" because the writers of both books were dead, and the dead cannot speak. Not to mention that, after a life of mystery, Shaozi was survived by only her mother, who passed of old age soon after the debate was ignited. After that there remained scattered sparks of interest, but the whole thing has since devolved into nothing more than an interesting anecdote from the past. No one takes it seriously anymore.

Either way, although The Fourth Person's reputation took a hit during that period of suspicions, sales of the two books in question once again rebounded and snaked up best-seller charts. Although it proved to be the books' swan song, their brief ascendance still became conversation fodder for the desolate literary world to come. Out of caution, future Chinese-language teachers and students of Shaozi commonly did not count *The Age of Goodbyes* among her output, since the veracity of the book's authorship had been called into question.

CHAPTER FOUR

—1—

That year, the boy Candlenut said he wanted to go to the capital so he could watch "The Greatest" Ali fight the European champion. Du Li An made a special effort to order a batch of charcoal-fired heong peng from Mi Shan New Village, which she asked Candlenut to bring along for Ah Sai. Little did she know that the good-for-nothing Candlenut would decide to linger in the city and refuse to return. Ah Sai called on his behalf. The pastries had indeed been delivered, but Candlenut had also asked to borrow three hundred ringgit, saying he wanted to stay and look for a job. "If I may bother you to tell my dad." With that, he turned and walked away.

Du Li An couldn't help cussing on the call. To Ah Sai's ears, her yelling contained some blame directed toward him: How could you let him just walk away? Although the relationship was a bit convoluted, Ah Sai was still Candlenut's "uncle" by name, and so held certain responsibilities befitting an elder. "Let's hear it. How do you propose explaining this to your brother-in-law?"

But Steely Bo's reaction surprised Du Li An. He nodded, then kept eating bowl after bowl at dinner, wolfing down meat, not saying much. As if he'd long understood that it is natural for birds to leave their nests when it comes time. And now, after The Greatest defeated the European champion in a game that was said to be incredibly boring, it was probably about the right time. Even Candlenut's sister Lau Lin was perplexingly calm. She still ate very little, occasionally put down her bowl and chopsticks to get her father more rice, then returned to finish her own tiny bowl with determination. Du Li An no longer put meat into her bowl. Not since Steely Bo suddenly became enraged and roared at Lau Lin to finish the meat sitting at the bottom of her bowl.

"You think I didn't see that? You, eat up every last bit!" Lau Lin had just stood up to put away her utensils when Steely Bo abruptly slammed his huge hand on the table, bouncing all the plates and bowls.

Du Li An and Lau Lin froze in shock, momentarily unable to comprehend what he meant. For his part, Candlenut leapt nimble as a monkey to safety with his rice bowl in hand. Everyone watched Steely Bo. With his eyes opened wide, he looked like a menacing temple guardian. "You, Lau Lin, sit down and finish that meat!" Only then did Lau Lin realize he was talking to her. She sat slowly down, her pale face turning green. But she didn't eat, she merely lowered her head to stare at the few pieces of flesh in the bowl. Steely Bo waited a while. Then he said, Fine, if you won't eat, then don't you ever get up. If you dare stand up I'll break your legs.

Then he continued to shovel rice into his mouth. Candlenut, gauging the situation and finding it none of his concern, followed suit and sat down to gobble his food. But Du Li An's heart raced with fear. From what she knew of him, Steely Bo was a man who'd gone through a lot. Over the past two years he'd gradually grown morose. The quieter he appeared, the more tension built, an explosion just waiting for a spark. She bit her lip, not daring to even take a big breath. From the corner of her eye she watched Lau Lin, still as a statue, her teeth gritted, eyes slightly bulged, as if trying to summon a strong jolt of willpower to disappear the meat in the bowl. Du Li An was almost afraid the girl would really stand up out of a moment's impetuousness.

When Candlenut was done eating, he disappeared from the scene with nothing more than a push of his bowl and chopsticks. But Steely Bo remained seated after his meal, one leg hitched across the other, asking Du Li An to fetch him a toothpick. When Du Li An returned, she heard Candlenut turn on the TV in the living room. For some reason Lau Lin's eyes grew red upon hearing the TV, and big droplets of tears splashed into her bowl. Du Li An noticed Steely Bo's brows were furrowed and his breathing increasingly harsh, as if the storm of the century was brewing within his throat. Her fear started giving way to panic. She cleared her throat and did her best to soften her voice.

"Ah Lin, go on, eat."

Her words seemed to make Lau Lin's crying a little worse, but she did finally lift one hand to deliver meat into her mouth. Du Li An watched Lau Lin's hand tremble; she didn't stop sobbing while gulping the meat, now mixed with tears and snot, into her stomach. Du Li An beamed a silent apology. In the end, Steely Bo really did exercise his patience. He didn't stand up until Lau Lin finished her few pieces of meat.

"I dare you to try this again in the future." The toothpick dangled from his mouth. Du Li An remembered this exact sight from many years ago, when she stuck her head out from cowering behind Sou Gei for a look. It was the very same expression, promising fiendish violence, as if he was intent on murder.

So with this current episode involving the boy Candlenut "running away from home," Du Li An couldn't quite gauge if Steely Bo's state of calm signified an impending thunderstorm. Before climbing into bed that night, she urged him to call the fishing village that was his hometown the next day. "You've got to clarify things. Can't have her thinking I kicked her son out." To her surprise, Steely Bo turned over in bed hugging a pillow and told her Candlenut had already phoned his mother. Steely Bo himself had been notified by the fishing village first thing that morning.

"No wonder you're so calm. You've known for a while." Du Li An was displeased to realize she was the last to find out. She turned off the light, her expression melting into darkness. Then she clambered into bed, groping her way, and lay down beside him.

"What else did they say? Did he get a tongue-lashing?"

"What's the use? His wings have grown tough." Steely Bo kept his back to her. His voice was a stream of mutters, like he was about to fall asleep. Du Li An turned onto her side so she was closer to him and put a hand on his arm. She said, You're not even a little bit anxious because you have two other sons over there, isn't that right.

His mumbled response sounded like sleep-talking nonsense. She wasn't really listening in earnest anyway. She said, Why don't you come with me to see a doctor. She gave him a little shove when she said it. He reflexively moved his arm away and hugged the pillow tighter. Soon, his snores rang out. She was somewhat suspicious he was pretending, but she didn't know what to do about it. With a low sigh that was almost a moan, she said, You're always like this. There was no movement from him. Outside the window, the chirps of insects echoed with his snores. Even in the dark, Du Li An could feel the presence of his back, hulking like a thick wall. It was solid, broad, and could absorb all sounds.

—

That year, Elder Zong finally made good on his promise and issued some money under the banner of the Toa
Pek Kong Society for Steely Bo to start a business. By
then Steely Bo was already fifty. His two eldest sons at
the fishing village had already started families, and both
their wives had given birth to children in the same year,
making him a grandfather. Ever since, Du Li An noticed
he seemed to have undergone a personality shift. Now
he showed extra interest in visiting his hometown. In
the past he'd visited once or twice a month at most,
doing nothing more than plunking down money for
their living expenses, eating lunch, and shooting the
crap. He always left by the afternoon, laden with fresh
seafood. But since the arrival of his two grandkids, his
visits to the fishing village were more frequent. He often
brought along new toys, and he even started spending
nights there on occasion. The worst part was that he did
it all spontaneously. What was so hard about making
a telephone call? Just say "I'm not coming back," and
don't come back. Simple.

Naturally, Du Li An was none too happy. They'd even
bickered a few times over some of her snider and more
provocative remarks. They both assumed their skir-
mishes were due to jealousy, not understanding that
underneath the sour-smelling, cold fire lay a hidden,
boiling current. Anxiety, yes, and panic, uncertainty,
and terror, mixed in like pebbles. When she delivered
the charcoal-fired heong peng Du Li An had ordered,
Guen Hou said, I never imagined Brother Bo would be
the type to adore children. I couldn't tell at all.

Guen Hou went with her to see a gynecologist. But
the doctor said these matters required both husband
and wife to be examined, and what's more, your husband

is already fifty. Steely Bo considered such suggestions taboo, and every time the issue was brought up, his voice got hoarse and his temper flared. After a few arguments, he went so far as to act deaf and mute. Du Li An itched to fight but had no outlet. She didn't really want to push him over the edge either, lest he escaped "over there." And so she maintained a mask of indifference, though she grew ever more fretful. It was right around this time that the Toa Pek Kong Society disbursed the money. Steely Bo was not enthusiastic about the idea of entrepreneurship. Not only did he let Du Li An make decisions about the venture, he even promised her full control over it. "You're the boss lady. Who better than you to take charge?" This more or less soothed her unease, and she thought keeping busy might help dissipate some of her worries. So she threw herself into planning, getting a head start on scoping out prime locations. She even consulted a fortune teller on feng shui and naming matters. The plan was to open up a grand restaurant.

Except there were road bumps, the biggest being that there wasn't enough money! The sum Du Li An received from Steely Bo was far below what Elder Zong had originally promised. The realization was like a bucket of cold water poured straight over her head. She stared in disbelief, so stunned she didn't even think to demand an explanation until a while later. Her question opened a can of worms. She'd assumed that Elder Zong had reneged on his promise, changing the amount of money at the last minute. But in truth, Steely Bo had "reallocated" funds to the fishing village.

"My two sons want to start a fish farm. I think it's a great idea." He deliberately kept his tone light, then spread his arms and broadened his stance while cracking his neck, topping it all off with a lazy stretch.

Du Li An stood shock still, wordless for a long time. She knew her face was hardening, and she felt as if ice water was injected straight into her spine. She trembled and her breathing grew frenzied, her chest rose and fell rapidly. After a spell, she finally opened her mouth and let out a series of dry, hoarse cries. Her crying was like a tube of unevenly squeezed toothpaste, emerging in fits, growing louder and louder until it was an earthshaking wail. Though Steely Bo knew full well that she wouldn't let things slide so easily, he was still flustered by the showstopping dirge now playing out. "Why are you doing this, stop that, you've gone mad." But Du Li An pressed against the wall and sank to the floor, her crying waning but not stopping. The weird thing was, she never once shed a single tear. Her crying was of a very dry sort, such that those wails sounded even more heartrending to anyone listening.

It was afternoon. Lau Lin was off sewing clothes in a factory. The neighbors on both sides heard Du Li An's crying and stirred, each one respectively issuing a woman carrying a child in her arms while dragging along other kids. They huddled against the chain-link fence and raised their heads to peer into Du Li An's house. Steely Bo's stony face appeared at the windowsill. He glared left and right, then shut the Venetian blinds with a loud smack, but Du Li An's cries could still be heard coming from the house.

That tearless storm sent Steely Bo running out the door. He did not return for three whole days and three whole nights. Du Li An cried on her haunches until her legs lost all feeling. It was only the thought of Lau Lin getting off work soon that made her slowly get up and grope her way along the wall to her dressing table. The oval vanity mirror on the wall resembled a transparent container, stowing away her person and her gradually darkening world, along with the loneliness palpable in the room. She looked at herself, stashed in the mirror. No trace of tears on her face, and yet it was so frail, suddenly aged. She couldn't stand the sight of it.

Du Li An mulled over many things while Steely Bo stayed away. Of course Lau Lin noticed his absence and the resulting change in the house's atmosphere. There were just the two of them now at the dinner table, but Du Li An kept on cooking his portion: three dishes and a soup, complemented by a large pot of rice, which sat next to two pairs of chopsticks. An impenetrable silence cloaked the table. It wasn't until the third day, when she initiated a conversation with Lau Lin, that Du Li An learned the boy Candlenut had found work doing odd jobs at a tire shop in the capital. She said, "Tell your brother if he needs any help with daily necessities, he should definitely seek out his uncle Ah Sai."

Lau Lin threw her a glance. Du Li An met that gaze head on, her spine straight. "I'm like you. I just want my family to have someone watching over them out there." Lau Lin gave this some thought, then nodded slightly.

"Your dad probably won't be coming home tonight. You eat as much as you can." Du Li An snagged a slice of grouper and thrusted it at Lau Lin. She hesitated a moment, just a moment, then extended her arm, too, holding out her bowl to receive the offering. Later, when Du Li An snuck a glance out the corner of her eye, she saw Lau Lin place the fish in her mouth. After some thorough chewing, she swallowed.

Du Li An was in the kitchen washing and chopping when Steely Bo returned the following day. He heard the sounds from the kitchen, but instead of heading in there, he turned on the TV in the living room and watched for a while. When he had driven up to the house, Du Li An had recognized the familiar sounds of the car engine. She combed her wet hands through her hair, puffed out her chest, took a deep breath, and continued rinsing rice for dinner. But he never did come in. She snuck side glances at the gray shadows thrown on the living room walls. A Malay film was on TV, and she could hear the faint dialogue between a man and a woman, accompanied by slightly melo-dramatic Malay music. Steely Bo, impatient, switched channels, but it was another Malay show. He waited a while, then switched back to the first channel, listening to the music undulating like a snake dance while bashful scenes of courtship played out. Then the music ceased and different scenes alternated. As the waiting stretched and the idling prolonged, Du Li An's heart grew cold.

He entered when she was sorting the water spin-ach. She felt his presence behind her. She listened as he lifted the thermos and poured water into a cup, drank all of it down in loud glugs, and then let out an exag-gerated sigh.

"Water spinach for dinner? What else?" He was up to his old tricks, as if pretending nothing had happened would cancel out all prior events.

Du Li An gritted her teeth. "Soy sauce chicken, yam stewed with pork belly, herbal soup," she said in a chilly voice. "And pan-fried shrimp left over from last night."

Steely Bo said nothing. Those were all his favorite dishes. The kitchen was suddenly very quiet, so quiet it amplified sounds from the TV, such as the music's kompang beats and the dialogue; all sorts of random little sounds from outside the house leaked inward. The people next door had already started frying in their wok. Children trotted past the house in groups, walk-ing each other home after school. Somewhere farther away a vendor sold popsicles from his bicycle, ringing his bell from perhaps a different street altogether. When Du Li An snapped the stem off a water spinach, it made an infinitesimal and hollow sound.

Steely Bo let out a long sigh that contained within it a flicker of capitulation. "Ah Li." He paused. "It's my fault."

She kept her head down and continued preparing the vegetables. Go shower, she said, so we can have dinner by the time Ah Lin gets back. He made no reply. Padding forward, he lightly grabbed hold of her arms from behind. Ah Li, I'm sorry, he said.

They'd been married only how many short years, yet at that moment, Du Li An felt that they were already an old couple. She'd had so many recurring thoughts while he was gone, and one of them was no less than divorce. But now, hearing an "I'm sorry" from Steely Bo, a man who had never admitted a single fault, she felt something stir in her heart. Without preamble, two fat tears suddenly fell fully formed from the corners of her eyes, as if they'd been suppressed for a long time.

She sniffled. She'd gone down so many mental rabbit holes, and in the end, all she wanted was simply this apology. Steely Bo embraced her from behind. She responded to his muscular embrace with chilly hands that emanated the delicate fragrance of green leaves. At that moment, the various noises that had tunneled into the kitchen like uninvited flying insects buzzed once around the room and then, one by one, flapped their wings in retreat.

—2—

The more you read, the more you get the sense that you've once known many of the novel's characters. It seems as if they float up from the words. While you fall asleep, exhausted, the army of ants in the book surreptitiously modifies its formation, surfacing characters on the pages like sculptures in relief. You can't help rereading the beginning of the book, but the odd thing is, those descriptions now seem unfamiliar, as if you'd never read it in earnest. For example, the man with mental illness who appears in the first chapter. When you first read about him, you got the impression that he is hastily sketched, almost like an afterthought, but now upon rereading you discover that he is expressively and memorably rendered. The writer even declares, before the man makes his debut, "perhaps this is Fate showing her hand."

The book mentions that he is the most well-known "lunatic" in the small town. Now that you think about it, you seem to remember seeing a similar person during your time, in your city. He's dressed in tattered rags and covered by innumerable layers of gray. Barefoot, he pushes a bicycle missing its chain, the handles crowded with dangling plastic bags half-filled with liquid the color of pee. No one can tell how much time is buried underneath that head of unkempt hair and the beard dominating his face. Even his race is obfuscated by his raw, brown skin and a profile rendered indistinct by accumulated dirt.

Why doesn't he speak? He knows only to howl, like Tarzan in the jungle. You seem to recall a similar figure from your childhood yowling at a crossroads in the city. He had been a taciturn, scrawny man, his eyes as profound as those of an Indian ascetic. He would occasionally and abruptly throw down everything he carried to stand among the rushing cars in the streets, his fists balled, his body arched backward. He let out long, drawn-out yells directed at shophouses lining the streets, his face aimed at upstairs windows, balconies, and roofs. His roars sometimes sounded angry, and other times like he was summoning someone who lived among the clouds.

Oh—

Ah—

You and mother were both startled by him. She immediately shielded you behind her. You followed the man's gaze to windows screened by wooden Venetian blinds with some slats missing. You saw something silver sparkle like spider silk among the blinds, almost as if there was a crowd of white-haired crones hiding behind the windows, observing.

This man, who feels like someone who could still be spotted in public not too long ago, suddenly barges into room 301 in Mayflower. He appears on the pages of the tome laid flat on the desk, the novel with dubious origins. On May Thirteenth, he breaks into violence, brandishing his bike chain to attack Du Li An at her post in the cinema. Steely Bo happens to be passing by and without hesitation yanks her into his car. This is the beginning of their courtship and marriage. Du Li An and Steely Bo feel familiar to you. You think about Mother and Uncle Sai, a little uncertain whether a pair of silhouettes resembling the fictional characters are stored deep within your memory. You close your eyes, quietly waiting for those silhouettes to surface from the limpid darkness. They finally appear, but it's like they're standing on the other side of a mosaic window. The man extends his arms and embraces the woman, who has her head down, from behind. Immediately the two colorful blobs melt into each other. They are silent, immobile. The vision grows blurrier and blurrier, like a splash of watercolor spreading out and dissipating on paper.

That must have been a dream. Your sleep is restless. A slight sound rings out from downstairs, dredging you up from the dream in which you'd sunk. You open your eyes and see two geckos chasing each other in circles on the ceiling, emitting mating cries. But in fact there is an unfamiliar sound downstairs, very dainty steps that may belong to a woman, though definitely not an old person. You bounce up from bed, out of that wok meant to cook you to death in your dreams.

Mana? Could it be Mana?

You burst out of room 301 and stop at the top of the stairs, holding your breath to hear better. The sound is coming from the second floor. You hear a door being closed, followed by the crisp click of the door lock's tongue flicking into its hole. On first listen, the noise seems to originate from Uncle Sai's room. You walk slowly down the stairs, but as soon as you reach the second floor, the floorboards there let out warning squeals, like rats tripping over each other at the sudden appearance of light. And so the sound, faint to begin with, that proof of the existence of an "other," abruptly vanishes. You tiptoe at a snail's pace right up to room 203 and lean your cheek against the door. You stop breathing and listen to the goings-on behind the door. You stay in this position for a while. The deep silence from within makes you doubt the existence of the room itself. Nothing but solid darkness through the keyhole and the crack between door and frame; the door begins to seem like a wood carving or artwork hung on the thick wall.

You wait patiently for a while longer, until you begin to suspect that all five rooms on the second floor have vanished, leaving behind only their doors, morphing into something like calendars or paintings. As you turn back toward the third floor, you can't help tugging at the handle of a particularly questionable door. The door opens with an answering creak. The curtains are not drawn in the room, which is storing moonlight; the furniture near the window are all sparkling with a splash of silvery-gray grandeur. You feel a little relieved, knowing the room still exists. You close the door and silently back out of this mysterious experience.

Back in room 301, you resume reading *The Age of Goodbyes*. But after trying for a bit, you realize you are unable to focus. Clearly you're still riveted by the slightest sound from downstairs, unable to repress your fantasy that Mana is intentionally playing hide-and-seek with you. Everyone has tunneled into their own separate spaces, as if their sole aim is to avoid you. This inexplicable self-pity takes root in your mind, triggering a sour response from the taste buds of your heart. Now you hear the front gate clanging on the ground floor. Uncle Sai is back. One, two, three, four . . . You count the footsteps underscored by the dragging of his slippers. It takes thirty-seven steps to go to room 203. But he stops on the landing between the second and third floors, for about five seconds maybe. You imagine the content of those five seconds. What is he thinking about? What caused him to hesitate, to pause before finally continuing on to his forty-seventh step.

Now he stands right outside the door. It isn't dinnertime, does he have something to say to you? Your page-turning hand pauses midair, awaiting the sound of knocking. But he continues to stand, rooted just outside. Maybe he stares at the numbers nailed into the door. Or maybe his knocking hand, too, is suspended in midair. He must know you haven't gone to bed. Even if he can't hear the cicadas in the tube light, still on, he can surely see the faint light seeping out under the door. Suddenly he leaves. His footsteps sound nimbler as he walks downstairs. Perhaps he is pondering certain things, and has decided to keep them from you, for now.

After Mother died, the two remaining old sex workers asked about your plans, one after the other. They each half-jokingly suggested adopting you as their son, so you'd at least have some kind of official standing to continue living in Mayflower. You gazed upon their faces, which had grown kinder as they aged. You imagined drifting to another and yet another mother's room after each one died. Every mother so similar to the others, with their approximate fates and body odor, like the many unmemorable little motels in this city or that town. These suggestions are anathema to you, but you understand their good intentions. Their sensory organs may be gradually blunting, but even so they are more sensitive than you to the slightest stirrings within interpersonal relationships. Maybe they've picked up something from Uncle Sai's quarters, or maybe it is solely the appearance of Mana.

There hasn't been a young woman in Mayflower for ages. Mana, the girl of the rumors, has been seen only once since she moved in with "a small satchel and a large duffle bag." Lately there has been no trace of her, and even the old man at the front desk cannot say for sure whether she has since left.

But the people of Mayflower are united in their belief of her existence, even if they haven't seen her. No one can provide any proof, yet; like you, everyone stubbornly believes the Thai girl "is just hiding." They theorize she may be an illegal immigrant who climbed over the border, or she may be a seed previously sowed over there by your Uncle Sai. This latter theory makes you see your own complicated position in harsh light. If Mana is Uncle Sai's daughter, then who are you?

No matter what, you are dead sure Mana is still ensconced somewhere in Mayflower. She's been visiting. When you're not around, she opens the door, walks into room 301, and carefully slides out certain drawers. She removed a nail clipper, then slipped back in later to restore it to its place. But she confused the clipper's original position. It goes in the mooncake box inside the left drawer, not the right one. This disappearing and reappearing nail clipper delights you. Mana must have some kind of curiosity about this room, which is after all unlike any other room in Mayflower. In here there are traces of the living, signs of life, the pungency of lamb curry, the knickknacks and clothing of a young man. She even flipped through the books and notepad on your desk, left them in slightly altered positions; *The Age of Goodbyes* has been left open on various different pages.

You imagine Mana standing here, right here in this spot, staring, as you are, at the lightly spotted mirror. She has once been in there, and now you are also in there. Of course you can catch her, root her out.

—

Maybe it's a dream. Tap tap. When you hear the sound, you think it's Uncle Sai knocking in your dream. But the door in the dream will not budge, even when you and the person behind the door both grab hold of the handle and exert yourselves, first pushing, then pulling with all your strength. You call to each other through the door, yet neither of you know who the other is, just as neither of you understand which of you is the one locked in. In desperation, you lift your leg and give the door a mighty kick. That's how you struggle free of that clinging dream and abruptly enter the waking world. Uncle Sai is standing by the bed, his eyes round and wide, face full of concern. He asks if you had a nightmare. With your hand you wipe away cold sweat from your forehead and neck. You nod once, leftover terror still coursing through you.

Uncle Sai said today is the forty-ninth day since your mother's death. Time to light some incense for her on this meaningful occasion. On the road with him, you finally find out this was what he'd wanted to tell you when he took the forty-three steps last night. But he didn't detect any movement inside the room, so he thought you'd fallen asleep with the lights on, tired out by studying. "Usually you rush to open the door before I even reach it."

Mother's ashes are in a temple located within a spacious, dim cave that lies beyond the city limits. You keep your eyes on the person in the porcelain portrait while Uncle Sai makes the preparations. She is obviously too young, her eyes limpid, a shy yet alluring smile on her face. The facial features don't quite match the mother of your impressions. You feel doubtful. But Mother picked out that photo. When she was on bed rest, her favorite thing to do was to reach into the drawer beside her and retrieve the only two photo albums she owned. She flipped through them, back and forth, removed the few photos within and arranged them on the bed. After several rounds of comparison, she finally handed this photo to you. She said, When I die, I want this at the front of the funeral procession. You took it from her and lifted the 4R-sized photo to compare it against the real deal. Mother's eyes were iffy by then, her eyeballs often seized and rolled upward. But she knew what you were doing. She sat up straighter, the eyes within her eyes smiling out at you, as if she were facing a camera.

You didn't tell her that the person in the photo doesn't look like her, though the other old sex workers all thought her eyesight was shot by then, and even

Uncle Sai said the photo really reminded him of his long-lost baby sister. Yet you still firmly believed Mother had been looking with another pair of eyes that were hidden. But on the seventh seven, the forty-ninth day of her death, as you stand in front of her altar burning incense, you suddenly begin to suspect this is another of Mother's tricks. She'd wanted to hide her whole life. Maybe the photo was a cover. She didn't want those who knew her in the past to know that "she" was inside the box right in front of you. Who is it you're hiding from, Ma, this time around?

Uncle Sai suggests breakfast on the way back to Mayflower. He drives the car into the older part of the city in search of an old kopitiam. "Their white coffee was your ma's favorite." You know which shop he's referring to. If he hadn't brought it up, you probably wouldn't have ever thought about it. You'd been there once on a Saturday morning before school started, not long after you moved into Mayflower. Mother said your shoes from the previous year were too worn out, and she wanted to shop for two new pairs with you. She wet a comb with water and helped you with your hair. When the two of you headed out, the sex workers in the hallway turned to smile at you, all playing along instead of stretching out their hands to ruffle your hair. It was only once you reached the ground floor that you discovered Uncle Sai and his car waiting on the street.

On that trip to buy shoes, they first took you to a kopitiam for breakfast in the old city area. You still remember the coffee cups were all porcelain ware from a bygone era that featured paintings of flowers or foreign gardens. Mother ordered white coffee. She lifted her cup and poured some of the coffee into the little saucer underneath. Then she passed you that coffee-laden saucer, saying her father used to do this too when she was a kid. You were bewildered. That wasn't the first time you'd had breakfast outside with Mother, but before this she'd never once shared a drink with you by pouring some of it into a saucer. You lowered your head to sip the coffee from the saucer, raising your eyes to gaze at Mother from time to time. She was in high spirits that day, voluble, her eyes sparkling. Uncle Sai was reticent as always, reading the weekend edition by the sunlight slanting through a window. You noticed that he, like you, had combed all his hair backward that day. Because of the hair gel he'd smoothed on, his hair glistened under the morning son, twinkling like the Kopi O in his cup.

The old city streets are busy in the morning. Uncle Sai drives the car slowly along the area's few branching alleys, looking for a place to park. You know that if Mother was along, she might suggest "waiting," i.e. stopping right in the middle of the street until someone left their spot. But Mother is no longer around. You look out at the street ahead and see window sills tottering on the higher floors of two shophouse rows. You ask Uncle Sai if he's ever seen a man with mental illness who pushes a bicycle everywhere and occasionally shrieks on the streets. He nods and says he has.

"Found it!" Uncle Sai exclaims. You look. The sun abruptly emerges in full force. People on the street melt into the sunlight's brilliance. Yes, there is indeed an empty parking spot not far away.

—3—

About that man with mental illness: A similar character appears in one of Shaozi's short stories, "Notes from the Left Bank." The character is a man who pushes along a bicycle day and night wandering the streets, who sometimes takes baths in a certain fountain in the city. Nicknamed "The Luminous Jade Goblet" after those rare vessels produced in Gansu since ancient times, that fountain sits in the middle of a traffic circle and is shaped exactly as its moniker implies. It is especially attractive after sundown, all lit up and sparkling. Maybe that's why, in the book, the "lunatic" has a penchant to wash himself there at night. The story is written in first person. On their way home after work, cruising on a bike, the "I" of the book would often see the lunatic climb into the fountain naked.

The lunatic brought to life by Shaozi's pen doesn't usually bother anyone, but he does have an "allergic reaction" to sirens. Whenever he encounters squad cars, fire trucks, or ambulances sounding their sirens, he loses control and becomes somewhat prone to violence. The book's narrator once saw him under such conditions, leaping out of the fountain and streaking on the streets.

"I" lives in the northern part of the city, which is the river's left bank. It's also where the city's low-income population is packed together in close quarters. I leads a perilous life, often runs into man-biting mad dogs on their way to work, or children distributing fliers for high-interest loans on behalf of loan sharks, not to mention lunatics triggered by sirens. But I likes to take the longer road home after work for the sole purpose of passing by The Goblet, to see whether the lunatic would be around. He likes sitting in the fountain and scrubbing himself with a rag. His eyes closed, he hums like music that no one else can hear is stuffed inside his ear canals. The sight of him conjures a shining, bejeweled Turkish bath right under The Goblet. A full moon rises out of the cup. The scene reminds I of some artwork they had seen before; I feels that of the dozens of thousands of people on the Left Bank, the lunatic is the happiest.

Naturally, you've never read "Notes from the Left Bank." All you can do is piece together Shaozi's original story in your imagination, based upon fragments of The Fourth Person's writing inserted by the author of *The Age of Goodbyes*. The Fourth Person generally has no praise for Shaozi's work, preferring instead to nitpick the details in her stories from a historian's perspective. Or he approaches the stories' plots, scenes, and characters through the lens of a psychologist, all so he can theorize about the dark rooms housed within Shaozi's heart. He also frequently switches hats and puts on that of a Taoist expert, before lashing out against Shaozi's moral values. But since "Notes from the Left Bank" has nothing to do with history, the tone of his criticism correspondingly softens. He even lets slip a rare anecdote about his personal life in his discussion of this story, mentioning that he'd once seen a similar lunatic in his very own city.[1]

This "universal lunatic" suffuses *The Age of Goodbyes* with a magical atmosphere. He is like someone with superpowers shuttling between reality and fiction, and also like a person with multiple aliases. You're reminded of the French artist Balthus, whose work often features a cat or a man seen from behind, the latter of which many say is the artist himself. You can't

1. ". . . Where I live, there too used to be one (maybe even more than one) such 'lunatic.' Every time I saw him, I had the vague feeling that he wasn't quite the same person I had last seen. Because of this, I'd sometimes have fantastical thoughts; for example, I'd wonder whether this was truly the same person I'd seen. After all, his unkempt appearance masked his original facial features, and thus I had no confidence whether I'd actually 'recognized' him. Could it be that the city held several similar lunatics? I myself discarded this train of thought later, because I'd never seen 'them' appear at the same time." See "Disappearing on the Other Shore—A Brief Analysis of 'Notes from the Left Bank,'" published in 2000 in *Of the Same Roots Monthly*.

help but start wondering whether the real author of the novel is the strange person pushing along a bicycle missing its chain on the streets. He stands yowling at a crossroads. Under The Goblet, he bathes with two palmfuls of moonlight-filled water from the fountain. He snatches up a bicycle chain and whirls it around his head like a cowboy. Recognizing you, he aims a smile your way, though you are oblivious.

The eeriest part of all this is—everyone has previously seen such a lunatic, yet no one can say when they saw him last. They are united in feeling sure he has long since "disappeared." In the book, The Fourth Person regards the lunatic in his memories with something like nostalgia, and because of this, the usual tones of censure are notably softer in his review of "Notes from the Left Bank." He was especially complimentary about the story's ending, judging Shaozi's refusal to elucidate the eventual whereabouts of the lunatic as a "cunning" move that moreover demonstrates the gentle and generous side of the author's personality.[2]

Too bad it's unclear to you how the story ends. You understand this much: "I" eventually loses the opportunity to observe the man on the Left Bank. Maybe The Goblet fountain is demolished, or maybe the man is confined to an asylum. Maybe either he or I moves to the Right Bank, or somewhere even farther. Possible, too, that one day he suddenly regains clarity of mind and assimilates into "normal life" on the Left Bank.

It's at this juncture that you begin to hate the author of *The Age of Goodbyes* a little. Because of the mysterious connection hinted at by the unwell man, you've developed a strong affinity for and curiosity about

2. Summarized from "Disappearing on the Other Shore."

"Notes from the Left Bank." Reading the story would scratch an itch, but you are unable to read something that has never existed. Yet it has embedded itself deep in your subconscious and thus acquired a meaningful "existence," all simply because you've read snippets of a review written by a fictional character. An existence, followed by a vanishing.

Something else confuses you immensely. Why did the author of *The Age of Goodbyes* choose to use this kind of narrative technique to sketch out Shaozi's existence? The more you read, the more you think Shaozi has become a shadow character attached to her own work, which has been dismembered and presented incompletely in various articles by The Fourth Person. This is a Russian doll structure; The Fourth Person is the outermost layer and hints at layers of other cores within. Meanwhile Shaozi, heavily wrapped, grows ever blurrier and insignificant.

As for Shaozi's real identity, Du Li An, your theory is that she alone stands outside of this whole Russian doll structure. As "Sister Li," she gallivants about town at leisure. When she occasionally feels out of sorts or encounters love troubles, she spends a night or two at a hilltop casino. On the other hand, if she's in a good mood, she'll buy a few takeout meals and feed them to stray dogs in back alleys. While the dogs eat, she squats next to them and smokes with her nose tilted up. Someone unaware might mistake her for a street prostitute, and it is true that certain folks have tried to chat her up, only to receive a barrage of curses for their trouble. You like this Sister Li. She reminds you of certain friends of Mother. There were a good many years when one such auntie would suddenly drop by, no matter where it was that Mother had chosen to temporarily inhabit, you by her side. The auntie would show up with bags of various sizes containing cookies and junk food, White Phoenix teapills, Yomeishu herbal liqueur, fruit baskets, and sometimes toys or clothes for you. You've seen her shove a small wad of rolled-up cash into Mother's palm. You often felt a wave of high-pitched excitement emanating from this androgynous auntie who favored Hawaiian shirts paired with over-the-knee shorts. Her habit was to open the windows as soon as she entered a room. She had ceaseless topics of conversation and smoked cigarettes endlessly. She stood with one leg lifted high and perched on a chair. Compared to Mother, the auntie carried about her an even more palpable air of the seedy and unsavory.

But since a time you cannot recall, this auntie with the hoarse voice no longer appeared. In truth, you might never have given her any thought again, were you not reading about Sister Li in *The Age of Goodbyes*. You remember the auntie now, her shiny short hair and her profile gilded by sunshine as she smoked by the window. You also remember that one time Mother reminisced about the past with her. Mother talked about someone who racked up gambling debts and was dragged by loan sharks to his father's for payment. You were on the floor then, eavesdropping while doing your homework. But Mother stopped talking right as she arrived at the tensest part of the story.

You raised your head and saw Mother dangling a slipper from her toes, looking a little bored. The androgynous auntie gazed silently out the window. The two of them looked forlorn under a dome of smoke, their expressions like bodhisattvas' wreathed by incense. You peered, transfixed, at the cigarette clamped between two of Mother's fingers. However much time later, the long, long block of ash finally dropped.

That anecdote about loan sharks abducting a son and

forcing him to beg from his father left a deep impression on you. That's why, when you came across similar events described in *The Age of Goodbyes*, you were so shaken that you felt like your brain had been bombed. There was a humming in your ears, as if the cicadas in the light tubes had crawled inside your ear canals. You discovered that the novel has some sort of mysterious connection to your real life; through twists and turns, the book leads you circling back to reality, right back to the starting point on which you stand. You drew a sharp breath and closed the book. To you, its rusty green cover looked remarkably like an ancient iron door.

And yet the similar events are not directly narrated by the author. Rather they appear in the book within the book, a plot playing out in Shaozi's posthumously published *The Age of Goodbyes*. The Fourth Person discusses the events in his review, "Victim of Multiple Personality Disorder," in which he criticizes the story's illogical parts with a detective's flair,[3] and in this way emphasizes Shaozi's lack of both the power of observation and meticulous reasoning. It is yet another step toward declaring *The Age of Goodbyes* a failed realist "magnum opus."

3. "In Chapter Nine, the eldest Chen son racks up debts due to a penchant for gambling and is then forced to the Chen family factory by his creditors, where they plan to threaten his father into repaying his son's debts. But because the father refuses to open the door, the goons start thrashing his son in front of security cameras. In the end the older Mr. Chen steels his heart and turns away, resolving not to look. While this plotline is moving, we see upon closer inspection that it is unquestionably pure sensationalism. This particular plotline doesn't reflect the realities of society at the time, and the author too has overlooked the local Chinese families' ironclad traditional attitudes. The older Mr. Chen in the novel is not only wealthy but savvy at business. As he has only two sons, he would absolutely never go through with a move akin to pedicide . . ." See "Victim of Multiple Personality Disorder."

CHAPTER FIVE

—1—

The kopitiam opened on a busy street, which, let's put it this way: The two rows of shophouses there had all kinds of businesses cornered and lacked only a place for people to have a cup of tea while they rested their tired feet, or somewhere for folks working nearby to get their meals. Du Li An had picked a corner lot and demolished one wall. This, combined with a few iron shutters and some bamboo curtains, opened up the space and maximized convenience. During peak hours, even the five-foot way was taken over by tables and chairs. The street was always bustling during the day. Moreover, the lane around the corner led to two cab stands, so it really was no overstatement to say that traffic flowed nonstop. Business boomed at Ping Le House from day one. Its prime location was obviously a factor, and the food and drinks on offer were as well-praised by customers as any established places in the old town area. But all this was owed single-handedly to the boss lady's management skills, something that even the men in Steely Bo's entourage discerned. This "Big Sister-in-law" had a good eye and adroit management abilities, making her no doubt an adept leader.

Naturally, Du Li An noticed how the men, both young and old, began to greet her as "Sis-in-law." Six or seven years ago, when the wedding hall had echoed with the men's roars, that moniker carried with it an undertone of teasing. Now there was no more insinuation, and no one blatantly ogled her chest while comparing her to Fanny Fan or Tina Leung. But it was also true that Du Li An had packed on a few pounds over the last two years. Her figure was not what it used to be. Guen Hou knew Du Li An was self-conscious about it and comforted her with talk about how it was much more appealing to be curvy—that way, she appeared well-off, the picture of prosperity, and plus it'd bring her husband luck.

Du Li An looked Guen Hou over. She, on the other hand, had grown ever thinner. In the last few years she'd become much wiser to the ways of the world, having worked her fingers to the bone. Now that she'd seen some things, her eyeballs bulged slightly and were webbed all over with tiny blood vessels. She didn't regain some ease in her daily life until her daughter, Eggplant Face, started primary school. Somehow Du Li An managed to squeeze an extra little space out of Ping Le House, where she allowed Guen Hou to put out cakes, fried noodles, and sticky rice for sale on a small, square table. She also helped serve drinks and clean up after customers, playing a dual role as mini stall-owner-cum–Ping Le House staff. By pinching pennies, she and Eggplant Face seemed to get by, despite their poverty. Ever since Ah Sai went south to the capital and Sou Gei exited the world of the living, Du Li An keenly felt the emptiness of her original home. With no one to turn to for heart-to-hearts, she gradually grew closer to Guen Hou.

Speaking of Guen Hou, she was basically an orphan. Her parents had borne too many kids and sent her to be raised by an old nun when she wasn't even a full year old. After that, she had zero contact with her birth parents. The old nun's body resembled tree bark, dotted all over with fleshy tumors of various sizes. She had a strange temperament and was extremely strict when it came to Guen Hou's upbringing. As a result, Guen Hou was initiated into nunhood with the bare minimum of coercing. The nun passed away when Guen Hou was just a teenager. Since she had no relationship with her parents, she took the nun's meager savings and rented a stall to sell snacks and Western packaged drinks at Old Majestic Cinema. And that was how she came to know Du Li An and, later, that unlucky bastard Chan Kam Hoi.

Guen Hou had not been a believer in fate while she lived under the old nun's thumb. It wasn't until Chan Kam Hoi's sudden death that Guen Hou started suspecting her life, just like her daughter's face, had been born crooked. Abandoned at birth, later rejected by the Chan family, she was clearly meant to be an untethered soul from her very first breath, intended only to belong with the likes of some monastic like the old nun. In recent years she thought back with special fondness on the old nun's kindnesses, and even harbored some regret for not sincerely serving and honoring her like a mother. Guen Hou chalked up Eggplant Face's exceptional cleverness and maturity to the blessings of the old nun, watching over her all the way from heaven.

As for Du Li An—because Guen Hou was a little older, she once treated Du Li An as a baby sister. Their intimacy grew after her marriage to Steely Bo, when they formed an unspoken understanding out of the shared experience of being someone's mistress. It was like they'd both been condemned to the same lower class. Guen Hou, recognizing this, initiated frequent visits, and thus the two became confidantes. Yet at the end of the day, people can lead the same lives and have different fates. Steely Bo treasured Du Li An far more than he ever did his first wife in the fishing village. He gave Du Li An funds to open a kopitiam, transforming her into the boss lady of Ping Le House. See her then, everything smooth sailing, triumph plain on her face. Every day she sat at the counter ordering others around, seeming for all the world like a legitimate spouse. Sheltered under the umbrella of her charity, Guen Hou quickly realized how much humbler her own position was. Du Li An was generous, but her speech now often betrayed a lecturing overtone. It was night and day compared to their previous mutual affection and trust. As for the looking out that she did—it was better characterized as a landlord's benevolence than sisterly love. Carrying this knot in her heart, Guen Hou felt the two of them were no longer as close as they used to be.

Such womanly matters were entertained only within Du Li An and Guen Hou's innermost thoughts. To Steely Bo, the "sisters" remained like two peas in a pod. Guen Hou still enthusiastically sought out all sorts of herbal remedies to nurture one's yin or supplement one's yang. She faithfully prepared these remedies and delivered them to Du Li An with various extolments of their effects on the reproductive system. Steely Bo detested these medicinal soups that came, one pot after another, but because he couldn't out-argue Du Li An, he downed several of them anyway. Once, his throat itched like crazy immediately afterward and he vomited for what seemed like eternity. That night his breathing was uneven and the itching spread from his throat to his lungs. It got to the point where he could hardly lay down to sleep. The torture persisted for a long period before he slowly recovered. From that point on, he finally had a valid reason for refusing to drink any more of the herbal soups that overelevated his internal heat. Du Li An, too, was frustrated after months spent witnessing his suffering. On top of that, the remedies never produced any results, and so she also lost all interest and told Guen Hou to stop preparing the remedies.

Intuiting the vague blame latent in Du Li An's latest instruction, Guen Hou was peeved. For many long years she'd helped shoulder Du Li An's anxiety about her barrenness. It was the absolute most intimate truth that bound them together. Now Du Li An was hinting that Guen Hou should back off, which made her feel both aggrieved and wistful. Without this link connecting them, were they still sisters? All that was left between them was more or less what passed as sentiment between "master and servant."

Du Li An did not have such complicated feelings about the matter. Being the boss lady of Ping Le House was nowhere near as easy as it looked from the outside. Steely Bo, uncouth meathead that he was, knew nothing about running a business. His daily cares revolved around the affairs of Elder Zong and the Toa Pek Kong Society, punctuated by occasional trips to spoil his grandkids in the fishing village. Ping Le House was merely a small investment that he left entirely in the hands of Du Li An. To think, she'd originally planned on opening a proper restaurant, with an alcohol license and everything. It was all to be very respectable, and she'd even paid someone to christen it Wui Hoi Grand Restaurant—such energy! She had thought that if Steely Bo became a restaurant boss, he would settle down and stop constantly roving all about town. And yet her best-laid plan went awry; Steely Bo had no time for a mere little kopitiam. Just think about it: It was a disgrace for the head of Kien Tek Hall to sit at a counter settling bills of a ringgit here, several cents there. Furthermore, it was utterly unbefitting his flashy gold and silver ornaments.

Ping Le House therefore failed to tame Steely Bo, though it did tie down Du Li An. Now she had no time or energy to mind his comings and goings. It was a good thing she managed the kopitiam to some success. With so many people deferring to her as boss lady every day, she experienced a secret thrill, though out loud she grumbled. She made it clear to Steely Bo: I won't ask about your sons' fish farm. And no matter what happens to Ping Le House's bottom line, there is to be no interference from anyone else. Steely Bo grasped what she meant; it was a drawing of lines. Stay in his own lane? That was exactly what he wanted anyway. He yawned deeply and stretched himself thoroughly, cracking every joint in his body. "For you women, running a business without losing money is already an amazing accomplishment." It suited him just fine to ignore the mountains of itty bitty bills and receipts that passed through Ping Le House.

Speaking of frustrating, what Du Li An feared most was the sight of her own old man. Left unchecked after Sou Gei's death, his gambling addiction had spiraled even more out of control, and his drinking habits had become downright outrageous. He was always complaining that Du Li An and Ah Sai weren't giving him enough to live on. Since Ah Sai was at a safe distance all the way in the capital, the old man instead hit up Du Li An every few days. Du Li An was not so much concerned about his freeloading as she was afraid he was fabricating illnesses or various excuses to scheme for money. Fortunately for her, the old man, thick-skinned as he was, did not dare cause a scandal large enough to become the town's laughingstock. She knew he was wary of Steely Bo, worried that once his temper flared there would be no mercy. After all, the back of the old man's left hand still bore the mark stamped by Steely Bo all those years ago. Whenever the old man placed a bet, it was a visual warning not to be too careless.

That said, she well understood he was slapdash by nature. Even Sou Gei hadn't been able to rein him in. Now that she was dead, it was only a matter of time before the old man caused trouble somewhere about town. Though Du Li An refrained from actively seeking out news about him, she couldn't avoid gossip and rumor from entering her ears, what with all sorts of customers coming and going through Ping Le House. Half a year ago, the talk revolved around the old man's frequent brothel visits, including that one humiliating episode when he claimed to be "short on cash." Recently, the gossip had evolved to hint at something going on between him and an Indian widow. Word on the street was he'd even brought her home to spend the night. Chin-wagging aside, Du Li An knew very well that no one would dare invent total nonsense out of thin air right in front of the wife of Kien Tek Hall Brother Bo. Therefore, whatever gossip that made its way to her must be close to being substantiated. But the thing was, the old man was fluent in only Cantonese and Hakka. Hard for her to believe that he'd somehow managed to woo an Indian woman with his smattering of broken Malay.

After closing shop that afternoon, she went out of her way to visit her old home. The sun was blazing. She was surprised to find herself slightly out of breath after almost twenty minutes of walking with a parasol. She'd not even felt as tired when she used to help Sou Gei push her tricycle. At the old house, Du Li An collapsed the parasol and dug out a handkerchief to blot away her sweat. It was only when she looked at the dim stairway that she realized how long it'd been since she'd last visited. The steps were filthy. Once she'd walked up those very same steps, half turning to wave at Lin Sang.

"Come here, let me see how much taller you are compared to me."

He really was a tall one. She climbed another step. Mmm, that made them almost equal. But after reaching that greater height, she realized they were now farther apart. Lin Sang. He stood against the light in the dark stairway, his facial features in shadow. But she knew he was gazing at her with a smile on his face, as if he were looking at those little students of his.

The old man wasn't in. Though she'd mentally prepared herself, she was still shocked by the absolute chaos in the house. Dust covered the floors and spider webs spanned the corners near the windows; broken cups listed drunkenly on the shrines, in front of a dirt-smeared Guan Yin and ashen-faced Du ancestors. The hot water bottle was empty, and the chairs leaned against the walls, burdened by loads of unwashed shirts and pants. She lifted a curtain to enter the old man's room, which was tidier than she'd expected, though a sour stench wafted from the long unaired mattress. The old man must be climbing into bed every night without first showering. She stood in the doorway, imagining the old man clasping the Indian woman on the bed.

Those bedsheets, they were ones Sou Gei had asked someone to sew from scraps of fabric she'd saved. The sheets had shone as bright as wedding night candles when they were first laid out. Now their gay patterns were faded. A big, oily looking patch shimmered in the middle of the bed.

Du Li An visualized the Indian woman as having dark, glistening skin.

Don't you damn well dare, oh, you. Don't you damn well dare.

Du Li An walked into the room next door. Hers and Ah Sai's bedding and pillows were still there, sitting tidily unmoved from their original places as if frozen by time. It felt like she and her brother had just left that very morning and would return anytime soon. An inevitable wave of emotion struck her. She lowered the doorway curtain.

She swept the floors, filled the bottle with boiled water, and straightened up the shrine a bit. Then she lit some incense and pressed her palms together, asking forgiveness from Guan Yin and their ancestors. Before she left, she gathered up the clothes strewn about and soaked them in a big steel basin she found in the bathroom. Didn't they say the Indian woman made a living washing clothes? Surely she'd pitch in to wash these when she visited?

Not too long after that, people said the old man was living with the Indian woman. Du Li An did not react to the news. When she mentioned it to her brother, Ah Sai paused for three seconds, then said, "It's good there's someone to wash and cook for him." Du Li An grimaced into the telephone receiver. She said, You haven't been home for so long, are you still going to stay over at the old man's when you come back next time?

Ah Sai mulled this over for quite a while. It was like an extra dimension had opened up between the two of them. Du Li An listened closely to the background noise on the other end of the line. She said, You must be very busy over there, so go on. Your sister has plenty of room here. Even if that boy Candlenut returns, you can be a little flexible and bunk with him.

Now that the topic had turned to Candlenut, Ah Sai started mumbling, as if there were words stuck in his throat. She had to force it out of him: Last month, Candlenut had lost his job at the tire shop. Then a few days ago he had turned up at the restaurant to borrow money from Ah Sai, and even asked if there were any jobs at the restaurant for them.

"Them? You said 'them'?" She raised her voice, then her eyebrows.

"There was a young girl with him. Big eyes, a bit tan, looks Malay."

"And what did you say?"

"I, I lent him three hundred ringgit. As for jobs, I said I'd keep an ear out for him."

Of course Du Li An was going to bring up this latest development with Steely Bo. She said, That boy of yours Candlenut, we don't even know if he quit or if he was fired. Either way he can't even support himself, but still he's courting and wooing like everyone else. It was obvious that Steely Bo had not been informed of this by "the other side." Although he seemed momentarily taken aback, in the end all he did was shrug, an attitude of "how bad can it be?" written all over his brow.

"Boys do what they want when they become men, and after all he hasn't found his footing yet," he said. "The boy reminds me of myself when I was younger."

She was about to insult the boy more, but then she intuited the sense of pride in Steely Bo's "myself when I was younger." A younger Steely Bo? She raised her eyes to their two overlapping figures in her dresser mirror. She was putting her hair in curlers. He sat on the bed behind her, clipping his toenails. The man was bald at the top of his head, and the surrounding ring of hair was sparse and shot through with white. She remembered that Candlenut did resemble Steely Bo quite a bit. Thick skin and firm flesh. Monolid eyes above a wide-bridged nose. A pair of horns was all that was missing for the image of a wild bull to be complete.

Maybe it was because of that? She thought Steely Bo probably loved his youngest son above anyone else. Candlenut had always been free to act as he pleased. When that punk lived with them, he'd once floated the idea of joining the Toa Pek Kong Society under Elder Zong's protection. Steely Bo agreed to it enthusiastically, as elated as if his son had scored straight *A*'s. For a few days, father and son draped their arms around each other and could talk of nothing else. Judging from his attitude, Steely Bo couldn't wait to pass on all that he'd learned and lived through over the past decades.

But he'd probably overlooked the fact that Candlenut had not yet found his footing. Even Du Li An's old man secretly pulled her aside to say, Heh, this youngster has yet to be tested. No surprise, then, that he quickly lost steam after joining the Toa Pek Kong Society, all because he wasn't elevated to the front lines immediately. He proceeded to "forget" that he was a member of Kien Tek Hall. All those aspirations and vows he made to Steely Bo before pledging were wiped clean from his mind too. Yet Steely Bo did nothing more than wrinkle his forehead and sigh. She'd never once seen him slam tables and take his anger out on Candlenut.

With all that in mind, she held her tongue. She'd never harbored goodwill for Candlenut. To her, his whole energy was of meanness. He had a chilling look in his eyes. Though ambitious, he didn't have the brains to match his goals. All in all he resembled that movie stereotype of a man who loved to stir up trouble and made things worse, not better, at any given opportunity.

In comparison, his two older brothers at the fishing village were much more dependable. As for his younger sister, Lau Lin—she was at least quiet and demure, if a little eccentric. Even her sneezes were soundless. Every day she sewed clothes at the factory, and every two weeks she visited the fishing village. Outside of that routine, her favorite activities were limited to buying *Sisters* and *Hong Kong TV* magazines, occasionally taking Guen Hou's daughter to eat cendol, and playing on the swings in the park.

Eggplant Face got along very well with Lau Lin. Eggplant Face would tug on her sleeve or yank on her skirt hem and call out, Sister Lin, Sister Lin, melting Lau Lin's heart. Little Eggplant Face did not possess adorable looks, but she did have a silver tongue and was sensitive to others' moods. If she were a boy, she'd have had Lau Lin's affection for sure.

Du Li An couldn't get out of her mind the sight of tiny Eggplant Face extending her hand to wipe away Guen Hou's tears. Du Li An thought that if she was fated to bear no sons in her life, then she'd be content with a daughter like Eggplant Face to keep her company. While Du Li An was lost in such thoughts, Steely Bo finished clipping his toenails and lay down in pursuit of sweet dreams. After she finished positioning the curlers on her head, she, too, turned out the light and went to bed. She was still not used to groping in the dark. From here to the bed was a distance of only around three meters. And yet it seemed those three meters took on a life of their own as soon as the lights were out. In the darkness, the distance silently expanded and distorted, becoming unknowable.

She climbed into bed and covered herself with blankets. While she waited for sleep to come, she let her mind wander unrestrained over inconsequential things. Just as she was sliding into the soft, silky tunnel of dreams, she heard Steely Bo's voice from the pillow next to hers, sounding as if it came from far away. He said, "I'll pay your brother back that three hundred ringgit." In a flat tone, she said, "You're his old man, so of course you should be paying him back."

She wasn't sure if she actually answered in that manner. Or, put another way, she wasn't sure if she'd already arrived in her dreams when she uttered those words.

—2—

As others have mentioned, she is very thin. But she has broad shoulders and jutting shoulder blades. You know she has to be Mana. This early in the morning, sunlight is still slowly soaking its way through thick piles of clouds. Who else could it be, on this street, headed in this direction?

She walks toward you, a large, colorful embroidered cotton bag swinging from one shoulder. The cloth bag draws your attention first. The fabric, somewhere between yellow and brown, reminds you of barefoot monks in Thailand. The bag's busy embroidery design features a gold-and-red bird that brings to mind a table-cloth meant for an altar. Your gaze naturally follows the bag's shape and glides up the girl's arm; her off-shoulder top reveals the curvature and angles of her shoulder blades. On such a thin girl, this wide pair of shoulder blades seems to be the full set of riches possessed by her body. After just one look, you feel your heart race absurdly and your ears blush, as if you have been confronted with a kind of nudity.

The girl throws you a glance when she brushes against you. At that very moment you lower your head and get a glimpse of skinny yet firm calves under cropped pants, and underneath all that, platform shoes decorated with what looks like woven Astroturf on her feet. The left shoe is obviously missing a blooming sunflower, an absence underscored by the right shoe, which is whole. The girl intuits your gaze, as if you've aimed a red-dot sight at her foot. She throws you a look over her shoulder. You feign indifference and widen your stride as you walk away, yet you can't resist turning back at the intersection to look at her. The girl bends at the waist and tears off the sunflower on her right foot with some vehemence.

She's Mana. She has to be. Your heart skips faster and you smile into the early dawn, which is still saturated with the previous night's chill. You check the time, then decide to double back and follow the girl to see if she enters Mayflower. For a stretch, you follow her from a safe distance, but when she reaches Mayflower she gives it only one quick look, then passes it without slowing. You are sorely disappointed by this, and for the rest of the day you are listless. You take the bus to the KFC at the city center. There, you fill out a job application form and squeeze in with the rest of the applicants waiting for an interview. There are a lot of you. Time seems to move more and more sluggishly, as if it's unable to fit through the throng of bodies. Suddenly, you feel exhausted.

You think about the girl's shoulder blades unfurling like a giant butterfly.

That afternoon, after you race to another interview, you buy a burger and a bottle of water. You work on both while strolling the streets. When you pass by Pizza Hut, you abruptly see yourself sitting inside. You're dressed in white and sitting with a group of graceful young men and women. You see yourself ordering food with a smile, your face so clean it could reflect sunlight. You are stunned for a long while before you finally understand that the person inside is not you. It's J. For some reason you're convinced he can't see you, just like you're sure that you're invisible to the person on "the other side" when you stare into the mirror every day. You take one last bite of burger and crumple its packaging into a ball. Sunlight descends like a curtain, separating you that much further from J's world. When you narrow your eyes against the window's glare, you see your own sorrow imprinted on J's smiling face.

You make it back to Mayflower before the kopitiam next door has closed, in time to order takeout for dinner. You'd mentioned to Uncle Sai that you want to handle dinner on your own. He nodded, and that was it, but it's been over a week and you still aren't used to the change. You'd also told him that you're looking for a job. Mmm. "Why not wait until the results for national exams are out?" You did not reply, and Uncle Sai did not follow up. He fished out reading glasses from his shirt pocket, adjusted his sitting position, and tilted the newspaper he was holding such that it was hit squarely by the sunlight slanting through the window. You stirred your coffee, head lowered, wondering whether to ask about Mana. In the end it was Uncle Sai who broke the silence first. He tossed the newspaper down and plucked off his glasses.

Your ma passed on any messages in your dreams?

You shook your head, bewildered. Mother was gone; that's just how it was. You asked him, What about you? Did you dream about her? Then you immediately regret asking. You didn't really want to know whose dreams Mother was hiding in. Whose bed she was diving into. Who she smiled at while opening up her body. Who ejaculated on her soul. It'd been forty-nine days and she hadn't once checked on you.

Uncle Sai shrugged. A wide stretch of empty silence followed. You each stirred your own drinks, concentrating hard on your respective whirlpools like two mystics divining.

You swing a plastic bag laden with a Styrofoam box of food and walk step by step to room 301. Yes, that's right, you too need only forty-three steps to reach it now. A few years ago you noticed you'd grown taller, and after that you liked taking the stairs two at a time to make room 301 seem closer. But that was when Mother was alive, and you wanted to let her detect your lumbering steps whenever you returned. Even so, she liked to assume an ambiguous posture somewhere between deep sleep and death when you entered the room. If you paid her no mind, she quickly lost patience and switched to other ways of attracting your attention, like coughing or humming. And if you ignored her further, she slumped on the bed with her eyes open, quietly and painfully continuing her existence.

Ma.

You call out to her in your dream. The dream is emptiness incarnate, nothing but darkness. You can't see them, but you can feel the endless stair steps on which you stumble. The dream is so crooked, so cramped. Ma. You thought you were walking in one direction, but the stair steps follow no rules, sometimes leading up and sometimes sloping down. You bump and scrape, falling countless times, and in the end you plummet from somewhere dizzyingly tall in the dream, though you never hit ground.

You have no choice but to open your eyes. Apparently the sky has gone dark. You don't move. Your body waits for the pain transmitted by the dream, and your mind waits for hollow blankness. There's an unusual scent in the air. You smell it. It grows ever thicker, ever closer, ever realer, almost solidifying into something quotidian. You struggle to sit up. Another wave hits you as you sit on the edge of the bed. It really is the smell of durian—cloying, extravagant, pungent.

You walk out of room 301 and follow your nose downstairs. As the smell intensifies, you feel as if you are walking into the heart of it. Who would bring durian back in today's Mayflower? Uncle Sai never touched the stuff. He said his body's base leans hot; in it swirls the fire of suns and the qi of bagua gold elements. Just one or two pieces of durian flesh caused him to suffer dry coughs, difficulty swallowing, or tinnitus. Once he even spat up blood. As for the two sex workers on the ground floor, they were too old to eat durian. Not only would the thick, dense fruit gum up the inside of their mouths, its fiber would also clog the gaps separating their fake and real teeth. Not to mention it would agitate their diabetes.

You descend to the second floor. Here, the fragrance is riotous, permeated with a smell of something like a fermenting toddy. You can't contain the stirring in your heart. It must be Mana eating durian. A Siamese cat sneaking off food.

This time you're sure of it—she's in room 204, right next door to Uncle Sai. You can even hear the sounds of someone greedily slurping what's left of the flesh from a seed. Eavesdropping outside the door, you're so excited you lock your palms into each other as if you're praying. Now you are so close, you and your prey, Mana. Only the door to room 204 stands between you, seemingly as fragile and thin as cardboard. You feel instinctively that the door isn't latched. All you have to do is press down on the handle, and the door will instantly yield. But you know you shouldn't. You think maybe you should knock, but you can't imagine what you'd say to her if she opened the door.

Hi, Mana.

You dither outside the door for a while, unable to decide how best to flush out Mana. Then the sound of someone opening the shutter gate drifts up from downstairs. You know it's Uncle Sai returning. You lose your cool, as if the hunter has become the hunted. Your first thought is to rush back up to the third floor, but that kind of speed requires such exaggerated movements that the building's old bones will revolt, which will alert Mana in her room and also Uncle Sai, now climbing the stairs. With no other option, you open the door across the hall into room 205. In a flash you dive into that gaping, dark maw, like leaping into a giant toothless mouth.

Uncle Sai makes his way to room 203, and you hear the jingle of keys as he unlocks the door. But he doesn't push it open right away. You sense a kind of hesitation. He takes two steps forward and stops outside the room you're in. You hold your breath, your hand wrapped around the door handle, wishing for all the world that your heart would pause its beating.

Knock knock.

You let out a long, slow breath. The door opposite opens with a squeak. You hear Uncle Sai telling Mana to open the windows, his voice low. Mana, the durian smell is too much, you hear me. There seems to be an answering grunt. Uncle Sai stands there and watches her spin on her heels to go open the windows. She must be barefoot and moving lithely; her footsteps barely make any sound. Every part of you listens as the Venetian blinds, long untouched, make a clumsy, crackling sound. Uncle Sai mutters something indecipherable. Then he finally closes the door, turns, and goes into his own room.

The air moves ever so slowly, still circulating the durian's fervent essence. Held in room 205's dark mouth, you feel an inexplicable sense of comfort. The three of you are very close, gathered up in the voluptuous bosom of the durian's smell. You think of Mother, of all people. You suspect this is her doing from beyond the grave; you question whether the scent of durian could actually be her body odor. She knows what you want, which is why she's left you Mana. You feel her presence in the darkness as she whispers into your cochlea: Go find it, why don't you. Her voice is so close, like a fluttering moth perched on the rim of your ear. Just like that one day sometime before her death, when she suddenly giggled as you carried her on your back down the stairs.

"You've grown so much. To think you can carry me now." She smiled, her muddled breath moistening the folds of your ears.

You've never once voiced the grief you experienced in that moment. By the time you carried her to the bottom of the stairs, you could no longer hold back your tears. You didn't even feel that kind of sorrow after she died.

Now, in this dark space permeated by the fragrance of durian, you remember the time you carried a small knapsack on your back while trailing behind her. She struggled with a heavy, oversized blue suitcase, her upper body listing to counteract its weight. She kept having to switch the suitcase from hand to hand for short stretches while she walked. For some reason you liked being on the side without the suitcase, and so every time she paused to switch hands, you unthinkingly swerved to the other side. At first Mother tried to clasp your hand with her free one, but the suitcase seemed to grow heavier and heavier, and in the end it required both of her hands. Even then she took more and more breaks, each one lasting longer. The two of you stood under the scorching equatorial sun, the shadows under your feet forever hiding behind you. Mother panted. Beads of her sweat fell and dotted the street.

"Are we there yet?" You lifted your head and were blinded by sunlight.

"Almost," she said.

She told you to keep watch over the luggage while she went into a store for bottled water, but then she ducked out again immediately. With some trepidation, she lifted you up and seated you on top of the suitcase. "That way I can see you." She smiled, tousling your hair. "Why are you so short? You tiny little winter melon."

You pouted and brushed her hand away. Then you followed her into the store with your eyes. Quite a few people trundled past on the five-foot way. You hung your head, your back against a wall. You stared blankly at the ground, watching pairs of feet and shoes saunter across your field of vision.

Mother came out of the store with bottled water. Sunlight poured in from an angle, flooding the shallow grooves demarcating the street's tiles. Slumped over like a teddy bear, you'd become part of the luggage.

—3—

After Shaozi's mother passed away, some busybodies entered the house in which she and Shaozi had lived in for years, under the guise of helping with funeral affairs. One thing astonished them. The double-story row house had four rooms and an open living space, all of which were neatly decorated. But there was nothing like a study or a workspace, like everyone assumed.

They found nothing to prove the existence of a learned person, an author. They thought it was a given that Shaozi loved to read, yet the entirety of the reading material found in the house consisted of a few tabloids and stacks of old newspapers readied for recycling. The few rooms upstairs held furniture like beds and dressers, while the only room downstairs was smaller and piled full of assorted junk. That turned out to be the old woman's bedroom. There was absolutely no trace of a study. They couldn't even find copies of Shaozi's own work, nor any of the prizes she'd won. Many of those were in the form of heavy copper objects; a couple of them were made of delicate glass. Where would Shaozi have stored them? No way she'd lock them away in a safety deposit box, right?

This matter was so mysterious that even The Fourth Person could supply no explanation. According to his reviews and analyses of her oeuvre, this writer who "excels at mimicry and group authorship"[1] would of course have been exposed to the works of many other writers. Yet not only was there no trace of books in her house, even the city library had no record of her ever checking out a single item. There *was* a street vendor near her house who sold printed material. The vendor recalled Sister Li would stop by for a newspaper now and then, sometimes tacking on a tabloid. Once, she even bought two Sudoku puzzle collections. There was also a hair salon owner who knew Sister Li well. He described her as chatty and especially generous with flirtatious remarks. She drank a lot of tea but rarely flipped through the magazines strewn about the salon.

The foppish hair salon owner reminisced that it'd always been a pleasure to shoot the breeze with Sister Li. Her conversation topics were eclectic, occasionally crossing the veil into supernatural territory. She

1. See "The Immortal Du Li An—Myths of Womanhood Woven by Shaozi."

could even describe places she'd never visited, such as Tokyo, New York, Northern Ireland—they came to life when she talked about them. Therefore he was not the least bit surprised when he later learned that she wrote novels.

It wasn't just the hair salon owner. A few of Sister Li's primary school classmates also recalled that Du Li An was a master storyteller. Without fail, each day at recess she was surrounded by little kids clutching lunchboxes, who clamored to hear ghost stories she made up on the spot. The passage of time had erased the stories; all they remembered now were the gasps and shrieks of the girls. Some of them would have nightmares.

The legend of "the novelist who doesn't read" shrouded Shaozi in yet another layer of mystery. People started painting her as a magician who could perform impossible feats, a literary witch.[2] Rumor had it that certain young writers eager to make a name for themselves would place Shaozi's books under their pillows—or even use the books as pillows. For these writers, dreaming of Shaozi was an auspicious sign that indicated they would soon be awarded prizes. In time, a branch of dream divination not far off from black magic sprung up within the country's Chinese class-rooms and writing circles. For example, dreaming of Shaozi, of bras, or of pirated DVDs on the eve of the biannual Hua Zhong Literary Awards was a premo-nition of triumph. As for books, high heels, lipstick, school uniforms, or purple hair ties—these were all precursors to total defeat. The divination's internal logic was somewhat complicated, requiring reconciliation with the time of one's dream alongside other symbols

2. The poet Boatcarver explains in their award-winning "Last Night I Conversed with the Witch" that the witch referenced in the poem is none other than deceased novelist Shaozi.

present in it, to be chained together like messages from Tarot cards.

Of course, this was just a game young people played. Mature scholars and professional writers treated it as ridiculous superstition. They would rather believe Shaozi was a "humanist writer" born with natural talent, who plucked her material from and beyond real life. Because of this, although most of Shaozi's writing existed in the space between nonfiction and its opposite, her work also incorporated realism, modernism, and postmodernism, not to mention elements of classical, sci-fi, stream of consciousness, fantasy, rural, urban literature, etc. But reviewers and the few historians in charge of editorializing "the phenomenon of local writers" nonetheless classified Shaozi as a "realist writer"[3] out of habit. Of course, due to the shape-shifting quality that made it so difficult to classify her work, there were dissenting voices that referred to her as a "no-ist writer," "freedomist writer," "post-postmodernist writer"[4] and so on.

The Fourth Person was unfazed by these abounding theories. He never wavered on his position around either Shaozi's work or "the figure of the author as deduced from her work." Right until his death he firmly believed that Shaozi "excels at mimicry and group authorship," though he could find no proof from Shaozi's residence to corroborate this claim. This was a sore point for him, and some joked that The Fourth Person died in bitterness over it.

3. *The 300-Writer Phenomenon*, *108 Must-Know Local Writers*, and *100 Most Moving Local Stories*, all published after 2000, unequivocally labeled Shaozi as a realist writer in their introductory remarks.

4. Ever since the popularity of The Fourth Person's *Always by Your Side*, numerous literary scholars have published articles in which they attempt to redefine Shaozi, thus resulting in this proliferation of labels.

CHAPTER SIX

—1—

When rumors about Lau Lin finding love first reached her ears, Du Li An simply twisted her lips and shook her head. Her eyes roved but never left her ledger and calculator. Was it not crystal clear to her? Every day Lau Lin left on time for work at the garment factory, and every evening she returned home at the same hour, down to the second. At night, she could be found either reading romance novels by Chiung Yao or Yi Shu in her room, or else watching TV in the living room. They'd just upgraded to a color TV, and Steely Bo had brought home a VCR player. Lau Lin had even skipped her fishing village visits a few weekends in a row for the sake of binging *Shanghai Bund*. And even so, after she was done with the videotapes, she'd voluntarily help out at Ping Le House or take Guen Hou's daughter window-shopping nearby. In what way were these the actions of someone in love? "Hmph, unless they're meeting up in their dreams."

Then the gossip gained some weight. A lot of concrete details emerged, though their veracity could not be confirmed. One detail stuck in Du Li An's mind: the man was said to resemble Chow Yun-fat. This made her snort. "Oh, all of you—" she hit the pause button and looked up, "have been brainwashed by soap operas!"

But as similar information continued to trickle in, she had to admit there must be some truth to the rumor. She compiled the gossip she'd heard and analyzed it based on her instincts. The "man who resembled Chow Yun-fat" must be the garment factory's new financial executive. He seemed to be much older than Lau Lin; the age difference had to be at least eight or nine years, if not a whole decade. People said he was handsome, with a sincere smile and a silver tongue. All the women working in the factory had a crush on him, falling over themselves to serve his every whim.

Du Li An shut her accounting book and let out a sigh.

It was afternoon tea time, and Ping Le House was bustling. Guen Hou had passed by the counter endless times holding a serving tray. With each trip she observed how Du Li An was completely absorbed in her thoughts, a stark contrast to her usual self, who was perpetually in motion, resembling none so much as the deities Nezha and Erlang with their respective eight arms and magical third eye. Guen Hou couldn't help rapping the counter and asking, Hey, Ah Li, did your soul leave your body? Come on, someone's asking to settle their bill.

As soon as they hit the kopitiam's closing hours, Du Li An hurriedly took care of the day's receipts and waited for her driving instructor to pick her up. It was her third day taking lessons, and she was still clumsy. Her mind was all over the place, too, and she stalled the car several times at various intersections. The instructor was so annoyed he had her aimlessly drive for a bit on a secluded little path, then called it a day. When he drove her back they passed through Old Street, taking the lane dotted by many dry goods stores. Du Li An lowered her window. She'd always enjoyed the salty fragrance of dried shrimp that hung in the air there. Even after so many years the place was still the same.

That narrow alley leading to Pei Hwa Primary School still lay quietly in its original spot. There was even a tricycle modded with an awning, transformed into a mobile snack stand, parked in front of the alley. It was the same old view, except the vendor had been replaced by a woman of moderate height. She was dressed like a miner panning for tin, a straw hat on her head and a towel wrapped around her neck. Du Li An watched her tidy up her kuali, plates, and other utensils. This was it, the end of yet another day chasing a living.

Back home, Du Li An rushed into the kitchen. There was no time to rest. They'd started employing an Indian woman to help out with laundry, and Guen Hou had also helped her find a middle-aged Chinese woman to handle other major housekeeping chores on a weekly basis. But cooking was the one thing Du Li An insisted on doing herself. She'd developed the recipes passed down by Sou Gei, such as Kwong Sai stuffed tofu and yam stewed with pork belly. These improved dishes had Steely Bo slurping up the juices at the bottom and sucking on his chopsticks, even after he'd finished all the rice in his bowl. She knew, too, that he loved Hakka cuisine, and so got to work learning how to make salt-baked chicken and yam abacus seeds. Her oily and flavorful renditions won the praise of everyone who tasted them. That said, it was impossible for a mere few dishes to guarantee Steely Bo's presence at home every night. Although he professed to love eating home-cooked meals, he inevitably wined and dined outside when he ran around town in the name of Elder Zong. One day he ate jumbo shrimp at this little village; the next day he sampled wild game and local brews at some big town. He claimed to have tried aphrodisiacs like bear paws, monkey brains, and tiger meat. Du Li An clucked her tongue at him. He stole near her, a smile spreading across his face, huffing the alcohol on his breath onto her neck.

"You don't believe me? Come test it out yourself."

When she flung him off, he let the momentum topple him onto their bed. There he lay, and soon he was snoring loudly, not even bothering to take his socks off. Sometimes he slurred drunkenly in his dreams, his mutterings wadding up like chewing gum into a jumbled mess. She felt as if he was speaking secret society slang. No matter how she tried, she couldn't understand him.

But it was as Guen Hou said—Du Li An should consider herself lucky he never called out for other women in his sleep. Of course she agreed; she wasn't naïve. This man's world was chock full of cigarettes, alcohol, and cash. Of the three major vices (whoring, gambling, and drinking), how could she count on him to only dabble in two out of three? When her thoughts turned in this direction, she felt somewhat more forgiving of his frequent trips to the fishing village. After all, it was much better for him to entertain his grandkids than put his mitts all over some floozy.

"Ah Lai, you really have it pretty good, as far as being a woman goes." Guen Hou pulled a long face when she said this, as if threatening to wield her own fate as a cautionary tale once more. You really have it pretty good. He cares about you. You have a house, you have Ping Le, and look, you're even learning to drive. Soon you'll have your own car. Yours was the first house on the block to have a color TV and a refrigerator. You're still the only family with a VCR. Just look how many kids from the neighborhood jostle outside your windows each weekend to catch your soap operas.

Du Li An smiled weakly. It was precisely those kids who had driven a wedge between her and the neighbors. The children came in waves, like flies and bees hovering over sugarcane drink stalls. Not only did the kids block all the windows, they were also rowdy to the point of distraction. She was so frustrated she couldn't even cry when Damian Lau was about to die in the finale of *Yesterday's Glitter*.

She was therefore making plans to buy a new house. Developers were building a dozen or so semi-detached double-story houses nearby, and from what she'd seen of the plans, they were much more impressive than her current home. "The yard is big enough for two cars. Now that's befitting a man like the leader of Kien Tek Hall." One night she draped herself across Steely Bo's back and sucked on his huge earlobe. Entirely defenseless against her move, he melted as she held between her lips both his earlobe and his ego as leader. Occasionally she nibbled gently. He gritted his teeth and resisted for a while, but finally he couldn't bear it any longer. He flipped over and pressed her down between his legs, where she lay biting her lower lip. A shallow smile graced her face, and scarlet blushes bloomed across her cheeks. That night she didn't bring up his promise not to touch her after drinking. It didn't cross his mind either. Once he was done he plopped down next to her. She curled into him, using his shoulder as a pillow, and then she heard him mutter, "A woman is really something."

She intuited that the "woman" in his sentence did not refer to only her. There had to be someone else involved. It might be because they were skin to skin, but it was the first time she'd managed to understand his dream talk. To her, the sounds originated from his chest instead of from his mouth. She felt a faint wave of despair. The passion and tenderness that had been aroused in her body quickly dimmed, leaving behind a chill that lingered in the soles of her feet. She heard mosquitoes buzzing in the darkness. After patrolling the space, one of them landed like a dragonfly on her toe, exposed outside the blanket. It must have been a brawny mosquito. When it stuck its stout proboscis into her skin, she felt a sting. But she stayed immobile, and in fact did not want that minute yet genuine pain to dissipate. In that moment she focused on imagining herself as a corpse, so as to avoid analyzing Steely Bo's sleep talk. The fatigue that follows sex overtook her. She sank heavily into a dream woven from smoke, alcohol, and sweat, and anticipated waking up the next day with the itch that circulated throughout her body via her bloodstream, along with the bite mark's miniscule pain and numbness.

She never asked where his money came from. But she knew that he was typically profligate, his money appearing in one hand only to disappear from the other. She knew it'd be an uphill battle if she asked him to fork over ten thousand ringgit as deposit for the new house. And so she read his moods and applied pressure every now and then. In this way, the requisite sum was finally collected. Though police stations and hospitals did not intimidate Steely Bo, he was afraid of office buildings. Therefore she was the one who handled trips to banks and law firms, and hers was the signature on all the loans and legal documents.

She was very excited about the new house, but she suppressed her feelings and told no one. Even a close confidante like Guen Hou had no clue. After the past few years' experience, Du Li An knew it was better to act without rousing any attention. Ah, people should keep a lower profile the higher they fly. Take Guen Hou for example, a friend who was almost like a sister. Du Li An realized that after she shared some good news Guen Hou was happy in the moment, but her attitude shifted in the days following. A look of deliberate coldness entered her eyes, and her expression signaled an intention to keep her distance. As for Lau Lin, though she gradually thawed after Candlenut's departure and she no longer wound herself up tight like a porcupine, Du Li An was always conscious that Lau Lin was a witness to the luxury and love showered on her by Steely Bo. Hard to say whether Lau Lin would turn what she observed into gossip and wag her tongue to "the other side." Thus, even though no one could have a bone to pick when it came to Du Li An's treatment of Lau Lin, the level of care bestowed was restrained, even somewhat businesslike. Neither party would deign be the first to treat the other as kin.

"I'm only the mother in name, right? We're not blood after all, to be blunt. There's no need for anyone to go through hell or high water for the other." That's how she described it to her brother, Ah Sai. Even though no one else was home at the time, she still instinctively covered the telephone transmitter with a hand, as if afraid of secrets leaking. That boy Candlenut couldn't cut it in the capital. He switched jobs every three or so months. His girlfriend couldn't stand him and had left him in the middle of the night. The worst part was, he spent more days lazing about than he did working, and whenever he ran out of money he simply sought out his "uncle" at the restaurant. Though Ah Sai didn't complain much about this, the situation incensed Du Li An, who nagged her brother to "stop indulging him!" She was so dismayed she almost tore her hair out. "He's an adult. His life or death has nothing to do with anyone else."

But she knew Ah Sai did not take her advice to heart. From conversations with him, she detected that a kind of relationship had sprung up between him and

Candlenut. She understood it was less the kinship between an uncle and a nephew and more a brother-hood between two young men. Therefore when Ah Sai gradually stopped bringing up news about Candlenut, she saw more and more clearly that her brother had started treating Candlenut's affairs as "matters between friends." Meaning Ah Sai was now a willing accomplice who refused to "betray" the other party.

Fine, she would watch and wait. She knew full well it was a mistake to go on the offensive when it came to the strange bond between men. The greater the external pressure, the more such bonds strengthened, creating a backlash. Yet weren't those rapports mostly hot air? Deep down, they were hollow. Let the passing of time and the facts of reality wear them down, and they would slowly deflate. Just wait.

Elder Zong celebrated his seventy-fifth birthday that year. Rumor was he planned to announce his retirement right after his birthday banquet and would hand over all of Toa Pek Kong Society's dealings to his son. The news caused much anxiety within the society. Steely Bo especially squirmed like he was sitting on a carpet of needles. Day after day he sought out Elder Zong for private discussions, and even roped in a bunch of his triad buddies to help sway the elder. Du Li An adopted a see-no-evil approach, but even from the little she glimpsed, she could hazard that the outcome had long been etched in stone. Elder Zong was now old, and Steely Bo was a mere parasite, a fern squatting on an ancient tree. And if the tree's days were numbered, then how much time in the sun for the fern? Not to mention Steely Bo himself was old too.

During the banquet, Steely Bo gave a venerating toast that was rewarded by a smile and a pat on the shoulder from Elder Zong. The elder said, Steely Bo, you're no young'un. We were at the front lines together, and now we should pull back together.

Du Li An immediately raised her cup when Elder Zong turned toward her. The elder still beamed beatifically, his face shining bright and red. He said, Ah Li, you're his wife, you gotta take good care of him for me. She downed her drink as a sign of deference, expending all her effort to make her own smile as brilliant and enticing as Fanny Fan Lai's. Steely Bo wasted no time grumbling as soon as he returned to his seat. "Look at him. The older he gets, the more he looks like a eunuch when he smiles." Du Li An's heart leapt into her mouth when she heard this. Under the table, her hand shot out and gave Steely Bo a sharp pinch. She was entirely sober. All night her cup had been filled with nothing but tea.

After the banquet, Steely Bo continued the celebrations elsewhere with his inner circle, while she took a cab home. It was already past ten at night. When she got home, a car she'd never seen before was parked outside the gates. In another glance she took in the Venetian blinds unexpectedly drawn in the living room. The wooden door behind the iron grille was half-open, presenting a wedge of deep darkness that faintly sparkled with glimmers from the TV screen. The whole scene seemed somewhat obscene. Now she saw, too, the men's leather shoes on the front steps. Acting on a hunch, she silently nudged open the front gate and tiptoed to the wooden door.

It was hard to get an accurate look because of the angle. And yet it was just as she'd thought—on the sofa were two . . . no, it was a bundle of entangled shadows. *The Brothers* was playing on the TV, the screen filled with a close-up of Chow Yun-fat's expressive face. His voice boomed so loudly that Du Li An didn't hear the mingled moaning on the sofa. She cleared her throat in an exaggerated way, then vigorously shook her handbag to make her keys and assorted objects inside jingle and clang. Immediately the shadows on the sofa bounced apart. She heard a weak, breathy cry belonging to a woman.

"That you, Ah Lin?" Du Li An asked. "Who else is there? Why don't you have the lights on?" She dug out her keys as she talked.

She said she wanted light, and so let there be light. With the lamp on, the living room's white walls looked especially pallid. When she swung wide the half-open wooden door, she was greeted by a shell-shocked Lau Lin standing motionless, her hair tousled, her face the exact same shade as the wall. Her hand was still on the light switch. Du Li An glanced at her, and this was when the shadow on the sofa stood up too. "How do you do, Sister Li."

A male voice.

Tall figure.

Slightly dark skin, a mouth of good teeth.

Neat brows as straight as twin blades.

Warm eyes bearing two pools of clear water. Because of his height, he bent his head a little, making whomever he looked at feel like a child.

She stood rooted to the spot, as stunned as Lau Lin. Du Li An felt her blood congeal and her heart freeze. It no longer beat; instead it was suddenly heavy, as if filled with lead. Heavily it sank, down and down, pressing upon her other organs. Her hands, so cold, like she was gripping a pair of ice cubes. She forgot to turn the key she'd already stabbed into the iron grille door's lock.

"Auntie Li, he's the financial exec at the factory. Mong Sang, Yip Mong Sang." Lau Lin spoke timidly, her shoulders shrinking.

Du Li An had no idea how long it took for her to gather her wits. Mong Sang? Yip Mong Sang? She'd once heard this name, knew this man. That thought restarted her heart and restored her breathing. When she finally moved to unlock the grille, the two people in the living room were exchanging looks, seemingly at a loss after witnessing such a long pause from her.

She strode into the room, closing the gap between them. The lamplight afforded her a good look. My god, there could be no doubt they were twins. It was unbelievable they looked so much alike. She glared at Lau Lin. "Mong Sang, is it? It's so late, and my man isn't around," Du Li An said. "Sorry, but it's not convenient for you to be here."

She felt as if the words she spat out were ice cubes that clinked and clanged upon contact with the air. After saying her piece, she politely ducked the man's stare, instead training her sight on Lau Lin, who stood next to her with head lowered and lips pressed together. The man took his leave courteously. "Sincere apologies, Sister Li, I'll come visit another day." Du Li An raised her head and saw him nod with a smile, no trace of embarrassment in his expression.

She sent him away woodenly. Lau Lin trailed him to the door and watched him bend over to put on his leather shoes. Du Li An stayed in the living room, removing her earrings. She witnessed him briefly hold Lau Lin's left hand just before departing. His movement was swift, and Lau Lin matched it with a rapid grab at his thumb. She was almost reluctant to release him, as if the thumb were a tiny floating log. Yip Mong Sang blinked, sending her an understanding, resolute, and comforting look. It was only then that she hesitatingly loosened her grasp.

Du Li An turned on the TV and ejected a tape

from the VCR. "Were you two watching *The Brothers*? I thought it was *A House Is Not a Home*," she said. The car beyond the gate drove off. She listened to the dead silence left in its wake. Lau Lin made no reply. She continued standing and gazed intently at the world outside. They kept their backs to each other.

Du Li An announced she was taking a shower. She turned the faucet to fill the water tank, then plopped down on the toilet. With her eyes she tracked a gray-brown moth as it repeatedly dive-bombed the fluorescent light. The tank overflowed. Water spilled in curtains onto the floor. She remained still with her head angled up, like an animal hung up for slaughter. The moth must be frantic, unable to immolate itself on the fluorescent tube's cold fire. All it could do was bash itself until it was wounded all over, and then it would die with broken wings. She asked herself, *What are you thinking?* She said, It is much more torturous to die like that instead of flinging yourself into fire. The moth didn't hear her. It kept on rushing the tube light.

Someone knocked on the bathroom door. Lau Lin was out there, nervously calling for her. Auntie Li. Du Li An did not respond. Gurgling water streamed downward. She stepped both feet into the puddles eddying on the floor. Auntie Li. Lau Lin summoned a bit more courage and rapped the door harder. Du Li An replied, Ahh, what is it?

"What happened tonight, can you not tell my ba?" Lau Lin's voice was so weak; what little bravery she had was fast disappearing.

"If everything was above board, why would you be scared of your ba finding out." Du Li An answered in a stentorian voice.

Silence on the other side of the door. After a long while, Du Li An got up to turn the faucet. Only when the water stopped did she hear Lau Lin's low sobs. "Auntie Li, I'm begging you."

For a split second, the scene of Lau Lin crying while choking down the few pieces of meat in her bowl flashed through Du Li An's mind. *How pitiful*, she thought to herself. "Relax. Your ba will probably be drunk out of his mind by the time he's back." After announcing this she ladled some water and started washing, aggressively splashing cold water onto her body. She shivered and gritted her teeth until her body acclimatized, numb and chilled as the water.

When she was done showering, the moth in the bathroom had exhausted itself. Still it tossed about the cold fire with what little remained of its strength. She turned the light off. She wasn't sure if this would save the moth, or if it was just a form of torture that would cause the moth to lose its sense of direction and fall into the water, where it would die in darkness.

Lau Lin was no longer outside the door. Du Li An headed for the bedroom and sat in front of her dresser. She cleaned her face and put her hair in rollers, as was her routine. The person in the mirror sat with blank eyes and a stiff expression, docilely letting her do as she wished. The more she looked, the more she found the person fat, and this was hard for her to bear. Yip Mong Sang was so elegant, while she had grown plain and overweight. She'd allowed him to see this version of her under that mercilessly pallid lamplight.

The sky was already faintly lit up when Steely Bo returned. Meanwhile, Du Li An's soul freely floated on the hot and humid air. The roots of her hair were soaked with sweat. Steely Bo disturbed her dream when he lay down. She opened her eyes for a look, then swiftly retreated back into the dream, a recurring one, to salvage scraps of memory and desire. When the alarm clock blared, the engorged dream shriveled like a sensitive mimosa plant. She awoke panting heavily. A sense of terror that she might not be able to wake up lingered. The person in the dream had stuffed her mouth with a passionate kiss, had declared to her with a tone of determination: Don't move, don't make a sound.

—

Two months passed without Yip Mong Sang gracing them with his presence. All Du Li An did was privately and briefly tell Lau Lin off. She wasn't very stern, more instructional than anything. The girl nodded in her timid way. Du Li An knew she was really full of gratitude. Meanwhile, Du Li An continued to maintain a low profile. After all, how would telling Steely Bo benefit her? When she conveyed news about Candlenut, all she gained was his displeasure. Who knew, it might have even earned her the accusation of trying to drive a wedge between him and his family, thus inviting ire from the fishing village. She was much more cunning now, all thanks to soap operas. After two years of watching those dramas, she'd learned quite a lot about the psychological jockeying and maneuvering waged within families.

Yet it was unclear, even to herself, whether she wanted to see Yip Mong Sang again. Would he appear at the door as if he had nothing to hide? Cradling a fruit basket, following Lau Lin's example and addressing her as "Auntie Li"? She dared not imagine it. If fate dictated it be so, then all she could do was cross the bridge when she came to it. How could she, a mere mortal, know what game the powers above were playing? And in the end, he did come. He rapped his knuckles against the counter and called her Sister Li.

Du Li An felt a violent pluck on her heartstrings. She recognized that voice. Turned out she'd been waiting to hear it for two whole months. She lifted her eyes. No one else knew how much effort it took, how heavy her eyelids were. She assumed her cheeks must be fiery red, though they were not. Head tilted, she feigned a moment of hesitation, as if she couldn't immediately place the other person. But in her heart she was astonished; she couldn't figure out how, with just one look, she'd identified the person in front of her as Mong Sang and not Lin Sang.

"Oh, it's me, Yip Mong Sang." He raised his eyebrows and smiled. "Ah Lin's financial exec."

"Ah, it's you." She put some change for a customer on a little tray. "Yip Mong Sang, yes, I remember you. Isn't it still working hours? Why are you here?" She twisted her head to look at the clock on the wall. Three-thirty.

"A supplier is visiting from the south, and the boss wanted me to show him around, sample some local delicacies."

She gave him a slanting look. "That much esteem? Thank you, then."

He grinned wide, as if to show off his beautiful teeth. "Ping Le House, that's all he'll remember from now on."

He turned to leave, but as he approached his table he doubled back. She'd been following him from the corner of her eye, and now, seeing him weave through the benches and stools packed full of people, her heart started to race for no reason. She was so nervous she upturned the loose change from the little tray into her palm. She made a show of counting the money, then returned it all to the tray. When she looked up again, Yip Mong Sang stood once more before her.

Knock knock. He rapped the counter. She gazed at

him. She thought her eyes must be flashing huge question marks, but they were not. All she did was stare at him.

"Sister Li, there's something I have to say." He met her gaze. His eyes were profoundly deep, like an ocean welcoming its tributaries. "You've lost weight. Did you know that? It looks good."

Du Li An met this unexpected shock with a calm smile. She was the only one in the whole world who could hear the overjoyed cheering in her heart. Yes, she heard it. "You sure know how to flatter. Looks like your tea will have to be on me." She handed off the little tray weighed down with coins to a passing worker. "Table ten," she said.

"No, next time." Yip Mong Sang shook his head once and left.

The bill for table twelve came to three and a half ringgit. She took the five-ringgit bill brought by an employee and turned to fiddle with her cash register. Ding. The cash drawer sprung out. She put a ringgit and fifty cents into the tray, and the worker walked away with the money. She shut the cash drawer. The cigarette cabinet next to her was fitted with a mirror, on which a calligraphy couplet had been printed. She spied on the enchanting reflection in the mirror. *May business prosper to all four corners of the world / May fortune and wealth span rivers and oceans.* There she stood, behind the two rows of calligraphy. Yes, she had a seductive figure now. The past two months of exertion had not been for nothing.

Guen Hou walked by and asked who that person was. "The one just now?" Du Li An furrowed her brows and put on an expression of nonchalance. Guen Hou twisted her head to look at Yip Mong Sang sitting on the five-foot way. "The man out there. Tall, refined."

"Oh, him." Du Li An snuck a glance, following Guen Hou's line of sight. "That's Ah Lin's coworker."

Du Li An had not forgotten that was how he had been introduced to her: the financial exec at the factory. Wasn't that so? Any other label would come off fishy, illegitimate. She pressed a button on the cash register. Ding. Such a crisp, clear sound.

The cash drawer sprung out. Coins and paper bills flooded the eye.

—2—

Surely Mana will notice the African daisy on the cabinet next to the bed. You'd wanted sunflowers, but the florist said it was impossible to find fresh ones in a place like this. He thrusted an artificial stalk at you. It was furry and did look very realistic, its head as large as a washbasin. In the end you bought a peach-colored African daisy and stuck it into a green soda bottle. It sits on the bedside cabinet in room 204. At dawn, sunlight will seep through frosted windows and strike that exact spot.

She sees it. She's adding water to the vase. But all flowers wilt eventually. At that point she sees a mini nail cutter. It has an apple-green sleeve and nestles among the African daisy's fallen petals like a grasshopper. Mana uses the cutter to trim her nails. The unpainted half-moons of her nail clippings are spotlessly clean. She tosses the clippings and what's left of the flower into a small trash can in the corner, the one meant for customers' used condoms. Often they thoughtlessly discard condom wrappers on the floor, or else they leave the wrappers on the bed. Sometimes they stuff them into the half-open drawers of the bedside cabinet. But after finishing their business, they always pack up their own semen, solemnly tie a knot around the opening, and then ceremoniously place the condom into the little trash can lined with a plastic bag.

In the trash can, you'd also find wads of toilet paper from sex workers wiping themselves down, empty containers of Vaseline, four-pill packs of Viagra, cigarette butts, empty cigarette boxes; sometimes there would be candy wrappers or other junk once squished into and then fished out from pants pockets. Things such as expired lottery tickets, receipts, theater stubs, balled napkins. And lipstick, almost entirely melted, abandoned by a sex worker.

Next, you place a maroon African daisy into the now-empty soda bottle. You can just imagine the way she spreads her lips wide into a smile. She is Mana, the girl with a giant butterfly beating its wings atop her shoulders. You recognize the shoes she's placed under her bed. They're the Astroturf platform shoes; now both are missing their little sunflowers. In their places are tiny balls of superglue, frozen solid. Your next move: wait until she's out, then stick a couple of fabric daisies you bought from a needlework shop onto those shoes.

You place the fabric daisies and a small tube of superglue into your backpack, which you carry to your job at KFC. You're responsible for the fries, and occasionally the salad and mashed potatoes. Putting on your uniform makes you feel almost identical to the other male workers. You're all like copies of clones, handling chicken pieces, drinks, hamburgers and such under shadows cast by the brims of your baseball caps. Yet J, the one who truly resembles you, is not there. He looks like he's from money. Perhaps he's traveling overseas with his parents. It could be early winter in Europe— could he be skiing? Of course he might also very well be swimming in Pattaya City with other beautiful boys and girls; on the beach, he slips his feet into delicate and slightly moist sand. He has a penchant for places where the sun blooms with abandon.

You quietly enjoy the scenes served up by your imagination when there's no one around to disturb you. You visualize Mana crouching and spotting the shoes hiding under the bed, the ones that have sprouted daises instead of ferns or mold. You've discovered that the large duffel bag under her bed contains T-shirts small enough to be child sized. You also saw the cropped pants she was wearing the day you bumped into her. The back pockets have butterfly designs sewn in silver thread. She's just like Mother, who also liked placing her luggage under the bed, as if she might hit the road again at any moment, without a second thought. But you know Mana now wants to catch you, just as you want to draw her out of her shell. You believe she will not leave Mayflower before one of you grabs hold of the other's wrist.

But she's more composed than you are after all. She flies under the radar, often leaving early and coming back late, or else leaving late and coming back early. Like a ghost, she dwells among the shadows of others. Mana. After getting off work and returning to room 301, you extract the daisies and superglue from your backpack, then wait for night to fall with some excitement. You halfheartedly flip through the book on the desk. *The Age of Goodbyes* is due soon, but you never once planned on returning the book. You now see it as an heirloom from your father. It is something he intentionally left for you to claim at the library. The tome hides certain secrets for you to unlock, and besides, you've fallen under Shaozi's spell. She has a haughty expression and seems distracted, looking just like Mana; she sails on wind currents toward you, showing off her shoulders.

You awake and clean up your nocturnal emission. The semen sticks to the crotch of your pants like superglue. These days, Mana's arrival is prefaced by countless erotic dreams. The scenes in the dream are so real that you suspect she has actually come by after you've fallen asleep. She holds you down by your shoulders, pressing you into the undulating folds of your dreams. Nimbly she dives into its currents and sucks you off like a mermaid. In those dreams you feel a sense of suffocation. Often you can't help yourself and you suddenly, explosively ejaculate, and then your soul floats up gradually, swimming toward the dream's exit. You awake and clean up after yourself, exhausted and satiated.

You eat your takeaway dinner. The rice has already hardened and dried. You imagine Du Li An's yam stewed with pork belly, fermented bean curd juices flavored with five spice powder and star anise mingling with fat oozing from the meat, piping hot and gushing into your rice. Mother loved the dish too. It's served with a hot bowl upside down atop a bed of raw lettuce in the center of a plate. She raised the hot bowl to reveal maroon yam and pork belly displayed on the jade-green lettuce. How sumptuous it was to watch the fermented bean curd juices overflowing onto the leaves.

No wonder Mother let herself go later on. She was self-aware enough to know she wasn't fated to meet her Yip Mong Sang. All Uncle Sai could do was indulge her and let her give everything up without worry, until in the end she turned into limp mud that couldn't even be smeared up a wall. On that final night in Mayflower, when you sat in the room watching over her body and smelling that stink emanating from the pus pooling on her swollen knee, you momentarily believed she would utterly melt away into a puddle of pus and blood by daybreak. You've read Bi Shumin's flash fiction piece "Purple Doll," in which a husband and wife, both severely burned, die in each other's arms on their bed. You thought it might be like that in the end, with Mother seeping into the mattress and leaving behind a shape the color of fermented bean curd, transforming the bedsheets into rich, luscious batik.

After confirming Mana's absence, you sneak into room 204. The maroon African daisy is still in full bloom. The bedding is rumpled; she must have rushed out. Two of her tops have been flung willy-nilly onto the bed, as if she'd tried them on before leaving but found them wanting. You pick up one of them, which is a gaudy red. It fits the image of what fresh bloody clothes look like in your imagination. The fabric is soft. You bring it to the tip of your nose for a sniff and detect a chemical scent common in laundry detergent powder. You make the bed and fold the two tops, neatly stacking them on the bed. Then you take the shoes out from under the bed, taking your time as you affix the two fabric daisies. While waiting for the glue to set, you can't resist dragging out the duffel bag from under the bed and subjecting it to mindless inspection. You discover that she'd left wearing a white blouse and a bohemian maxi skirt, paired with that bright, monk-ish bag. Beneath the blouse is a thin lotus-colored bra, and farther down is pink underwear rimmed with lace. She's wearing accessories, at the very least an ivory ring and a cheap bracelet featuring fake seashells. Where did she go, dressed like this? Who is she seeing?

The white daisies have taken root on the platform shoes. You give the flowers a yank to make sure they are secure. From now on Mana can match these shoes with her long, loose skirts or flowy blouses, completing your picture of her as a colorful butterfly dancing over daisies. You put her things back where they belong. The bag you shove into the depths, while the shoes you place on guard in front. The daises do not require sunlight. They keep watch in the dark. You turn off the lights and return the room to ignorance, its original state.

Back in your own room, you sit under an artificial lamp and listen to the light's hymns. Uncle Sai comes back and heads straight to his room, 203. After a few long minutes he emerges once more, wearing slippers to wash himself in the second-floor bathroom. You listen as he hums an old Cantonese ditty in the hallway, his mumblings containing almost no lyrics save for this one phrase: *Someday you'll have what's fated to be yours, but what's not yours can never be forced.*

You rally your concentration to focus on Mong Sang and Lin Sang in earnest. Twins who look almost identical. There's something suspicious about them, which makes you think of yourself and J. Although the connection between you and J has not been confirmed, you've already decided he is one of those things Mother forgot simply because she kept it hidden for so long, like the laser gun and other items. Maybe Mong Sang and Lin Sang carry genes predisposed to generate twin offspring, and one of them might very well be the author of this magnum opus. Mother fell for him and bore him sons. You go as far as to visualize Mother seducing him in that library piled high with books, writhing with him on top of the unfinished manuscript of the masterpiece. Yip Lin Sang has the air of a scholar, making him the likelier candidate for the author of *The Age of Goodbyes*. As for Mong Sang, he has the cavalier aura of a rebel about him, and that makes him the only possible choice for someone who would flirt and commit carnal acts in a library. At this moment you don't know which of the brothers dwells in the library housed within your heart. You don't think Mother knew either, which one of them whispered sweet nothings in her ear while tunneling into her body, and which one remained in her memory by the end. She may never even have known that there were two people, a pair of brothers.

You fall asleep and jerk awake. Because the sky is still dark every time you open your eyes, you suspect you are simply "waking up" into a different dream. You believe the overarching dream to be a kingdom not unlike an ant colony, crowded with ditches branching off every which way. Tiny rooms shaped like beehives proliferate, and you can never be sure of your position, nor can you locate the exit. But finally, you really, truly awaken. Though you understand that can never be a proven fact, you trust that the real exit must surely feature a wide expanse of bright, blinding light.

You get ready. You're tired after treading the dreamscape that rolled out infinitely last night, though you're also thankful you were able to return and face this mirror splattered with toothpaste stains. Maybe because the dream created a misguided sense of having survived a disaster, or maybe because you keep thinking about Mana discovering the flowers blooming under the bed, you are actually in a sunny mood. After showering you return to your room, put on your uniform, gather up your backpack, and carelessly flip through the notes you made last night. A piece of paper slips out from the notebook and glides to the floor. You pick it up. It's a 3R-sized color photo of a skinny girl with copper skin who smiles at you. She's wearing a white broad-brimmed hat with a ribbon around it. Perhaps it's a little windy, because her left hand presses down on that overly delicate hat, as if worried it will fly off. Her mouth is so wide when she smiles. All of the light in the photo is focused on her, as if she is a sunflower and can summon sunshine.

Mana was in here and now she's gone, and she left behind a photo. Very likely while you were washing up.

You stare at the person in the photo, suddenly touched by an emotion you've never experienced. It's a glorious and yet sorrowful feeling between your heart and lungs, like a bunch of infinitely expanding balloons filling you up. You feel as if you've been found. Is this the same amorphous sense of fulfillment that Mother felt when she died willingly? She closed the eyes within her eyes. *I'm satisfied with my time on earth.*

You want to cry. This is a blessed day. Young men and women on holiday hold hands while they walk on streets paved with sunshine. You've passed through a night of thick fog that oscillated between light and darkness, and you pushed open a great gate that leads to tomorrow. It's sunny outside. You walk downstairs. When you reach the metal shutters, the sky pours down glorious light, and the sounds of the great wide world wash over you in waves.

—3—

Shaozi wrote a story that touched upon same-sex relationships called "Only Because the Durian Blossomed." At the time, the literary world experienced a surge in sensual depictions of same-sex love, and writers were happy to be identified as ambiguously queer. But it was surprising that Shaozi, who usually "stood apart from the world," did not avoid the bandwagon and instead published "Only Because the Durian Blossomed" during this peak of queer representation.

The Fourth Person naturally looked down his nose at this. In addition, he was not shy about expressing his "deep aversion"[1] to such "trend-following" handling

1. See "The Well-Trodden Pilgrimage toward Queerness—A Review of Shaozi's 'Only Because the Durian Blossomed,'" published in 1999 in *Coconut Rain*.

of queer subjects. For this reason, "Only Because the Durian Blossomed" was placed second to last in his personal "ranking of Shaozi's notable works," ahead of only "Last Words from Last Night."[2]

But this queer story of Shaozi's was a favorite of readers for several reasons. The ranks of queer literati were growing by the day. There was also the turbulent political situation of the time, coupled with the sodomy scandal involving key politicians that provoked heated reactions from the people. In this climate, Shaozi's story was praised as "an exceptional work that most capably reflects the society and generational spirit of our times," as well as "a lasting metaphor in response to the political farce at the tail end of this millennium."[3] The story even garnered Shaozi a nomination for that year's Outstanding Writer Award. As one of the judges, The Fourth Person vehemently opposed granting the award to such a "faux-postmodernist piece," and went so far as to submit evidence stating the story either plagiarized well-known foreign works, or at least invited suspicions of "group authorship." But the other judges dismissed him, and in the end Shaozi won the award with the highest number of votes. The Fourth Person stormed out, vowing to never again judge any such awards.

This particular controversy was leaked by an internal source and then unabashedly confirmed by The Fourth Person, which only led to higher acclaim for Shaozi's story. Because of its "vast, multipronged, and uncertain subject matter that remains open to interpretation," "Only Because the Durian Blossomed" was subsequently included in many anthologies of diverse

2. See addendum at the end of *Always by Your Side*.
3. For the former, see the introduction to Shaozi's short story collection, *The Durian Blossomed*. For the latter, see a blurb on the aforementioned book's cover.

themes over the years, eventually breaking the record for "most anthologized short story" within the local literary scene. Because it was read by a vast number of readers, the story is commonly considered Shaozi's signature work.

After some research, The Fourth Person concluded "Only Because the Durian Blossomed" contains certain autobiographical elements, and so it is entirely plausible to read the work as Shaozi's "semi-autobiography." But his point mainly builds upon the fact that the story sets up a "female writer" as its main character. You find his conclusion hard to swallow, seeing as it's based upon just that one factor. Further, you, like everyone else, suspect The Fourth Person was only trying to imply that Shaozi had same-sex tendencies through his shallow theory, as if this somehow implicates her.

This might be the eeriest part of *The Age of Goodbyes*'s second half—though Shaozi herself never makes an appearance, you start to develop a liking for her through "the works of Shaozi" that you've never read. The feelings that grow in you are akin almost to pity, or a desire to protect the weak. Because Sister Li was verified to be a romantic lover of men, you don't believe Shaozi to be a lesbian. Yet the few excerpts of "Only Because the Durian Blossomed" as quoted by The Fourth Person in his analysis made your heart race. The excerpts' depictions of the female writer as a child and her later adulthood actually correspond completely with the Shaozi you conjured in your imagination.

At twelve, the female writer was of medium build, her face betraying the ravages of hunger. Sporting a bowl cut fresh from an afternoon barber visit, she accompanied her mother to a wake at her friend's house. No one paid attention to the quiet, shy, and unremarkable girl with a novel in her hand. Even if they noticed her, they would remark only that she was reading a book. Little did they know she was really drafting a story from the future the entire time she sat there.

In that short story, another female writer is attending a similar event. She sits alone on a plastic chair closest to the exit, a smirk on her face, her arms crossed in front of her chest. Silently, she observes the comings and goings of people. She notes, too, the deceased's age, over-reported and sketched on white lanterns, as is tradition. It might be drizzling; diagonal wisps of rain land on her back or on the shoulder exposed to the outside. But the female writer is not bothered. She stands tall among the crowd with a distracted air and a posture signaling chilly, remote arrogance.

As if she understands very well that she's on planet Earth only as long as it takes for the next spaceship to carry her back to outer space.

On second thought, every funeral seems to mark the presence of one such female writer, or at least someone like the female writer. She'll refuse to light incense for the deceased. From start to finish she'll sit with her legs crossed flippantly, instead of doing what everyone else does, which is to pay their respects by giving the dearly departed one last look, or else by uttering a word or two of comfort to the surviving relatives. Though she clearly came with others and will sit with everybody, her silence makes her appear eccentric and eye-catching, like a jarring spot of blankness amidst the busy "wholeness" of a mosaic artwork. She gradually sucks up all attention in the room by utilizing an unreasonable method, a distinct special quality called "personal style."[4]

4. See "The Well-Trodden Pilgrimage toward Queerness."

To you, Shaozi is exactly that "person" carried by a spaceship into outer space. Her existence is corroborated solely by *The Age of Goodbyes*, which is by no means a reliable source of truth. It is chock full of contradictions, constantly negating itself; though it relies on the power of fiction, the result is nothing more than a castle in the air. It's just as the sentiment expressed in "Only Because the Durian Blossomed" goes: the book is like a "story from the future" that was written long ago.

But you've taken a shine to Shaozi. You like her the same way you gaze, through a reflection thrown on a cabinet's glass panels, at a girl who walks past behind your back. You can't make out her facial features clearly, but you like seeing her swim quietly across the cabinet's glass screen like a fish. You like that novelist who somberly records the common scenes of life. You're quite sure that it's Shaozi you're obsessed with, not your own image. Oh yes, you're certain that you are not the mythical Narcissus falling in love with his own reflection.

At the same time, you start to form some insight into The Fourth Person, who hovers between existence and nonexistence. You discover that you're actually shoulder to shoulder with him, both of you facing that same cabinet. You have never met, separated by the ages. Both of your inner thoughts exist not inside the cabinet but on the surface of the glass panels.

Now you recognize The Fourth Person as the medium between you and Shaozi. The author, through The Fourth Person's writing in his collected criticism, *Always by Your Side*, has summoned Shaozi as if performing a séance. You know one day the author will finish detailing all the analysis written by The Fourth Person, which will spell the end of everything related to Shaozi in the novel. Having detected the possessive hold The Fourth Person has over Shaozi, you feel a little jealous. He is the key to Shaozi's entire body of work, having stuffed it all into his analysis. This is akin to wizardry. He is using his body as a vessel to contain Shaozi's soul.

CHAPTER SEVEN

—1—

Imagine, right there, a jackfruit tree that stretches all the way into the stratosphere.

Du Li An raised her head, as if she could already see time passing through the gaps between the leaves. She said no, when the jackfruit tree grew larger, its roots would eventually ruin the open drains next to it. "Then how about a mango tree in the backyard?" She said no to that as well. Mango trees were nothing to scoff at once they grew stouter. The moment their branches extended and their leaves spread, they would block out all the light going into the upstairs windows.

But would anyone even be living in those two rooms? She and Steely Bo were the sole occupants of the double-story Western-style house with five bedrooms and two living spaces. Lau Lin was just a temporary lodger after all, and Ah Sai would probably end up making the capital his home. What, was Du Li An supposed to move the old man and the Indian woman in? Setting aside all this, Du Li An finally decided to plant a few royal palm trees in the front yard, with pots of sago palms and bougainvillea arranged under the trees. "Why plant things we can't eat? Waste of soil." Steely Bo was obviously displeased. "Also sago palms have thorns. Have you seen them? They're like wasp stingers."

She did not respond, instead continued to balance her books with her head down. Steely Bo knew there was no chance of swaying her as long as she maintained this posture. Ever since this woman got the hold of running Ping Le House, she'd developed a will of steel. Yes, there would indeed be royal palm trees, sago palms, and bougainvillea. She could just picture the scene. There would be everything desired—leaves, flowers, trees, and fruit, a harmony of yin and yang.

Steely Bo, on the other hand, had no imagination. He couldn't even deduce his own standing once Elder Zong stepped down. Oh well, it wasn't like he'd officially announced his retirement anyway. His eldest son had thrown himself into business and was already an important executive in the tin mining town's Chinese Chamber of Commerce. The second son had also made a name for himself in politics. Neither of them were interested in the affairs of the Toa Pek Kong Society. That said, both of them had occasion to lean on the Toa Pek Kong brotherhood from time to time, but they went about it carefully such that their names were never directly linked to the triad. As for the young'un born to the Zong mistress, he was said to be a spoiled good-for-nothing through and through. It was only a matter of time before he pissed away all the family had built.

In reality, Elder Zong was taking a step back and gradually handing over his responsibilities and power. Steely Bo harbored dreams of succeeding as leader of the entire Toa Pek Kong Society. His restlessness did not escape Du Li An. She saw, too, the tension that flared whenever he hung around his society brothers. But she failed to comprehend the danger herein, and so she did not rain on his parade.

Perhaps it was because the country was switching prime ministers that year. Steely Bo saw an auspicious sign in the old PM's retirement. The deputy PM would replace him. Steely Bo felt that his day, too, was due, after so many years of loyally following Elder Zong.

Du Li An did not spare much thought for such remote matters. She'd just gotten the keys to the new house and was consumed by renovations and move-in details. Business was still booming at Ping Le House, too, and so she could only manage to rush over and supervise work at the new house after the kopitiam closed in the afternoon. The carpentry man came recommended by Yip Mong Sang, who sometimes dropped in for a look if the house was on his way. If he came during afternoon tea time, he often brought along cold drinks and snacks for whomever was on site. He was always gone by the time Du Li An arrived. The workers praised him for being attentive, and some of the apprentices even mistook "Mr. Yip" for the homeowner. Du Li An always spent an hour or two there. Steely Bo was tied up with efforts to build his base anyway, and seldom ate dinner at home. Having lost the motivation to prepare dinner, Du Li An stayed at the new house into the evening, going home only when the workers and their supervisors left. She made her rounds in and out of the house before leaving, collected the workers' drink containers hung carelessly here and there, then threw them into the garbage pile.

It'd been a long while since she'd seen Yip Mong Sang, she thought.

That fellow had stayed away from Ping Le House for a stretch of time. Du Li An found out through subtle inquiries that he'd quit his position at the sewing factory. Supposedly he was now in the construction supply business with a friend. But she couldn't tell any of this from observing Lau Lin, that secretive and taciturn girl. Ever since Yip Mong Sang's abruptly interrupted night visit, Du Li An had little to say to her, and the girl similarly kept mum. Her daily schedule appeared unchanged. Occasionally as she was leaving the house, she would mention catching a movie with her coworker after work. The few times Du Li An spied on Lau Lin through the blinds, she was always alone in the cab that dropped her off. But Du Li An understood that Lau Lin's "coworker" must be none other than Yip Mong Sang.

Because Du Li An had connections everywhere and Ping Le House was a hub of information, hearing bits and pieces about Yip Mong Sang was unavoidable. Although there was no hard evidence, the man must have had his fair share of romantic entanglements. People said he was a womanizer and always had his finger in at least two pies. "Two pies? It must be more than that?" Du Li An remembered how tightly Lau Lin had held on to his thumb. Oh, what a hard-headed, persistent girl. Du Li An feared that if something were to happen one day, Lau Lin would slit her wrists like Carol Cheng in *The Brothers*.

Well, what was that promiscuous Yip Mong Sang doing right at this moment, and who was he doing it with? Du Li An drove once around the town center and saw that Old Majestic Cinema was showing Sam Hui's new movie. Lights blazed throughout the building and threw looming shadows cast by the crowd, making the place seem even more bustling than it was. To think people used to say the cinema was haunted. Clearly no one took that seriously anymore, now that enough time had passed. Did the deceased Chan Kam Hoi still linger in the women's bathroom? Looking at the crowd's shadows overlapping under bright lights, she felt an agitation come over her out of nowhere. She didn't especially want to go home. After driving aimlessly along the streets for a bit, she steered the car toward her old home to check on her father.

For the past two months the old man had been limping because of arthritis. Since his mobility became limited, he'd almost entirely stopped making a scene at Ping Le House, granting her a period of peace. Now she stood downstairs from him and suddenly felt uneasy for the relief and freedom she'd enjoyed while her own father was suffering. It made her embarrassed to go up, and so she hesitated for a while on the five-foot way. The stairwell's dim lighting made it seem forbidding in the dark night. It was ghost month, the seventh month of the lunar calendar, and she could feel unholy presences enshrouding the entrance. Strange—how had she ever managed to walk up those stairs before? She'd never felt this on edge.

She drew a deep breath and groped her way along the banister. Then she realized she didn't have the keys on her. Nothing to do but to slap on the door. Old man, old man. It was the Indian woman, Vati, who opened the door. She wasn't yet fifty, but with gray showing at her temples she seemed to Du Li An much older than when they'd first met two years ago. Vati possessed astonishing linguistic talents; her Cantonese was even more fluent than Sou Gei's. Vati opened the two layers of doors with practiced fluidity, all the while telling Du Li An about door locks and the neighborhood's safety, or lack of it. It was only then that she noticed the massive, brand-new lock docked around the door's latch. The lock seemed sturdier than the iron grille. An odd sensation arose within her as she waited outside. This Indian woman, practically a stranger to Du Li An, was now acting like the woman of the house. Du Li An felt a whiff of rejection emanating from both the door lock and Vati.

Earlier that year, Ah Sai had come home as usual for Lunar New Year celebrations. Du Li An made her appearance on the second day of the new year, per the custom for married women. Vati prepared a whole spread of lamb and beef, all dowsed in curry. Ah Sai and the old man couldn't get enough. Du Li An alone felt that the dishes weren't appropriate for new year. But the house was undeniably much cleaner and tidier since Vati moved in. Ah Sai said that she ground her teeth all the while doing laundry, as if she had a bone to pick with the clothes. Unable to withstand her scrubbing, the old man's Pagoda shirts and Ah Sai's Eagle-brand singlets lost their shape after just a few washes, and yet they all shone bright as new.

"You see, even years of sweat stains are gone," Ah Sai said and turned his back to flip up the collar of his shirt.

After the New Year meal, Ah Sai left to visit his old mentor, Uncle Wah Zai. Du Li An walked out with him. In the corridor they ran into two Indian youths climbing up the stairs. Ah Sai greeted them and told her, over his shoulder, that the two were brothers, Vati's sons. "There's a ton of leftovers. They're here to help finish it up." She sidled sideways to let them pass, aiming nods and smiles at the brothers, all the while concluding that this must not be the first time they'd come for a handout. How else to explain her brother's familiarity with them?

"I played badminton with them yesterday. The older one has great technique." Ah Sai kept walking ahead, the back of his neck like a patch of mossy grass. "I was no match."

She glared at him. How could he still be so naïve? She turned around and watched Vati let the two teenagers in. Then she said, unable to hold it in any longer, "Can you believe it, such strapping young lads freeloading at the house of their mother's lover." Ah Sai didn't catch what she said and asked her to repeat herself. She looked at him twisting his neck to see her. His hair, fresh from an army cut, gave him an air of tender innocence. She said, You must have gotten your hair done at an Indian shop, right. Ah Sai smiled and scratched the back of his neck, a little self-conscious. "You got it. They don't raise their prices at new year. Cost only a dollar."

"That's enough for a cup of coffee at Ping Le House." Du Li An reached out a hand and brushed it against his nape. It was prickly, as she'd expected. For some reason Yip Mong Sang came to her mind then. No, maybe it was Yip Lin Sang. She liked the fresh look that haircuts gave them. Mong Sang even lathered on lots of wax, rounding out his outfit of neatly pressed long-sleeved shirts and pants. No matter the occasion or the place, he always presented an image of immaculate tidiness.

Now she caught sight of the old man prone on his recliner before she even stepped foot in the house. His arthritis must be more serious than she'd thought. He'd lost a lot of weight in just two months. Skin and loose flesh drooped limply from his cheeks and underarms. Du Li An pulled over a chair to sit beside him. The old man said, Ah Li you're here so late, have you eaten? He had been born with a booming voice and he still spoke with plenty of brass. Hearing it relieved her. She chatted with him for a while, until he yawned twice in a row and she realized the hour. She waited for an opening, and when Vati walked into the kitchen Du Li An fished a few fifty-dollar bills from her handbag and shoved them into his palm.

"See a Western doctor if a Chinese one won't do. Maybe it'll all go away with one needle."

The old man pursed his mouth and shook his head. Reflecting on the moment later, she agreed that she might have sounded too flippant. The arthritis had dragged on for years, after all, and at his age, there was really nothing to do but let his ancient bones wear down. As she left, Vati emerged from the kitchen cupping a bowl of Chinese medicine in her hands. Du Li An asked what it was. Vati replied that she'd brewed a licorice and wolfsbane concoction to help with arthritis. Du Li An eyed the steaming black soup emanating the scent of Chinese angelica and admitted, reluctantly, that the Indian woman's Cantonese really was excellent.

Vati put down the bowl of medicine to open the iron grille door for Du Li An, then locked up again. Du Li An meant to ask for a key to the new lock, but she saw Vati rushing to feed the old man his medicine, and the words stuck in her throat. The moment passed, and then it was too late.

About a fortnight later, kneeling with Ah Sai in front of the old man's coffin, she dwelled on the mysterious impulse, out of nowhere, that had driven her to visit home that night. Yet all she did in the end was glance at the massive lock on the front door. Its size was really ridiculously out of proportion for their thin old iron door, like a slender necklace burdened by an oversized pendant.

Vati was present when the Taoist priest began performing the rites, though she was tactful enough to keep a wide distance from start to end. Sometimes she sequestered herself in the back to help fold joss paper money. It was only what was due a few years of companionship. Her two sons stopped by too. The three of them sat in a corner and conversed in Tamil through the night. Meanwhile, Du Li An kept returning to her chat with the old man that night she visited. She should have noticed the various signs. A black moth had circled the shrines in the house, death's cursed shadow stealthily lurking in the background. The old man even brought up Sou Gei's possessions. That was unusual, wasn't it? He said, You're taking good care of the gold necklaces and rings and whatnot your ma left behind, aren't you? This had raised a flag for Du Li An. She thought he was asking for Sou Gei's things.

"Of course, they're in a safe place. Those were her prized possessions her entire life." Du Li An peeked at

Vati, watching TV off to the side. Later, Du Li An told Ah Sai she thought the old man wanted to give the jewelry to Vati. "You know how much Indian people love gold."

Ah Sai merely nodded. Du Li An couldn't understand his reticence. Now, head bowed, he separated the bunched-together piles of joss paper money, then threw them one by one into the basin of fire. He was so attentive, like he was cleaning sea cucumber in a restaurant kitchen, or maybe preparing bird's nest. She, on the other hand, felt her senses scattered, her emotions unable to cohere. Perhaps it was because something was amiss with her husband. For the past few days he'd popped in and out of the funeral hall, saying only that there were matters requiring his attention at the Society. Even when he did show his face he never stayed long, always rushed off somewhere with a few of his Society brothers without saying goodbye. The Society brothers came bearing messages, their faces stony, their footsteps rapid, and whispered into his ears. It finally alerted Du Li An to the thick tension in the hall. She hadn't forgotten the fuss that had been made over Sou Gei's funeral. This time, Elder Zong had simply delegated someone to bring over a wreath, while he himself never made an appearance.

The presiding Taoist priest, on the other hand, was the same one, unchanged. As a longtime acquaintance of the old man, the priest performed his tasks with extra zeal. Whenever he took a break he regaled others with cryptic tales about the underworld. He revealed that Sou Gei had summoned the old man. Du Li An nodded gently in the face of this fervor. Staring at her, the priest said that everyone must face the three major misfortunes and six key prosperities, oh boss lady.

Yip Mong Sang came the night before the funeral procession. Ah Sai rubbed his eyes in astonishment when he saw him walk into the hall. It was only after she noticed her brother's expression that she too saw Yip Mong Sang standing at the entryway with his head bent, whispering away with Lau Lin.

Really, it had been ages since Du Li An had last seen him. She suddenly felt a sharp pang of sadness, though she couldn't quite grasp the roots of it. The feeling grew uncontrollably, and her nose prickled with suppressed tears. She narrowed her eyes. Everything in front of her became hazy. Yip Mong Sang turned into a blurry, distant figure. He was there, so close and yet so far, untouchable.

"He's not who you think he is. That's Yip Lin Sang's twin brother, Yip Mong Sang." She acted nonchalant. "He used to be Lau Lin's coworker." She turned her face to gaze directly at Ah Sai, hoping he would understand. "I never told him I knew his younger brother."

Ah Sai might not have been able to probe the depths of her feelings, but he nodded with understanding. Secrets were for keeping, wasn't it so? Du Li An smiled bitterly. It was unclear even to her why a fact had turned into a secret. She felt a little lost. The content of the secret was too obscure. Did it center around Yip Lin Sang? Or was it Yip Mong Sang? She couldn't explain it to herself, had no way of beginning to untangle it.

Yip Mong Sang didn't stay long. He lit some incense and came forward to offer a few words of comfort. Du Li An kept her head down while acknowledging him, though from time to time she strained her eyes upward to sneak glances at various details of Mong Sang's body. Wrinkles on the long-sleeved shirt. Armpit stains on such a hot day; maybe he had been bustling about outside and hadn't had a chance to shower and change at home. As if on cue, Mong Sang said he'd been busy with affairs in the capital the last few days and had rushed straight to the funeral hall. She wasn't really listening. She spied a small fuzzy ball that looked like a dandelion stuck to the front of his shirt. After that, her gaze never left the little tuft. There was a persistent urge to pluck it, but she never acted on the impulse. He made his excuses and left after the customary pleasantries. She watched him go and saw him stop by Lau Lin at the entrance. While the two of them spoke, she leaned forward to fluff his shirt.

The old man's funeral was an even grander affair than Sou Gei's had been seven years ago, and even more people came to pay their respects. But something was obviously off in the atmosphere within the funeral hall. There was tension drawn tight, and also dejection. The Society brothers fluttered in and out, always in a hurry, giving off an uneasiness, like an impending storm. Du Li An was agitated by the unnamed apprehension. Guen Hou had been coming to lend a helping hand several nights in a row. On that very last night she brought along her daughter, Eggplant Face, because it was the weekend. The girl seemed entirely carefree. Since Lau Lin was occupied, Eggplant Face sat reading alone under the iron awning near the entrance. She'd gone through a growth spurt that year, although she remained all skin and bones. Her hair, though, was extraordinarily lush. This, combined with her puffy mushroom haircut, made her head appear giant perched on her tiny body. She looked like a matchstick.

Du Li An passed some time standing by the entrance. The rain, suppressed for the last few days, finally poured down. Surprisingly there was neither a gale nor thunder, only heavy raindrops exploding on the iron awning. People under it moved one after another into the funeral hall to continue their tea drinking and peanut shelling. Du Li An told Eggplant Face, Why don't you move your chair forward a little, the rain is going all over your shoulder.

The next day, a misty rain fell for the entirety of the old man's funeral procession. Du Li An stood on the side of a bare hill under her wide, black umbrella, eyes trained on the rain, her thoughts elsewhere. The eccentric priest mumbled in a low baritone for an eternity, as if transmitting his past and future lives to his old friend lying in the hole in the ground. Du Li An had been told to move away when the body was placed into the coffin. She turned to stare at the mountains undulating like waves. The sky was so high, so far off, the wisps of rain floating down seemed like unyielding lotus fiber connecting heaven to earth. After the ceremony, she returned home and promptly developed a cold and fever. She awoke after days of troubled sleep to see Guen Hou, her face full of anxiety, saying something about bad news from the Toa Pek Kong Society.

Du Li An, still groggy, received only bits and pieces of Guen Hou's information. Du Li An had to force herself to pay attention, and after some patient listening, she finally deciphered that two days ago Elder Zong had announced he was handing over major responsibilities to his nephew. A group of Society brothers led by Steely Bo rebelled on the spot, putting on a farce of a mutiny in the Toa Pek Kong temple. Steely Bo even stepped forward to denounce his godfather in front of everyone, enraging Elder Zong so much that his breathing failed and he collapsed from a stroke. Then the brothers apparently twiddled their thumbs even though the whole place was thrown into high panic; if it weren't for a few veterans taking decisive action, the elderly man might have died where he lay.

Finally Du Li An grasped the ins and outs of the situation. Exhausted, she closed her eyes. She believed she slept for a long time, but when she opened her eyes again time seemed to have stilled in the air around her. Guen Hou remained in the exact same position as she had previously. "And Steely Bo?" Du Li An asked calmly. "What did they do to him?"

Guen Hou shrugged. "He ran off." Her face was a picture of pity.

Du Li An used all her strength to swivel her eyeballs. She saw Lau Lin standing by the bedroom door, hands behind her back, shaking her head, bearing an expression of innocence.

Not a trace could be found of Steely Bo after the whole hullabaloo. Lau Lin asked around at the fishing village, but no one there had news of him either. He maintained radio silence all through Du Li An's recovery, even for the duration of Elder Zong's hospitalization and subsequent discharge for his stroke, which had paralyzed half his body. Naturally various rumors began to spread around town. Some said the new leader of the Toa Pek Kong Society, Elder Zong's nephew, had sent men to "take care" of Steely Bo, whose body had been trussed around a huge rock and thrown into the old river. Others said he must have followed a plan B; he'd taken a boat to lay low on some remote Indonesian island. Still other gossip claimed he was hiding on a fishing boat back at his childhood home.

Du Li An maintained an appearance of complete composure, brushing off each and every rumor. Other than two trips to visit Elder Zong, she did not vary from her routine of dolling up each day to sit at the cash register in Ping Le House. Cha-ching, cha-ching, cha-ching. She did, however, grow somber and taciturn, and remained illogically calm. Because of that, Guen Hou told others behind her back that the boss lady no doubt had some idea of Steely Bo's whereabouts.

In truth, Du Li An was simply numb to it all. The bigger and more complicated the matter, not to mention the more embarrassing, the less one should shrink from it. At the same time, one shouldn't ever reveal one's hand. For a whole month she returned straight home after closing shop at Ping Le House. Since she was in no mood to make dinner, she let Lau Lin eat as she pleased. After dinner Du Li An turned on the TV and sat in the living room, idly listening to every pip and squeak in the house. The neighbors, busybodies that they were, loved to peer in from outside, and so she put on a show of cracking sunflower seeds. She even had Lau Lin bring home rental VHS tapes so they could broadcast the soundtrack to her normal daily life for the neighbors' benefit.

Du Li An kept thinking Steely Bo would send her a message, or at least make a call home. But more than thirty days came and went. Her heart grew cold as she waited. It wasn't that she was worried for his life. After all, Elder Zong had said to her, face muscles spasming, Ah Li, I am not an extreme person. The poor old man's mouth was now crooked after his stroke, and he bit his tongue whenever he spoke. But the tone of his voice was steady, determined, and his eyes remained clear and intimidating, just like they'd always been. She nodded.

Let Steely Bo gaze upon those eyes. He'd understand then that he was but a rash bull with no plan whatsoever, and no moral backbone to boot. He was no leader material.

Du Li An had even rehearsed what she'd say, every word traversing the spectrum from shouted accusation to rebuke to jeers, all the way through interrogation, exhortation, and forgiveness; she came up with a new set of talking points practically every day. But Steely Bo never did contact her, leaving her to torment herself with imagined scenarios and wild guesses. All she could do was grind her teeth and wail in her dreams. She woke up filled with bitter hate, begrudged as an abandoned wife.

Now that something of such magnitude had happened, she keenly felt the absence of a confidante by her side. If the old man were there, she might have been able to drag a few coherent ideas out of him, befuddled as he was. But he'd left without saying goodbye. After he'd died in his sleep on the recliner that night, he'd tunneled into a hole in the ground to lie beside Sou Gei. Someone told Du Li An that the Indian woman remained in the old family home and had even moved in her two strapping sons. "One happy family." Surprisingly, Du Li An was unperturbed by the news. After half a moment's silence she said, Well, someone needs to watch over that house. "She's a woman, it's not like she can just stay there all by herself."

The gossipmongers instantly felt as if they'd put their feet into their mouths. "Aiyoyo, who'd have thought the boss lady of Ping Le House would turn into a philanthropist?" They forced sneers onto their faces and awkwardly left her counter.

Du Li An couldn't be bothered by such trivial matters. For the past month her nerves had been worn paper-thin by the telephone constantly ringing at Ping Le House and at home. On top of that she couldn't sleep at night, all of which left her bone-weary. They closed the shop late one evening. She watched her workers pull down Ping Le House's shutters and walked to her car alone. By that time, most of the neighboring shops were also done for the day and few cars went by, giving the street an air of desolation. Her attention was drawn to the streetlamps that suddenly shivered into brightness, like a row of giant, erect lightning bugs. She paused her steps, raised her face, and concentrated on the last streak of sunset blending into the sapphire-blue sky. Such beauty. She let out an earnest, admiring sigh.

That precise moment made her give up on the idea of going home to sit by the telephone.

Instead, on that night she drove around town to take in its views. She even went out of her way to go by her old home. There were indeed lights on in the windows upstairs. As she craned her neck to stare at the dim yellow glow, she felt sad and moved at the same time. Ah, someone was at home. No matter that the wavering figures were putting on an entirely different show behind the curtains and lighted window that resembled a shadow play theater.

She suddenly thought of her new property on the way home. The renovations had been put on hold since the old man's death. Du Li An drove to the newly paved roads in that area and saw that the owners of some other new houses had already started gardening. Certain front yards even boasted fruit trees. She got out of the car and stepped into the unkempt wilderness of her new house, where weeds frothed and spilled everywhere. Add to that the junk left scattered around by the construction workers, and the place looked just like a forgotten graveyard.

It was then that Mong Sang barged in. At the very time in her life, just when she was filled with melancholy and had fallen to lamenting the bleakness of life, the vagaries of fate—at that exact moment she abruptly saw light. She raised her head and saw two headlights heading straight for her front gates. The twin beams were dazzling, and the accompanying engine was thunderous. A man emerged from the car and stood outside the gates. She recognized the gangly figure. "What a coincidence," the man said.

"I was driving by these parts and wanted to see how your house was getting along."

She recognized this voice too. This smile. These eyes. She remembered this person once walked toward her filled with love. Weaving through the dappled light cast by angsana trees in front of Pei Hwa Primary School, through dark shadows slanting in alleys; through violent policemen and agitating citizens;

through tables and chairs and bodies crowded in Ping Le House; through the barren corridors of the funeral hall; and then through lush dreamscapes and the desolation of reality. He'd been walking toward her, and all this time she'd never taken her eyes off him. She'd always liked summoning him. Come, let me see how tall you are.

"I haven't seen you in such a long time." She finally released them wistfully, these words that had been suppressed for ages.

—

They chose the bedroom suite upstairs and padded the floor by breaking down boxes that once had held construction materials. Yip Mong Sang kissed her, placing her within the blue moonlight as if releasing a fish into water. Du Li An stretched out her neck, using every sensory organ in her body to receive his passionate kisses and fondles. The man was gentler and more patient than she'd imagined. His slender fingers played her body like a piano. She heard a meandering ballad flowing back and forth like a lukewarm brook between her body and his, brought alive by their caresses. She let him undress her, let him bite her earlobes softly, let him kiss the corners of her mouth, lick away her tears. She arched her back in greeting when he entered her. She writhed to meet his collisions. The world sank gradually into peace and quiet. The sounds of the natural world rushed in and circulated their bloodstreams. Looking to the walls, she saw a carved windowsill transformed into a deep-blue painting, a full moon suspended in its upper right corner. The whole world had quieted down to listen to them, to the repeated calls mingled with her moans. Mong Sang. Mong Sang.

Softly, he answered, I'm here.

You can see the fireworks. They shoot into the night sky like arrows loosed from a bow. Then they bloom in the black expanse, taking the shape of mango flowers. The fireworks' lifespan is so short it rivals that of queen of the night cacti; they're often disappeared by the night before they can even plummet to earth. You hear the crowd cheering. Every single person has stuck out their neck to anticipate the next explosive bouquet. The pyrotechnic performance has stunned the city and frozen time. Only you and a very few others uninterested in the display weave through the gaps between people, sweat pooling on your backs.

You know Mana must be here somewhere on this plaza. You know she left this evening wearing the platform shoes adorned with white daisies. She'll stand out with her beauty, just like Emily in the novel. You have no doubt you'll be able to find her on this plaza crammed with people. How exhilarated you were when you saw Du Li An and Yip Mong Sang embrace naked in *The Age of Goodbyes*. She opened herself up for him to slip in, uniting with him. You couldn't hold it in any longer. It has to be today. What else are you waiting for? You want to catch hold of her wrist. You want to call out her name. *Mana.*

She wasn't in her room. After checking the duffel bag under the bed and the makeup kit in the drawer, you knew she'd dressed up and gone out. The faint fragrance of perfume wafted in the room, bringing to mind fresh jasmine blooms swaying in the breeze. You lay down on her bed, closed your eyes, and drifted off for a bit. No dream descended. Then you remembered how the novel described Du Li An narrowing her eyes and calling out your name, and you're almost tempted to masturbate. This yearning alarmed you. No, the one you want is Mana.

Odd that you were so riled up. Just like how the novel described rain that's been repressed for a long while. When it finally poured down it was accompanied by wind and thunder, an unstoppable force. You paced room 204 in consternation until you heard the call to prayer from the mosque. Suddenly, as if through divine intervention, you remembered it was New Year's Eve, which meant the plaza in the city center would host both a night market and a fireworks show. You didn't know where the certainty came from, but you were positive Mana must have headed there. Wearing those platform shoes that make her proud, perhaps latched onto somebody's arm, she first sauntered through the night market, and then stood in some spot on the plaza, her head upturned to await the neon flowers that would soon unfurl and die in the sky.

So then you left the building as well and dove into the jam-packed city at night. The world beyond was abuzz and ostentatious, while Mayflower stood empty and silent like a towering graveyard. Even after you walked out you could still hear your frantic footsteps echo in the motel. There remained some dusky light in the sky, though the streetlamps lining the broad road and the decorative holiday lanterns hanging between telephone poles were already lit up. All the shops were closed, and there was scant foot traffic about. The street stretched out, long and lonely, in sharp contrast to the lustrous lights. You recalled Shaozi in the novel. In her story "Only Because the Durian Blossomed," she described such dark corners as "the backstage areas of a city."

When you arrived at the plaza, you found that the temporary night market was larger than you expected. There are so many people they form an almost watertight mass. You squeeze into the congested flow of bodies. At a loss for what to do, you let yourself be pushed forward by those coming up behind you. In reality, you don't have much say in the matter. It is only after being cast into this sea of souls that you realize how puny you and Mana are. It might be a matter of luck after all, whether you find her, or if you find each other.

You are marched forward like this for who knows how long. You glance at the backs of the people ahead of you as well as everyone coming toward you from the opposite direction. You look, too, at the girls standing in front of the stalls picking through clothes, accessories, snacks, or other items. You pay extra attention to the shoes they wear. Two white daisies, Mana's trademark. Even so, this doesn't lessen the difficulty of the search. The girls' feet dart out of sight, and then the window for scrutinizing their faces passes. Maybe there's simply too many people. Each person added into the mix negates another's existence, until everyone's uniqueness is cancelled out, making this an impractical space for finding a person.

Yet you stubbornly cling to the belief that tonight is your best possible opportunity for meeting Mana, even though you understand better than anything that *if* Mana really were here, you are still like two drops of water in an ocean. You're both rubbing shoulders with the entire city's population, meeting every single person and then immediately losing them again. The deeper you wade into the night market's belly, the tighter the crowd becomes. Faces waver in front of you, filling up your field of vision, suffocating you. Subconsciously, you angle your head up and puff out your chest to breathe. It feels like some aloof god exists beyond the night sky, casting a cold gaze down upon this choked plaza.

"For His eyes are on the ways of a man, and He sees all his steps."

Like driftwood, the phrase floats suddenly up to the surface of your mind. The speaker is an old woman who often appeared to convert the sex workers at the motel. She had a clean face and white teeth, and she loved children. You remember that when she listened to others, she often liked to interject an abrupt "praise the Lord" or a "Hallelujah" in the tiny gaps between their sentences. For instance, when Mother once indignantly recounted how you had been separated from her at a night market the previous night. She said she searched for two hours and was worried out of her mind. In the end she found you outside a model toy store near the night market.

She called out to you. When you turned to face her, you were inexplicably calm, as if you hadn't yet realized that you'd been lost.

"Praise the Lord!" The old woman patted your back tenderly. "This child right here, lost and then found." Then she locked eyes with you and recounted a story from the Bible about a shepherd who left his flock in search of a missing lamb. She spoke very slowly and softly, as if trying to hypnotize you. Lacking patience, you turned your back before the story was over to play with a Rubik's Cube you'd just found. You didn't catch the story's ending. Before she left that day, she pulled you toward her and trapped you between her knees. She raised an index finger and you couldn't help but look outside the window, in the direction she pointed. The old woman said right into your ear, For His eyes are on the ways of a man, and He sees all his steps.

In your memory, the old woman always had a smile on her face, which gave her some magical power that was hard to resist. She liked having your mother and the other sex workers chanting Bible verses with her. You stood next to Mother, your little hand in hers, and often you couldn't help but follow along. "The Lord is my shepherd; I shall not want."

I shall not want.

"He makes me lie down in green pastures; he leads me beside quiet waters."

Quiet waters.

"He restores my soul; he guides me in the paths of righteousness for the sake of His name."

Restores my soul, paths of righteousness.

"Even though I walk through the valley of the shadow of death, I will fear no evil; for You are with me; Your rod and Your staff, they comfort me."

Fear no evil. You are with me, comfort me.

"You prepare a table before me in the presence of my enemies. You anoint my head with oil; my cup overflows."

In the presence of my enemies. Oil, cup overflows.

"Surely goodness and mercy will follow me all the days of my life, and I will dwell in the house of the Lord forever."

All the days of my life, forever.

The first bloom of fireworks resembles a fast-disappearing golden palm tree. Everyone lifts their heads and releases admiring sighs. As if receiving a divine message, you suddenly recall that this was the exact phrase Mother recited before her death: all the days of my life, forever. Was she thinking of that kindly old woman in that moment? Or was she gazing upon the throne of the Lord?

Now that the fireworks have started, the night market crowd boils over onto the plaza. You're swept up and onto the plaza alongside everyone else. People are already packed like sardines there. Bang bang bang— the screen that is the sky displays trees of fire and petals of silver. They look like flares and cast bright lights that travel across people's faces. You, too, stop your feet at some point. It looks almost like meteors of fire are streaking overhead. Fireworks scatter into star clusters.

Time pauses. You look around you. Everyone seems so somber at this moment, as if making silent wishes upon the ephemeral splendor in the sky. You can't resist soundlessly reciting the girl's name too. Mana.

You make your way through the complex formations composed by human bodies, in search of Mana. Was this how Mother looked for you all that time ago? My child, though the ocean of humanity is boundless, no one can deny your existence. Finally she caught sight of you. She rushed forward, calling you.

You heard your name. You turned and were slapped ferociously across the face. Cradling your cheek, you still had no self-awareness about your status as a lamb, lost and then found. But because your face was on fire, and maybe because you felt you'd been treated unfairly, you eventually broke down into loud wails when she twisted your ear with all her might.

You bump into quite a few acquaintances before the fireworks display ends. Even Mayflower's ancient doorman is here, standing in the middle of the plaza with his grandchild. The duo, old and young, stand agape, awed to silence like two statues. You also see two classmates holding hands, a boy and a girl, plus the Sikh teen everyone calls Black Jack who works with you at KFC. None of them notice you, and you pass right by them like a stranger. You think you see the back of Uncle Sai too. The last bunch of fireworks jets toward the sky, dozens of rapid-fire crackers. Bang bang bang, bang bang bang. It's a brilliance of falling blossoms. The people on the plaza, dazzled, raise their voices in uniform cheers. But Uncle Sai walks off alone without even lifting his head.

You loiter on that plaza until midnight, sitting on stone steps and watching people leave with their arms around each other after counting down to the new year, their smiling faces bearing traces of dejection. The fireworks and the exuberance of the festival were a mere interlude between two calendar years. When you leave the plaza, you feel just as despondent and exhausted as anyone else. Like cotton candy, all that lovely hopefulness cannot withstand any actual enjoyment.

Mayflower retained its Zen composure from last year. Uncle Sai's snores waft from the second floor. The toilet tanks continue to leak, and the building's floor joints still groan. You return to your room. The light is on, and you see right away that there's a takeout foam container placed on the desk. On the box lid is red marker ink spelling out "Happy New Year" in English. The marker pen is yours, originally stuck into a pencil cup but now perched atop the cover of the "magnum opus." You open the container to see two exquisite pieces of kuih lapis. One of them has a corner missing, a crescent of faint teeth marks. She's taken a bite. Perhaps at the "golden moment," just when you were sitting on the stone steps looking up into space, your ears resounding with people raucously counting down to the new year. Ten, nine, eight, seven, six . . . Mana sat right here, fuming and taking a bite out of your new year cakes. You can't help but laugh, can't stop yourself from licking that bite mark. From that lick you devour the kuih.

What Mother said was this: "Don't stray far in the future. Stay where you are and wait for me to find you."

"You hear that? Answer me!" She held your ear in a twist, her face very close to yours, as if she wanted to aim her shouts right into your cochlea.

Was that what the shepherd said to the lost lamb?

Mother didn't know. But later in life your ears often rang and you had mysterious dizzy spells, and you vomited for no apparent reason. After you were diagnosed with peripheral vertigo, Mother suspected that she'd ruined your ear when she smacked you across the face years ago. She was filled with regret. During many boring, empty afternoons, when drowsiness suffused the air, she'd half listen to the radio with one leg perched high, chin resting in her hands, and she'd stare at you in a trance, trying to recollect scenes from that fateful day to sort out once and for all which ear it was that she'd slapped.

Maybe the two pieces of kuih are overly sweet. In your dreams that night, you keep having the sensation that your upper and lower jaws are glued together by some cloying, sticky liquid. Someone pushes open your door in the small hours. You're not sure whether that sound is from reality or from the world of dreams, but you think the person must be Mana. Therefore you're reluctant to make a single move, for fear that you'll pierce the dream or scare her away. She stands a moment by the door, as if hesitating over whether to enter. You lie on your side, your back to the door, feeling like an earthworm strung up as bait. Time passes exceedingly slowly. Does she really have that many misgivings? Then she finally pads in, though she pauses a while by the door after softly closing it, as if ready to burst back out again at any moment.

Mana. You called for her in your dream. She heard you and so tiptoed toward you, yet now she's still and silent by your bedside. You're almost certain this isn't a dream. Though your back is to her and she holds her breath so carefully, the two of you are so close, close enough that you can feel her gaze lingering on your spine, the same way you can sense the eye within the eye. The book within the book, the novel in the novel.

In your dream, with great difficulty you pry open your mouth glued shut by cloying, sticky liquid. Your ears pick up dreamy voices. Happy New Year, you say in

English. The person by the bed lets out a snort of laughter. She climbs in, burrowing under your blanket and adhering her face to the back of your neck. This, too, has the trance-like quality of a dream, but then again you can so clearly feel her fresh breaths huffing against your vertebrae. She snakes a hand across your waist. You grab hold of her hand lightly, wrapping it in your palm. Instead of struggling, she affixes herself closer until she's like a tame macaque riding on your back.

You open your eyes. The dimmest moonlight shines through the window, giving everything the feel of a fantasy. But Mana's hand is indeed in your grasp, and you feel her body heat against your back. Both of your palms are sweating slightly. You want to turn around, but she hugs you tighter when she senses your movement, clearly reluctant to let you flip over. You let her have her way, continuing your hold on her hand. In silence, the two of you watch the foggy moon beyond the window, like twins in a womb anticipating the real world.

You have a very peaceful night's rest, so dreamless that you feel digested into nonexistence. Around dawn, Mana awakes to the mosque's sunrise call to prayers. She leaves. The mattress retains her smell and a fragrance lingers under the blankets. A sweetness remains in your mouth, as if coated with honey. You wake and sit up in bed, your eyes stuck on a strand of wavy hair gracing the pillow. Early sunlight seeps in and you are unable to stop the waves of desire that wash over you, making you erect.

—3—

The woman writer in "Only Because the Durian Blossomed" falls in love with Emily, a mixed-race city girl.

She says she has Portuguese, English, Indian, and Chinese heritage. The woman writer responds, Ah, so there must be several generations of prostitutes in your bloodline. She always speaks like this, a smile conveying her ill intentions curving her mouth. Emily is the only one in the whole wide world who doesn't care a whit, who even plants her hands on her waist and throws herself into wholehearted laughter.

Thus she dissolves the woman writer's callousness. Later, in old age, the woman writer is unable to forget that girl who let a cobra twine her wrist. The girl astride an elephant, the girl who kissed a crocodile. In her writing, she describes Emily as "resembling an Indian deity." A deity who saved the writer with morphine, who ensnared her with love.

The first quarter of the story describes the women taking a weeklong trip across Thailand. The young woman writer disembarks at the Malaysia-Thailand border, where she meets Emily. They travel by bus, making stops at Songkhla, Krabi, and Hua Hin District on their way to Bangkok. The woman writer records scenes from their journey. Rice fields with water buffalos roll out under an open sky. Shy smiles from numerous young women blooming in the fields. Every view was flagrantly dyed and worked upon by the sun like cloisonné, until they popped with feverish colors like pictures on a postcard. It was the writer's first encounter with blue skies and jade sea. The long and narrow coastline along the Gulf of Thailand unfurled in front of the bus windshield like a carpet, giving the whole scene a vibe like an elopement.

Emily sits beside her. The girl seems to be in a good mood no matter the time or place. Her backpack is a bottomless well of snacks and fruit. She even gives the writer a few cigarettes. She's only seventeen, and throughout the trip she tells the writer everything that has happened to her in her life. She was once with a bald white man for six months, and it was he who named her Emily. The writer jots it down—he marked her like God naming a rib Eve.

The weeklong trip ends with the writer returning alone to her country, while Emily stays in Bangkok to be with an American punk. The middle of the short story details how the writer revisits Thailand three years later, where she is received at the bus station by Emily. At the Hua Lamphong station, the girl wears a peach broad-brimmed hat (you've now grown very fond of such hats) to distinguish herself amid the gloomy mass of people. Hey, I'm over here! The writer turns toward the voice. Emily looks to have grown much taller. Incredibly, her slender body seems to exude a metallic essence. She plucks off her hat and waves it enthusiastically, as if showing off a huge butterfly she's just caught.

The writer watches Emily windmill her arms and swim toward her through the crowd. Emily's limbs are long and her gestures exaggerated. Her smile and voice are, too, which causes heads to turn. Quite a few white people crane to gaze at her, their eyes full of interest or the desire to possess. The writer notices their admiring and jealous expressions. A girl as vigorous and eye-catching as a sunflower.

Why would the inevitability of wilting cross anyone's mind at that point? Who would think of darkness and misfortune, which seem to have nothing whatsoever to do with the young? In reality they lurk, always, just behind youth. The writer stares at Emily moving against the current, her peach broad-brimmed hat bobbing on the surface until it finally floats right up to her. Emily almost flies as she leaps forward to embrace the writer. You're finally here. You, I've missed you to death.

Later, after her suicide attempt, the writer continues to travel frequently. That last scene often comes to her when she stands in various stations around the world. Caught in the moment, touched and heart brimming with joy, she forgets herself and kisses Emily on the forehead and cheeks. Emily, you've grown. What a pretty Emily.

They squeeze into Emily's blue Volkswagen Beetle. They roll down the windows, letting in gushes of sun and wind and raucous street noise. This, combined with their chatter and laughter, fills the little car to the brim. The peach hat is now on the writer's head, its long ribbons streaming and flapping in its wake.

That may very well be the one and only time the writer experiences the pleasures of life on earth. The Beetle crawls clumsily along Bangkok's chaotic streets, passing many flamboyantly decorated cows and tuk tuks laden with tourists. Clouds proliferate in the sunny sky, which resembles a concave firmament or a massive wok turned upside down. The Thai king is as omnipresent as four-faced Phra Phrom, always watching over from up high. The writer's pen records it this way: "This city feels like it's been installed within a glass ball pumped full of a celebratory atmosphere. The world spins leisurely along clockwise, while the radio tremblingly oozes the manic ecstasy and fury of electric guitars. What can the ambiance of a foreign country gift us? No less than the thrill of escape."

When the writer describes Emily later on, her image is inextricably linked to the blue Beetle. They spend a total of three weeks together in that car. Emily uses her elbow to blare the car's horn. She kicks her high heels against the car's doors and tires. "Shitty car, rotten person." The rotten person is a reference to the Beetle's previous owner, her most recent ex. Other details include sunlight scissored into confetti on the Mekong River; giant catfish ogled by crowds; the Zen trance of crocodiles; the eerie similarities between an elephant trunk and a python; the frosted red lips and riotous feather boas on trans women. Against a backdrop of raging music, tabasco peppers roll and roil in tom yum soup, as red as the trans women's painted nails. Emily guffaws with gusto at the sky, repeatedly exclaiming to the writer in English, "Welcome to Bangkok!"

Bangkok really was Emily's world. She leads the writer into the backstage areas of the city. There, it is as dark as the deep shadows cast by a lamp; it is a darkness born of light and nestled tight against it, a darkness curtailed by surrounding brightness. Following Emily, the writer walks under numerous light bulbs, passing through an entire alley of dressers and erect human bodies on display. The people living in the mirrors are busy applying eyeliner or else angling their faces to stare into their own blank eyes. The writer watches herself and Emily stride from this mirror into that one, as if entering door after door, or as if they're beasts leaping through successive hoops of fire. The mirror people are so absorbed in painting their faces. Perhaps they are sketching from memory their selves of a day ago.

This is all you can manage to piece together. This Emily character—if you were to travel into the story, you might very well fall in love with her. Her flirtatious nature, her recklessness and worldliness; her broad experiences, learnedness, connections, and the charm that means she gets freebies everywhere she goes. You might fall in love with that Beetle and her excellent sense of direction, her courage in letting snakes curl around her body, her ability to seamlessly combine and wield several languages at once, and her smooth handling of police who harass them on the road. When you summon Emily in your imagination, your brain occasionally supplies the image of your mother's deep-voiced, androgynous friend. You remember how she sat by the window, her profile snipped out by sunlight and gilded with a golden burr, wreathed in fog-like smoke. Once, she teased you, "This kid. His pubic hair hasn't even come in yet."

But Emily doesn't exist, and neither does the female writer. "Only Because the Durian Blossomed" is just a work of fiction. It doesn't matter that every image triggered by the story in you feels completely real. Many times you've witnessed the writer and Emily from the back, observing them while they stand on a bridge, shoulders touching, looking down upon the Mekong's bustling floating market. There's an overabundance of details in this scene. The boats passing under the bridge always hold vendors hawking fruit raised over their heads, and on the bridge are copious blond, smiling, strolling tourists, their exposed arms roasted red by the sun. Standing in the midst of all this, Emily starts to talk about a young man chomped to death by a crocodile, a topic incongruous with the lively, thriving scene surrounding them. The writer isn't really paying attention.

"By the time they snatched him back from the croc's jaws, his neck was barely connected to his body. You could twist his face so that it was turned around, 180 degrees."

This narration is interrupted by an enormous catfish being transported along the river. The fish is so large, it's practically prehistoric. Throngs of people push forth to watch. Even the canoes laden with goods on the river seem to float toward the spectacle. Gazing at sunlight reflected on the river, the writer experiences a sense of irreality. The crowd cheers and gasps. Tourists jostle to raise their cameras. Emily sweeps off the sunglasses perched on top of her head and says, Come back next May. I'll take you to eat giant catfish in Ban Had Krai. You'll fall in love with it. You really will.

The following May, the writer pens a confession in her hometown's rehab center. She says that she clasped a dying Emily to her breast in a rumah panggung situated within a durian orchard. At that point Emily weighed so little she was like a corpse, her previously glossy skin gone dull, big eyes sunken and utterly blank. The writer describes her, "Like a girl pictured in a brochure soliciting donations, anticipating death more than she hopes for rescue." Before dying, Emily told the writer things she'd never told anyone else, like how she gave birth to her own brother and then abandoned him, or how she once pushed that "rotten person" into a pool of crocodiles. The writer hugged her so tight their ribs smashed into each other. The writer wrote down what she was thinking about in that moment: Kangiten, two elephant-headed bodies embracing to form one god. Because of this, she titles the story she writes in rehab "God of Bliss," to commemorate Emily's death and her own rebirth.

You look it up on Google. Kangiten, or Ganapati, appears as husband and wife in a tight union. The male is the eldest son of Maheshvara and a god of famine that endangers the world; the female is an aspect of Guanyin who embraces him, winning him over and taming his violence. Thus arose the moniker, God of Bliss.

The writer and Emily's very last moments together are spent on a hill dense with durian trees. They want to pick up the first durian to fall that season, but it is still so early. It is the writer's first time seeing durian flowers. To Emily, she says, Who knew such beautiful flowers bear such ugly fruit? Emily leans her back against the thick branches of an old durian tree, her fathomless eyes filled with empty dreams. She looks just like a tarsier.

"Is the world short of beautiful flowers? The durian flower knows it's valued for its bad seed, which grows of course into evil consequences," she says.

The durian planted throughout the hill is of a strain called "Golden Pillow." Shaozi titled the story after a scene featuring durian flowers blooming all over the orchard. This "semi-autobiographical story," with its duo female main characters and its theme of "feminism + queerness," is unsurprisingly labeled by The Fourth Person as one of Shaozi's "myths of womanhood"[1] and also as the closing chapter of the entire "myths" series.[2]

1. See "The Well-Trodden Pilgrimage toward Queerness."
2. See "Dream within a Dream—On Shaozi's 'Last Words from Last Night,'" published in 2006 in a "Special Edition Commemorating Shaozi" by *Literary Plaza*.

CHAPTER EIGHT

—1—

It was indeed an auspicious day. The skies were clear and everything went smoothly. The move was finished before noon. The same old Taoist priest said that moving to a new place on a propitious day and at a favorable time guarantees lifetimes of prosperity. Generations would flourish. He led Du Li An in prayer at all four corners of the property. They placed Guanyin, Tudigong overseeing the soil, the Kitchen God, and the Jade Emperor in their rightful places. The altar in the living room was an exquisite item made to order from another city. Intricately carved from solid, reddish wood, it seemed to glow like jewelry under bright light. The only thing was, it was a little too large. With only a lone Guanyin perched on top, it gave off an air of desolation and scarcity. Du Li An's original wish was to surround the Guanyin with a fleet of ancestors. It wasn't until the altar had been transported here that the priest found out about the very same ancestors currently being honored in the fishing village. Du Li An was thus forbidden to re-invite their Lau ancestors onto her altar.

"What about my own parents then? Surely I'm allowed to have our Du ancestors up there?" She was annoyed and angry at the priest for not laying it all out earlier, for making her face this embarrassing predicament now.

The priest furrowed his brow and made himself smaller. "That won't do either. That's something only your brother can take care of. Boss lady, you *are* married."

She had no idea there were so many rules and regulations just for worshipping somebody. Her eyes bulged, and she barely suppressed the swear words clamoring inside her. "So am I nobody? Even if the saying goes that a married daughter is water down the drain, I don't belong anywhere now. I'm neither a Du daughter nor one of the Lau family."

Despite her raging, there was nothing to be done. She arranged a good many items on the altar, such as a ceramic vase, a jade cup, copper candlesticks, a stone incense pot, green and tender fern-leaf bamboo, a couple of pink lotus lamps, and a crystal tree. But her plan backfired. Enclosed on all sides by such riches, the lonely white ceramic Guanyin seemed even paler. The priest suggested that Du Li An pair it with a Guan Yu, but when she imagined the warrior god's red face and bushy beard, she knew it would clash with Guanyin's unadorned clothes and face. Not to mention that she was unsettled by Guan Yu's outlaw aura and that menacing broadsword he carried. The priest, noting her long face and her hands wrung together, smiled and said that a house's feng shui depended on nothing so much as the owner's intentions.

"We make our own luck," he quoted. "Our thoughts and desires shape the earth. Take heart, boss lady."

After the gods were installed, Du Li An followed his instructions to a T and carried a vat filled with Thai jasmine rice into the house. Once that was done, they left every light on in the house for three days and three nights. Later, Guen Hou and Lau Lin came by to help cook a large batch of sweet red bean soup. Because the priest said a move required liveliness and warm bodies, Du Li An closed Ping Le House for a day. She ordered a whole suckling pig with crispy skin, fried noodles, and soft drinks. She asked employees and stall owners from the kopitiam to come over, and went door-to-door inviting her new neighbors, since many of the nearby houses were now occupied. And it did turn out to be a dynamic scene, her house filled with the young and old while the high noon sun glared overhead.

She led batch after batch of visitors through the lavishly decorated new house, tromping upstairs and then back down. The Ping Le House crew was dazzled by the matching sets of furniture and electronics, not to mention the eclectic variety of lamps and other accessories. More than half of the gawkers had already disbanded by the time Yip Mong Sang arrived. When Lau Lin offered to give him a tour, he laughed at her naïveté. "You'd be stealing the scene. The tour should be conducted by the owner." As he said this, he gave Du Li An a sly look.

"Isn't that so, Sister Li?"

She felt all the blood in her body rush toward her heart. She said, Come on then, and so he followed, Lau Lin trailing him. They first made a loop downstairs. Here's the kitchen, here's the dining room. Yip Mong Sang gave the eight-person dining table crowned with a marble top a little shove with both hands. He said, This table is so stable, you could use it as a bed. His words swelled Du Li An's insides and made her dizzy, as if the blood pooling in her heart was now jetting into her brain. She thought she must have blushed, but she didn't. It was Lau Lin who turned bright red and imme- diately buried her face into her own chest.

Du Li An extended a hand and brushed the marble tabletop. It was smooth as silk. She could see their reflections, all three of them. Standing at the back, Lau Lin sulked and shyly plucked at his sleeve.

"It *is* a little too big, what with so few of us eating at home," Du Li An said.

Upstairs was a small sitting room and four bedrooms, which naturally only made her heart pound wilder. She didn't step inside the primary bedroom. Instead, she simply stood at the entrance and announced it.

"Master bedroom." He didn't cross the threshold either. He stood beside her and repeated what she said, Master bedroom. He said it like it bore a hidden meaning. He was too close, his voice almost a whisper in her ear. She felt another wave of wooziness. Her ears seemed to ring.

"There's an AC unit, you see?" Lau Lin said.

He nodded, a wicked smile on his face. "Of course, it's the master bedroom after all."

They turned and made their way to Lau Lin's room. Aside from a single wood bed, the rest of the furniture was mostly stuff they'd moved over from the old house. Lau Lin had meant to stay on by herself in that little row house, but Du Li An wouldn't allow it. First of all, it was best that a single woman didn't live alone. Secondly, she wanted to rent out the row house to help pay off the new mortgage. She gave Lau Lin two choices; one was to move in together into the new house. "Plenty of room there. Or else you can go back to the fishing village."

"As long as you stick around, you are my responsibility." Du Li An's forehead smoothed out as she said this and sighed. "Since your dad isn't here, why don't you see it as keeping me company."

She'd thoroughly grasped Lau Lin's sensibilities by now. The girl was stubborn and unyielding on the outside, but soft and pliable inside. She needed both carrot and stick, wielded with exactitude. In the end it went as planned. She bit her lip and thought it over, and after much deliberation agreed to move into the new house. Du Li An had known from the start she wouldn't choose the fishing village. How could Lau Lin stand to leave Yip Mong Sang? Also, since Steely Bo left, they'd both felt more or less abandoned. They had no choice but to look out for each other when it came to matters of daily necessity. Maybe it was the passage of time, or maybe it was because Yip Mong Sang had exerted some influence out of sight, but Lau Lin had become slightly more affectionate. She no longer hid from Du Li An or turned her back on her as if she were a harbinger of bad luck.

But was he really the one who'd untied the knot? Du Li An cast him a glance. An untying implied a knot in the first place. And he was the one who'd stealthily tied an intractable knot between Lau Lin and Du Li An. From time to time he pulled it taut, yanking at her heart.

"Isn't it more convenient for us if she doesn't move in?" He kissed Du Li An's neck, his warm breath gathering first behind her ears, then at her temples. She felt herself go numb, her addicted flesh trembling. Ha. She twisted her head to glare at him, to dive right into his limpid gaze.

"For us? You mean convenient for you, don't you?" She sneered. "I won't make it so easy for you two."

The more she kissed him, the more she understood him. When she'd previously consulted the priest to pick the best day for moving in, she'd also taken a certain Ba Zi for him to divine its corresponding fortune according to the Four Pillars of Destiny. The Ba Zi belonged to someone else, a male born under a Yang year. After some ambiguous writing and doodling on a piece of paper, the priest concluded, "An abiding desire to explore outer realms, yes—an unsteadiness and impatience with constancy. With such a recalcitrant person, whose heart is fickle as an ape or monkey, the only way to tame him and regulate his desires is by unleashing multiple strategies at once." Guen Hou happened to walk in at that moment. Having heard only the last part of what the priest said, she assumed that Steely Bo was the one whose chart was being read. Du Li An merely smiled and said nothing, for fear of digging herself into a hole. Secretly, she was impressed by the priest. Yip Mong Sang was indeed like an oversized monkey; he had charming looks, quick wit, tact enough to handle people and relationships smoothly, and a honeyed tongue that could melt you into syrup. Most likely his life would take off like a rocket. Who could tie such a man down?

The priest instructed them on this moving-in ritual: All the lights in the new house had to be kept on for three days and three nights. She'd made plans to move in with Lau Lin after the three days were up, but now Du Li An was uneasy about the brightly lit house being left unattended. Coincidentally, Yip Mong Sang overheard her discussing the matter with Lau Lin. "There should be a man on night duty," he volunteered. Then he mimicked a night watchman from a movie, pitching his voice high, "Tuk tuk tuk, qiang qiang qiang. Lock your doors and watch your shutters; beware unattended fires!"

Du Li An and Lau Lin laughed. Guen Hou and Eggplant Face, off to the side, couldn't hold their amusement in either. Encouraged, Yip Mong Sang extended his dramatic performance. Lau Lin laughed so hard she suddenly choked. Hand pressed against her chest, she coughed and hacked. Du Li An was just about to rub her back when he reached out and ran his hand lightly over her thin back, asking, Are you all right? Lau Lin nodded, but she couldn't control the coughs that kept coming.

"I'll go get her a glass of water." Du Li An swiveled on her heel and headed for the kitchen. She thought, *This man is incredible.* He effortlessly made a houseful of women guffaw with laughter, and then with just one simple gesture he chilled her heart inch by inch.

By afternoon, the whole roasted pig was gone and the guests had disbanded. After cleaning up, she drove Guen Hou and her daughter home, Lau Lin tagging along. For some reason Guen Hou was unusually energetic and talkative. She sat in the back seat with Eggplant Face, chatting loudly, landing now and then on the topic of Lau Lin and Yip Mong Sang.

"Give some advanced notice before the wedding, okay? I have to save up for a red packet."

Lau Lin blushed deeply, her head sank lower and lower, and she said nothing. On the other hand, Du Li An was irked to no end by Guen Hou's chatter. Du Li An found a cassette tape and shoved it into the stereo. Sam Hui sang "The Genius and the Idiot." Who is the genius, and who the idiot? She turned the volume way up and said, "Sam Hui was the old man's favorite."

Lau Lin nodded.

Du Li An gave her a side-eye and said, smiling, "I'm talking about my dead dad, not your deadbeat dad."

Even though it'd seemed lighthearted when she'd thought of it, any humor in the joke evaporated as soon as the words left her mouth. Du Li An was the only one laughing in the car. At least Guen Hou received the message and finally shut her mouth. Du Li An glanced at the rearview mirror. Eggplant Face sat ramrod straight, yanking at her mother's sleeve as if giving a warning. Beyond the windows lay a sunbaked day. Du Li An's smile disappeared as she hummed along to Sam Hui. She really was thinking about her own old man. She remembered how he stumbled along the streets one night singing "Romance of the Phoenix Chamber" at the top of his hoarse voice.

Ah, poor me, how lonely I am. Ah, poor me, how lonely I am!

She and Lau Lin said nothing to each other after they dropped off Guen Hou and her daughter at Mi Shan New Village. The cassette looped through one rotation and went back to the singer asking, Who is the genius, and who the idiot? Du Li An thought back to her joke. It suddenly struck her that she and Lau Lin had gone down some twisting roads together, but no matter how jumbled and convoluted their relationship, they were still mother and daughter by name.

The phrase "mother and daughter" froze Du Li An's heart, numbed her skull. This was a relationship courtesy of Steely Bo. Everything had seemed so simple in the beginning, but then that rogue Yip Mong Sang tied a dark knot between them. It was a waltz with three people. He led the women in circles and spun them in strange patterns, complicating their relationship. There were no numbers on this bill, no score to settle. The more Du Li An thought about it, the more muddled she felt.

"How old are you now, Ah Lin?" she asked.

Lau Lin started, perhaps because the question came out of nowhere. "Twenty-five."

"Oh, that makes me a whole decade older than you." Du Li An sighed. "I was twenty-six when your dad married me."

Hearing this, Lau Lin's face flushed again. She thought Du Li An was probing her courtship with Yip Mong Sang in a roundabout way. Averting her gaze,

Lau Lin looked out the window. Her right hand grasped her left index finger, folded it, yanked it, massaged it, tormented it. Du Li An took it all in. "Don't worry, Auntie's not asking you to get hitched."

"Marriage can determine someone's whole life. You have to think hard and clear about it," she continued. "They say a man's biggest fear is entering the wrong profession, and a woman's biggest fear is marrying the wrong partner. You've seen it happen yourself, I'm sure."

She pretended to focus on driving, her eyes never leaving the road, doing her best to keep the tone of her voice casual. She honked at a stray dog hesitating in the middle of the road, unsure whether to advance or retreat. But all the while she could not avoid thinking of Sou Gei and Guen Hou. And herself—was she also a part of this band of misery? Maybe she was putting herself forward as a cautionary tale, much like the advice Guen Hou gave her years ago, with Eggplant Face cradled in her arms. The child's face smeared with snot, her mother's streaked with tears.

"He . . . I mean Yip Mong Sang—word is he's a womanizer. Isn't that right?" A yellow light turned red. Du Li An brought the car gradually to a halt.

Lau Lin looked straight out at the street unfurling ahead. She shrugged weakly. "I don't know . . . Auntie Li, I don't know." She blinked. Daylight pierced her chocolate-brown eyes. Those eyes were too clear, as if they contained glass marbles with distinctive patterns, incapable of hiding anything.

Du Li An nodded. "Some men are just born that way, like giant monkeys only the Buddha can tame." She continued, "The Buddha, you hear? It takes that kind of power."

Lau Lin did not reply, and Du Li An lost the enthusiasm to continue her train of thought. The sun was in her eyes. She'd woken up very early that morning, and she was beat after a whole day bustling about. She thought she'd nap once she got home. What was Sam Hui singing? *Truth or lie, it's so hard to decipher / the world is full of heartless deceivers.*

Long before they reached the gates of their home, she saw from a distance the outdated Mercedes parked by the side of the road. The black sedan looked clumsy, heavy. It was dusty too, like an ancient tank stalled in the desert, covered by swirling sand.

Lau Lin let out a shocked gasp. She shot up in her seat, her eyes bulging and her mouth agape, unable to speak for half a moment. "That car. Auntie Li, Ba's back!"

Du Li An blinked. She thought her face had become ice. Indeed, she was neither surprised nor overjoyed at that moment. A disdainful snort emerged from deep within the cracks of her bones. See that? In the novel, a crow's shadow flits across the car's windshield, behind which Du Li An smiles like a sad queen on a poker card. Calm, aloof, uncanny. She made Lau Lin get out to open the gates, so that she could park the car in the yard. Lau Lin exited the car. For a split second, Du Li An had an urge to step on the pedal and speed away. But she was a cooler cucumber than she ever was. She could tune in to her inner voice.

And so she let it rip.

"Back so soon? I thought you'd died somewhere out there." She barely spared him a look before striding through the living room for the bedroom, leaving Lau Lin standing at the threshold and Steely Bo sprawled across the sofa. When he called after Du Li An, she neither stopped nor looked back. A figure darted out from the room next door as she approached the bedroom, almost colliding with her. She took a closer look. A bony, topless man, face yellow as wax, resembling nothing so much as air-dried lean jerky. She was at a loss until the man called her "Auntie Li." Then she recognized him as that boy Candlenut.

"Today is really the luckiest of lucky days," she scoffed. But she couldn't help staring a few more beats at Candlenut, so drastically different from the sparkling, energetic boy of her memory. "Well, if it isn't a happy family reunion." She walked around the jerky-like Candlenut and closed the door to her room.

She did manage to fall asleep. It was evening when she woke up. The light in the room made her mistake the time as dawn. She needed a period of adjustment to traverse from her dreams into the waking world. Eyes open, she continued lying on the bed for a while, allowing the reality marinating in her thoughts to resurface slowly. Steely Bo had obviously gained weight. Or, no, maybe his skin and flesh were just hanging looser. A single year had laid waste to all his previous physical training. She'd also noticed, of course, that the gold necklace with the Phra Phrom pendant was gone from his neck, and his fingers were now bare except for a lone jade ring, framed in gold. Clearly he hadn't been living in luxury. Candlenut, on the other hand, seemed to have been flattened by time to become a thin husk with soulless eyes. She recalled how he'd once wanted to watch a boxing match. Back then he was muscular and had skin thick as bark, charged with a daredevil energy from head to toe.

She'd been keeping tabs on him via Ah Sai. Over six months ago Candlenut had left the capital to look for jobs farther south, and after that even Ah Sai had lost contact with him. At the time she was secretly cheered by the news, but now Candlenut was back, swinging between her and her brother like a pendulum, foretelling ill luck.

When she got out of bed, her head still felt like it was stuffed with glue, unable to make sense of the situation no matter how hard she tried. All she knew was that Steely Bo was no longer the Kien Tek Hall boss of yesteryear, and Candlenut seemed even more downtrodden than his father. Their return was more distressing to her than their disappearances.

It was almost dark. She combed her hair in front of the mirror. The two-hour nap had done her good, gave her a glow. She understood that what would happen next was unavoidable. Problems were never solved by ignoring them. But still, she needed to shore up some energy before she could face the days to come. She gave the person in the mirror a faint smile. The corners of her mouth rose high, higher. Yip Mong Sang had told her, You look so becoming when you smile like this.

Guen Hou's eyes were impossibly wide the next morning. She couldn't believe Du Li An had really gone and taken a nap at such a juncture. "My god, but it's your man come back. After how long away? Where did he go? You didn't ask him anything?"

Du Li An maintained her smile. Ding. The cash box bounced out. She pushed it back in. By now she knew the cash register's rhythm inside out, to the point that she could almost use it as a musical instrument. Ding. Guen Hou remained rooted to the spot, her expression one of urgent curiosity. Du Li An beamed again, her smile now even more confident than the one from the previous night.

"Why ask? I'd rather not know."

Guen Hou stared in disbelief, but it was true that Du Li An had not demanded a single answer. Last night, Steely Bo had gone out of his way to bring home charcoal-fried hor fun from Tuk Gei, hoping to pacify her with the fragrance of lard, shrimp paste, and chili that suffused the whole room. She sat down and ate graciously, but she treated Steely Bo and Candlenut as if they were invisible, didn't even look directly at them once. She did make small talk with Lau Lin, mostly about some TV dramas. "Patrick Tse really has no self-awareness. Look at him, hogging the main role and playing such a young man at his old age, geez." She was talking about *Love and Passion*. "The theme song from the soundtrack is quite good though, isn't it?"

Lau Lin nodded timidly. After eating, Du Li An went out to rent some tapes. When she came back, she watched two episodes of *Love and Passion*. Then she took Steely Bo's pillow out of the wardrobe and placed it on the sofa, after which she went off for her bath, humming the main theme from the drama. It was this same song that floated softly from her throat when she left the house in the morning, passing by the sofa bearing Steely Bo, an alluring scent of perfume in her wake. Eyes made bleary by boogers, all he managed to catch was a faint snippet of the song and an aromatic, colorful figure floating past. She still had not looked at him once. *La la la / God decides if we stay or separate / I won't blame Him nor will I lament fate / All I ask is for mountain and sea to bear witness while I wait.*

That afternoon she had her hair done, cutting off her loose curls in favor of a shorter style, lightly permed. She emerged looking sprightly, more with the times. When she debuted this hairstyle back at Ping Le House, she was greeted by successive waves of praise and even some wolf whistles from frequent customers. She puffed out her chest and her smile grew ever more alluring, drawing unblinking and covetous stares from the men in the kopitiam. On the other hand, Guen Hou and a few other women who worked there could be seen crookedly pouting. From time to time they exchanged looks that seemed disapproving. Du Li An had the foresight to understand that Guen Hou would give her the cold shoulder in the days to follow, preferring instead to insinuate herself with the other women, who often gathered in a corner with their arms crossed as if forming a secret alliance, combining their icy expressions to counter Du Li An's fiery glamor.

Du Li An had long realized what lay behind such schemes. Guen Hou may be a friend in need, but this was because she saw them both in the same boat of misfortune. While she wasn't without gratitude for Du Li An's aid all along, Guen Hou's feelings toward the other woman were mixed and contradictory; since they emerged from similar backgrounds, some comparisons and secret competition were inevitable. When Du Li An was laid low, Guen Hou did everything she could to help and shield her. Yet Guen Hou more often than not went green with envy when Du Li An soared to new heights, so much so that she'd lead efforts to ostracize the boss lady.

Once she grasped the rhythm of this behavior, Du Li An could handle it all without breaking a sweat. She didn't let it get to her. Everyone had their turn with the three major misfortunes and six key blessings after all, and so she was happy to lend a helping hand whenever it was Guen Hou's time in the ditch. No debts owed either way. Like last year when Eggplant Face was hit with a double whammy of acute appendicitis plus jaundice, Du Li An not only opened her wallet but volunteered her time as well. No one could criticize her for not doing what she could. Back then Guen Hou had been so thankful she'd shed actual tears, but look at her now, her feathers ruffled because she couldn't stand to see Du Li An's beauty turning heads and dazzling the whole room. It was "the rhythm" after all, with its own fixed cycles, just as the moon waxed and waned.

In reality, Du Li An had internalized that praise from men necessarily made women envious. Moreover, male admiration was much purer and simpler than female admiration. The quality of a woman's life could be ascertained by examining the attitudes and appraisals of other women around her. Over the years she'd grown to savor the cold looks and resentful one-liners from women. She was not bothered by Guen Hou's stony face; she even enjoyed seeing it. For the next few days, Du Li An decked herself out whenever she left the house. In her platform shoes, bell-bottoms, and large hoop earrings paired with a cute little handbag, she deliberately swung her hips as she strutted about. Let those ineffectual Ping Le House women grind their teeth clean down. That would only please her more.

But the biggest gratification of all came from Steely Bo's lusty gaze and frustrated expression each morning as he watched her leave the house. The man had beat a hasty retreat after pulling off what he thought was an incredible feat. In reality, a whole year had passed without a peep from Elder Zong. After his nephew took over Toa Pek Kong Society, everyone had carried on with their usual business, as if none of them were the least bit put out by Steely Bo's actions. For Steely Bo, this was a much bigger blow than if they'd called a hit on him.

After much subtle asking around, Du Li An learned Steely Bo had first spent time in a Malay fishing village on the east coast. There he hid in a hut and walked on eggshells, subsisted on salted fish and sea breeze. Later he went south and met up with that boy Candlenut. With nowhere to turn, father and son frittered away some time at the hilltop casino, which almost entirely bankrupted them both. At this point, despite Steely Bo's delusions of grandeur, he had to face up to the fact that Toa Pek Kong Society had no plans to come after him. With the end of the road in sight, the pair gritted their teeth and made their way home.

Steely Bo had been squeezed completely dry by his year in exile. Since his return he was tired to his bones, his whole being deflated like a balloon. Du Li An took a leaf out of Elder Zong's book and put up a front of indifference. In fact, she went even further, parading her looks so that he could have a taste of how zesty her life had been since he'd abandoned her. This proved to be an effective trick. To Steely Bo, it seemed everyone was thriving, even Lau Lin, whose face had a rosy tint and a softer expression. He alone was battered and bruised. He finally saw things for what they were: Nothing but a comedy of errors had come of him staking it all on that one big move. He'd thought he was going for the big guns, but he was nothing more than a forgettable sidekick.

It was one thing to come back with his tail between his legs, knowing he'd pissed away the Society prestige he'd painstakingly built over half his life. It was quite another to realize that even his status within his own families had morphed into that of a clown. Du Li An was in her prime, her nose turned up so high it was practically facing the sky. Though she had invited him and his son to move into the new house, she made Steely Bo sleep in a separate room and wouldn't allow him anywhere near her. Meanwhile his fishing village family had long written him off. When any of them saw him their expressions were distant, even a little disdainful. No one even bothered to ask him where he'd been.

One day he was forced by Du Li An to beg forgiveness from Elder Zong. She never entered the room, but she heard from others that Steely Bo knelt in front of the elderly man and loudly condemned his own crimes, after which Steely Bo gave himself a series of rapid-fire slaps across the face that sounded like firecrackers. Afterward he was even more of a shell than before. His hair, already thinning to begin with, turned ash gray, as did his eyebrows. The fire of ambition that had burned and sparked in his eyes was gone. He seemed even more ancient than Elder Zong.

Naturally, news of his return brought a flock of busybodies to Ping Le House, hungry for details. Instead of asking an employee for the check, they went up to settle their bills at the counter so that they could tap Du Li An for information straight from the horse's mouth. She knew how to counter their inquisitiveness with grace, deploying her cash register as needed. Ding. Ding. Ding. Her employees watched with admiration. They had to admit it was quite something that she could deflect any nosy prying with just a few words. The busybodies' favorite saying went something like this: Oh, but to err is human, boss lady.

"Sure, and in this case, lightning struck twice," she replied, referring to Steely Bo and his son. All the while she kept a flirtatious smile on her lips and tossed off meaningful looks. It dissolved the men to marrow.

Ding.

Some of the busybodies loved sticking their heads forward in unison while leaning on the counter, asking in stage whispers, Hey, is he going to live with you? He's not going back to his other family?

"Surely the fishing village isn't as comfortable as it is here?" She smirked. "Men aren't stupid. They're calculating."

Ding.

The days passed that way, big stretches of it mired in verbal sparring. Du Li An lifted a hand to massage her own shoulder. She rotated her neck. Her eyes accidentally met those of someone in the crowd. Ah, it was him. Ping Le House in the afternoon was bursting at the seams. Yip Mong Sang sat among this sea of souls in all his lanky glory, staring at her without reservation. Her breasts, her neck, face, ears, eyes. A flame raged in his eyes, yearning to melt her.

She was no longer as helpless under his scrutiny as she used to be. No way was she ignorant enough to make eyes with him under such public scrutiny. But still, she had her ways of keeping him looking.

She leaned forward slightly and supported her cheek with one hand, resting her elbow on the counter. Pretending to be lost in thought, she let her gaze become unfocused, so it was difficult to determine whether she was looking at him, or rather through him at the street outside. A hot and muggy day, with the threat of impending rain. Almost all the men in Ping Le House had their eyes glued on the boss lady. Guen Hou frowned. The other women caught on and contorted their faces as well, signaling to each other to look in the direction of the counter. Look, look at that tease. Du Li An noticed everything. She let her elbow glide forward on the countertop, bringing her upper body along, angling it even lower. Treasures abounded within her V-collar top. The men arrayed before her gulped down saliva, their Adam's apples bobbing. The women bulged their eyes and gnashed their teeth dramatically. In that moment at least, everyone on the scene was united in their desire to devour the boss lady.

"Bill of two fifty." Guen Hou walked up and placed three ringgit on the counter, conveniently blocking the view with her washboard back.

Du Li An gave out the change. By the time she turned around, Yip Mong Sang had left. His seat was empty, the table bare save a coffee cup and an empty plate. In no time a newly arrived customer occupied the space, and in the next instant an employee approached to clear the table. It was only then that she realized the three ringgit she just took were from him, and he'd left without waiting for his change. Probably he was ticked off? Irked that she'd shown everyone her cleavage, had freely distributed the goods. She *had* harbored some intention to provoke him, but now that he'd stormed off without a word, she found there wasn't the same thrill she experienced when she aggravated Steely Bo. Instead she felt a vague sense of loss. Abruptly she became vexed.

Two more small bills settled. Ding. Ding. Storm clouds gathered inside her, mirroring the weather outside, the thunder and rain stewing in the atmosphere. She no longer found any of it amusing. Gloomily she looked at the cash register, the name "Yip Mong Sang" taking over her brain. She sensed, in a groping, foggy way, that she was willing to give up everything for that man then and there. And it was at that moment the phone next to her suddenly blared, startling her from her confused thoughts.

She picked up the receiver. Hello. Silence on the other end. Listening to the background noise filling up the space, she intuited somehow that it was him. Is that you? she said. She stood up and looked out through the window at a little path nearby. There was a pole of a figure planted at the telephone booth by the taxi stand. She couldn't help the surge of smugness. "I know it's you. I see you." The person in the booth did not turn around. Have you had your fun? he said to her.

Such a weird scene. Later on, she thought about it often and for no reason. That man standing across the street, blanketed by the looming shadows of the buildings. Her line of sight zooming across the tops of her customers' heads. A huge distance spanned between them. There were overlapping hordes of people in the kopitiam and cars crisscrossing outside. But his voice was so close by, like a teaspoon of sweet ice cream melting in her ear.

"I had my fun." Yes, she'd indeed lost interest in the game since she saw that empty seat. "I miss you," she couldn't help admitting sadly. I miss you, Mong Sang.

They could no longer rendezvous at the new house, and the old place was about to be rented out. Neighbors knew her by sight, making the entire area unsuitable as a meeting point. Let's go where we went last time, he said. Five thirty, same room.

She hesitated a beat. She didn't like the place. It seemed unsafe to her. But she understood there was no better choice.

"Okay, five thirty." She twirled the cord connecting the receiver to the rest of the phone.

—

The motel in the novel might very well be where you live, situated in one of the tin mining town's corners, a pocket of silence within its overall bustle. Mayflower. Du Li An walks up the stairwell by the side door. Something stirs in you, as if it's you she's walking toward. You hear her footsteps, the platform shoes of her era as heavy and clumsy as wooden clogs. Your ears perk up as you count her strides. She walks very slowly, cautious and hesitant. With each step the tiny bells on her anklet ring out clearly, the crisp sound of jade cracking. One, two, three, four, five . . . Du Li An has arrived. She pauses outside the door for a few seconds, perhaps glancing left and right, on high alert. Relax, it's dead quiet in the stairwell and the corridor. No other soul in sight. Finally, she raps on your door carefully. Knock knock.

—2—

You have no idea how many motels there are named Mayflower in this sprawling country. But you've seen quite a number of them at least. Every town and city with a Chinese presence may harbor one or two rundown motels called Mayflower. There's no connection between them, yet they resemble each other so uncannily they could be part of a chain. All of them appeal to everyday citizens. They have similar management styles and long histories, as if they'd been established to provide shelter to the merchants and laborers who traveled the country of yore for work. Your guess is that the name comes from the famous *Mayflower* ship in history books. Wasn't the ship's cargo basically the poor, people like carpenters and the indentured?

All those Mayflowers could not avoid being squeezed by an ever-expanding city into its shadowy seams and sunless corners. Sleazy-looking and humble, the motels did not fit in with the city. They share your Mayflower's fate, unavoidably and gradually turning into places for illicit liaisons or sex work. They pivoted from daily rates to charging by the hour, thus completing a transformation from their original identity as inns to what many call "no-tell motels." And now they have been left in the dust, what with the stylish, modern motel chains popping up in the city. Their lobbies feature floor-to-ceiling windows and a rotating cast of sharply dressed men clutching young women decked out in high heels and backless outfits. You sense that all the Mayflowers in the world have wilted. Only the sex workers long past their prime are left, saddled with various illnesses, sitting on the beds examining their dry vaginas, occasionally followed upstairs by day laborers or migrant workers without much disposable income.

You assume it is not such a room whose door Yip Mong Sang opens to usher in Du Li An. Surely a Mayflower of their time is not so ominously dim and filthy. Surely there is no spider filtering sunlight on the windowsill with webs of white follicular strands. The room of their time must be passably clean and bright, though that doesn't endear it to Du Li An. She feels the place is akin to the Cave of Silken Web from *Journey to the West*. Yip Mong Sang, on the other hand, is as comfortable as if he were returning to old stomping grounds. His familiarity makes her shudder. When he places her on the bed, she can't help imagining him and some other woman making love in this room. Could Lau Lin have also sprawled across this very bed? Du Li An is both overjoyed and tortured by the thought that she's no different from another woman, just a piece of meat laid out on a chopping board.

Yet even when she gathers all her willpower she can't resist his summons. With practiced motions he dissects her, lifting out her virgin-like soul, shy and pure, and setting it aside. He renders her simply a body, a sack of flesh and blood that knows no shame. She obeys him. She worships him with lust. Clinging tightly onto the bedsheets, she endures the numb ticklishness brought on by the tip of his tongue. It's like a row of ants crawling across her skin, following a trail left by his saliva. She's suffered long stretches of emptiness just for this short burst of fulfillment. Brazenly she asks and demands of him, letting him hear her moan and cry out like a prostitute.

In his deep voice he says, I'm here.

You imagine them right where you are. The springs on the mattress patiently bear their weight, pressing down. In truth, *The Age of Goodbyes* does not mention the number of the room where Du Li An and Yip Mong Sang rendezvous. The writer never even mentions Mayflower. It's your own wishful thinking that overlays yourself and the two of them in the same space across two different time dimensions. This brings you so much closer. All you have to do is close your eyes to see, right in this room, right on this bed, Du Li An pushing you and J out of her vagina like squeezing toothpaste. Maybe after one of her sexual escapades with Yip Mong Sang, she returns to the scene where life originated and gives birth to you two.

You confess this theory to Mana. But the idea is too outlandish, and your word choices too intentionally learned and obscure. She probably doesn't get it. Like a Barbie doll, she simply smiles and blinks. But those eyes are as all-knowing as cat eyes. Although she stays silent, her skinny face carries a perpetual expression of semi-translucent omniscience.

She still likes to sneak in at night, tunneling under the covers to embrace you. She likes listening to you recount the many stories from the novel, speaking as if to yourself. Her favorite is "Only Because the Durian Blossomed." She's mute, never says anything. When you are with her, you hear only yourself and two heartbeats. You don't mind. No matter how curious you both are, you will never ask after each other's background or origin. You place an extra pillow on your bed and get into the habit of reserving space for Mana before you fall asleep. She especially likes to spoon you, clinging onto your back with all she's got.

You smile faintly in your dream. Mana, you're fast becoming a koala, you say.

You know she's crooking her mouth into a smile too. There's a huge heart inside that thin chest of hers. Sounds like there's a ticking alarm clock in there, you say. Sometimes it reminds you of a bomb. You roll over and press your face against the left side of her chest. Her heartbeat is obviously elevated. With your face, you massage the petite breasts inside those pajamas. Her heart thumps even faster. "Might your whole heart leap out from your chest?" You say as you kiss her. She flicks her tongue in response. Two little snakes entwine in your mouths. This kind of kiss reminds you of the saying about fish spitting on each other to stay alive when the river dries up. It reminds you of love too, of Du Li An submerging into her obsession.

But Mana often disappears without your noticing, leaving when she thinks it's time to go. You wake up under the covers from which her body heat is gradually dissipating and feel like all of existence is but a dream. Twice you caught her in the act of leaving. You grabbed her wrist, asking her to stay. At the intersection of moonlight and the first shimmers of dawn she looked back, smiled, and then gently but firmly withdrew her hand.

All this makes you feel that Mana does not belong to you. That feeling of something slipping through your grasp brings you back to primary school, when a classmate lent you a new gadget they'd brought to show off in class. It was a handheld gaming console. Just when you were getting into it, he suddenly snatched the console from your hands. You were furious, but you stood stock still and watched as he pressed the Off button and effortlessly erased all the progress you had painstakingly earned.

It's rare for you to have something that truly belongs to you. Growing up, there was only Mother. Between you and J, she'd picked you. But one day even Mother was lost. In the end you still had to return her to her true possessor.

Mana blinked her curious eyes. Who? Who is the true possessor?

The universe, destiny, dark fate.

The two of you are obviously too young to be discussing life and death. Mana writes down her age on a piece of paper. She's a little older than you. You tell her she is the age at which Du Li An makes her first appearance in the book. At the time, she had a crush on a teacher at a Chinese primary school, a man younger than her. Yip Lin Sang. Mana flips through the tome on your desk, head tilted to one side. She doesn't know the language used in the book, so she's not so much reading as she is using her eyes to scan its symbols, as if that were a way to unearth some secret.

You look at her. The skin on her hand glows with the sheen of ancient copper, topped off with fine, thick hair. Your gaze climbs along her hand like an invisible snake, slinking from wrist to arm, then crawling up her long, graceful neck. Her protruding collarbones and elegant shoulders; her chin and that discreet little mole by her lips. Mana is the sexiest, most vibrant girl you've ever seen. You have an urge to take her out and show her off. You want to hold her hand and walk along the broad paved streets where a multitude of glass windows and doors reflect sunlight. You want to meet her gaze at an intersection and smile at each other under traffic lights, squeezing in a kiss right there in the open while the walk signal still hasn't turned green.

Mana, smiling, continues to turn the pages of the book, neither agreeing nor disagreeing.

You can't resist going up to hug her from behind. You stick your nose behind her ear and onto the back of her neck, catching a whiff of her clean-smelling sweat. Yip Mong Sang does this same thing when Du Li An is dressing to leave. From behind, he catches hold of her hand clutching the comb. She looks into the small round mirror on the wall. Inside, a woman is staring at both her and the man behind her with a surprisingly sorrowful look. Meticulously he fixes her hair, returning to her the soul that had been temporarily abandoned. But she understands deep in her heart that the soul can no longer dissolve back into her flesh.

Your fondest wish is for J to see your Mana, a lover who, like Emily, can arouse pride and self-satisfaction in every man. When you work in the KFC kitchen during the day, you like to watch people walking by the windows whenever there's some downtime. You think that surely one day you'll catch Mana walking under the brilliant sunshine in all her glory. You want to see the pedestrians' double takes as they turn and watch her with stunned admiration. Like the others, J will snap his head around like he's just belatedly noticed the treasure in a store window he's walked past.

"How about this? Spend some time with me on my birthday next week? Share a meal, browse the shops?" When she gets up to leave that dawn, you suddenly clench her hand in a vise-like grip. She smiles amid thin light and morning prayers. When she tries to draw back her hand, you clamp down like a leg-hold trap, pinning her, cutting off her escape. Mana sighs. Biting her lip, she sits on the edge of the bed, silently and attentively watching some spot in midair as if there is a hole you cannot see. Sunlight thickens. For a brief moment you have the confused sense that she will disperse from your palm. Perhaps a spaceship will come through the deep hole you cannot see and beam her up.

The standoff persists a short while. She can't see a way out. Half turning, she glares and pouts at you, then nods.

If time could be frozen in that instant—if it allowed the two of you to melt into one when you are so equally joyful and contented—what a happy couple you and Mana would make! Yet life's stories, be they comedies or tragedies, always hinge upon the point in time when they end. And more often than not these stories dither on for too long. All because no one can bear to spit out the wad of chewing gum just when it is at its most flavorful.

From that moment on you anticipate the following week. You ask for time off from your manager and swap shifts with a colleague. Deliberately you mark your calendar hanging on the wall, drawing an unmistakable red heart in dry-erase marker. You move the calendar to a conspicuous spot by the door so Mana can't miss it. Indeed, she stands before it as she leaves one day, scrutinizing it for a while.

Many years later you travel north alone on a business trip. On the long-haul bus to the Thai border you reminisce those days and can't help grinning at yourself in the window, beyond which night falls. The bus is crammed full of men in a hurry to pay for sex in a neighboring city for the weekend. They sit on the narrow bus seats, slumped in all sorts of positions, heads back and snoring, resting in preparation to unleash their seeds upon someone else's country. The bus runs along, neither fast nor slow, carrying a load of snores in different pitches and tunes. You might be the only insomniac onboard. Through the drawn-out night you think about Mayflower and the Mana who weaved in and out of room 301. She dragged the duffel bag out from under the bed. The bag is simply too large for the handful of

—714—

things that belonged to her. You imagine Mana tucking herself into the bag like a wide-eyed doll, folded up. Belonging to no one, she can be abandoned by nobody.

She walked into room 301, exchanging her green grasshopper for your bare-bones, clunky, old-style nail clipper. Right at the very end, she took out a bloodred lipstick and scribbled on your mirror in English: "Time to say goodbye."

—

The day before your birthday, out of nowhere Uncle Sai suggests getting dinner together after your shift at KFC. At first he wants to get dinner on the following night. Somewhat taken aback, you tell him about your night shift the next day, which means you'll eat at work.

"Then let's go out tonight." He rubs the back of his head. You sense that he's manufactured this opening for a talk, or a discussion around some matter. This makes you anxious. But you understand that certain kinds of conversations are unavoidable. The woman who'd always stood between the two of you no longer exists.

Back when Mother was gravely ill, you'd already harbored the worry that Uncle Sai would one day force the two of you to leave Mayflower. Mother didn't think much of it. She still smoked then and propped up the leg with the swollen knee on her other thigh, jiggling her foot with effort. She huffed out a burst of smoky fog and narrowed her eyes at the blurry foreground. "Your Uncle Sai isn't that kind of person."

You ripped the cigarette from her grasp and put it out. Like an amazing magician, Mother always managed to get her hands on cigarettes and hide them from you, no matter how much you tried to stop her. You searched her bed and the surrounding cabinets, and occasionally you uncovered a few sticks, but somehow she still materialized more out of nothing, as if all she needed to do was pinch her right index and middle fingers together, and poof—a cigarette out of thin air. She liked to show off this talent in front of you, as if smoking's greatest pleasure was in annoying you. You knew she loved the sight of you rushing up in consternation to snatch away her sticks. Yet if you held back, she smoked them down to their tips without a care in the world.

Seeing you throw the extinguished cigarette into the trash can under the desk, Mother put on an expression of faux regret. You ignored her, bent your head down to continue with your homework. After what seemed like a long time, Mother's voice drifted wistfully from behind you like sluggish smog. Don't worry, your Uncle Sai isn't that kind of person, she said.

She revealed that he was often turned out of places when he was young. "Back then he was so dirt-poor he couldn't get enough to eat. He knows what it's like, having nowhere and no one to turn to."

Maybe she was right. At least he never drove you out while she still breathed. He set aside room 301 for the two of you, even added a study desk on your behalf. He stayed in room 203, where Mother often spent the night before her knee swelled up. Once, you heard Mother say to the Hawaiian shirt auntie, "Can you imagine, first time spending the entire night with a man at my age."

The auntie seemed indifferent. She extended a hand out the window to flick off some cigarette ash, lost in thought.

Maybe Uncle Sai had been acting out of nostalgia for his bygone relationship with Mother. If so, her death would have rendered all of that mere scattered clouds. Ever since you wrapped up her funeral affairs, you've avoided him under the assumption that one day he'd cut ties with you. Over the long years the two of you, both introverted and reticent, had seldom spent time alone. You had even less to say to each other once Mother rescinded her role, as if she took away your lines and dialogues, stranded you without an audience on the rundown stage that is Mayflower.

That evening, you steel yourself as you get into Uncle Sai's car. He says the AC is broken and tells you to crank down your window. Of course it has to be an especially muggy day. Overhead, thunder and lightning sharpen their knives and polish their guns behind increasingly thicker stacks of clouds. Soon it will rain, and heavily. By the time you get to Old Zhang's restaurant both your foreheads are dripping with sweat. You wipe it away with the restaurant's paper napkins. When the auntie wearing wooden clogs comes to take your orders, Uncle Sai swipes at his sweat and says, Let's eat something nice tonight. This makes you even warier. You're convinced this dinner is meant as a kind of farewell.

He orders a whole catfish, yam stewed with pork belly, pan-fried prawns, bean curd with celtuce leaves, and a jumbo-sized bottle of beer to top it off. Have a glass, he says, you're not a kid anymore. The unexpected bounty of rich dishes makes you even more jumpy. Watching him swallow a large swig of beer, you guess that he's about to say something that he finds difficult to deliver.

Instead he drones on casually about inconsequential fluff. So-and-so hotel is opening next month, he says. This place, Old Zhang's, used to be just an open-air food stall with iron awnings set up on a roadside slope. Back then they were extremely popular, when he and your mother were regulars. "Sometimes you'd be half-way through a big beer bottle before anyone comes to take your order, and then you gotta wait over half an hour once your order is in." But later, after Old Zhang's moved to a new construction brick-and-mortar shop, their business began to suffer. They've been struggling for a few years, and now they're almost unable to make ends meet.

Uncle Sai moves on to a jumbled assortment of other topics. You listen without quite comprehending as he talks about the hullabaloo since the latest elections, Indians setting fire to mosques, the mafia backgrounds of certain Chinese politicians, and rants about how migrant workers cause societal problems. He's unusually chatty, and the output of his words keeps pace with his input of beer. You think he must be attempting to treat you like an adult, as if he believes you've matured and can now stand on your own two feet within this messed-up society as a grown man.

You drink a little beer with him and polish off the steamed catfish almost all by yourself. By the time Uncle Sai asks for the check, the table is littered with quite a few beer bottles and an abundance of leftovers. Go on, eat, he says. The braised pork here was your ma's favorite. "Last chance. Won't be able to taste this in the future." He lets out a beery burp, releasing a sad, sour flavor into the air.

The rain starts on your way back. Chilled wisps of it slant through the half-open car window, lashing your faces again and again. You say, The car has seen many years, hasn't it? Might be time for a trade-in. Uncle Sai smiles bitterly. "Oh, it'll do. If there were money to spare, I'd sooner buy a decent house." You turn these words over in your head, trying to locate a hidden meaning you suspect lies between the lines.

"Mayflower is ancient. A building that old doesn't fetch much," he says.

"Not to mention the termites."

Uncle Sai nods. He activates the wipers. On the windshield, neon lights dilute and bloom apart, further blurring the view. The city at night is lurid and beguiling. Neither of you speak, your eyes focused on the unseen road ahead.

His footwork is not the steadiest when he gets out at Mayflower. His movements are clumsy, and it takes him too long to deal with the lock on the iron shutters. Patiently, you follow behind him as he lumbers upstairs. At the second-floor landing he abruptly turns around and takes an object out of his pockets, slightly ham-fisted.

"Spend it however you like for your birthday tomorrow."

Without further elaboration, he shoves the object into your shirt pocket. You catch a glimpse of a red packet, folded over. This is the first time he's directly given you money. You're embarrassed but don't know how to decline. I have a job, Uncle Sai, you say. He seems uneasy as well. He laughs hollowly and says, Take it, take it. I had some luck at the lotto yesterday. This is nothing, a small gesture.

"Your ma was worried I'd forget your birthday, so she marked this big ole reminder on my calendar long ago." He swings a hand back and forth, tells you to go upstairs and stop acting like an old woman.

The rain does not fall freely that night. Noiseless, wet wisps cut across the window like cold blades. It's not until midnight that a true downpour begins. You sit in bed waiting for Mana, uncertain that she will appear. She finally walks in past three, her hair wet, her thin white shirt clinging to her body. In flashes of lightning she looks like a spirit floating up from watery depths. You hug her to your chest, feeling her metallic hardness and cold clarity. She stares into your eyes and softly kisses their corners. She knows you've shed tears. You place your face on her chest, in that spot where a ticking bomb is buried.

"Mana, what should I do? I miss my Ma so much."

All Mana can do is embrace you and kiss you to express her sympathy. Her kisses fall in dense clusters like rain. Her snake-like arms twine sometimes around your neck and limbs; other times they swim rapidly all over your body. She gives you what Mother never could, a deep-seated comfort that settles in your marrows and softens your soul. You're sure that you'll make love tonight. Mana, I'm yet another year older, you say. But nimbly she extricates herself, not letting you go any further. Her gentleness is so practiced it scares you. Her lips and tongue, her fingers; she narrows her eyes as if to say, *Though I have not allowed you to possess me, I have already surrendered everything to you.*

Sparks of lightning flash one after another. Mana, you're really like a venomous snake, you say, as you watch semen trickle from the corners of her mouth. A snake with lethal poison and brilliant streaks adorning its length. It coils itself around you and gyrates intimately, full of nothing but gentle and piteous love, and yet you are aware, after all, of its deadly fangs. It flicks its tongue at you, forked tip and sharp fangs grazing your body, making you uneasy about the hurt and pain to come even while you are wrapped up in this wave of tenderness.

—3—

"Mayflower" makes frequent appearances in the works of Shaozi, a fact that naturally did not escape The Fourth Person. Basically, Shaozi applied the name to all small motels of the same type.[1] According to The Fourth Person's calculations, "Mayflower" is the name of the motels in one novel, two novellas, and four short stories written by Shaozi.[2]

Among those works, you are most interested in the Mayflower that appears in the short story "Opening the Attic Window." This is one of Shaozi's early pieces, which The Fourth Person disdains for its overemphasis on the pursuit of plot. He moreover dismisses the story as being "deeply influenced by writers of the mainland Chinese literary boom; the language used in the story is obviously borrowed from a specific author's style, and yet the attempt to blend it into the story's background, which is full of local color, is entirely unsuccessful."[3]

But all you care about is simply the narrative in the story. In it, the main character, Xiao Ai, gives birth to a bastard in the attic of a Mayflower. Afterward, she "takes care" of the baby in the bathroom. Although The Age of Goodbyes doesn't expend much ink on this short story, those few sentences set you off on a fantasy that your personal Mayflower contains an undiscovered attic. The image of an attic is night and day compared to the cellar you've imagined in the past, the two combining

1. The type meant here is described in the following passage from The Age of Goodbyes: "Be it in a metropolis or a small town, anyone can stumble upon a Mayflower that's subsisting on meager business in an unexpected alley, or in an area where shadows congregate." In other words, precisely the kind of inn with "an absolutely inconsequential name" in which "you" and Mother moved into and out of many times. For detailed depictions of such motels, see chapter 8 of The Age of Goodbyes.

2. Namely the novel The Age of Goodbyes, the novellas The Lefty Who Lost Her Right Brain and The Tree Would Prefer Stillness, and the short stories "Rainless Town," "Opening the Attic Window," "Only Because the Durian Blossomed," and "Last Words from Last Night."

3. See "Mainland Soil on the Malaysian Peninsula—My Thoughts on Reading Shaozi's 'Opening the Attic Window,'" published in 1993 in the Literary Arts section of Politics Review.

to form a pseudo heaven and hell. And Mother? Which one will she be in?

Many literary critics have been interested in the "Mayflower phenomenon" within Shaozi's work. They commonly view the Mayflowers as forming "a weighty and yet highly precise historical symbol."[4] The conclusion is that the name represents the effects of British governance and culture imposed during the period of colonization, and at the same time more or less reflects how the Chinese population of the time pinned its hopes on the building of an egalitarian society. While The Fourth Person did not necessarily disagree with this reading, his opinion was that it resulted from a "lucky coincidence" sans authorial intent.[5]

Mayflower was the first pilgrim vessel to sail from England to North America. It landed at Plymouth on November 21, 1620. Before going ashore, the ship's poverty-stricken masses drafted and signed the Mayflower Compact in the cabin, which laid the foundation for self-governance in New England.

Uninterested in this piece of history, you absentmindedly scan these passages before promptly turning the pages. Being purely a reader, you intuit that many critics can only manage to be just that—professional critics, never real readers. They are more inclined to show off their so-called unique perspectives and contrived reading attitudes. Among them, The Fourth Person is the crème de la crème, and yet the more he invests in seeking various channels into a story, the

4. See "The Mayflower Stranded on the Shores of History," authored by a certain overseer of a university's archives, published in 2007 in *Southern Literature*'s "Special Memorial Edition on the One-Year Anniversary of Shaozi's Passing."

5. See the addendum titled "Recurring Symbols and Tropes in Shaozi's Body of Work" in *Always by Your Side*.

more violently a story resists him, applying an opposing force in reaction.

You begin to pity The Fourth Person. You think he must be the loneliest reader in the world. Perhaps even lonelier than a writer. He is a reader abandoned by stories, fated to spend his whole life reading what exists only in his own imagination.

CHAPTER NINE

—1—

The afternoon when Candlenut was driven out of the big house by Du Li An, Steely Bo was engaged in a life-or-death gambling session at the club. The lamp suspended over the card table suddenly emitted brightness when it became dark enough to turn on the lights. He and his gambling buddies massaged their eyes, the bags underneath swelling with each rub. It was only under the harsh white lamplight that they noticed each other's fatigue and haggardness.

When one of the club's workers went out on a food run, Steely Bo asked for congee with pig blood curd, which he ate distractedly. He drove home after the gambling party disbanded, releasing bloody burps in the car. He kept nodding off. Because of that, he rear-ended someone on the way. He had no choice but to get out and argue with the other party. Back in his prime he got excited when he found himself in such situations, often pushed up his sleeves and cracked his knuckles before he'd even stepped out of the car, a threatening aura gathering about him. When people saw the triad tattoos upon those arms of steel, they'd back down a few notches even if they were in the right. But now Steely Bo was getting along in years. The mythical beasts engraved on his arms had aged, as had his muscles, so everything was loose and atrophied. What remained were limp worms and flaccid fowl. It didn't help that he had spent the last twenty-four hours giving it all at the gambling table, which left him now with a shriveled expression and trembling cheeks. He looked like an old lion that had entirely lost its grandeur. Even his voice no longer carried as far as it once had.

The other party drove a lightly used Japanese car. When a skinny youngster with thick-framed glasses pushed open the door, Steely Bo at first felt a wave of delight. He was hoping to borrow some of his old splendor and make a mountain out of this molehill, so he could relive his glory days. Except two rotund women clad in kebaya emerged from the car before he could even take up the proper stance. One of them was old and the other young, but both had fair, glowing skin that gleamed as bright as the reds and greens on their Malay outfits. They opened their mouths and let loose long English sentences that flowed like water. In the face of this, Steely Bo was mute and defenseless. It was a good thing the skinny, bespectacled man interjected with a few phrases in Cantonese. Otherwise Steely Bo couldn't have gotten a word in even if he'd wanted to apologize. Roaring at them was definitely out of the question.

In the end, to settle the matter he had to open his wallet and surrender the fruits of his exertions from the past twenty-four hours. Even so, the two women were dissatisfied. Before getting back in the car they made a show of inspecting its bumper, glared at him, and pursed their lips as they muttered away.

At this point in his life, there was nothing Steely Bo feared coming up against more than this type of well-dressed woman with sly looks and merciless ways. Over the past year Du Li An had really shown him what a woman could do. When he drove home in the Mercedes with the slightly concave hood and the license plate hanging by a thread, he had in mind the Du Li An he'd first seen selling tickets in a cage at Old Majestic cinema—shy-faced, full of grace, like a canary. At some point, who knew when, she'd turned into a coquettish boss lady who earned the praise of anyone who crossed her path. "Oooh, that boss lady at Ping Le House . . ."

Modern, captivating, pinched waist on a wasp-like figure; smart, cunning, great with numbers, precise in all business calculations.

When such assessments reached her ears, she didn't pout in anger. "Oh? They haven't caught on that there's murder behind my smile? That I can kill without shedding blood?" After saying this she'd quirk up the corners of her mouth and toss off suggestive, alluring glances, stealing away snippets of everyone's souls.

After a year of aimless wandering, Steely Bo had returned home to find her off-limits. His eyes were not yet cloudy then, and he discovered, to his surprise, that she grew lovelier by the day. Despite being a year or two from forty, she bloomed like a fresh red rose. She was thorny like one too. When she got mad the air around her seemed to curdle with her rage. When Steely Bo's gambling buddies brought her up, they invariably harbored dirty thoughts, which translated into uncouth phrases when they talked: Oh, speaking of your wife, they say women are wolves at thirty and tigers at forty, so you gotta store up some of that vital essence during these years. Steely Bo knew what they were hinting at, and yet there was no way he could confess that, even if he wanted to, he was no longer capable. Once, he happened upon her as she exited her room in a towel. Her exposed flesh was smooth as white jade and yet lush and bouncy, as if it would yield a precious elixir with a gentle squeeze. Heat rushed upward in his chest, and yet his dantian were cool; the heat did not reach his energy centers. Absolutely nothing happened from the waist down. She displayed not one iota of intention to engage either. After looking at him for a beat she walked back into her room. She even latched the door.

What else was there to say? Back when he was engorged with vigor she was the one who often put up blockades, such as a rule that he was not to touch her after drinking. He'd had no idea she'd take it so seriously when he promised her. Later he often encountered this iron rule while burning alive with desire. It almost made him go off the deep end, so angry he came close to physically hurting her. After this torture had happened frequently, his enthusiasm was snuffed. He'd sooner turn off the lights and be embraced by sleep. Anything was better than trying to cajole and beg her into submission atop the sheets.

"Is it so hard for you to take a shower and brush your teeth?" Du Li An would grumble from her half of the bed.

And now, even if she were to bare her body and let him ogle those voluptuous breasts, even if she were tiger or wolf, Steely Bo knew full well that his flesh was weak, despite his willing spirit. Because this was so deflating to think about, he preferred to gamble away entire nights at the club, where he had the company of an old clock in a wooden box that counted down to daybreak. Win or lose, it was only a matter of a hundred or so ringgit. And though the poker cards featured four dour women, they did not make him feel nearly as bad as the queen at home, with her airs and her verbal barbs.

He'd practically written off Candlenut. His youngest boy, formerly the apple of his eye, was now a lumpy gallstone he couldn't pass. Du Li An never held back when she insulted the youngster. In fact, several times she ridiculed father and son as a combo to their faces. Even when Steely Bo lost his temper, Candlenut remained like soft mud, too lazy to either rally his spirits or return to the fishing village for help from his two older brothers. Instead, he holed up in his bedroom and slept away the hours, day and night. Or else he buried his face in a pile of serialized comics and martial arts novels that he'd already read many times over.

It was hard to believe, but Steely Bo had actually tried to advise this son of his. Once, Steely Bo marched into Candlenut's room and made space on the bed by pushing aside the stacks of *Oriental Heroes*, *Drunken Master*, and *Buddha's Palm*. Steely Bo plopped down across from Candlenut, who knew at once that this was an unusual visit. He lowered the comic he held in his hands, revealing a pair of protruding, yellowing eyeballs. His nose and mouth remained concealed. Father and son stared wordlessly at each other. A mosquito out patrolling way too early in the day flew by shakily, as if it'd feasted on a drunkard's blood. The two men couldn't help tracking the mosquito. It was only after it'd buzzed past that they began to feel embarrassed, and yet neither knew how to break through the standoff.

Steely Bo was as clumsy as ever with his words. He'd walked into the room on the spur of the moment, without quite understanding what it was he wanted to say. Now, just for something to do, he picked up a martial arts novel pinned under his thigh and flipped through it. The book was several hundred pages long, as thick as an almanac and filled throughout with dense text. You did go to school after all, he said with a sigh. For a bit anyway. You know so many words.

Candlenut did not reply. He simply continued staring at Steely Bo.

The curtains in the room were half-drawn, allowing scant light into the room. Steely Bo looked into his son's wary eyes. The kid was still so young, and yet those eyes were like iron balls that had rusted over. They sunk heavily into sockets that seemed too wide and loose. When Steely Bo's gaze slid onto Candlenut's left shoulder and rested on the long-tailed bird there, he couldn't help but twist his head to locate his own. The bird's tail was about the same length as its body, but its wings were impossibly tiny in comparison. How could it fly? Steely Bo lifted his tattooed arm and rubbed the image vigorously with his other hand, like he might wipe off a smear of dirt.

"It looked good when it was new, right? The color was like cloisonné," he said. "Then after a while the color changes, becomes dark and faded. You don't like it anymore, but you can't wipe it off even if you want to."

Candlenut, still not responding, blinked occasionally. The drunk mosquito was back, weaving left and right on its return voyage, sounding like it was humming a song that could barely be heard.

"You're still young, with so many days ahead of you. A life stretches out long like a rolling river. You can't spend yours like this." Steely Bo flicked his wrist and sent the martial arts novel flying onto the mound of books on the bed, where it landed with a loud smack. Candlenut kept silent. The cogs in his brain turned slower and slower. It felt as if his skull was filled with mud and stones, like a lumbering cement mixer. His body was heavy and sank downward, while his mouth seemed crammed full of concrete. This was all made worse by the awkward situation playing out now, his father sighing and lamenting like an earnest, evangelizing old woman.

Eight or ten years earlier, the old man would never

have let things drag out with such patience. Instead he'd have promptly yanked Candlenut out of bed and delivered a severe beating, or else locked him in the room to starve for a couple days. Growing up, he and his two brothers had tasted their share of the old man's iron fists. Especially Candlenut, who'd been as stocky as Shi Hei Long in *Oriental Heroes*. Everyone said that was a result of Steely Bo's "coaching"—the old man was the steel to his stone.

All of these musings were impenetrable to Steely Bo. All he saw were those yellowish, graveyard-dull eyes, which reminded him of the eyes on fish that had been dead for a while. Candlenut was still wordless. Steely Bo let out one more sigh and then stood up, patting his son's shoulder. "Why don't you think it over." Steely Bo experienced an eerie moment of déjà vu when his hand made contact with Candlenut's shoulder. Even the light and shadows in the room seemed familiar— the way they fell, the length of their arches. It was as if he'd lived through this day in a dream long ago. Or as if, even further back, his old uncle had on some afternoon parted a curtain to walk into the room and said to him in the dialect they shared, A life stretches out long like a rolling river. And then his uncle stood up and patted Steely Bo's shoulder in a resigned way.

If that was a shred of an actual memory, he would have been just a youngster at the time. Maybe he'd suffered injuries from a fight and had been lying low at home to recuperate. He did remember once hiding out on a fishing boat for half a month. He ate clams to replenish his blood and the days passed in a blur. But then his wound became infected and oozed pus. His arm turned purple, the color of jam, and swelled up to the size of his thigh. He had no choice but to go ashore for a doctor when he developed fever, dizziness, and nausea on top of that. The village's traditional medicine doctor and his son both held their breaths as they squeezed pus out of Steely Bo and let his blood. A rank stench wafted from his wound. Blood gushed so dark it was almost black, smelling like a basket of rotting clams.

That long bout of suffering earned him Elder Zong's esteem. Steely Bo was allowed to officially kneel in the temple and swear oaths during a tea ceremony that cemented their pact. He received a set of golden bowl and chopsticks from Elder Zong, and from that day on they could refer to each other as adoptive father and son. Was it then? His father had lost his life at sea earlier in the year, and so it was an uncle who came into the room. Skinny, tall, with skin tan as a shadow from several decades' exposure to sun and rain. The old uncle sighed and patted Steely Bo on his shoulder, gave him counsel in the dialect that he'd never been able to master his entire life. Back then, charged with rebellious energy, he must have fired off some rash retort. Fuck! Y'all depend on god and fate for the rice and congee you eat. I look to Elder Zong. It's all the same!

It seemed to have happened that way, and then again maybe not. The memories of his youth had run away from him. Steely Bo scratched his head and thought fiercely, but all he could recall were the tones of that unpronounceable dialect. For the life of him, he couldn't remember the features or outline of his uncle's face buried in dark shadows.

No matter what, his "chat" with Candlenut seemed to produce some effect. The next day he accepted Steely Bo's suggestion to help out with odd chores at Ping Le House, like serving tea and washing cups. Her misgivings notwithstanding, Du Li An nevertheless agreed to the arrangement without hesitation. Steely Bo was rather excited for a few days. He invited his gambling buddies to have afternoon tea at Ping Le House, the pretext allowing him to monitor the situation on the sly. Du Li An did not care for his feelings. She bossed Candlenut around as if Steely Bo and his buddies weren't there and treated him exactly like a common helper picking up odds and ends. First, Steely Bo felt his chest tighten. Then he thought it might actually do Candlenut good to undergo some indignity and endure a few hardships, so he bore it all silently alongside his son.

Except after a few days of this, even the old-timer in charge of making drinks became bold enough to yell at Candlenut. He called him sluggish and picked at the way he dragged his feet when he walked. "Slowpoke! Lazy ass!" the veteran jeered. Steely Bo felt he was losing face but had no outlet. His enthusiasm evaporated. He'd also come to realize that Candlenut was really just picking up scraps at Ping Le House. There was nothing humbler than that. Though it was framed as the chance to turn over a new leaf, what he was doing was but a tiny step up from turning the pages of comic books in his room. This train of thought brought Steely Bo rapidly back to the gambling table, where time passed in successions of bridge, mahjong, and pai gow, followed by his return home, where he fell immediately asleep.

"You could at least bet on horses," Du Li An mocked. "Otherwise you're becoming more and more like my old man every day."

The day of Steely Bo's little car accident, Candlenut had been helping out at Ping Le House for less than a month. It was the afternoon of that very same day when Du Li An caught him doing heroin in the bathroom. She had long detected something fishy, and the other workers had repeatedly made complaints to her about how often Candlenut snuck into the bathroom with a comic under one armpit, and how he stayed for ten, twenty minutes. It was clear he wasn't shitting in there. That was a bathroom everyone shared; sometimes his hogging it made even customers grumble. Her many reminders had no corrective effect on him whatsoever, no matter how biting her words. After that she kept tabs on him. Guen Hou contributed leg work, informing her that Candlenut entered the toilet each time with the same exact copy of *Oriental Heroes* under his armpit. That comic was wrinkled like pickled mustard from mainland China, as if it was a volume of secret kung fu techniques he'd read to tatters. Obviously, something was up. Du Li An sent Jignesh, the youth who worked at the chee cheong fun stall, on a task. While Candlenut monopolized the bathroom with his book, Jignesh carried a wooden bench to the back alley and climbed up so he could spy through the bathroom's small window. Then, panting, he delivered his report with the bench hugged to his chest. There's a candle, he said. Candle; fire; tinfoil; paper; white, white powder, white-colored powder dust.

Her face turned green when she heard this. She gave Jignesh some money and told him to keep what he saw to himself. Then she summoned Guen Hou for deliberations. After putting their heads together, the close friends decided that Guen Hou would find an opportunity to get her hands on Candlenut's treasured book. Guen Hou became even more unnerved than Du Li An when she found out it was as big a deal as drugs. This only made her movements slow and rigid. Multiple times she missed great openings, and it wasn't until almost closing time that she achieved her goal. Hot potato in hand, she rushed furtively to the counter and shoved the rolled-up issue of *Oriental Heroes* straight into Du Li An's lap. She unfurled the comic in a drawer and, sure enough, the tableau was there in its entirety.

And so in the big house, right that afternoon, Du Li An hurled the bundle of evidence at Candlenut's feet. "Looking for this?" He stared unblinkingly at the objects, head hung low, his eyeballs looking like they would fall out of their sockets at any moment. He alone knew how arduous that moment was for him. He wanted to defend himself, and at the same time he wondered whether he should apologize and admit fault, but his mind was immediately stalled by these questions. With effort, the puddle of mud in his brain surfaced a few bubbles.

Du Li An had prepared for a scene of chaos. She'd brought along Lau Lin on the assumption that Candlenut's face and ears would burn red, that he would muster one last drop of aggression. Instead he didn't utter a single word but merely crumpled meekly at the waist, and sunk to his knees to gather up his tools scattered across the floor. From Du Li An's vantage point, she could see his bowed spine and his thick, fat tailbone, like warped bamboo, each individual segment protruding through his thin singlet. That shriveled, slavishly, dutiful posture reminded her of an old person's hunched back.

She let out a long, whistling sigh. "You should go back to the fishing village! Let your ma and your brothers be the ones to school you," she said. "Look at the state you're in. Your Auntie Li doesn't have it in her. She can't rein you in, and she can't raise you either."

To her, there was no path forward for a drug addict. She'd seen her share of youngsters in that predicament. Other than Elder Zong's impeccably fashionable youngest son, all of them ended up looking barely human. Didn't there used to be one such heroin addict clinging to life around the Old Street market? Several times he robbed passing women of their purses and gold chains, and was then chased and caught by community members. There was a sundry shop located at a dead end. Sometimes the workers there tackled him, abusing him with punches and kicks in broad daylight. Once they beat him so badly they broke one of his arms. Du Li An had been there, having wormed her way into the crowd that had gathered. Later she was convinced she'd heard a loud crack, clear as a bell, as if what lay beneath the addict's skin were rotting wood planks. After recovering from his injury, the heroin addict continued to linger around the Old Street market. People said he'd managed to get clean but doing so turned him into a befuddled beggar. Sometimes he'd show up at Sou Gei's stall and thrust out a hand for food. Du Li An would give him stuff they couldn't sell that day, usually ham jin peng or youtiao, since both varieties of fried dough leaked oil overnight; it wasn't like they could be sold the next day.

At some indeterminate point the beggar stopped appearing at the Old Street market. Sou Gei said he'd died in who knew what alley after contracting rabies from a violent dog that bit him. "One way or another, he was heading for a bitter end," she said through her buckteeth. But for some reason Du Li An always believed that he'd instead discovered new stomping grounds. She suspected him of transforming into the homeless man who often appeared in the stretch between the bridge and Old Majestic Cinema, the one who walked around barefoot pushing a bicycle. He'd disguised himself under strata of dust and soot, layers of hair and clothes, and an accumulation of time. Sometimes when she bumped into him outside the cinema, he'd narrow his eyes and stare at her as if remembering something from the distant past. She used to bring him leftover fried dough and Nyonya kuih. He'd seem overjoyed and stuffed the snacks into his shirt without hesitation.

Because she'd shown him this bit of kindness, she assumed that this "madman" retained some clarity of mind and maybe even harbored goodwill toward her. Therefore she could hardly believe he would repay her as he had on May Thirteenth, when he swung his bike chain and attacked her, forcing her into Steely Bo's shiny Mercedes.

This same Mercedes now looked like an ungainly tank. The front license plate clanged and bucked wildly, clinging on for dear life by the grace of a single screw on the left. Steely Bo sensed something was wrong as soon as he drove the car into the yard. Lau Lin came out of the house, green-faced. Third Brother left us, she sobbed. An explosion went off in Steely Bo's head when he heard this; he thought Candlenut had died in an accident of some sort. Not one for words to begin with, Lau Lin more often than not spoke in timid, incomplete sentences. By the time she explained everything through her tears, Candlenut had gone who knew how far.

But she really hadn't expected her father to become so agitated by the news. Candlenut had packed up what few clothes he owned, she said, and left holding a plastic bag. He didn't respond when she followed him and called out, "Third Brother!" several times. She even asked him, Are you going home? Back to Ma's? Without replying, he pushed open the gates and walked toward the main road.

Steely Bo's eyes bulged, revealing blood vessels like leaf veins. His expression shocked Lau Lin, who thought he looked as if he'd been electrocuted and a live current still coursed hither-thither within him, singeing his organs. She couldn't help but whimper and swallow whatever loose words still lingered on her tongue.

Steely Bo burst into the house and sped upstairs, where he slammed open Du Li An's door. The fuzzy sounds of someone talking poured from the radio at the head of the bed. She was sitting in a chair by the window, in that spot where the sun's rays met lamplight, holding a small round mirror and painting her brows. When the door crashed into the wall with a loud bang, she did not turn her head but simply glanced at the mirror in her hand. There he was in that tiny round glass, humble as anything. He roared at her through the mirror, You, you—how cruel can you be!

"What about it? Just ask Ah Lin. I gave him five hundred ringgit. That's above and beyond." Du Li An raised her chin. "Count for yourself how many days he worked at Ping Le House. I gave him five hundred!"

To her it was a matter of dismissing an unskilled worker. To him it was the exile of his son, the Lau family's third-born. And yet he was awed by her imposing manner. Five hundred ringgit was indeed a fair deal, Steely Bo thought, then sensed something was awry about this logic. He maintained the distressed expression on his face, though his eyeballs continued to spin, making him look like one of those rakshasas writhing under Guanyin's foot in temples.

"You could at least have waited until I got home."

"Waited?" Du Li An plucked a single eyebrow hair. This had the effect of raising that arch of hers, giving her an air of cockiness. "You knew all along, right? You knew your son is addicted to drugs. Still you brought him here without so much as a heads-up. Who am I to him? And I can't believe you let him loose at Ping Le House."

She twisted around, displaying a left eyebrow raised to the heavens. "You've really outdone yourself as a dad. Now it's time for his mom to worry about him."

Though Steely Bo and Lau Lin both guessed that Candlenut would not return to the fishing village, they had no clue where he would go instead. When Steely Bo drove out to find Candlenut, Lau Lin threw herself into the car as well. The car sounded its horn all its harried way to the bus depot. There, the two of them waited for almost two hours, until the very last bus heading for the fishing village left in a spurt of black smoke. No trace of Candlenut. By then the lights were on in every house. The night sky looked like the black screen after a movie had ended. Steely Bo shook his head. Let's go, he said to Lau Lin. I'm hungry.

The car ride home was somewhat bumpy. The two of them heard a sudden clang. What's that sound? she asked. Though he knew it was the wobbly license plate finally falling off and hitting the street, he felt only fatigue coursing through his body. His head was heavy, the insides a can of cement that had hardened beyond any possibility of mixing. So he neither replied nor stopped the car to retrieve the plate.

Two months after that, he finally and reluctantly replaced the license plate after he was pulled over by police. They let him go with a warning after he paid them twenty ringgit in "coffee money." As for the concave hood, if it weren't for rainwater seeping in and causing the car to break down, he would have left it in that state forever. For two months he'd been using a temporary plate improvised out of cardboard and hung in front of the car. Seeing him in that huge, old-fashioned, beaten-down, and ludicrous pile of metal scrap, Du Li An had a hard time figuring out her feelings. Once upon a time she'd sat in that car, the trunk laden with gifts he'd bought to endear himself to her family: durian, preserved seafood, bolts of fabric, clothing, and even live fish and shrimp he wrangled from the fishing village. He'd stopped the car in front of her house and she opened her door to shout at the upstairs windows, Ah Sai, Ah Sai, hurry down and help us. Everyone in the neighborhood had heard her. People stuck their heads out of doors and windows to gawk, the extra nosy ones sauntering forth with their hands crossed behind their backs to watch Steely Bo lift treasure after treasure out of the trunk like a magician. Sou Gei had rushed downstairs in wooden clogs while Ah Sai and the old man dragged their feet behind her. Du Li An waved at them. No matter how she tried to restrain herself, she could not stop her eyebrows and the corners of her mouth from arching up to form a smile.

Those generous gifts, that sparkling, spotless car, and that man were supposed to be a preview of life's banquet.

She probed him now, assuming that he was too broke to fix his car. He replied tiredly, "I have money. I'm just lazy."

Not long after he returned from his "daring escapade," they reached an agreement that absolved him of any responsibilities toward the mortgage and household expenses. He had exclusive use of their old place, and in exchange, he transferred the deed for the big house to her name. He was definitely no match for her calculating cleverness. Not to mention that, since his return, he felt that he was simply living out the rest of his days. He had no energy left to fuss over the endless financial obligations and was happy to accept her suggestions. The two of them settled the paperwork at a lawyer's office, after which he lived on rent collected from two little row houses, which stretched enough to cover his gambling and drinking needs. Of course, he realized his glory days were over. When it came time to distribute red envelopes to the younger generation at Chinese New Year, he was no longer as generous as before.

Du Li An noticed that his trademark necklace and showy watch, both gold, had disappeared. Only a gold-framed jade ring remained on one finger. Steely Bo had devolved like his steed into old metal scrap, rough around the edges. That car used to be his baby, driven every week without fail to the Old Street market, where it was washed by children squatting roadside with a pail of water. The car-cleaning kids recognized Steely Bo and knew he wasn't stingy with tips. They eagerly yelled out, "Boss!" every time they saw Steely Bo, and they always cleaned the car with extra enthusiasm. Du Li An had even once witnessed two squads of children come to fisticuffs over Steely Bo's patronage while he looked on with a smug smile.

Now, who knew how long it'd been since the Mercedes was last washed? Every day Steely Bo took it dithering on big streets and unpaved paths alike, its handmade cardboard license plate sporting crooked numbers scrawled in black marker. At first glance, the plate looked just like the "Best Offer" and "For Rent" signs hung on old houses. Then came the new replacement plate, but it was too shiny, its black against white too stark, looking utterly out of place against the car's faded paint. Steely Bo didn't give a shit. When Du Li An occasionally fired off sarcastic remarks about the car, he'd respond with stuffy, literary sayings that were out of context: A centenarian's life must needs come to an end; a thousand-year-old tree yet has to burn. Where once he'd had all sorts of tricks and hacks to style the piteous amount of hair on his head before leaving the house, he now didn't even care to dress himself properly. He wore durable plastic sandals on his feet and paid no attention when buttons popped off his shirts.

When Lau Lin collected them from the clothesline, she noticed the missing buttons, and it fell on her to sew them back on.

Du Li An no longer referred to him as Steely Bo when she talked about him with others. He'd been renamed "that old fella." "He's crossing his legs and doing nothing except wait for the end. What's that called again? Yes, killing time until he dies!"

He sort of identified with that hopeless sentiment. His body was failing just like his Mercedes, which malfunctioned in myriad little ways and emitted strange noises from every corner. It was no different from the phlegm stuck in his throat, hard to expel, or the pinging and twanging of his joints, or his lungs that sounded like ancient bellows. Sometimes he even heard his own snores after he'd fallen asleep. He suspected he didn't have long to live, and this unexpectedly made him miss Candlenut. When Steely Bo made his daily rounds between the club and the big house, he sometimes drove to the fishing village, glancing left and right all the way on the off chance he'd bump into Candlenut.

But Candlenut never returned to his childhood home. It seemed no one ever saw him again. The fishing village received not so much as a phone call. Du Li An suspected that he'd turn to Ah Sai in the capital once he ran out of options. Acting on this hunch, she called the restaurant in the capital and told Ah Sai what had gone down with Candlenut.

"It's heroin—you know how scary those people can be. He's a good-for-nothing now." She paused, thinking she'd overstated it. It might rub her brother the wrong way and actually provoke sympathy in him.

"If he hits you up, just do what you can. Don't get caught up with all that red-blooded honor or loyalty stuff and try to be a hero. What he has is a problem for life, and you can't just give a man a fish. There's no sense helping him, and if you try, you'll only bring trouble on yourself."

Ah Sai mumbled a halfhearted agreement. She sighed. "Ah Sai, are you familiar with the three major misfortunes and the six key blessings?"

Of course he wasn't. If it weren't for that Taoist priest prattling on and on about them, she would never have retained the information either.

"The three major misfortunes are the failing of the body, the failing of family, and the failing of luck," she explained. "A person who has fallen into misfortune will drag down his whole family and also everyone around him."

She didn't catch a response from Ah Sai, but she sensed that her brother must have nodded on the other end of the line.

The priest had embraced Taoism as a teen, and so had only a few years of schooling under his belt. It was only natural that his interpretation of the three major misfortunes and six key blessings contained some errors. But his theory did play out, and Du Li An was the unsuspecting witness. After Candlenut experienced his failing of the body, the fishing village went through a series of ill-fated events, proving the part about the failing of the family. First, Candlenut's eldest brother got into an accident during a midnight motorcycle ride. After several surgeries his legs remained of mismatching length, giving him a strange appearance. Then the son and daughter of the second eldest were diagnosed with thalassemia and were told they would have to rely on blood infusions, injections, and medication their entire lives. Worse, the doctor predicted they would not live beyond their twenties, a diagnosis that shrouded the fishing village in an atmosphere of tragedy. Their parents were so beset by medical bills they had to sell their fishing boats. Later, after some introductions, they found a local newspaper correspondent who helped them publish a plea for help from the public.

Steely Bo blew his top when the news article was printed. He threw down the paper in a rage, picked up the phone, and roared at his wife there, almost severing ties entirely with that family. Du Li An knew he was furious about the loss of face. He was, after all, the "former leader of Kien Tek Hall!" He knew full well he'd made scores of enemies in his past. Now that his family was pulling long faces and begging for charity, those who hated him would naturally feel triumphant. The neighbors and his former sworn brothers were probably joking about his downfall, calling it karma. This whole thing destroyed the last shreds of his reputation and whatever remaining dignity he imagined he had.

Du Li An sneered in silence. She sent Jignesh to buy a copy of the day's paper so she could see the story and photos for herself. It might have been the effect of the black-and-white photos, but the Lau's second-eldest and his wife looked tanned and provincial, exactly like what you would expect of villagers exposed to constant sun and rain. The two sick kids were whip-thin, like willows in the wind. Their skulls seemed overlarge, their eyes too wide-set, and their foreheads protruded; the girl had conspicuous crossed eyes. It was Du Li An's first look at the people "over there," but she didn't feel anything extraordinary. Among the boundless sea of souls, strangers will always outnumber acquaintances.

"My god, what a terrible thing to have happened." She shared the newspaper with Guen Hou. Together, they lamented the cruelty of fate. Du Li An also learned from Lau Lin that her mother's health was suffering, especially from the rheumatoid arthritis she'd had since she was young, which had worsened so much in the last two years that her two knees became deformed. "When it rains, it hails, and it's definitely hailing over there." That was how Du Li An put it to Guen Hou. Then even Steely Bo was struck by disease and had to be taken to the hospital in the middle of the night, after which Du Li An changed her tune: "That Lau family is cursed."

Steely Bo's initial diagnosis was gastric ulcer. His turds were black as coal. After a few days in the ward, they discovered he also had internal hemorrhoids filling up his cavities with thick, oozing blood. The saying goes, even heroes fear the ravage of disease, let alone Steely Bo, who was already sapped of his will and strength before his hospital stay. All the time he had spent toughening himself up had been wiped away by two years at the gambling table. After ten days on a hospital bed, he was reduced to relying on a walking stick. Every step had to be carefully planned. Lau Lin almost asked for a wheelchair from a nurse, but was shushed by Du Li An. "You think your dad will really sit on it? A wheelchair? You must want him to vomit blood from anger."

During his hospital stay, she still held court over Ping Le House from her counter, and brought him food only after closing time. She peeled oranges and cut apples for him. She poured takeout noodle soup into bowls and put them by his bed, arranged chopsticks, soup spoons, and forks within his reach. He sprawled on the middle bed in a three-person room, right across from the TV bolted to the wall. Back then there were only two national channels that played Malay programs almost all day. Steely Bo didn't like listening to Malay all day long. He acquired a tiny portable radio from who knows where, which he placed next to his pillow for his personal amusement.

Du Li An sat at the foot of the bed and half watched

the TV. Occasionally she heard him say something or other about his visitors that day. Visits from the fishing village weren't frequent, since it was such a trek, but his second-eldest had come once with his wife. All of them nagged Lau Lin to take care of Steely Bo. Though she never had much to say to him, she dutifully showed up every single day. Once, her mom from the village came along with sons, daughters-in-law, grandchildren, and assorted friends and family. The group of ten coincided with two of his triad friends on their visit, and together they formed quite the tableau. Then the other two patients in the room complained there was too much noise and too little airflow, causing a minor fuss that had to be resolved by the nurses.

"Speaking of noise . . ." Steely Bo glanced at the Indian man to his left. "Three visitors from his family are equal to ten from ours."

Du Li An didn't react. She looked first at the old Indian man lying there, then at the Malay youth attentively watching TV on the remaining bed. Steely Bo wasn't done. He continued, "Making noise is one thing, then there's . . ." She interrupted him. Eat your noodles faster, she said. I want to go home after I tidy up here.

Ten days in the hospital meant ten days without any gambling. Immediately following his discharge, Steely Bo hurried to the club to build cities out of tiles and cards, even though he was still unsteady on his feet. Du Li An had no thought to spare for his well-being, though Lau Lin, face full of anxiety, couldn't help telling him to watch his hemorrhoids. "Ba, it can't be good for you to sit and play cards all day?" Impatiently he waved her off, not at all alert to his daughter's care and worry. He trotted out that same old line, "A centenarian's life must needs come to an end," then bent over to scoot into his car. The old diesel-powered thing gyrated its rear and, like a cuttlefish, sprayed black smoke all over her feet.

Du Li An took in the scene from the balcony. Her heart shuddered. For some reason she thought about Eggplant Face pressed against Guen Hou's chest all those years ago. *Daughters are the best,* she thought with feeling.

Lau Lin indeed had a heart of gold. After living so many years with her, Du Li An knew the girl simply had no clue how to stand up for herself. She withdrew part of her bank savings to help her second-eldest brother pay off his kids' medical bills. Every Chinese New Year she bought two pieces of fabric and used the factory's equipment to make her mother a couple of new outfits. Once her nephews and nieces started school, she didn't forget them when she shopped for fabric. The one person she couldn't bear to spend money on was herself. Her plastic wardrobe contained the same few T-shirts and pants, plus a few skirts and dresses unfit for formal occasions. Now that the fishing village had been hit by a series of misfortunes, her mother's days were turbulent. Every time Lau Lin visited she made sure to bring formula, canned sardines, ketchup, soybeans, Milo, saltine crackers, instant noodles, etc.—seemingly random objects, much as if she were distributing donated goods.

Ah Lin, why don't you open a sundry shop back home? Du Li An teased her.

That very day, after dropping Lau Lin off at the bus depot, Du Li An made her way to Mayflower. Time passed light as a feather in the motel. She dozed off then woke up and fell back asleep; her dreams were shot through with footsteps on floorboards and snatches of conversation from beyond the door. Yip Mong Sang embraced her tightly from behind, massaged her back, nuzzled the sensitive spot between her earlobe and neck, making her shiver all over. "What kind of feeling is that?" He blew on the taboo area again.

"Like an electric shock," she said. She felt herself melt, gradually liquefying, slowly seeping into the mattress.

The man smiled and said nothing, as if digesting her answer. She lowered her head. His two hands rested on her lower abdomen. She covered them with her own palms and said, Mong Sang.

I'm here.

She liked this refrain of his. She closed her eyes and savored that phrase, "I'm here." It was warm and sweet, like a lick of flame burning within her melting heart.

"I want a daughter," she said.

"A daughter? You want to adopt?"

His hands on her abdomen retreated. She caught them. "No, my own daughter."

This sank him into a long silence. When she slowly released his hands, he didn't immediately move away, as if using his ten little fingertips to probe her stomach for movement.

"Don't worry, I'm not going to bring you trouble." She turned over and smiled at him. The smile was the picture of lightness, but her look conveyed a seriousness that sank like an anchor into his eyes.

"Didn't you hear me? I said I want my own daughter, not 'our daughter.'"

Now he understood. She had no wish to spend the rest of her life with him. No desire to grow old together. But he was still confused; a life, his blood and essence, a whole human being brought into the world, an identity? It involved so many factors and would become a huge, complicated lie. No, only the beginning of a lie. There would be no room for sloppiness and rashness. Still encircling her waist, he tried to think how to change the subject. His hands drifted upward and he began to once again tickle the baby hairs on the back of her neck with his breath, but all that did was raise goose bumps on her skin. Her shoulders shrank and lifted upward.

She cast aside his hands, releasing herself. Standing up, she smoothed the messy hair pressed against her temples. Then she picked up a porcelain cup from the bedside table, lifted the cup's lid, and took a sip of tea. Yip Mong Sang sat on the bed and observed her slow, methodical movements. He watched her pluck a chrysanthemum petal stuck on the tip of her tongue. How beautiful she looked in that moment. He'd seen it before, this serene expression of hers, and he had never forgotten it. It was the time she said she wanted to start a business without anyone knowing. He'd acted as go-between and taken her to negotiate with a business owner. She'd sipped her tea in this exact same manner, peeling Tie Guanyin leaves off her tongue. Without raising her voice or deploying any aggressive verbal tactics, she managed to secure two storefronts at great locations and at a discounted price. Once the t's were crossed, she gave Yip Mong Sang his broker's fee, unprompted. Right there in the car, she fished out a stack of bills from her handbag, as graceful as if she were pinching tea leaves from the tip of her tongue.

"Why cash? Isn't a check more convenient?" He took the money and stashed it carelessly into his pants pocket.

"I have my reasons." She started the engine and put on her sunglasses.

Now she stood half-lit by the bedside lamp, her face in shadows. Her naked body glowed, showing off the perfect curve of her lower abdomen, below which bushes of fragrant grass formed a delta. She looked like a sculpture posed under spotlight. She was no longer the Du Li An he knew, that Du Li An who trembled easily, a woman he once led with his own hand under moonlight.

"Didn't you say you wanted to get out of business with someone?" She sipped another mouthful of chrysanthemum tea, the corners of her eyes lifting with her smile. She was wearing her boss lady expression, one that seemed sure the world was her oyster. "You want to buy up their shares, right?"

That was indeed what he'd said. He asked her to lend him a sum, and also tried to persuade her to invest. She lied, telling him that all her liquidity had gone into real estate. In truth she simply did not trust him, and furthermore was not interested in his line of business. Yip Mong Sang was a clever, carefree man who had no use for practicality, and he was vain to boot. What he aspired to was the lifestyle of a rich socialite. There had been problems with the books when he was the financial executive at the sewing factory. His reputation did not improve when he next went into the construction business. Given her broad network of connections, she'd long known him for what he was. Rumors swirled around his motives to buy out his business partner, something about how the partner had discovered that Yip Mong Sang was diverting company funds. Should he fail to fill in the gaps on the books, he might very well end up in court.

"I'm already thirty-eight." She set down the remaining half cup of tea, long since cooled. "I'd be a geriatric mom if I had a baby now." She folded her arms across her chest and forced a smile, twisting one corner of her lips. Not once did she divert her gaze from his eyes. "But still, I want to give it another shot."

He stared at her wordlessly. Time passed. She didn't

move an inch, but stood there like a beatific wax figure, her expression dignified and authoritative.

"Know what I'm thinking about?" He lay back down, resting his head on folded hands. Now he was at an even lower angle.

She simply blinked.

"The way you're standing there, you look like an antique vase. So expensive that no one dares risk a touch."

After that day, Guen Hou received orders from Du Li An to resume her herbal remedy treatments. Du Li An also visited an ob-gyn this time for an accurate sense of the "best" days. Though Guen Hou was both excited and confused, Du Li An maintained an air of mystery, unleashing her seamless coping strategy in response to any inquisitiveness, determined not to reveal anything. Guen Hou's rudimentary probing and roundabout questioning produced absolutely no results. Of course she felt a little aggrieved.

The herbal remedy was a midwife's recipe passed down through generations. It asked for a bunch of odd ingredients meant to promote one's yin and yang. Guen Hou had to order mutton from the Indian butcher in advance. She went early on specific days to retrieve and store it in Ping Le House's sizeable fridge. After the shop closed, she took the mutton home and forced herself to wake up around 3 a.m., at which point she placed the meat into a clay pot, added herbs from the Chinese medicine shop and four bowls of water, and simmered all of it over low heat until it was done. She emphasized that it must be drank immediately while hot, and she also insisted on using charcoal as a heat source. This stewing routine, done once a week, invariably resulted in dark circles under her eyes on the designated days. Yet it also returned her relationship with Du Li An to its previous intimacy, since they now had a hush-hush topic to whisper over together. Whether out of admiration or jealousy, the other Ping Le House workers started to tease Guen Hou every so often. One of them came up with a nickname they used behind her back: "The Twenty-Four Filial Exemplars," a sardonically lofty moniker with the weight of Confucianism behind it.

—2—

Eleven in the morning. The sun warms bit by bit, as if placing all living beings into a huge clay pot to simmer over low heat. Outside on the busy street, vehicles flow unceasingly, like a rushing river. Your eyes sweep the intersection while Mayflower retreats into hiding, enveloped by dense urban shade.

As if out of thin air, Mana emerges from the back alley behind the shops. She's dressed simply that day, though her feet sport those platform shoes topped with daisies. You stand at the intersection, waiting, watching her come toward you with a smile. Her calves exposed by her cropped pants are long and slender, and she looks full of grace and beauty, like a model towering on a catwalk. She makes you feel proud. The back alley, filthy and old, threads behind Mayflower. A tabby saunters along the wall, stepping like a high-wire artist. From time to time it lowers its head to see whether mice are zooming out of the sewer drain under the wall.

This is your first time meeting Mana in broad daylight. Under harsh sunlight she looks haggard, but she's taken pains to enhance her looks with some light foundation, peach-colored blush, and glossy brown lipstick. You extend a hand for her to hold. Let's go, you say, flinging your head. Your ten fingers lock together; hers are slender and her palms are broad. You like touching her hands in the darkness to feel those ten obstinate, uneasy parts of her. You keep saying her hands belong on a musician. Piano, maybe, for these dancing fingers. Now, yours locked into hers, you discover your two hands already seem familiar with each other. They are mutual admirers. They press into one another, docile, the fingers like five pairs of lovers unwilling to separate.

You go see a movie, then have lunch together. Mana prefers your time together in the theater. The cinema is located on the top floor of the mall. Before heading there, you hold her hand and idly window-shop, lingering in front of lavishly decked-out store windows. Mana walks and pauses as she pleases. While she examines the goods on display, you look at your reflections in the glass. In the mirrors, you and Mana are two dark blurs, devoid of almost all details. When you smile, it's too subtle to show up in the glass.

It's slim pickings when it comes to daytime movie options. The two of you pick an English-language movie that seems heartwarming. A happy, cozy family visited by tragedy and the shadow of death; though those who leave are no longer present, the survivors cling onto their memories. Love defeats all. The audience is tiny at noon. People start to sob before you're even halfway through the movie. When the final scene rolls, the two of you can't help swiveling your heads to look at their faces lit up by the silver screen. Almost every viewer's face bears the mark of tears. But you and Mana smile at each other, your hearts like stone. The world of the movie must be too distant for you: that kind of family, with a gentle father, obedient sons, and loving sisters; the sort of family that gathers on meadows and beaches; the tender care and playful teasing between people closest to each other; the summer sunshine that pours and spills as if without end; the gradual death surrounded by that kind of contented happiness, eyes closing in the throes of angels' blessings.

But Mana was clearly more absorbed in the movie than you were. You caught an earnest expression on her face, her eyes shimmering with stark, bright light, like two oil lamps. During several scenes, you noticed her smiling along with the dying girl. You grip Mana's hand resting on the divider. Sensing the hand's iciness, you rub it, massage it, give it warmth.

Outside the theater, Mana has trouble adjusting to the exterior brightness. She looks even more tired than when she'd first left Mayflower. You pick a unique little restaurant and listen quietly to the piano music played inside. The sound of tides is mixed into the melody. You say you know this tune, called "Tears." Then you tell Mana many things about movies, including how the novel *The Age of Goodbyes* begins with Chan Kam Hoi dying in a theater. When you were little, you always felt that cinemas were a mysterious place, a gigantic black box that allows people to sit in darkness and spy on the lives and events playing out on the silver screen.

You remember your first time walking into a cinema. Uncle Sai was in line for tickets. Mother dragged you by your hand to the snack vendor and bought a small box of colorful candy dotted all over with powdered sugar. You sat in your seat, box in hand, and by what light there was, you very carefully distinguished each individual candy by its color. When the curtains parted, all the lights abruptly went out in the theater. You pinched a single candy between thumb and index finger, holding it up against the bright screen. After that, you could identify the candies only by your taste buds.

Mother hadn't been to the movies for many years. She was even more excited than you were. From the moment she walked in, she kept exclaiming, "Cinemas

these days are so much better than they were before."
At supper afterward, she still brimmed with enthusiasm and insisted on telling you all about cinemas of the
past in full detail and with great urgency, as if afraid
you would forget an era that didn't even belong to you.

Back then, theaters were divided into upstairs and
downstairs seating, she said. Because you didn't need
to angle your head up when watching movies from
upstairs, those tickets went for higher prices. Both
kinds of seats featured foam cushions wrapped in
maroon faux leather, which automatically bounced
up and folded inward when the customer stood. The
seats were often sabotaged, the pleather cut with sharp
objects, creating jagged cracks that exposed the foam.
The wooden seat dividers concealed fleas that weren't
shy to bite. To save money, many parents perched their
young children on the dividers. The kids had to multi-
task and scratch at their bites during the movie. After
the show, their thighs and buttocks were predictably
swollen, carpeted by red rashes.

Later, you found out Mother had been to a cinema
only a handful of times. A memory that stayed with
her forever was when she caught *Liu Sanjie*, a movie
of the Shan'ge Chinese folk song genre and her own
mother's favorite. It was during that particular showing that your mother's little butt was stung by fleas. She
itched for two days and two nights. Because she was
so young, she didn't retain much of the movie's plot.
All she recalled was a couple dressed in Hanfu singing
while steering a boat through water running alongside
fog-wreathed mountains. And you, you are the same.
You have forgotten what movie it was that the three
of you saw that night. All you remember are glinting
knives and flashing swords. The terrifyingly loud sounds
of clashing weapons, fists, and kicks. Curious, you kept

looking this way and that, trying to see what others were doing during the movie. Partway through you felt the urge to pee. Mother had Uncle Sai take you to the bathroom. You prudently put the lid back on the box of candy and followed him across many strangers' knees. When he reached down to steer you, you grabbed only his index finger as you walked the long corridor toward the bathrooms. He waited right behind you at the urinals, and the two of you stood in that formation for quite a while, until you couldn't bear it anymore. You turned around and said to him, "I can't pee if you're looking at me."

Later, he must have told Mother what happened. Told her how you swung your little dick around when you pivoted and talked to him. How it was right at that moment your bladder chose to exert itself. An arc of pee shot toward him, and though he jumped aside immediately, urine splashed on his old leather shoes and even on the hems of his pants. Uncle Sai didn't tell you off, but still your face was flushed red when you followed him back to your seats, your head low. After just a few minutes, when the movie was at a duet scene, Mother erupted suddenly into a series of loud cackles. Those sitting a row ahead of you turned their heads to stare.

At this point in your story, Mana can't suppress a wide grin, showing off two rows of extremely neat teeth. You smile too, yet a sudden sorrow follows. What you just narrated was quintessential familial love, only you had been so obtuse and careless back then you didn't realize it. A few days after the three of you watched that movie you found out it had been Mother's birthday. No wonder she'd smiled all night, her face lit up like a new bride.

"But my Ma's teeth aren't as good-looking as yours," you say. When Mother smiled, her mouth cracked so wide it completely exposed her yellow teeth, which weren't too obvious otherwise. During supper she teased that you "poured tea" for Uncle Sai in the cinema bathroom. Then she said you gifted him the treasure that was virgin urine, and while she said this, she yanked on the rubber elastic band around your shorts, making as if to undress you. The other customers and restaurant workers all turned to stare. You shrieked sharply and wriggled your body to break free of her. You felt she was too ostentatious. Her lips were so wide when she smiled, her voice carried so far, and her movements were so exaggerated. As if she was taking pains to make sure the onlookers would mistake you for a happy family.

Orchestral music plays in the restaurant when you and Mana are about to leave. She lingers at the counter over a particular piece, but in the end she pulls you toward the exit before the music stops. She refuses when you suggest a stroll. Rubbing her temples, she makes a pained expression, then folds her palms together and cushions one cheek against them, letting you know she needs to rest. So all you can do is hold her hand as you hop into a cab. Outside, the opposing forces of sunlight and shadow are equally matched, both proliferating lushly. Mana puts on her sunglasses. They seem ridiculously large on her broad face, reminding you of the compound eyes on flies. She has your arm in hers and leans crookedly against you, your shoulder pillowing her head. She seems to fall immediately asleep. Scenes on the street move across her sunglasses like a silent film. You notice the Malay driver's eyes constantly roving in the rearview mirror to take stock of you two. You shut your eyes and tilt your neck until your head gently meets hers. Like a canoe bumping into a pier.

You think that if you ever write fiction, this scene would surely appear in your work.

When you get off at the intersection, Mana is reluctant to walk with you; she seems anxious about something. She loosens her fingers and withdraws her hand from yours, then walks alone into the narrow alley from which she'd earlier emerged. At its mouth she twirls around and waves you away, wanting you to go your separate way. So you do, but then quickly retrace your steps and sneak back to the alley. You peer around the wall and watch as she walks right up to Mayflower's back entrance and opens the rundown iron door that has long rusted over. Through all your years at Mayflower, you've never seen anybody open that door, which is secured by an ancient-looking yet sturdy padlock. When you were young you wanted to open that door because you found the alley beyond full of mystery, as fantastic as the world within mirrors. Back then, you often imagined that a magical child lived in that alley. You told Mother this and she declared that you'd encountered the supernatural.

Uncle Sai said he'd misplaced the key because the door had been out of use for so long.

Mana opens the iron door that stands guard over Mayflower's abandoned backyard. Weeds and cogon grass squeeze out of cracks in the cement floor, which is littered with mushy pigeon shit. She has to open yet another iron door before she can enter the kitchen under Mayflower's stairs. That kitchen is another abandoned place. Though the tap above the sink is occasionally usable, the gas tanks under the stove are empty, and the kitchen god shrine has not seen incense in many years. From there a spiral staircase stretches upstairs—Mayflower's fire escape. The iron steps and handrails show signs of decay. Impossible to climb for the sex workers, overweight and weakened by age. It's usually utilized only by neighborhood cats to scale the heights. No wonder Mana has managed to evade the sleepy old doorman and the few old sex workers who sit under the big tree out front. She goes upstairs via the fire escape.

Back in Mayflower, you can't resist a detour to check out the kitchen and backyard. Now you see the two iron doors have new padlocks on them. That must have been Uncle Sai's idea. He lets Mana slip in and out of the back entrance so she can have her own exclusive passageway. He doesn't want anyone in Mayflower to see her; as suspected, he's hiding her, making her his very own secret.

At work that afternoon, you try to figure out what goes on between Mana and Uncle Sai. You know too little about them. The story has too many gaps, resulting in endless possibilities and turning the guessing game into a matter of pure fabrication. You make a bunch of mistakes on duty that day because your mind is somewhere else. Just before closing time, a coworker everyone calls Black Jack lights a tiny candle on a left-over piece of fried chicken breast, brings it to you, and starts to sing "Happy Birthday" at the top of his voice. A few other coworkers immediately join in the commotion. Unable to fend them off, you actually, earnestly make an impossible wish on a piece of fried chicken before blowing the candle out.

The ringleader, Black Jack, starts chatting with you while you eat the chicken. He says he saw you at noon. "That girl was a ten, stupefyingly beautiful." He emphasizes his words by slamming a fist on the prep counter, then follows it with a punch to your shoulder; he grinds his teeth, his expression full of both admiration and jealousy. Amused, you shake your head and laugh.

"That must have been a pricey cake too!" He raises his eyebrows. "In my head I cussed you out pretty savagely when I watched you hold such a pretty girl and blow out your candles with her. Ha, you rotten fella, lucky bastard."

You freeze and all your good humor dissipates. Immediately you realize you are not at all the person Black Jack chanced upon. It must have been J? It's true, then, that you two were born on the same day. You and him, living in the same city, one of you on the front stage, illuminated by a bright spotlight; the other backstage, among the city's moldy, sinister shadows. You both held close the girls you respectively treasure as you celebrated your joint birthday. You dislike this imagined scene with its displeasing facts. You're reminded of this one thought that bothered you constantly when you were little: a mirrored world branched off from your own reality. You stared at the background behind the boy in the mirror, daydreamed about some hidden button or handle, perhaps a secret password. Something that would make the child in the mirror open a door to admit you. There, within, would be everything you had ever lost without first possessing it.

It's midnight by the time your shift ends. Black Jack volunteers to take the birthday boy home on his motorcycle. As soon as you climb on the back seat, the bike dashes off along the empty streets like a wild horse throwing off its reins. Black Jack is clearly reluctant to head home. Going against your wishes, he insists on taking you around town. There have long been rumors spread by other KFC coworkers that he's gay. You're not concerned about this. It's just that you're thinking about Mana returning to Mayflower in the small hours. Will she tiptoe into your room? You don't want her to be greeted by a somewhat chilled and empty bed. You don't want to miss the warmth of her body.

Black Jack drives like he's playing Russian roulette. The city's streetscape is a field of silence at midnight on a weeknight. As if wanting to show off his new bike's features, he lets it scream to its content. If there's a bend in the road, he'll take it. Again and again he accelerates in the split second before a traffic light turns red, and occasionally he brakes so hard the bike squeals. If this were a weekend, his performance would surely have attracted a bunch of street racers, and he would have been egged on by young people screaming at the road-side. Perhaps such people were at that very moment crowding Black Jack's world. Otherwise he wouldn't be this excited. He arches his back high, as if the finish line is in sight.

You pat his shoulder at a traffic light that's about to flash red. I'll get off here, you say.

Instead of obeying you, Black Jack revs and runs through yet another red light. Only after the intersection is behind you does he slow down. The bike ceases its growling, restoring the city to its deserved quiet. Black Jack is still lost in his own world. He's tuned in to music only he can hear, something with a rhythm heavy on bass drums. Then he breaks out into song. It's "Isabella," a Malay pop tune that once took the country by storm. The song describes a love that traverses two worlds. During the verse his voice breaks as he bellows, Mengapa kita berjumpa, namun akhirnya terpisah. *Why did we meet, only to part in the end.* You ask Black Jack if he's been unlucky in love. He lets out big guffaws.

"Come on, I'll show you the real city." He starts talking rapidly, like an enthusiastic tour guide. He wants to take you to see "prostitutes who have totally lost their figures but still want to wear tight dresses," who stand around stairways smoking, bored. Once, he saw his own alcoholic father lying on the five-foot way of some shops, fast asleep.

"He was lying there with his limbs all spread out. I thought he was dead."

You don't say anything. You sense Black Jack is opening the gates to his world inch by inch, inviting you in. But that world holds no charm for you. It looks just like another dark place devoid of all light. You think about the memory of Mother once coming to blows with a drunk customer. She tried to kick his nuts and yanked on his hair with all her might, taking a fist to her face in the process. The bruise persisted for days. But in the end the man was kicked out. Uncle Sai and the sex workers who were not with customers came to help, everybody all fists and legs until the man was shoved out of Mayflower by the crook of his elbow. You climbed on a wooden bench beneath a window and peered downstairs. The man squatted by the roadside, vomiting, one hand massaging his chest.

"The variety here is of the exotic kind. Very high quality!" Black Jack turns into a side street next to a small retail plaza. A long row of three-story shophouses comes into view. All of the shops on the lower levels are closed, whereas the businesses upstairs begin only after dark. You've long heard that this is a well-known spot in the city where trans sex workers gather. You've seen them in the flesh too. They're clad in backless tops, miniskirts, and stiletto heels. Though their makeup is extremely sophisticated, their asking prices are the same as those charged by old sex workers in dark alleys who don't even bother to apply their lipstick properly. You once shared a cab with several trans sex workers. Surrounded in the back seat, you watched the driver put a palm on the thigh of the heavily made-up front seat passenger. It made you nauseous, as if a gecko were crawling up your windpipe.

Most of the trans sex workers in this city are from across the border up north. They form a rotating cast, switching out members every few months, like the merchants who used to go from port to port. They band together to make a living in places such as this row of shophouses, forming a display for customers to make their selections. Right now, several options are poised under the lamps lighting up each stairway. They are all on the skinny side, with narrow hips and slender legs, though their upper bodies are curvaceous. Another thing they have in common is thick makeup, eyeliners sketched so thick they look like a cross between Indian dancers and Chinese opera actors. Taken together, they form a colorful, vibrant picture.

Black Jack slows down and wolf whistles at the women, who can all effortlessly pass. He impudently runs his mouth with some off-color, teasing phrases, riling himself up so much he starts losing his grip. The front of the bike wobbles. This makes you dizzier than when he was speeding. It feels like your stomach has been shaken loose and is rattling around inside your body. Hey, let's go, you say. I want to go home. He detects a determination in your words. "Fine, all right, just one last stop so you can feast your eyes on something minty and refreshing!" He peels off, not waiting for your consent. Yanked forward by the momentum, you feel the earth tilt and the stars shift. An aftertaste of KFC Original Recipe gushes up from deep within your stomach.

"Look! The one there, wearing a long skirt!" Black Jack yells at the top of his lungs and lets out an aggressive, drawn-out whistle.

Gathered at the stairwell ahead are three younger-looking girls who are dressed less ostentatiously. One wears tight jeans, another a short skirt. The one in the Bohemian skirt has her back to you, a figure-hugging T-shirt making her look especially tall and slim. The three girls turn their heads when Black Jack whistles and you think, *I know her.* Even if you don't recognize the long skirt, nor the back, nor even that face, there's no way you can't identify the shoes on her feet. Those platform shoes are adorned by intricate white daisies, marks made for her with your very own hands.

You exchange a single glance with the girl in the long skirt. Black Jack revs and the bike lurches away into the interminable night, whizzing like an arrow leaving its bow. That one glance was too short for the girl to register any astonishment. But what expression does her face bear now? When you turn, all you can see are three slender figures in the stairwell; they grow smaller and smaller, ever blurrier.

Black Jack still seems to be telling you colorful tales about the sex workers. But the bike is howling something fierce, and the wind sharpens sound into blades that slice past. All you hear are his words cut to pieces. Maybe he's singing, his voice cracking as he loses himself in the song. *Oh her, Isabella, love lost and falling like dead leaves.*

Night air and night scenes jam into your mouth, nose, ears. You shake his shoulders forcefully. Stop! Stop! Black Jack brakes with urgency and his wheels screech piercingly against the road. You jump off, your dizziness making you feel like your legs are treading soft mattresses woven from empty dreams. It's like someone up high, beyond the skies, has picked up this world of yours and is shaking it in a bottle. Black Jack's face floats up in the air above you. What's wrong with you? he asks, face full of concern. You shake your head. Another wave of fried chicken spurts upward from your stomach. You burp, then throw up violently.

—3—

It was something that happened not long after Shaozi made her debut. That year, a group of high-profile foreign media and culture personalities launched the monthly *Federation of Literature* magazine to great fanfare. The inaugural issue included a short story titled "Butcher" that exhibited a unique style and daring (for the relatively puritanical times) content.

In the story, a young butcher named Shi Shuangxiu inherits the family business selling pork at the market. In middle age, after their wife's death, Shi starts appearing in public dressed as a woman. Their children break with them as a result. Shi continues to make a living selling pork, and moreover competes with their son and daughter-in-law who also set up shop vending meat nearby. For a time, the family is the talk of the market. Near the story's end, Shi Shuangxiu is diagnosed with late-stage breast cancer. Before their death, they have their portrait taken at a photo studio and express in writing that the portrait is to be used at their funeral. Furthermore, they explicitly instruct that they are to be laid to rest dressed as a woman. But after some discussion, their children and other family members decide to "maintain one last shred of dignity for Shi Shuangxiu," and so not only were Shi's wishes defied, the family also saw fit to create smoke and mirrors with a declaration that Shi Shuangxiu had passed away from testicular cancer (some others heard it was prostate cancer).

The above is just a rough sketch; the story itself is naturally much more intriguing. Apparently "Butcher" is a showcase of complex writing techniques. The writer liberally employs stream of consciousness layered atop frequent time jumps, and moreover depicts sex scenes with "a high degree of realism,"[1] demonstrating avant-garde sensibilities. All this was underscored not only by the story's appearance in the highly anticipated inaugural issue of *Federation of Literature* but also because the story was singled out for praise by the editor in chief. A wave of attention descended upon the story. To create hype (or due to miscalculation of market size, as some opined), the magazine's publisher pursued a strategy whereby the inaugural issue was given away more often than it was sold. Its print run far exceeded its sales figures, and about 70 percent of the issues were complimentary copies distributed to various cultural organizations, schools, and libraries in different countries. Some copies made their way first to the homes of regular households, then into the hands of recyclers and junk collectors. Because of this, "Butcher" was very widely distributed and left a lasting impact. Later, many scholars and critics offered it as a key example of a "pioneering work during the transformational period of local literature" in their articles.

Yet none of these were the main reason "Butcher" left such a deep impression. Everyone who read the story remembers the writer going by "Shi Shuangxiu," same as the main character. In an appendix, the editor clarifies that the writer did not include a personal bio with their manuscript. The editor further urged the writer to contact the editorial department as soon as possible with their address and contact information, so that accountants could release payment for the work. Alas, *Federation of Literature* ceased publication after

1. See "Editor's Note" from inaugural issue of *Federation of Literature*.

only two issues due to "internal problems," cementing its fame as the most short-lived major literary publication in history. It also turned *Federation of Literature*'s only two issues into rare treasures. According to follow-up reporting, the writer of "Butcher" never made contact again with the magazine, and no one has since come forward to claim authorship of the story. The real identity of Shi Shuangxiu remains an unsolved mystery.

After both Shaozi's and The Fourth Person's deaths, some people drew a connection between Shaozi's colorful life and the unclaimed "Butcher." Because she was such a legendary eccentric, they very naturally and unanimously believed she could very well be Shi Shuangxiu, despite there not being any plausible explanation or proof. When these theories reached the ears of her friends and family, they came forward with an anecdote. Growing up, Shaozi lived in a new village settlement, where there was a large family whose only son loved playing dress-up with his sisters. Later in life he married and had kids with his wife, and it wasn't until his middle age that his children discovered his stash of female outfits and shoes, hidden alongside a box of feminine perfume and makeup. After the discovery his family spurned him. Backed into a corner, he abandoned all caution and started facing the world dressed as a woman. His thick lips, painted chili-red, and his high heels "long as coffin nails" became a legend in the village.

They said that Sister Li was on good terms with this cross-dressing person. They often shared drinks and meals.

Going by The Fourth Person's research, Shaozi has a penchant for writing characters that go through existential predicaments caused by huge contradictions between their internal and external selves.[2] The female writer in "Only Because the Durian Blossomed" who "waits to be beamed up by a spaceship" is one example (the main character of *The Lefty Who Lost Her Right Brain* apparently being another). There are also secondary characters who display characteristics of "multiple personality disorder" to greater or lesser degrees, such as the old medium in "Weedflower" who "isn't sure whose soul is housed within her body," the digital Romeo in "Last Words from Last Night," and the ER doctor in "Snail" who makes the hospital their permanent residence because they suspect themselves susceptible to genetic onset cardiac arrest. The Fourth Person also opines that the pair of twin brothers who appear later in *The Age of Goodbyes* is yet another representation of split personality disorder.[3]

The Fourth Person points out that the twin brothers are a further projection of self on the author's part. From "two selves, one body" to "separation of cells," and via "waving the old self goodbye" through "the final split in the womb," it is clear that the author's own personality disorder grew worse by the day. Through it all, Shaozi's wish for a clean break from her original self, Du Li An, is startlingly clear.[4]

The Fourth Person had expended much effort poring over critical works in psychology. He consulted the 1980 version of the *DSM* and landed on its definition of multiple personality disorder, namely "the existence of two or more distinct personalities within the individual,

2. See "Multiple Personality Disorder—An Analysis of Shaozi's *The Age of Goodbyes.*"

3. See "Multiple Personality Disorder—An Analysis of Shaozi's *The Age of Goodbyes.*"

4. See "Multiple Personality Disorder—An Analysis of Shaozi's *The Age of Goodbyes.*" In the original text, the "original self," Du Li An, is clarified to be "(Du Li An = 'Ah Li' + 'Sister Li')."

with each personality assuming executive control at specific times. These personalities are independent of each other and respectively exist as autonomous, complete selves."

Under this definition, Shaozi and Sister Li, whose paths never cross, fit beautifully into the model. In "Victim of Multiple Personality Disorder," The Fourth Person classifies "the vendor Du Li An who sells underwear at the night market" as the "main identity," and "the author Shaozi" as a result of the former's fragmentation. He even boldly theorizes that Du Li An/Shaozi's sudden death could very well have arisen from "mutual hatred and sabotage" between the main and fragmented identities, or some strong will in them to destroy each other. In short, a kind of "subconscious suicidal behavior."

His research indicates that Shaozi/Du Li An was indisputably a classic case of multiple personality disorder. His work in literary analysis was further enriched by the colorful legends surrounding both Shaozi and Du Li An (due to the names they made for themselves in, respectively, the literary world and the seedy underground), not to mention the clues and "evidence" provided by Shaozi's writing. All of this, compelling enough on its own, is married with his "novelistic writing style that combines facts with fiction"[5] to make for highly readable work.

The Fourth Person probably never expected that the culmination of his life's work would later bring on similar suspicions concerning him. Because there remains

---

5. Excerpted from "A Crucible of Creativity and Analysis—On the Artistic Techniques of *Always by Your Side*," presented in 2010 at the Southeast Asian Literary Analysis Conference by a graduate student in Chinese literature.

doubt as to the authorship of *The Age of Goodbyes*, quite a few people believe that this so-called posthumous work by Shaozi could very well have been a monologue acted out by The Fourth Person from start to finish. Although this suspicion was never verified, it is difficult to write off. Therefore, "The Fourth Person as yet another victim of dissociative identity disorder" was a new angle pursued by psychologists and psychiatrists.[6]

If *The Age of Goodbyes* was indeed written, produced, and controlled by The Fourth Person, then his psychological symptoms and mental states surely go beyond the garden-variety multiple personality disorder. Many medical professionals believe that his case demonstrates extremities of love and hate, plus overlapping personality changes that contradict each other. They do not rule out delusional disorder and a desperate wish to "let Shaozi live on." "Was this wish built upon conscious admission, or repressed in subconscious? This is the key to determining whether The Fourth Person is a victim of multiple personality disorder."[7]

6. This issue was first raised by Japanese psychologists on a website advertising a "Club for Discussion of Detective Novels, Religion, and Psychology." There was broad discussion among local psychology researchers and detective novel enthusiasts.

7. Translated excerpt from local Malay psychologist J. Aminah's article "The Fourth Personality."

CHAPTER TEN

—1—

Eighty tables had been booked at Chin Woo Hall for Elder Zong's eightieth birthday. The festivities would start at 8 p.m. sharp. Invites were sent to Ping Le House, addressed to Steely Bo's legal name, Mr. Lau Siu Bo, and Ms. Du Li An. She looked at the unfamiliar handwriting on the peach-red envelope, the black words written in pen with such force it embossed the flip side. Emotions welled in her. She stood at the counter, distracted for an entire afternoon. She couldn't have explained what she felt. It was only that she'd suddenly realized the transience of glory. It alarmed her, and it also made her fiercely miss the octogenarian, a sentiment that was mixed with gratitude. He'd been at Sou Gei's funeral. In the funeral hall, he said to Du Li An in front of all those triad boys, Ah Li, it must have been hard. She was incredibly moved. Even if she had to suffer more exhaustion and more injustice, his words seemed to make it all worthwhile.

By then she'd learned how to hide her emotions, but she was certain that Elder Zong could detect her pleasure at his words. After all, the old man had seen it all. They said that the longer a person lives, the shrewder they become, just like a ghost grows its power as it lingers.

When the invite was put in Steely Bo's hands, she knew he was more shaken than anybody else, though he showed no external signs of it. She dispassionately observed him as he pored over the invite repeatedly as if trying to crack some hidden code. Afterward he couldn't sit still. First, he said it was too hot, then he complained about mosquitoes, his attention completely diverted from the TV even though it was playing *The Legend of the General Who Never Was*, a drama series he'd been closely following because it featured his favorite actor, Alex Man Tze Leung. You keep the invite, she said. Steely Bo nodded, then claimed to be sleepy and went upstairs to bed. But later, when the VCR ate the tape while she was watching *Hong Kong Nocturne* with Lau Lin, he came back downstairs and announced he was going out for cigarettes.

Du Li An had not seen him smoke even once since his hospital stay two years ago. She exchanged a glance with Lau Lin. Neither questioned him. The odd thing was, he returned home with two boxes of mosquito coil. Didn't you say you were going to get cigarettes? Du Li An asked. He looked down at the insect repellant in his hands, seemingly a little astonished himself.

"It's all the same," he said. "I just wanted to create some smoke to drive away mosquitoes."

Du Li An and Lau Lin couldn't help but exchange another look.

After two episodes of *Hong Kong Nocturne*, the women took the stairs up two at a time. They saw the light spilling from under Steely Bo's door.

As the saying went, rare was the person who lived to enjoy the ripe age of seventy. It was rumored that no expenses had been spared for Elder Zong's eightieth, which meant the birthday gift was a serious matter not to be taken lightly. Du Li An assigned the task to

Steely Bo, who did not refuse, freeing her up to spend all her thoughts on what to wear. At the hair salon she frequented, she sat under the perming machine's glass dome and flipped through magazines until they became tattered. She even tore out a few color pages. On a weekend afternoon, she made Lau Lin accompany her across the bridge to the Old Street market, where they browsed several large fabric shops. By that time Lau Lin's sewing skills were nothing to scoff at. Right before New Year, Du Li An had bought her a Singer sewing machine, saying, Now wouldn't it be much more convenient, making clothes for your ma? Lau Lin gave the machine's leather wheel a gentle spin. A smooth clacking sound rang out, even though the needle wasn't yet in place. She covered her nose and mouth with one hand and blinked twice, summoning a thin film of tears over her eyes.

Du Li An took up Lau Lin's other hand and patted it. How long and slender it was, this hand of hers. "All these years you've helped me with countless chores around the house. Auntie Li never forgot."

By then Lau Lin was twenty-eight, no longer that weak, skinny teenage girl tailing close behind Candle-nut. She was plain and self-disciplined, and content to be so. Every day she rose early to sweep the floors, do the dishes, and take care of the ancestor altars. Then she took to the tables, cabinets, and windowsills with a feather duster, and after that she rushed to work clutching bean paste– or coconut-filled buns prepared the night before. Same routine every day, except when she visited her childhood home, and even then she surely helped her old mother with housework. When Du Li An examined Lau Lin's hand in hers, she noted the markings of time, the dry skin that resembled green onions laid out too long under the sun.

It was clear Yip Mong Sang now seldom took Lau Lin to the movies, as he was occupied with endless business pursuits. Yet her sights remained single-mindedly pinned on him, leaving room for no one else. When they didn't go on dates, she either binge-watched long-running drama series on the VCR, or else turned to sewing, her only hobby.

Undoubtedly she knew all there was to know about making clothes. Du Li An picked out a few patterns from books and turned to Lau Lin for her opinion, even invited her to shop for fabric together at the Old Street market. Lau Lin especially loved browsing fabric shops. At the time, Kwong Fatt Department Store was a good place to visit; the fabric shop downstairs had an especially comprehensive inventory, though its prices were on the high side. Lau Lin often went into the store just to feel the high-end fabric between her hands, but because the ghostly presence of slightly hostile store employees always lurked right behind her, she was thoroughly uncomfortable and never stayed long.

On this particular visit, several bolts of quality fabric caught Du Li An's eye at the Kwong Fatt shop. One was brocade, one had flowers fashioned out of lace, and one featured large peonies with green leaves straight out of a traditional Chinese painting. Lau Lin, on the other hand, bought some fabric scraps that were decent though cheap. She pounced as if stumbling upon rare treasure, declaring there was just enough to make a blouse for her second-eldest brother's daughter.

They headed back, weighed down with their purchases. Back home, Du Li An shoved a bundle of sparkling, ocean-blue woven silk fabric toward Lau Lin. "Don't always just think about sewing clothes for others. Here's three and a half yards, enough for you to make yourself a skirt."

It was a top-quality piece of fabric, soft and breezy, the texture of wispy clouds when held. Lau Lin knew quite well she should reject the gift, but in her heart of hearts she simply couldn't bear to, and so she stood frozen, unsure what to do. Du Li An suppressed her snickers. Earlier she'd observed how Lau Lin handled this piece of cloth at Kwong Fatt, pinching and caressing it with two fingers, putting it down only to pick it up again after another stroll around the store, indecisive. Du Li An shoved her lightly. "Auntie Li's going to have someone sew my clothes, but I was hoping you'd help with any alterations after that. This piece right here counts as your compensation, so don't you be picky or polite with me now!"

Lau Lin had no defenses against Du Li An's craftiness, especially when that artfulness was wrapped around a core of genuine, caring sentiment. Du Li An sent her chosen fabric to Yoke Giu Tailors. Perhaps because it was a rushed job, she ended up having quite a few bones to pick with each finished dress. Luckily, Lau Lin willingly skipped her drama series and stayed up nights to work on alterations, managing in the end to finish several outfits before Elder Zong's birthday celebration. She even washed and ironed them before hanging them up in Du Li An's room.

Du Li An particularly favored the peony-patterned cheongsam, which Lau Lin had modified by replacing the cloth buttons sewn on by Yoke Giu with true lover's knots she made out of the original fabric. The knots showcased impeccable handiwork and were seamlessly sewn on, elevating the dress to new heights of luxury. Du Li An put it on and felt elegant and curvaceous, like a mermaid. When she couldn't help but bring up the topic of her new clothes at Ping Le House, she was a fountain of praises for Lau Lin.

Guen Hou inferred from this that Du Li An and Lau Lin had grown close, which pricked her heart and made sour grapes of the words coming out her mouth. To Guen Hou, shopping for fabric together was a bonding activity between sisterly friends, and yet Du Li An had never once brought up the matter of making new clothes with her. Probably Du Li An thought little of Guen Hou's style sense and assumed she wouldn't be able to offer any suggestions. "Why are you telling me all this? It's over my head. How many good outfits have I ever touched in my entire life, after all?" She pouted and marched to the kitchen. For the rest of the day her face bore a chilly expression, and she barely interacted with anybody.

Du Li An noticed Guen Hou's old jealousy flaring, but she had no time to deal with it, and furthermore she wasn't in the mood. Guen Hou wasn't too far off the mark either; she really didn't know much about fashion. The outfits she wore to banquets were mostly outdated hand-me-downs from Du Li An. Often they were so ill-fitting that Lau Lin altered them as favors. A couple of them remained unsuitable even after alterations, but Guen Hou refused to have them worked on further. Instead, she folded them and planted them deep in her wardrobe, claiming she was saving them for Eggplant Face.

At sixteen, Eggplant Face was slowly growing into a tomboy. No one had ever seen her in a skirt or dress outside of her school uniform. That year she was due for her PMR exams, but even though she had been a precocious child, her grades had been mediocre since secondary school. She was especially lazy when it came to homework, reading only what suited her fancy. Guen Hou said the girl often made excuses to skip class or even miss school entirely in favor of messing around at the roller skating rink with some good-for-nothings. At night, she hid under the covers and read novels until the sun came up. Her teachers couldn't keep her in check, and neither could Guen Hou, who felt her hold slipping by the day. This daughter of hers was almost ready to leave the nest. Even when the Sister Lin she once adored stepped up to offer gentle words of reproach, the girl laughed it off, not at all stung.

Guen Hou had counted on Eggplant Face to provide her with an easier life after retirement. But in the past few years, she felt like she was watching her daughter grow from a good sapling into something crooked. Guen Hou became anxious and increasingly restless. The only bright spot in her life was the Teochew widower who'd started renting a stall last year to sell popiah at Ping Le House. He was attentive to her, and during the day they regularly traded pleasantries. It seemed they were sweet on each other. She felt that he was overall acceptable, with no undesirable habits other than a love of cigarettes and a weekly lotto habit. She knew full well that at forty-plus, a connection like this might be the very last of its kind. Du Li An encouraged Guen Hou to be bold and open. Even the best daughters end up marrying, Du Li An said. Better to find a stable partner for your golden days.

Ping Le House being the size it was, the other workers of course took notice of the push and pull between the Teochew widower and Guen Hou. No time was lost turning them into a topic of conversation. The employees caused a ruckus and seized every opportunity to tease. They asked the widower why Guen Hou's orders of popiah always had extra filling, and joked that his spring rolls surely added a spring not just in the customers' steps, etc., which embarrassed Guen Hou to no end. Behind her back, the gossipmongers made eyes at each other and cruelly joked that the Twenty-Four Filial Exemplars' chastity paifang was about to be toppled; from then on her new nickname should be "the old coquette."

As the boss, Du Li An obviously had to stay out of such matters. Even so, she could not resist reminding Ms. Potty Mouth to tamp it down. Ms. Potty Mouth sold laksa and was often the instigator, first to spread gossip and sow discord. She was amply assisted by the two women who sold wantan mee and rojak, respectively. Du Li An restricted herself to sharing a tidbit with Lau Lin. The widower had four intact limbs and didn't shy away from hard work, Du Li An said. "If she waits any longer she's gonna hit menopause, and who will want her then?"

Seeing as both parties were showing interest, Du Li An thought it was a done deal. How could she foresee that Guen Hou would be hot and cold toward him? Her old bad habits took over, fueling her paranoia and suspicions, making her behavior intolerable. The Teochew widower, having been single half his life, had no experience with this particular tango. In the face of her on-again, off-again treatment, he was as clueless as a mouse trying to drag a turtle. His original outpour of hopeful passion burned out after a few rounds of cold shoulders and harsh words. In no time at all his fire smoldered to ashes. First he grew distant toward Guen Hou, and then he swiftly found a new target: a girl who had a sweet demeanor but did not seem very bright.

Only seventeen, she'd been hired to help out at the chee cheong fun stall. She was said to have come late in her mother's life, and from a young age she exhibited signs of developmental delays. Unfortunately, her mother passed away from illness not long after the girl was born. Her father was over eighty and long past his prime; he practically already had one foot in his coffin. A cousin from her mother's side took pity on her and got her work at the chee cheong fun stall. That stall had moved to Ping Le House half a year ago. From the start, the girl seemed shy and reticent, and so was usually ignored by everybody. But now that the widower had transferred his affections, all eyes were on her. Not only did he give her popiah with extra filling, he also brought her fried spring rolls made at home from a special recipe.

This drove Guen Hou up the wall. The widower was no longer receptive to her moves. He put aside the Wuyi tea she brought him, left it untouched all the way through closing time. The wagging tongues in the kopi-tiam went to work, claiming the old coquette was after all a wilted flower that could not compete with a fresh, dewy spring bulb. Du Li An knew Guen Hou suffered, even though she was too proud to pour her heart out. Therefore Du Li An wrote off Guen Hou's increasing irascibility as part of her mood swings.

Until things came to a head on the morning of Elder Zong's birthday. Like a volcano, Guen Hou abruptly erupted and started howling at the chee cheong fun girl, accusing her of intentionally knocking over a tray she had been holding. "You're evil to the core! You did it on purpose! Don't you play dumb!"

The girl was timid and clumsy with words to begin with, and she'd never seen Guen Hou bare her fangs. She was shocked, frozen on the spot, her head hung low, her eyes fixed on the coffee cup smashed against the floor. But her silence only emboldened Guen Hou, whose tongue-lashing grew crueler and crueler until its target included the girl's octogenarian father. The girl's employer, a wizened old lady, was so short of breath she couldn't get a word in edgewise. When the widower rushed in to defuse the situation, it was like pouring oil on water. He was promptly dragged into Guen Hou's "conspiracies" and received a thorough cussing-out.

There weren't many customers at the time, and those who did stay around were regulars. Du Li An assumed Guen Hou's rage would dissipate after a brief tantrum, and so pretended to be busy while she observed the situation from a safe distance at the counter. She hadn't expected Guen Hou's tirade to behave like athlete's foot, which itched the more it was scratched and swiftly became uncontrollable. The Guen Hou she knew was narrow-minded yet did not lack in self-control. That Guen Hou might toss off a few snide remarks here and there, but she would never descend to such barbarity. Meanwhile, the Teochew widower was not slow-witted, and moreover, as the saying goes, a cornered dog will leap over walls! At first, he'd meant to be the bigger person. Perhaps worried that Guen Hou would continue on her trajectory of escalation and become physical, he stepped forward and reached for the girl, pulling her so that she was shielded behind him. Though it was a slight movement, Guen Hou experienced it as a stake hammered into the very core of her heart.

For a split second, Du Li An thought she could hear Guen Hou's teeth grinding all the way from the counter. Then came the unrestrained string of filthy insults. "Animals!" Guen Hou screamed. "You'll protect her, will you? Go ahead and protect this dimwit! She's fresh all right, warm and fragrant down there! If you protect her, she'll let you touch, let you claw, let you fuck!"

Du Li An was up on her feet in an instant, but she was too late. The widower slapped Guen Hou across the face. "Crazy bitch!" He roared, his voice shaking the ceilings and floors.

By the time Du Li An hurried over, the widower still

stood in front of the girl, his right palm raised high, ready to give Guen Hou another taste. She stood rooted to the spot, her left cheek a field of red. Then she took in the surrounding rubberneckers, her gaze alighting briefly on Du Li An's face before training on the widower's. The tip of Guen Hou's nose tremored. Suddenly she howled hysterically, "You can all go to hell!" She shrieked as she launched herself forward, maybe to land blows on the widower, or the girl behind him. Either way, she was thwarted by the multilimbed crowd reaching out to block her.

At this hour, there were quite a few curious pedestrians peeping in from outside the kopitiam, as well as some customers who were hesitating, wondering whether to walk in. Du Li An knew that if she didn't put a stop to it now, it would soon become a runaway disaster. She grabbed Guen Hou's arm that pointed at the widower and with all of her strength, cranked it down as if working a wrench. "That's enough, Sister Guen Hou. Ping Le House is still a place of business, all right?" She pierced Guen Hou with a stare, eyes fixed on that face flat as a book for several long seconds. Slowly, Guen Hou's expression shriveled, her features crumpled and twisted like plastic dropped into fire. She seemed to be crying, yet there were no tears. Squeezing Du Li An's hand tight, Guen Hou began to sob drily.

Du Li An had seen Guen Hou shed tears before, but this arid wailing was new. "You must be tired. Go on, go rest up at home." Du Li An pulled Guen Hou through the crowd and led her to the kitchen in the back.

"You must have lost your mind!" Du Li An gave Guen Hou's palm a hard pinch. "Causing such a scene! If we lose some business, it'll only be a concern for this one afternoon. But whether you can live with yourself, that's something you'll carry for the rest of your life!"

Hearing these words, Guen Hou's expression bunched up again. Finally, two large teardrops squeezed out of her eye sockets, like ripened fruit falling to the ground, and rolled from the corner of her eyes to her chin. She sniffled, her cries no longer as parched as before. "Even you won't take my side! Ah Li, you're not on my side!" Broken, hoarse screeches squeezed through Guen Hou's tightly gritted teeth. She thumped her own chest with all her might. From the loud drumming coming from that flat chest, Du Li An could tell that Guen Hou was not holding back at all. Hastily she caught the pair of beating hands, clucking her tongue.

"Are you crazy? You think you're punishing someone else, but really you're only making things hard on yourself." She patted the backs of her hands. "Sister Guen Hou, would I really not be on your side? Am I not helping you right this moment? How many years have we known each other? Tell me."

This line of questioning shut Guen Hou up. She took store silently. Indeed, they went way back, to the time Du Li An sat in that cinema ticket counter that looked just like a pigeon cage, while Guen Hou herself sold sweets and snacks near the entrance. Back then Chan Kam Hoi often flirted with her under the pretext of buying chewing gum or packaged drinks. Who knew that she would eventually have his daughter. And wasn't that daughter now a woman in her own right? Guen Hou and Du Li An had been like sisters for almost two decades.

Under the influence of nostalgia, Guen Hou's wrinkled forehead and knitted brows slowly smoothed. Now her tears came in a torrent, as if those eyebrows were valves unleashing snot and tears across her whole face. "Ah Li, you have to help me! You must!" This bout of crying, too, was like an attack of athlete's foot. Guen

Hou abandoned all decorum and cried with everything she had, two hands rending her own clothes.

Du Li An grabbed a roll of toilet paper and tore off a huge handful for Guen Hou. "Go home for now. Don't come back until a few days have passed."

On her way back Guen Hou's eyes were red and swollen. Her head felt like lead and she staggered, dizzy, spent from wailing hysterically for the larger part of an hour. To avoid running into others, she'd left through the back door. She had not said bye to Du Li An, who sat at her counter discreetly observing Ms. Potty Mouth and the other busybodies. All afternoon they were in high spirits, huddling together to whisper and bark out the occasional loud laughter. The Teochew widower continued his workday with a stony face. The girl, on the other hand, seemed completely unaffected. When business was slow she pulled over a chair and sat at her stall with her head lowered, fidgeting with her fingernails as usual. Her mother's cousin, the old woman running the stall, spoke a few words to her now and then. Several times the aunt went over to the widower too, the two of them speaking in low voices.

Meanwhile, the busybodies gave him the side-eye, their eyebrows dancing and their tongues wagging. Du Li An watched Guen Hou disappear through the back door. In her wake, the veteran in charge of making drinks leaned in to his helper and the two began whispering. Du Li An sighed. Guen Hou should not have left with her tail between her legs that way. Now how could she ever walk back in with her head held high?

—

Steely Bo put on the outfit Du Li An had prepared for him to wear for the banquet that evening. Dressed in a

Western shirt and pants accessorized with a new leather belt, he couldn't get used to how neat and put-together he looked. As for her, she'd permed her hair into rolling waves and draped herself in gold and jade to complement the peony dress, as befitting a rich, sophisticated lady. Even Lau Lin, normally so reserved, stared with protruding eyes and complimented the look. Though Du Li An was not concerned about being dubbed the beauty to Steely Bo's beast, she refused to step foot in his old clunky car no matter what. So he drove them in hers, bringing with him a work of embroidery depicting longevity, as well as a Buddha statuette made of jade. There was an anxiety about him when they left the house.

During the short drive, she intermittently chatted on about Ping Le House and Guen Hou. But he clearly was not listening. Instead he fiddled with the radio, turning it on and off. He cranked down the windows, then he changed his mind and wanted the AC on instead. She watched beads of sweat appear on his forehead and observed the trail descending from his crown to his spine. Taking out a few tissues, she wiped the sweat clinging onto the back of his neck.

"You've seen some things in your time. Why so nervous?"

He muttered an acknowledgment. Her hand was so unusually gentle it made him uneasy. He felt his neck tense up, as if she were holding a shaving knife instead of tissues. Thanks, he said. The word came out stiff as rocks. Hearing it, she experienced the full distance between them. How far they had drifted apart. She pretended not to hear him. Winding down her window to toss out the tissues, she said as if to change the topic, "Time really flies. Elder Zong is eighty now."

They'd gone all out for the birthday festivities. The

banquet hall was newly renovated and still carried a whiff of fresh paint. A pair of calligraphic couplets celebrating longevity graced the stage, one on each side. The left read, "See crane and deer eternal as springtime; spot pine and cypress forever lush green. Ages undulate like flowing water; good fortune and long life combined bring joy." Correspondingly, on the right, "Longevity grows with heaven's cycles; wealth piles up as good luck floods the earth. Happiness greets this eightieth birthday fete; the setting sun paints this cheery hall red." The gold letters shimmering on red paper were written in flashy, broad strokes that gave the couplet a grandiose air. Elder Zong's son and daughter-in-law were stationed to greet guests at the entrance, both of them seasoned players of the underground world. When they saw Steely Bo, they naturally remained welcoming and courteous, their handshakes firm, and their smiles carved deeply into their faces.

Yet their hospitality could not dispel Steely Bo's fearfulness. As soon as he saw someone from the Zong family he tensed up, his neck shrunk into his collar, his expression froze. Even his walk became unnatural, and he looked as if he'd become noticeably shorter. Du Li An slipped her arm into the crook of his elbow and, half holding him up and half forcing him along, led him around the room to greet various other Zong family members. Once they entered the hall proper she propelled them straight to the head table and delivered him right up to the elderly figure.

There sat Elder Zong, surrounded by several guests, everyone eager to ask after him and convey their wishes. The old man looked well, as he'd received the best care after his stroke. On top of that, he had much fewer worries since he'd handed over the keys to the Toa Pek Kong Society. Day after day of being fed tonics and herbal supplements had given him a glowing face and an aura of wellness. Although his mouth remained crooked, which was a pity, his hair shone silvery bright and his eyes were unclouded. When his gaze landed on Steely Bo and Du Li An, he shouted, Oho! Ah Bo, Ah Li, you came!

Hearing such a warm greeting, Steely Bo felt a surge of heat in his chest. He couldn't help but be moved. Walking forward, he bowed at the waist to grab Elder Zong's hand. The elder exchanged pleasantries with him and asked after the fishing village. Because Elder Zong's crooked mouth made his speech somewhat unintelligible, Steely Bo had to bend his knees and lean forward until their two heads almost touched. Watching the exchange, Du Li An felt a wave of pitiful sorrow. The tip of her nose soured. She'd seen them go over plans and strategies like this many times in the past, except now they were both white-haired seniors. Steely Bo looked especially decrepit with his wilted, beaten-down countenance. From a glance the two men seemed to be from the same generation. Ah, in the end it'd been an intimate relationship lasting several decades after all.

Since Elder Zong and Steely Bo were godfather and godson by name, he and Du Li An were arranged to be seated near the head table. With them were two distant Zong relatives and a few long-retired mafia brothers, plus their families. The stylish, dolled-up Du Li An stood out like a sore thumb at that table full of the old and washed-up. The men had no shortage of conversation among themselves, while the few unfashionable old ladies clung together like birds of a feather. After greeting Du Li An with polite nods, they quickly tossed her aside to cheerily chat about their grandchildren and shopping trips to Thailand. Du Li An put on a vague, soft smile and pointed her face in the direction of the old ladies, whose chatter grew increasingly disjointed. But her attention went around them, curving toward the guests all about her with great curiosity, landing every so often on the various people just coming in through the door.

Among the guests that night were many notable businesspeople. She also recognized quite a few politicians of no small importance from their newspaper and TV appearances. When Zong family members approached them, she caught glimpses of the sparkling jade and diamonds adorning their hands and heard their booming laughter ring out. She had a sensation of being in a lavish movie scene peopled by impeccably dressed and groomed actors who, though they looked familiar, led lives that had nothing whatsoever to do with the audience. She remembered how she had loved sneaking into shows at Old Majestic cinema. She'd wait until the lights were dimmed before slipping into an empty seat. Guen Hou had watched many free movies this way with her as well, except Guen Hou preferred period fare with Huangmei-style opera, while Du Li An's absolute favorites were contemporary Cantonese drama. Guen Hou had crushes on actors of bitter tragedies like Zhao Lei and Betty Loh Ti; Du Li An had eyes only for Nicholas Tse and Lui Kay.

At that time, Nicholas Tse had a classic hero look, in contrast to Lui Kay, whose thin brows and narrow forehead gave him a faintly devilish air. Occasionally close-ups of them appeared on the silver screen, their handsome faces humongous in the camera lens' scrutiny. Du Li An's face would flush and her heart pound. She'd felt exposed in the giant black box that was the cinema, the two men unrelentingly staring her down.

Having opened memory's black box, she nearly missed a face she never wanted to misplace amid the people swarming into the banquet hall. She'd caught only a quick glimpse out of the corner of her eye—an unremarkably dressed party of people who looked like experienced teachers or white-collar peons working in the same office building. She almost didn't realize she'd seen him, that tall, lanky man now being greeted by the Zong family's second-eldest. Her gaze swept around him to evaluate the two women following behind. Only then did her brain light up in recognition. He was right there! This figure, this face, this person!

She gathered her wits and sought him again in the crowd. He'd turned and walked with his companions to the right of the entrance, where the guests who were not close to the Zongs were seated. She managed to catch only his profile as he weaved between the tables and chairs that were rapidly filling up. But the profile was enough to confirm that it was him, and not Yip Mong Sang.

It's you. It's you.

Throughout the rest of the evening, she glanced surreptitiously at his corner again and again. He sat with his back facing her, yet his faraway figure seemed to crystallize just a bit more with each look. On either side of him were the two women who'd walked in with him. He often turned his face to chat and joke with the one to his right. Once, he bent down to pick up the chopsticks she'd dropped on the floor and summoned a waiter to get her a new pair. Because of this attentiveness, Du Li An couldn't help but also scrutinize that woman. She was average and moderate in both build and looks. With her inoffensive short bob, she could be considered cute in a pinch.

Du Li An realized that the woman's eyes kept locking onto him. But so it was for Du Li An herself. Now she saw clearly that he and his older brother Mong Sang were not as similar as she'd thought in the past. They were two different people, after all. While she'd been separated from him for over a decade, the years she'd spent with Mong Sang had given her a false sense that they more or less still resembled each other. She'd long thought the two brothers were of the same height and moreover possessed extremely similar facial features and smiles, yet reality contradicted this. Time had developed them into different people over the last ten-plus years. This person she was looking at was skinnier and darker than Mong Sang, brighter, with a more sincere smile. Where Yip Mong Sang was careless and indifferent, a city person whose entire being exuded privilege, this other man had a neat, bookish aura and a woodsy touch of the provincial.

She had heard more from Yip Mong Sang about what had gone down between the brothers. He casually brought up the topic from time to time, and she'd feigned nonchalance as she listened. They were a pair of twin brothers no closer to each other than distant relatives. Their father was a communist who had fought Japanese imperialism. He went deep into the jungles to take part in guerilla warfare, before the brothers were even born. Mong Sang said he never once saw his father, but Lin Sang had clear memories of the man sneaking into their home one night. Their mother had shaken awake the twin brothers and their two sisters from deep sleep one by one, so that they could meet their father. Lin Sang remembered the man picking him and Mong Sang up, cradling them one under each armpit. Because they were afraid and reluctant to leave the warm safety of their dreams, the two boys wailed in unison.

This must have been before they turned five. By the time Mong Sang was five, he'd already been left with an uncle to be raised. With a son and a daughter already in his home, the uncle wanted to avoid complications, and so had Mong Sang also call him "dad" while referring to his birth mother as "auntie." The uncle also thought it wise to maintain a careful distance from Lin Sang, who remained in his original home, though some aid was occasionally sent to tide them over. From that day on the brothers grew up apart; they lived in different villages within the same township, attended different schools. They met only briefly twice a year, during Chinese New Year and over the graves of their ancestors on Tomb Sweeping Day.

And so a sense of strangeness began to build up between them. Their resemblance to each other made them both afraid. "I always felt peculiar when I saw him as a kid. It was like seeing another me, one that I didn't really like." That was how Mong Sang put it, then he planted a kiss on Du Li An's forehead. Her head was nestled on his arm. Smiling faintly, she looked at the mirror hanging in the motel room. How many people had been reflected in this glass? She recalled what Lin Sang said long ago: "Seeing him was like seeing a person who'd escaped from a mirror."

The adults, as if fearful the two boys would forget they were once two peas in a pod, often clad them in identical outfits during the annual New Year gatherings. This only made the two children feel even more unnatural and creeped out. No matter how the adults "matchmade" them, they hated playing with or even sitting next to each other. They'd instead clasp their own cups of Sarsi and eat their kuih bangkit or achu murukku from safe distances, all the while eying the other person warily. It was not until they became teenagers that they ceased finding each other novel. Although it remained difficult for friends and family to tell them apart, they understood very clearly that a huge difference existed between them.

"Even when we were dressed in the same clothes, I no longer had the sense that this person resembled me." Mong Sang caressed her hair from behind, slipping his fingers into her dark waves.

In Lin Sang's memory, the uncle did much better financially compared to their mother. "My brother had a silver tongue, and so my uncle and aunt spoiled him with treats and toys."

They were by a man-made lake in a park, Du Li An and Lin Sang. She watched him throw a pebble into the water, rippling and blurring the view reflected on the lake's surface. "He wasn't like me. My ma always said I was wooden, even as a kid." He turned to face her, exposing a mouth full of good teeth. She thought he was about to kiss her, but all he did was place a palm over her hand. She spread her fingers to let his slip in smoothly, like a key gliding into its lock.

It wasn't until later, when she reminisced about this scene, that she realized the meaning hidden behind his movements. *Though I lacked treats and toys, what I have is you.* That's what he was saying. But at the time she was laser-focused on savoring every bit of physical intimacy between them. She still thought he would kiss her. He didn't.

"Wooden indeed!" She sighed.

By the time he was in secondary school, Mong Sang had moved out of town with his stepparents, and the two boys no longer had regular opportunities to meet. He remembered a morning at the humble train station in their small town. His mother had brought Lin Sang and his two sisters to send him off. Despite his protests, she shoved a bag of star fruit and guava into his hands. They'd been plucked from her own little orchard. In his heart of hearts, said Mong Sang, the dark-skinned auntie with calluses all over her hands actually did feel just like some relative they seldom visited.

Quite a few people had come. His sisters were relatively friendly, but his younger brother stood silently at the periphery of the crowd. After Mong Sang boarded, he looked out at the throng from his window. Everyone was waving at the people onboard, and those in the carriages raised their hands in response. He discovered his brother was the only one with his arms and hands down in the crowd. Even toddlers carried in the arms of adults were coaxed into shyly batting their little hands about, but there his brother stood, hands clasped behind his back, head raised, looking somewhat arrogant, like a prefect patrolling school grounds.

Of course Mong Sang waved. His waving had no specific target beyond the little town, to which he was saying goodbye. His "auntie" was in a straw hat and a floral-patterned shirt that she usually wore to work at the fruit orchard. Together with his sisters, she stood among the rustic, unfashionable townsfolk, their faces frozen in place while their pale hands flapped back and forth. The train began to take off slowly. It was his first time riding one.

After his mother died of illness, Mong Sang had even less contact with the small town. He remembered how he went back to sit at the wake for his "auntie." Once in the funeral hall, his stepparents wanted him to put on marks of mourning reserved for immediate family. They also wanted him to sit on the floor next to his sisters and younger brother. Mong Sang was reluctant to do so, but could find no reason to refuse. Together with Lin Sang, he carried flowers and prepared purifying water for the woman lying in the coffin. Following the Taoist priest's lead, they walked around her in endless circles.

From then on they went their separate ways. Mong Sang's stepparents died one after the other. The inheritance went entirely to their birth children. Mong Sang fought with his brothers and sisters by name over this, almost irreparably damaging their relationships. Meanwhile, he had also lost touch with his birth brother.

Du Li An noticed that neither of them mentioned the whereabouts of their father. She herself never thought to ask. There was one thing Mong Sang mentioned. When their mother was laid to rest, the family buried her with a few items that had been important to her, among them a red identity card issued to permanent residents. "That red IC is the closest thing to a wedding certificate she had."

Mong Sang had few updates on his brother. What news he did receive was conveyed by people from the small town, whom he bumped into on certain occasions. He knew this much: Lin Sang was once a key figure in the Labour Party of Malaya. He often organized large meetings, participated in many protests and appeals, and was in and out of jail. Rumor had it that he was locked up for a time on Jerejak Island.

"Jerejak Island," Du Li An repeated softly. It was an unfamiliar name, as distant-sounding as the paradise of Penglai referenced in movies.

"Yup, a small island specifically for keeping political prisoners. It used to be a leper asylum. I thought he'd die in there for sure." Mong Sang turned around and took up the watch he'd placed by the bed. "It's eight o'clock."

She grunted a response and picked herself up from the bed's soft mattress, into which she'd sunk farther and farther. "I should get going," she said.

Looks like it wasn't true after all, what people said about blood being thicker than water. In the past she'd heard people talk up the mystical connection between twins, as if they were destined to share a single life and the same fate. For example, if one of them fell and hurt their head, the other would encounter some coincidental misfortune. Mong Sang claimed something like that had happened with him and his younger brother, a side effect of the adults' determined meddling. Because they kept worrying he and Lin Sang would forget the connection between them, they often, intentionally or not, exaggerated the bizarreness of those coincidences, big or small. Through this the adults meant to caution the boys: You two must love each other.

Now she firmly believed he was him, while Mong Sang was Mong Sang. It hardly seemed possible they had once spent ten months whispering secrets to one another in their mother's womb. Du Li An stared at that back across the room, her thoughts weaving among countless jumbled versions of Yip Lin Sang and Yip Mong Sang, as if traveling back and forth through the past decade. Even though those years had whipped by in a frenzy, there was a sense that they had taken place in a past life, and then again in the present.

She withdrew her gaze when someone touched her elbow. When she turned, a haggard old man's face appeared in her vision. Steely Bo? Such an ancient, wasted man. In that moment her entire world became soundless and bleak, as if she'd been plunged underwater. She saw his mouth moving, morphing with the slight changes in his facial expressions, but she could not tune in to his voice. She felt he must be reciting an incantation for summoning lost souls.

"Listen, this song. It's your favorite."

Suddenly she regained her senses. It was like she'd lost the power to remain in the present earlier, while slipping and sliding in time's turbulent waves. When she blinked, a sluice lifted and the aural weight of the banquet hall gushed torrentially into her brain. The hosts had invited modern Chinese orchestras from two Chinese independent high schools for the night, as well as a song and dance troupe from a charity organization. The older people in the crowd were practically drunk on the series of opera performances accompanied by loud gongs and drums. Then, while she wasn't paying attention, the era onstage shifted. A woman in a bloodred cheongsam took over, her slender waist snaking to the music's beat. The song she sang was "Love and Passion."

God decides if we stay or separate; I won't blame Him nor will I lament fate. All I ask is for mountain and sea to bear witness while I wait.

Du Li An couldn't help but be amused. Wasn't Liza Wang, too, a relic of the past? Now everyone worshipped Anita Mui, she of "Bad Girl" fame.

Du Li An kept thinking someone onstage would sing a couple of Mui's hits before the banquet was over. But charity organization singers were obviously on the more mature side, with limited range for modern pop songs. By the time dessert was served, the spectrum on stage stretched to include only Roman Tam and Paula Tsui.

The guests began to depart after dessert. Du Li An saw Yip Lin Sang and his tablemates get up in preparation to leave. The woman to his right was slower to rise. He waited a while by her side. When she got up, he briefly supported her elbow. Du Li An remained in her seat, feeling lost and empty, still unsure whether she was hoping he would turn his head and at least give her one single look. It would be a reunion of sorts. The last time she saw him he'd been this mere blob of a figure, out of reach. He'd stood under a tree and ruffled Ah Sai's hair, then walked farther and farther away, his arms around a big, thick book, never once looking back.

So be it.

Better this way.

Back home later, she unexpectedly had a good night's sleep, devoid of dreams, though a slight sourness lingered on her tongue and throat. Probably it was from drinking some Cordon Bleu at the banquet, which caused her to go to bed tipsy, a bitter smile on her face. Steely Bo, on the other hand, barely drank. For one thing, his body had been thoroughly battered, and his liver was no longer up to the challenge of strong spirits. For another, his eyesight had deteriorated but he still had to drive them home afterward, and he was worried if he drank it would cause an accident. His brother-in-arms from his glory days certainly understood, yet this didn't stop Elder Zong's youngest from making a couple of snide remarks when he and his two brothers made their rounds on their father's behalf to toast the guests. "It's not every day my ba makes it to eighty. Brother Bo, what do you say? Will you be downing a drink of respect or a drink of penance?" Caught off guard, Steely Bo's sagging face flushed red. He gritted his teeth, grabbed up the bottle on the table, and sloshed liquid into his cup. "I volunteer three cups as punishment!"

Of course Du Li An wouldn't let him do any such thing. She wrested the half-full bottle of Cordon Bleu from him and poured it for herself. "I'll take Steely Bo's place, since he's driving. But I'm just a woman, so surely one cup will do?" She kept up a steady flow from bottle to cup while she talked, and soon her cup was over half full. "How's this? Is this half cup good enough? Should I fill it to the brim?" The guests looked at each other, agog. Then the two eldest Zong sons moved to stop her with a few practiced, polite phrases. Swiftly, they led their younger brother away to pay their respects at another table.

On the way home, neither she nor Steely Bo had any enthusiasm for small talk. They didn't turn on the radio either. The car's interior filled with a chilly silence. Du Li An stared at a pair of tiny ornaments on the car's dashboard and the long street rolling out ahead. For some reason she began thinking of a teenage Yip Mong Sang sitting in a train compartment, beyond which numerous palms waved endlessly, like so many clock pendulums. She suddenly felt fatigued.

—

Oddly, the next time Du Li An saw Yip Mong Sang, she found she'd lost all of her previous rampant love and raw desire for him. In truth, it had been many days since she'd thought about him at all. It was the end of the year, and everyone was busy with their own affairs. When he occasionally crossed her thoughts, she understood that the person projected hazily by her mind was not him but his younger brother Lin Sang, the Lin Sang who'd left chatting and laughing with his companions without once looking back or waving goodbye to her.

It was already the day marking winter solstice when Yip Mong Sang next appeared at the counter of Ping Le House. The kopitiam was closing two hours early to observe New Year celebrations. Knock, knock. He rapped a ring on his fingers against the counter. Du Li An shifted her attention from a stack of bills. It was still a face familiar to her, its same old arrogance inflected with flippancy, those eyes that looked straight into yours without any sense of decorum. He was him. He was not Lin Sang. Because of this fact, she finally discovered a strangeness she should have detected much earlier on this familiar face.

Lau Lin was home preparing tangyuan for winter

solstice. Du Li An had said she'd help out as soon as she got back, but she still headed to Mayflower that afternoon for a tryst. Unlike Lin Sang, this particular person was not as easily dismissed. He was possessive over what he thought belonged to him. He knew how to squeeze every last drop out of it.

As usual, she handed her body over to him, let him muss up her hair. That's what he liked—to transform someone into a mad dog during lovemaking. As if detecting her inner turmoil, he was more vigorous than ever, loosening her at the seams again and again in the motel room, making her scream as if he wished to tear out her very soul. But her soul was no longer where it was supposed to be. She opened up her ecstatic flesh and welcomed in this man, and gradually he pushed his way in until he was almost entirely tunneling into her body. "Mong Sang . . ." she moaned, tears seeping from the corners of her eyes. Mong Sang.

I'm here. I'm here.

Thus went the winter solstice celebration, marked by the feasting of two physical bodies. Like two fish stranded together on land, they sustained each other with their respective moistures. Du Li An imagined her clit as fish lips gasping for breath onshore; *all is void and the void is all,* as the Buddhist chant went. They carried on until both of them were exhausted, each dreaming that they fell asleep cushioned by the other's shoulder. In her chaotic dreamscape she spotted Yip Mong Sang, but why would she be dreaming of him? She suspected she had mistakenly slipped into his dream because their skulls were so close to one another. Sorry, she said. Turning, she searched for a door through which she could leave. But there was no door. The wall held only many elaborately framed full-length mirrors. In each mirror there appeared a vague, blurry human figure, as if clothes had been hung inside the glass, flapping. Yet she knew instinctively that she was looking at Lin Sang.

The room was pitch black when she awoke. It took her some time to recall scenes from the dream, and longer still to identify the surrounding darkness. She was reminded by Yip Mong Sang's snores and the laborious creaking of a bed from some room down the hall that, yes, this was Mayflower. What was Yip Mong Sang seeing in his dreams? She smiled bitterly in the dark, then raised herself. A backflow of semen trickled between her labial lips onto Mayflower's bedsheets. She sat up straight, spilling everything, letting loose hundreds of millions of sperm cells that had flocked to the fecund soil she'd offered up to them. Then she got out of bed, tore off wads of toilet paper, and carefully wiped her private parts.

Yip Mong Sang, too, stirred awake. When he opened his eyes, he saw a glowing female body wavering at the foot of the bed. He almost assumed he was still dreaming, but before he could be sure, he was sucked back into the quicksand-like world of sleep. Du Li An was practically pulling her car into her yard when he finally woke up. She felt sticky all over. Clumps of hair stuck to the back of her neck, and her clothes gave off a kind of rotten, impure scent. Lau Lin was already done rolling out the tangyuan flour and boiling the accompanying dessert soup base. The sweet fragrance of pandan leaves wafted through the kitchen. Wait for me, Du Li An told Lau Lin. I need a shower first.

Yip Mong Sang sat up and switched on the small desk lamp next to the bed. He'd spotted a brown leather envelope left on top of the sheets by Du Li An. She knew there was no need for a courteous exchange between them. Anything she said would come across as too insincere, too affected. Yip Mong Sang thought it was best that way too. He tipped the envelope and out fell a wad of cash, which he counted with utmost seriousness in the dim corona of the small desk lamp. It was only later, when he stuffed the cash back into its container, that he saw the word "Goodbye" written on the envelope.

That was unexpected. Like the parting words at the end of a movie.

Dinner was an especially bountiful affair, which suited Du Li An's ravenous appetite. She polished off two bowls of rice and a big serving of tangyuan before bed. Steely Bo, on the other hand, was preoccupied with setting up the karaoke machine he'd bought earlier that afternoon. At first Du Li An and Lau Lin brimmed with enthusiasm. But Steely Bo knew absolutely nothing about electronics, and here he was with a gigantic gadget and its tangled, complicated-looking bunch of cords. In the end, after fussing the entire evening, he was unsuccessful in hooking it up to the TV. Worse, now even the VCR machine was malfunctioning, rendering their rental cassette tapes unwatchable. Du Li An and Lau Lin were both miffed, though one look at Steely Bo's pained expression and the sweat dotting him from head to toe was enough for them to realize the futility of either complaining or badgering him. So after supper the three of them listlessly watched whatever was on TV, yawning the whole time, and that was how winter solstice came and went.

Before going upstairs, Du Li An said she'd call the electronics store tomorrow and have someone over to fix the karaoke machine. But the next morning she was startled awake by the sounds of singing from downstairs. Mic in hand, Steely Bo was delivering "Fatherland" at the top of his lungs. He was ridiculously off-key, though his facial expression was as smug as could be. Later, when she got in the car and drove to Ping Le House, her mind supplied her with the colorful words and phrases that floated across the TV screen. *The river bends, and bends again; how these casual words capture my worries . . . Between heaven and earth humans writhe like ten million little ants . . . Though jade-green grass sprawls across my dreams, my temples are already dotted with snow.*

Lin Sang would definitely like this song, she thought. A song like this, with lyrics about soil and homeland paired with a swelling, cascading melody. A manly song brought to life by the voice of Michael Kwan, which sounded like it'd been polished to a shine by the passing years.

And what about her? Though she'd heard the song long ago when she watched the corresponding drama series, and would sometimes even hum a line or two of its tune, it wasn't until today, when she saw the words change color one after another across the karaoke song screen, that she became enlightened, as if touched by a higher power. Word by individual word, she began to understand the meaning of the song.

And because of this, Du Li An thought about that tome. She couldn't remember its title, but she felt that if she were given that thick novel with the green cover again today, she might be able to finish it now.

—2—

In all your years on earth, you'd always thought nights were longer than days. When you were little, you used to lie in pitch-black rooms and listen to your mother and the other sex workers walk downstairs. Every day after dark, they had to squeeze themselves into tight tops and miniskirts that exposed half their butts, then descend the stairwell together in cheap high heels bought from the night market to await johns on the ground floor. The women were like spiders perched and waiting on the same web. Sometimes they fought over customers, but after a few days they'd make up again over the generous offering of a single cigarette. Mother especially liked gifting cigarettes in exchange for more restrained moans and groans. "Please, the brat has to go to school in the morning."

Mother worked that way till dawn. Before the day turned bright she'd return barefoot to your room, high heels in her hands. You always pretended to be asleep, so that she'd believe you had a restful night.

The night Mother died was of course the worst one. But every night since that you've waited for Mana hasn't been easy either. In your current state, you aren't sure whether you want her to visit, and you can't tell either whether she's going to come. To you, this is the utmost torture. You are completely unable to fall asleep. All you can do is read *The Age of Goodbyes* in bed or scribble nonsense in your diary. Sometimes you fall asleep out of sheer exhaustion, but even then you enter the realm of sleep like a child onshore, one foot tentatively dipping into still water. Any wisp of wind or shudder of grass startles you.

Mana? Is it Mana?

Mana does not come. It's been several nights. *I miss her, but I don't really want to see her,* you write in your notebook. But she stays away even from your dreams, which have formed a puddle of dull water that cannot reflect reality. The only presence in the pool is your own reflection. You start imagining J as the figure on the water's surface. You stare at each other, both thinking about what Yip Mong Sang says to Du Li An in the novel. "They used every trick in the book to place us together, but we were very uneasy, being so unused to each other."

The dream drags on, and then even J disappears. All that's left is a looming spiral staircase with you in the middle. You sense its precipitous height and cannot see either top or bottom. You're like Jack on the magic beanstalk, except you can't reach either end. A sudden terror grips you. In the dream you wait and wait, but not a single soul passes by. Vast blankness unfurls in all directions. You are terrified by a feeling of colossal and fathomless emptiness, and so you grasp onto the rusty staircase and bawl.

You forget whose name you were shouting. Mana? Ma? In the dream, there is no answer.

Someone switches on the light. Brightness filters into your dream alongside the cries of cicadas. When your eyes open, room 301 is in its usual cramped and cluttered state. Uncle Sai stands next to the desk. He pours steaming fish congee into a giant steel mug. You caught a cold, he says, and you're running a fever. He walks to open the window, then squats by your bedside to light a mosquito coil. You clamber up in bed to eat the congee and listen to his nagging. "Who knows, it might be dengue. If the fever isn't gone by morning you gotta see a doctor." Then he halfheartedly tidies up your room and gathers up some dirty shirts and pants tangled on the floor. Before he leaves, he reminds you, "I've set an alarm for you. Medicine and water is next to the bed, so make sure you take those at midnight."

You're startled awake at midnight by the alarm's blare. You have a fierce headache, as if your skull houses a hive of industrious wasps. *Bzz bzz bzz.* You swallow the medicine by the bed. The water makes you choke and you start hacking violently. Then you accidentally overturn the leftover congee sitting nearby. The steel cup clangs to the floor, spilling its thickened mess of cold congee across the floor, scattering pieces of pale fish fillet that are starting to smell off.

Uncle Sai pushes the door slightly open without knocking. "Anything wrong?" He stands beyond the threshold, his voice traveling through the gap between door and frame.

You shake your head. "Just water going down the wrong pipe."

"Ah, get some rest then. Whatever was spilled can wait till morning." Softly, he closes the door.

The night drags out, longer than usual. You're rolled into a dream as if bundled within a thick duvet. In the damp, moldy dream, you watch over a faceless corpse. The corpse starts out as a boundless jigsaw puzzle that's missing pieces. Sitting on your knees, you try to solve the puzzle in a frenzy, sweat dripping off you like it's raining. The wasps in your brain vibrate all night amid the cicada chirps, digging countless secret tunnels through your gray matter. It seems to you that Uncle Sai walks in a few times, but it's also possible he never enters the room, instead simply pushing the door open a little to observe everything through a slim crack. Each time you hear the door's hinges creak, you struggle to open your eyes into narrow slits. As your eye boogers accrue, you feel as if you are gazing upon the world with the eyes within your eyes. The lights blaze in the room, in contrast to the deep dark of the corridor beyond the door. Whoever stands there remains still as a statue.

You aren't sure what closes—the door or your eyelids. You're ensnared by the dream, as if wrapped in bandages, bound like a mummy, or maybe like inside a cocoon. The two are the same, concerned with the preservation of lives and souls; the expectation of rebirth; the pickling of past events in memory; the totality of loneliness; the existence and compatibility of another self; the impending embrace of the rest of humanity.

The dream reaches the end of its spun silk. It's almost noon the next day when you open your eyes again. The room is hot as a stove, as if the sun is hiding out between the ceiling and the roof. If this were a Shaozi story, there would be an attic in that space. You move your eyeballs and discover Uncle Sai standing by the bed. His two arms are planted on the small of his back, and he has the look of someone gazing upon a mummy or a lavish gold-embroidered shirt on exhibition. He's calling you, calling your name, waiting for you to send back an echo from the yawning canyon of your dream.

But you're not used to hearing your own name. It sounds like he's calling a stranger who happens to live in your body. Only when you realize you should reply do you discover that your vocal cords are stiff, your throat has transformed into a rubber tube that was exposed to high heat and has since lost its elasticity. All you can manage are coughs, and those take the wind out of you. Your lungs are like a desiccated air pump. You lack the strength to squeeze it.

When you wake next, you can't tell the time of day. Uncle Sai is nodding off at the foot of the bed, his mouth gaping, head swaying on its stem like one of those ornaments with springs for necks. People like to put these little toys in their cars, so that when they're in motion the toys will bob their noggins to the engine's vibration or the road's bumpiness. Somehow you haven't realized, until now, how old and faded Uncle Sai has become. The ash-white roots of his facial hair dot his dark face, like sugar scattered on top of brown bread.

It's good to be alive after all, you think. You get to reunite with the world after emerging from sleep.

The room was tidied up while you were out cold,

and now it's almost spotless. There's no trace of the fish congee on the floor. The tome of a book that used to be by your pillow is now on the desk. You rotate your eyeballs, sensing that sunlight has made its sterilizing rounds in here. Not only does the air in the room seem less damp, it even contains a vague insecticide flavor. Your clothes have been laundered and folded neatly on the wardrobe. Your KFC uniform shows obvious signs of having been ironed. It's hooked up behind the door alongside its matching hat. Together, they resemble a boy hanging his head in regret.

Uncle Sai trips over something in his dream and wakes up with a shudder. Eyes bleary, his face seems to convey an abrupt realization that it's great to be alive. "You're awake," he says, blinking.

Now you're all awake.

He continues to come at least twice daily for the several days you're confined to bed, bringing you take-out congee and noodles, and occasionally fruit or soda crackers that come in tin cans, all items one would typi-cally bring to visit the sick. Whenever you see the soda crackers in tin cans, you're reminded of eating colorful candy in cinemas as a kid, those tidbits stuck all over with powdered sugar and placed in an oval tin container that looks like a box of rouge. That was a snack only available for sale in cinemas, and because you can count on one hand the number of times Mother took you there, you always thought of the candy as preciously rare. On the other hand, there were those two mobile carts that sold lok-lok on the main street outside the cinema. Whenever you came down with a fever or had run-of-the-mill stomach bugs, Mother would take you to the Ho, Fong & Yap Polyclinic nearby. On your walk home to Mayflower after seeing the doctor, you'd stare bug-eyed with desire at the meat and seafood skewers displayed on the carts. Mother usually never gave in to you, but during those specific moments she'd always cave. She'd glare and shove you. "Go on then, pick out what you want, but you can have only three."

You favored the fishballs and water spinach with squid, while Mother couldn't help but indulge in a couple of fresh clams. The clams were bloody and stank of the rivers. After being dipped briefly in boiling water, they turned a purple-tinged ashen gray, the color of corpses. Mother said this was nourishing stuff for women, since clams reinforced yin energy and replenished red blood cells.

Mana left, perhaps right during your period of recuperation. It's odd—when she first moved in you had no inkling of her arrival, but now it's crystal clear to you that she's gone. Maybe it's because you get the feeling that Mayflower is, remarkably, more desolate than usual, so quiet that even insects like spiders and geckos have abandoned this place. Mana took even her scent with her. City Hall employees have been by Mayflower to indiscriminately spray clouds of mosquito repellant, and now its kerosene-like tang is the only odor drifting in her room. You kneel down on the floorboards and check. The shoes and large duffel bag under the bed have disappeared. This tears you up. It's like your heart's been gouged to reveal a hole that has always existed.

Is this a good thing? This departure without a goodbye, Mana letting herself melt into the crowd like a drop of water into an ocean.

No, not a good thing. Sprawled on the floorboards, you hug your knees and cry, because suddenly you know Mana did not actually go without leaving word. She'd been to room 301. She was the one who cleaned and tidied the room, who opened the windows to let in sterilizing sunshine and wind to drive away loitering germs. She folded your laundered clothes and even ironed that KFC uniform. Lastly, she sat in the chair you use daily and flipped through that tome of a book. Then she took the red fountain pen from your pencil cup and wrote down a sentence on the blank page before the novel proper starts:

This is my commandment, that ye love one another, even as I have loved you.

She's never coming back. She sat hugging her knees, chin resting on kneecaps, her eyes never leaving you. Though you distinctly felt her presence in your dreams, and understood how tender, how sorrowful her gaze must have been at that moment, you did not have the courage to open your eyes. You still had no idea how to confront what you imagined to be embarrassment and awkwardness, and you had a premonition that as soon as you opened your eyes, Mana would start speaking to you. Mana with a baritone voice.

It must have happened on the same day: you, pretending to be asleep until you dozed off, then, that very evening, Uncle Sai drove Mana to the bus station. Although time was a little tight, Uncle Sai still stopped on the way to buy a couple servings of buns and dumplings from a roadside stall, one for Mana, and the other for you. The heady fragrance of roast pork bun led you back to the waking world from your dreams. When you opened your eyes, Mana had already embarked alone on her long, protracted journey.

Many years later, as you sit on a long-distance bus headed north, you can't stop thinking about the Mana of that moment. Perhaps she was teased by some overeager john on the bus, or maybe it was certain foreigners in search of the exotic. Someone extended a cigarette toward her as a conversation opener. Who sat by her side? When she couldn't help nodding off from exhaustion, which way did her head droop?

But ultimately you're calmer than you'd imagined. Very quickly, you grow accustomed to the deeper layer of loneliness uncovered after the hole in your heart has been excavated. The trough of death remains on the bed mattress; your dreams are either completely devoid of human figures, or else crowded with strangers' faces. It's Uncle Sai who keeps seeing your mother in his sleep. "Ever since the day you fell sick, your ma's been reaching out in my dreams every night," he says.

In them, Mother appears as a much younger version who wears miniskirts that were popular in the seventies. "Really the spitting image of the woman in that photograph. I almost thought it was my younger sister who'd been missing for many years. I've said it to her before, the person in the photo looks so much like my sister. But she insisted she was your ma and not my sister. And she got mad over this too. She pouted and turned her back, wouldn't answer my questions, barely acknowledged me. She seemed to be crying."

To soothe the unease brought on by his dreams, Uncle Sai goes behind your back and consults a medium for a séance. The trip is no joke; he has to drive a whole hundred kilometers in total. Upon his return, he forwards the message your mother transmitted through the medium, telling you to take care of yourself. "She said if you get into a university, then you should go."

You and Uncle Sai both understand the medium is a fraud. Those definitely do not sound like Mother's words. You know all of it is made-up, that the medium conjured this version of your mother out of thin air, that Uncle Sai is editorializing Mother's advice. You even start to wonder whether the entire trip to see a medium is invented. Uncle Sai might simply be acting on something he read in the papers at the kopitiam. That something led him to tell you, in this circuitous, absurdly roundabout way, "Don't worry, Uncle Sai is here to help you."

You do understand what he means. The two of you are perched on Mayflower's second-floor stairway. Uncle Sai lights a cigarette. He mentions that someone wants to purchase Mayflower and renovate it into a café. You nod, though you still haven't quite digested the implications of Mayflower being sold. I have to get to work, Uncle Sai, you say. I'll miss the bus if I don't leave now. You turn and race downstairs, then abruptly stop at the corner where the steps curve. Swiveling your head, you gaze up at the faint shadow melting into dimness. "Uncle Sai," you whisper.

He hears you and steps out from darkness, like a translucent image solidifying into something tangible.

"What's that?" He exposes his mouth of yellow teeth.

"Mana? Is she not coming back?" You lift your chin, self-conscious of your own child-like, prayerful face.

—

That comes later. There's a story you must put down in writing. Later, you'll enter the story in a competition and unexpectedly win the grand prize. On the long-haul bus to Thailand, you resemble nothing more than a piggy bank down on its luck. The midnight journey shakes you and out fall abundant dreams, all broken into tiny bits. You dream of Mana and tell her about winning the prize. She remains as beautiful as Emily, still sorrowful, still smiling and silent.

In your writings, Mana's mother is a Thai girl named Rania. "Rania Sri." In the story, Uncle Sai pronounces the unfamiliar name with difficulty.

Rania is short and plump, her nose slightly flat. The bags under her eyes are especially swollen the night she leaves the man, and there's bruising on her face. The previous night she'd wailed, tears and snot flowing, that she couldn't stand to live with him any longer, and by dawn she'd exited the little house they shared. The man was very young back then and prone to oversleeping. What's more, he was in a drugged, drowsy state after a night of shooting both morphine and his load. Therefore, though he dreamed about Rania sneaking out, he did not manage to struggle free from slumber. When he woke up it was already noon. Rania had searched every nook and cranny, took all the money in the house with her, and left behind not a single coin. The man found a packet of instant noodles and a lone egg. It was while chewing on those that he finally remembered the fight he had with Rania the previous day, how Rania cradled her rapidly swelling face and said, No more, this is it. She said she was going to get an abortion, but between them they had only thirty-odd baht. What good was that itty bit of money?

That's why the man believes her when she later tells him she gave birth in her hometown, to a baby named Amphan who takes her last name. The man doesn't seek out this child of his. But upon his release from a final stint in prison, he finds both his parents have passed away back home, and he has no way to contact his only sister. It is then that he suddenly discovers the preciousness of family ties and turns over a new leaf. From time to time he sends some money to Rania and her child. Much later on, when Rania has cancer and is on the verge of death, the man makes the long journey to Thailand. There he meets the teenage child, now named Mana after her transition.

Rania breathes her last in the stilt house that was

her old family home. This happens not long after the man leaves Thailand. After a few stops here and there, Mana finds a job in an oceanfront bar. One day, the man receives a phone call from her. She's at the border, and she says she's on her way down south.

"I want to make more money. Then I'll head back by year's end for another surgery."

Mana walks through Mayflower's front doors. Upstairs, a sick woman lies dying on the bed in room 301. The man leads Mana in to say hi. Mana guesses that the woman with the tumor on her knee must be the man's wife, or at least his lover. That woman is your mother, who had long ago heard about this child, Mana, from Uncle Sai. Mother beckons Mana to her bedside and holds the girl's hand tenderly. It is the hand of an orphan from a faraway place; a slender, firm hand, with very long fingers and protruding knuckles.

"You are so beautiful." Mother very slowly opens the eyes within her eyes, her right hand lightly caressing the palm within her palm. "Really, Mana, you're so beautiful!"

Mana is delighted. The sick woman in room 301 is the kindest person she's met in this foreign land. This woman, whose facial features are already somewhat ravaged by disease, reminds her of her own mother, Rania Sri. That is why, when your mother asks her—"Child, are you carrying any smokes?"—she takes out every single cigarette on her and heaps them all upon this amiable sick woman.

Mana stays for half a year in Mayflower. It's her idea to use the back entrance for her comings and goings. Because Uncle Sai can't find the key to the old lock, he has it replaced with a new one. Like a light-footed cat she comes and goes freely, and because she keeps a nocturnal schedule, even Uncle Sai often feels unsure whether she actually exists. Her room and his are divided by a thin wall. Sometimes he picks up certain sounds from next door, like a sneeze muffled by a towel, or a humming that is as soft as a spirit's sigh.

Room 301 is a place she frequents. She listens to your mother mutter to herself and keeps her company while she smokes. Mother has Mana slide out the suitcase from under the bed. Then Mother recounts in detail the origins of every single object within, as if going over family heirlooms: plastic trophies of various sizes, award certificates from when you won math and composition contests in primary school, two yearbooks in which your essays were published, your itsy-bitsy face in a graduation photo. "My son." Mother points you out in the photo, from among a crowd of fifty. Her index finger strokes your face, her fingernail only slightly larger than the captured faces.

The suitcase also contains some clothes she seldom wears, along with a pair of thong sandals. She always seems prepared to leave, and if she really were to leave Mayflower, she'd probably bring those cheap, broken objects with her. But here they remain, the gold paint peeling and fading on the trophies, the certificates bearing brown and yellow spots from the humidity. You do retain an especially deep impression of a shining blue dress at the bottom of the suitcase. You remember Mother once mentioned it belonged to a close friend who'd died. It was clearly her absolute favorite piece of clothing. She'd worn it only once and with great ceremony. That was for your Standard Six graduation, when she went out of her way to see you receive a prize for academic excellence on stage.

The night Mother breathes her last, Uncle Sai conveys the news to Mana. "The auntie upstairs just died." Mana presses her lips together, then fishes out a carton of cigarettes from her cloth bag. She bought them for your mother, she says. Uncle Sai takes them. "I'll give it to her," he says.

Those who leave don't come back, and after all Mayflower is a mere transit station. The odd thing is, since your recovery from illness, your memories of Mayflower are gradually receding one by one. The spiders that reproduced for generations in the room's corners were wiped out in one go, alongside those mosquitoes and flies that had accrued countless cycles of life and death in the shadows. The scent of lamb curry that lingered in the air, the pungency of durian, nicotine, and Mana's perfume—all were overpowered by a smell that stung the nose a little like kerosene. Even the fluorescent light that doubled as broadcaster of cicada hums in room 301 was abruptly silenced when the circuit breaker tripped one day. From that day on, the light did not turn on and the cicadas stopped singing. It was as if the tube light had once housed a living being, one who recited verses to help the souls of the dead cross over into another realm. And now the being's work was done. Because ignorance has ceased, perceptual fields subsequently cease, as set down in *Awakening of Faith in the Mahayana*. And because the causes of erroneous thoughts and perceptual fields have ceased, the characteristics of the mind all end, leading to what is called attaining nirvana.

Uncle Sai detaches a tube light from another room to swap for yours. The light beams with a marked cheerfulness after being cleaned of its accumulated dust, making the room so glaringly bright it seems capable of banishing wandering, lost souls. You read and write under this light. With nothing to build upon, the cellar and attic housed within your heart inevitably, gradually fade, taking with them, one after the other, the treasures and truth they sheltered, those things you were never able to find.

You maintain your habitual silence. The work at KFC remains mechanical, everyone's facial expressions obscured by the shadows cast by their baseball caps. You can make out the sound of gears turning as time passes, audible in the gap between sunrise and sundown. The sound is like termites eating away at wood, rapid-fire and yet hard to detect. Though invisible to your eye, the hollowness of the passing days is made plain to you by that sound. Mosquitoes prosper once more in Mayflower, though the cicadas in the tube light are gone for good. At last you understand that saying about hearing a pin drop. In your dreams, you detect the hurried, shuffling footsteps of time passing through the night's stillness. Termites tunnel into your bedframe from the floor and begin to gnaw away at the bed's memories.

Soon after, the rainy season arrives. On nights that it downpours, flying termites swarm like locusts. These tiny souls, seemingly born out of thin air from pockets of darkness, cannot wait to rush headlong into lighted rooms as soon as they draw breath. There, they gorge on lamplight. Under siege by wall-to-wall waves of termites, you have only one recourse, which is to turn off the lights and dive under the covers for sleep. The winged insects lose sight of their north star in the darkness. They crash into the glass windowpanes as if committing mass suicide, trying their best to embrace the moonlight beyond the windows.

It's clearly raining. Yet the moon is bright as a conspiracy.

Mother's spirit never once visited my dreams, and Mana won't be coming back either.

You run into Shaozi in a novella. In that work of fiction she is the main character, a writer. You bump into each other in a crowded, noisy little bar that's the favorite of many poets and novelists. There, everyone either drinks and smokes while shooting the crap, or else they make huge, bitter deals out of the cutthroat and isolating nature of the literary world, as accusatory as any politician. They never neglect to proclaim their literary aspirations either.

You and Shaozi both know full well that such a place can exist only within a work of fiction. "Because there cannot possibly be that many poets and novelists in the entire world," she says. As you recall, this is a line that appears in one of Shaozi's stories. "Now I know who you are." You order a beer for her.

"Oh? And who am I?" She raises her mug of beer, half-full, and downs it in one gulp. "I would love to know too."

"Last night I conversed with the witch."[1] You lean forward and softly, very softly, breathe your alcohol-tinged answer into her ear.

That night, the two of you have sex in one of the novella's scenes. It takes place on a queen bed in a certain room within a Mayflower of a certain era. You keep a nightstand lamp on, though moonlight streams and spills through the windows. The earth-brown lampshade is veiled by built-up dust, ensnaring light such that only a puny, circular slice of brightness makes it to the head of the bed. This has the effect of making Mayflower look ancient. You feel as if the two of you

---

1. "Last Night I Conversed with the Witch" is an award-winning poem by Boatcarver, written after Shaozi's death.

are entwined in a condemned building scheduled to be demolished the very next day. You ask Shaozi whether this is a dream. Us making love in a motel that both of us have written about.

Shaozi makes no reply. Does she assume you to be the poet Boatcarver? Does Shaozi know she is Shaozi? The novella leaves all this unresolved. What the author does do is describe your lovemaking process in elaborate, painstaking detail, so much so that critics later deem Junichi Watanabe's well-known *A Lost Paradise* as an influence on the book. Obviously, for both of you, what the critics say are completely meaningless. They arouse absolutely no interest. After the two of you have wild, crazed sex twice, you lie in bed on your stomachs and talk about the characters and events in *The Age of Goodbyes*. You come clean to her: you never did manage to finish reading that tome.

Shaozi turns and stares into your eyes. "Are we not discussing the new work you're currently writing?"

For a moment, you are stunned. Then you think it through carefully and begin to suspect that you and she may not be talking about the same book. But then it hits you. The Shaozi you've met has not yet written *The Age of Goodbyes*.

"No, that one's done," you say. "The novel ends before the book is completed."

The Fourth Person never got to read this novella written about Shaozi, and so there was no chance of any critical analysis by him. Naturally he, too, is written into the novella by the author. Out of concern his estate might take legal measures, the author cunningly dismantles The Fourth Person into four different characters. At this moment one of them is crouched outside the door attempting to eavesdrop on you and Shaozi. Though of course all he cares about is her. Several times he has the urge to barge into the room and expose you to her; he wants to tell her how you've stolen her life's work, using your own words to flesh out every single piece of her work ever mentioned in *The Age of Goodbyes*, thus manifesting each and every one of those fictional stories. Then you have the shameless thick skin to publish them under your own name. You even submit them to contests.

You know The Fourth Person lurks outside. He's been trailing you for some time now. His eye's been on you since you made your debut with "Notes from the Left Bank" in the arts section of the country's best-selling Chinese daily. On the other hand, Shaozi seems to have forgotten she is the true original author of these stories. It's as if you and The Fourth Person are the only ones in this whole wide world who are aware of the stories' origins. You, too, seem to be the only ones who have ever read *The Age of Goodbyes*. You think he must be spending his days searching far and wide for that tome with the green cover, so that he can provide proof of your plagiarism. But obviously there's nothing straightforward about the matter. It's only now that he realizes even *The Age of Goodbyes* exists only as a fictional book, a prolix, monumental work conjured from the lightest ashes. Once you and he respectively read it, it dissolved once more into dust, scattered by the wind.

Later on, The Fourth Person in this novella descends into a hateful rage after multiple failed attempts to condemn you. His torment contains more than a tinge of envy. There's another Fourth Person in the novella, a hypnotist with a grasp on psychology who is put in charge of treating the stalker. The hypnotist sits down with you to discuss the patient's condition. It's from him that you find out his patient is working night and day to compose a fictional novel entirely in his head.

"He says the only way to prevent you from continuing to plagiarize Shaozi's work is to finish writing *The Age of Goodbyes* before you can."

By that point the stalker is teetering on the edge of madness. In his imagination, the version of *The Age of Goodbyes* he's abstractly composing will serve not only to foil your thieving tactics but will also restore and revive the one true original. You pass word to him through the hypnotist that his behavior undoubtedly counts as fabricating evidence. The hypnotist takes your side, but the patient brushes aside many attempts to talk him down. In the end you and the hypnotist have no choice but to join forces and stymie the birth of *The Age of Goodbyes*.

One of the remaining two Fourth Persons in the novella is a police officer handling the stalker's case. The last is a lawyer who later defends the stalker in court (charged on counts of libel and fabricating evidence). The novella sinks to such slapstick absurdity, with total chaos dominating the courtroom scenes, that in the end the hypnotist has to make an appearance. He manipulates the judge and the accused both into believing that the case does not actually exist.

Through all this Shaozi sits off to the side, listening. When you see her faint smile, as mysterious as the Mona Lisa, you know she is preparing to turn all this into a work of fiction.

You go to the bar in search of Shaozi before the novella ends. There, you run into the four Fourth Persons drinking together and making fun of each other. Shaozi is nowhere to be seen. You leave the bar to look for the motel you've both written about: Mayflower. There's a full moon overhead. You discover it's the same old moon dangling in the night sky, while all the Mayflowers in this city have been demolished.

CHAPTER ELEVEN

—1—

Vati's eldest bought a pre-owned house in a new village. The house sat on a riverbank and came with a pre-owned watchdog. Though slightly worn and old, the house was spacious. Plenty of room for Vati. After the old man's death, Du Li An let Vati stay on in the old family home on account of their relationship. This arrangement went on for almost eight years, with a symbolic monthly rent of a mere twenty or thirty ringgit. Fully aware of the situation's dynamics, Vati maintained a perpetual state of cleanliness in the house, and never forgot to freshen up the shrines and altars on the first and fifteenth of each lunar month. She even lit incense offerings for the Du ancestors every day without fail. Grateful, Du Li An presented Vati with a 22-carat gold bracelet when she moved out, and also sent her off with some old furniture she wanted from the house.

Vati's face bloomed into a smile as she cradled the bracelet in her palm. By then she was grandmother to four bright-eyed babies, and with the birth of a new generation, naturally she had no choice but to age into elderliness. Her once thick hair had turned sparse, and one of her front teeth had fallen out. Not only that, but she'd developed a tremor in her hands as well. Taking this all in, Du Li An experienced pitying sorrow alongside a large dose of terror.

For a while she had no idea what to do with the old house after Vati moved out. Du Li An's biggest headache was the entire lineage of Du family ancestors worshipped on the altar. She called up Ah Sai for the express purpose of figuring out what to do. He'd just bought a place in the capital, ahead of his wedding in the coming year. Du Li An tried to persuade him to host the Du ancestor tablets in the safe haven of his new home, but Ah Sai hemmed and hawed until finally, after prolonged squirming, he spat it out: His fiancée and her family were followers of Jesus. There was absolutely no way she would allow any Chinese idols into her home.

Hearing this, Du Li An's face darkened. She began viciously berating her brother over the phone. "Idols? Those are ancestors! Ancestors, as in our very own family members!" She called him heartless and unfilial, said he had zero morals whatsoever, and capped it off by venting about her own suffering. The longer she railed on, the sorrier and more indignant she felt for herself. Why did this younger brother of hers never do the right thing? Ah Sai mumbled some nonsense in acknowledgment, which only made her feel like he was twisting the knife in her wound. She hung up in anger. The more she dwelled on it, the angrier she got, until to her surprise, tears began to drip and splatter from her face.

It sure was an eventful year. Maybe it was destined to be one marked by misfortune, with things souring even on a global scale. For a while the papers were crammed every day with breaking news from China, multiple full-page spreads of black-on-white text and sprawling photographs bursting first with dark waves of students, then with marching soldiers and rolling tanks. Looking at them made one's heart race and pound. Du Li An kept quietly wondering, *How far away is China? Could the tanks one day reach these shores?* Older folks talked about how, back then, the Japanese army invaded Southeast Asia on bicycles. Bicycles! China seemed so very close by; for several nights in a row this thought turned her dreams black and white. In them, blood flowed black instead of crimson.

That same year the youngest Zong failed to turn up at home for Lunar New Year celebrations. Instead, on the first day of the year, he killed himself by jumping off a building on an island city a good fifty kilometers to the north. Various theories were floated, everything from drug and gambling addictions to revenge plots, even supernatural encounters gone bad. Local tabloids made much of his death, just as they always chased sensationalism. But the stark reality remained that, late in life, Elder Zong suffered the loss of a child. The agony of a white-haired parent seeing his dark-haired child to his grave overwhelmed Elder Zong, so much so that at one point during the funeral he gasped for breath and fainted on the spot. Once he was revived, they found that his mind was not what it used to be. He could barely recognize anyone. The few times Steely Bo and Du Li An visited the Zong residence, they found the elder's face clouded, his eyes glassy. He simply stared and gaped no matter who was presented to him. It was like he'd lost his will to live.

It was difficult for Steely Bo to see Elder Zong in this state. After every visit Steely Bo told Du Li An he had a premonition his godfather was not long for the world. She refrained from poking holes in this ridiculous premonition. Going by the lunar calendar, Elder Zong was already eighty-four years old. Who wasn't aware that his days were numbered? She heard rumors about how those in the business of bereavement all had their eyes on this big fish. It was obvious that when Elder Zong finally breathed his last, there would be a memorial so grand his eightieth birthday celebration would pale in comparison.

She also understood the self-pity beneath Steely Bo's tender feelings about Elder Zong. Steely Bo himself was over sixty, and his second son at the fishing village had just lost a child to thalassemia. That, too, was the pain of a parent mourning a child. From what Lau Lin let drop, her second-eldest brother laid the blame for the genetic disease squarely on his wife. The couple squabbled often and fought hard. Pots and pans flew; there was never a moment of peace in their home, which had practically turned into a scene from hell.

"Mark my words." Du Li An sneered. "Just you wait. Soon your second brother's gonna be putting his paws on some other woman out there."

After over a decade in business, Ping Le House could sort of bill itself as an establishment. Over the past few years, quite a number of shopfronts on the plaza had pivoted to become kopitiams, heating up the competition. There was a decree that the tin mining town had been upgraded to city status, but despite that there was no marked increase in its population. Supply outstripped demand, and many of the kopitiams hung by a thread. Fortunately Ping Le House could count on word-of-mouth from the last ten-plus years, and business was propped up by its many frequent customers. The entirety of the original crew remained employed, with the exception of Guen Hou.

The matter bothered Du Li An whenever it crossed her mind, stirring up wistfulness and some other feeling she couldn't name. Two years ago when Eggplant Face graduated from public secondary school, she'd taken a risk and partnered with some others to start a night market gig. They peddled women's fashion, each night in a different spot. Business was surprisingly brisk, and soon she was able to run a stall on her own. The girl's habitual chilly expression and masculine features would seem to work against her. Yet as soon as the stall opened for business, she transformed like a Cantonese opera actor crossing the threshold onto the stage. In the blink of an eye she turned into a sweet talker and was especially effective on women, many of whom became loyal customers. At first Guen Hou helped out only on weekends. Then, seeing how the money rolled in, she took the plunge and quit her job at the kopitiam, relinquishing her little snacks stall to brave the night market business alongside her daughter.

Du Li An made no attempt to change Guen Hou's mind. For one, she felt she had nothing to offer other than the unconditional support expected of a sisterly friend. For two, she knew Guen Hou still nursed resentment that Du Li An had not helped repossess the Teochew widower's popiah stall. Nor did Du Li An join forces with Guen Hou against the girl working at the chee cheong fun stall. Then there were those Ping Le House veterans with long memories who had a bone to pick with Guen Hou. She was predisposed to paranoia and had a bad temper to begin with, and moreover was sensitive to the opinions of others. Every time there was a disagreement, it inevitably devolved into a situation of one against many, as fierce as Lü Bu's battle against the three heroes. Yet Guen Hou never gained the upper hand, and so always descended into grievous self-pity. She also hated Du Li An for always looking out for number one, which intensified Guen Hou's sense of embittered isolation. With all this rancor piling up day after day, it was only a matter of time before she made her exit.

By then the Teochew widower had married the chee cheong fun girl after forking over three thousand ringgit in bride price, and the new wife's stomach was already rising like dough. Imagine the awkwardness of Guen Hou bumping into the newlyweds day in and day out. Coincidentally, the widower also won second prize in a lottery draw right around the same time. He was so pleased with his luck that he told anyone who would listen how he was "All hits, no misses." He treated his young wife like precious treasure, showered her with protective affection. This on its own was enough to pierce Guen Hou's heart, but of course the kopitiam gossipmongers joined forces to make it worse. They especially loved to kick her while she was down. They lavished the new bride with extravagant praise about how she was a harbinger of great fortune who brought her husband both wealth and offspring. They also emphasized how lovey-dovey the couple was every chance they got, and nicknamed the Teochew widower "Hubby Befitting Twenty-Four Filial Exemplars."

Though Du Li An knew full well what was going on, she could do little to stamp out the fire. It was within her power to chastise the tongue-waggers and remind them not to cross the line or say anything too hurtful. Yet she couldn't very well order a stop to schadenfreude, especially given the reason Guen Hou was unpopular at Ping Le House. Du Li An knew it was because the others regarded Guen Hou as the boss lady's confidante, a status that only made Guen Hou pleased with herself and led to vicious takedowns when she fell from grace.

And so, knowing words don't heal wounds, Du Li An did the math carefully and made sure not a cent was missing from Guen Hou's last wages, which she delivered with a hefty bonus tucked into a red packet. Guen Hou did not feign politeness, now that matters had gotten to such a head. After all, she counted herself among Ping Le House's first crew, and she had never skimped on her efforts, whether in the workplace or when it came to more private matters. She more than deserved the red packet. Du Li An had planned on taking it one step further by treating Guen Hou and Eggplant Face to a fancy dinner, but Guen Hou was disdainful of such theatrics. She made various excuses, claiming to be busy or else unwell. Once she left Ping Le House, she never stepped foot in it again. Du Li An never got a chance to make good on her dinner offer.

She couldn't help feeling melancholic about Guen Hou's departure. They'd known each other for over two decades, and Du Li An had thought they were close as sisters. Yet their bond was now in tatters. It had become crystal clear to both parties that their relationship amounted to nothing more than that of a host to her guest. The sentiments between them could be rung up like a bill and settled in full, just like that. And yet what had really happened to cause all this? Du Li An found she could not come up with an answer, and she thought Guen Hou might be just as muddled. Regardless, once a seed is planted, the day must come when the seed's relentless push upward forms fissures in the earth. Having regrets now was like closing the barn door after the horse had bolted. Du Li An once considered herself to be above the mundane sting brought on by life's inevitable separations and fallings-out, and yet with Guen Hou gone, she genuinely missed having someone she could really talk to by her side. When even the gossip-mongers felt a vague boredom pervading these times of peace, it was only natural that Du Li An experienced a deep solitude.

All in all, it seemed to be a year for young women. There was the Teochew widower's tender wife, who was finally living the good life. Then there was Eggplant Face, who in a way was fulfilling a great ambition. Everyone else was tortured by loneliness and middling, uneventful days. Lau Lin sat at home, all of thirty-two years old, watching time pass in tepid tedium. After hastily wrapping up his affairs in town, Yip Mong Sang had absconded to a big city in the south, supposedly to try his hand at quarrying with new business partners. Du Li An thought Lau Lin should have gone with him. That season, TVB station aired a mediocre drama called *The Sweetest Moment.* Du Li An went out of her way to make Lau Lin rent and watch it, as a reminder that she really shouldn't drag her feet any longer. But Lau Lin's cloying neediness was totally ineffectual. All she got in return was a pledge from Yip Mong Sang before he skipped town. She held onto his hollow promise, as devoid of substance as candy floss. Docilely she waited, passing time every day after work with serialized dramas.

Though all appeared serene on the surface, Du Li An saw how Lau Lin languished and couldn't help fretting on her behalf. Du Li An reflected on how she was already the boss lady of Ping Le House when she was Lau Lin's age. Meanwhile, Lau Lin was still drawing a textile worker's salary that was just about adequate to stave off literal starvation. Word on the street was that the past two years had been rocky for the textile factory; once, loan sharks barged in with the owner's son in tow as hostage, seeking payment. Any worker who had other options was soon out the door. Even the big boss's daughter-in-law had broken with the factory to start her own business. Only Lau Lin, afraid of any and all changes, clung to the familiar and feigned calm, unwilling to think beyond the very immediate future. Meanwhile, Du Li An's sentiments toward her ran genuine and deep. Not everyone and everything in this world deserves your undying loyalty, Du Li An advised.

In truth, she should have discerned that a supposedly peaceful life was nothing but a false ideal. Something else always brewed beneath the surface. She should have seen it coming: With her single-mindedness and her mouth shut tight as a clam, Lau Lin would eventually find herself on a path of no return. Or maybe Lau Lin did sense that she'd reached the end of *The Sweetest Moment*. Like the legendary yellow crane, Yip Mong Sang was gone without a trace. In over three months she'd seen neither hide nor hair of him, and he hadn't called, either. Given all this, Lau Lin's serenity was extraordinary, in fact ominous. But Du Li An was experiencing some ennui herself. It was not unpleasant, this prevailing calm born out of numbness and sweeping boredom. Only when she was forced to pry did she realize how much things had come to a head, and by then Lau Lin had almost reached the end of her path of no return.

Yip Mong Sang had "borrowed" what little money Lau Lin had saved, claiming it would go toward his new business. This did not surprise Du Li An in the least. She'd had a hunch that they'd seen the last of the faithless Yip Mong Sang. "It's just that . . . What are we going to do?" She sat down beside Lau Lin and rubbed her back. Just a moment ago Lau Lin had rushed into the bathroom and thrown up waves of sour-smelling vomit, after which came hysterical crying. Du Li An heard the unmistakable roiling and crashing of Lau Lin's stomach contents. Of course something more was going on. How many times had such scenes played out since the dawn of mankind, and how many times had she watched them unspool on-screen?

Aware that Du Li An was posted right outside the bathroom door, Lau Lin wrung her hands and hunkered down inside once she was done crying. Du Li An said nothing and simply stayed put until Lau Lin opened the door, her lower lip caught between her teeth. It took one glance at Du Li An for Lau Lin to see the writing on the wall. There was no chance of obfuscation any longer. Like a criminal caught red-handed, she gripped her own elbows and trembled in naked fear, unsure whether to remain on the spot or to walk away. Du Li An had no speech prepared. All she could do was stare the younger woman down until her eyelashes lowered like blinds and her eyeballs quaked beneath their filmy lids. And still she maintained that glare, taking in Lau Lin's face, white as bone china, on which the only bloom of color came from a half circle of blood on her chewed bottom lip.

The next day Du Li An took Lau Lin to a clinic at the far edge of the city. At the registration window, an old nurse slid a small glass bottle toward the women. The bottle was clearly repurposed; it carried a label for essence of chicken. "Which one of you's the pregnancy test for?" Du Li An gave the old woman a look and palmed the bottle. Later, the nurse opened another door and stood at the threshold shouting Lau Lin's name. Du Li An went in with her. The doctor, though young-ish, seemed to know what he was doing. After asking for details, he immediately deduced that the child in the womb had been there for almost four months.

"How big is a four-month-old fetus?" Du Li An asked with urgency.

The doctor made a fist. "Bigger than this, and growing nails and hair."

Lau Lin, who'd been hanging her head throughout, now lifted her eyes for a look. A mound of flesh bigger than a man's fist in her stomach—how petrifying. Probably enough to kill her if it were a tumor. Yet this mound carried life, contained sentience, encompassed fate. She suddenly seemed to wake up to the horror of the situation. An understanding that things would only grow worse from here struck her into a trance. Her eyelids twitched uncontrollably, as if somebody within her was convulsing in extreme terror.

They left the exam room, and the nurse from earlier called out Lau Lin's name from the dispensary window. In the nurse's mouth, Lau Lin's name spoken in Malay sounded like "love—lingers—" in Mandarin. Du Li An rushed forward to occupy the window and opened her purse to pay without being asked. Lau Lin understood her intentions. Du Li An was trying to cover for her; she wanted to give off the impression that of the two of them, she was the focus of this visit.

Back in the car, Lau Lin shoved a few red ringgit bills toward Du Li An. Auntie Li, she said, here's the money you fronted. Though Du Li An meant to refuse, she saw Lau Lin's clenched jaw and her fixed glance beneath lowered lashes. She felt, too, the intent in Lau Lin's fist that clutched the money. Sensing her determination, Du Li An did not tussle with her.

It was a dreary afternoon, the sky hovering on the brink of rain. The air hung heavy with humidity and piles of clouds descended thickly upon the roofs, just like the secret that weighed on both women's hearts. The two of them sat within the expansive gaps of language, feeling that whatever they said would sound irrelevant. In the middle of the drive, they ran into a snaking funeral procession. The deceased's identity was unclear. Surprisingly, brass bands from two separate schools and a few traffic cops on bulky motorcycles formed part of the procession. Based on the pomp and circumstance on display, the deceased might have been a major personality from the education sphere. Girls in snazzy uniforms held flutes to their mouths or struck drums while they crossed the road and marched in step behind the hearse. Du Li An was forced to give way, and the car idled while she and Lau Lin watched those girls in their short skirts and high boots go by, gold tassels hanging off their shoulders, red knots on their chests. It was like watching the prime of one's life unfold in slow motion. Under an overcast sky just before rain, wrapped up in an atmosphere of death, the brilliant youth walked away, raucous and yet plodding.

"Must have picked a bad route," Du Li An said. "This one's tough to get through."

Lau Lin seemed to assume some additional commentary lay behind those words. Du Li An realized belatedly how it must have sounded, even though she hadn't intended any double meaning. Now neither knew how to move on from the moment. The funeral procession inched past like a slow-moving train. The music, slightly discordant, drifted shakily farther and farther, pursued by the traffic cops on their huge bikes. Both women failed to realize when the light turned green. In unison, the two or three cars lined up behind them suddenly leaned on their horns—

It was indeed a bad route. Disruption after disruption greeted them ahead, including a series of red lights and a No Entry sign. But they could not remain forever in one place. They had to barge forward no matter what. Yet, just as Du Li An anticipated, Lau Lin only continued to make phone calls that went unanswered. What kind of a strategy was that? Still Lau Lin dragged her feet, guiltily evading Du Li An's inquiring glances. Lau Lin stopped watching the dramas in which she used to drown her sorrows; she turned in early each night as if convinced that when she woke up next, Yip Mong Sang would materialize at the front door.

But Yip Mong Sang was after all a figure who appeared only in dreams. He could never be placed squarely under the rays of reality. He was unable to bear the weight of mere sunshine. He evaporated. How delusional to try lassoing the man with one little life. It would only accelerate his disappearance. Once shocked by such overly harsh sunlight, he swiftly flees.

Even absconded in dreams Lau Lin was unable to avoid Du Li An's inquisition. Those dreams were as claustrophobic as an elevator, going up and down with no way out. Du Li An was the only person in which she could confide. Meanwhile, Du Li An was astonished by how heartfelt she was in the dreams. Her dream counterpart bulged her eyes and wrung her hands, her voice quaked and tears streamed when she spoke. When, really, these people and their affairs had nothing to do with her. As her old self would have said, "These are Lau family concerns." Lau Lin was not her blood. The relationship between them was not that of mother and daughter, nor that of sisters. Certainly they were not friends. Ever since Du Li An settled scores with Yip Mong Sang and cut off all ties with him, she had even ceased being Lau Lin's rival.

Come to think of it, Du Li An remembered a time when she bore Lau Lin some ill will. Of course in hindsight it was all just a tempest in a teacup, but still the episode was fresh in her mind, every detail vivid and stark. It started with Lau Lin wearing a newly tailored tea-length dress on her way out the door. Du Li An thought the sky-blue dress looked familiar. "Spin around so Auntie Li can have a good look!" she said, nudging Lau Lin with her elbow. Lau Lin rotated twice in place like a coin spun, sending her full skirt floating until it resembled delicate ripples spreading across a clear pond. "Does it look okay?" blushing, Lau Lin asked in a wispy voice.

Du Li An reached out and stroked the buttery, shining material. It really was like cradling a palmful of pure spring water. While her lips sang praises, her eyes were busy minutely scrutinizing the stitches running along the hem. "Oh wow, Ah Lin, looks like you have more tricks up your sleeve! This is some fine handiwork." Du Li An smiled sweetly and relinquished the palmful of sparkling spring water, though she held onto a perceived slight. For seven or eight months she did not have Lau Lin alter her clothes out of a feeling that the girl was deviously holding out on her. It was a good long while before that prejudice dissolved. Perhaps sensing something was off, Lau Lin helped matters along by seizing an opportunity to volunteer her skills and produce a beautiful skirt for Du Li An. Only then did the freeze thaw.

While these complicated, sometimes calculating inner workings of the heart entangled her, they were by no means connected to Yip Mong Sang. Besides, Lau Lin's usefulness became much more apparent after Du Li An got into minor tussles with two different seamstress shops over some alterations. And didn't that sewing machine at home count as an investment? It'd be her loss to hold on to a grudge. The more she thought about it, the funnier it seemed. Lau Lin wore the shimmering sky-blue dress only once or twice. Du Li An watched Lau Lin lift up her skirt hem and slide into Yip Mong Sang's car with a blooming smile. To think, what had bothered her was the dress—the dress! Not the man in the car but the fabric she'd bought and gifted to Lau Lin.

It'd always seemed straightforward to Du Li An. She and Yip Mong Sang, she and Guen Hou, even she and Lin Sang way back when—she assumed a finality when things ended between them. A clean cut. But unlike her, Lau Lin was born dogged, loyal to the bitter end when it came to the people and things she loved. It was a common condition afflicting ordinary folks of small means. Just look how that one blue dress became her pride and glory, to the point that she treated it almost as her bridal gown. Naturally Yip Mong Sang carried the same weight for her. She only wished she could stash that beautiful and eye-catching man like a piece of clothing in her wardrobe. But of course the dress was something she'd custom-made to fit her body. No matter how envious Du Li An grew, it was useless for her to possess it. On the other hand, Yip Mong Sang was a man customized to suit every woman.

Want love? Here's love. Want sex with no strings attached? There you go. He dispensed whatever was desired, fulfilling every woman's shallow yet ever-burgeoning vanity. He made them feel as if their wishes were being granted, yet inevitably they sank further and further into ignorance and self-hatred. He planted seeds of obsession in women's bodies, be it addiction to flesh or addiction to matters of the heart. The seeds were deposited where the women were softest and moistest. Ultimately, those muddy fields yielded only countless marks of his trampling and ravaging.

Du Li An sent out eyes and ears to unearth Yip Mong Sang. But no one could trap that sly rabbit when he resolved to be undiscoverable. They did, however, manage to expose some of the ungentlemanly conduct and romantic affairs scattered in his wake. Lau Lin's fate differed from those of the other women only in minutiae. One was a widow in a faraway town, another a hair salon assistant in some new village near the capital. None of this surprised Du Li An. She could easily believe there were such ill-fated women up north and down south. Basically, in every place Yip Mong Sang had ever made a pit stop, there lived at least one woman who had given up everything for him, surrendering both body and cash. Why did these women never realize that he was replicating their fate someplace else in the country? Would they gape and stare dumbly as Lau Lin did, when all this was revealed to them? Would they tremble all over, overcome by emotions?

Du Li An stopped talking about her findings, afraid they would agitate Lau Lin so much the fetus would be affected. Plus, although Du Li An was quite sure Lau Lin had never heard about his exploits, she nevertheless must have long held suspicions. This was the ultimate form of idiocy, driven not by obliviousness but by knowingly giving free reign to one's own ignorance.

Like a moth throwing away its life to ludicrously charge at the cold fire housed within a fluorescent lamp. Though unsinged, it leaves covered in bruises, wings crooked, limbs broken.

When there's too much water, it must overflow. As slender as Lau Lin was, there was no hiding her protruding stomach. Du Li An grew frantic on her behalf. She tried every rhetoric under the sun. "That extra flesh and bone isn't growing on *my* body. What I mean is, you've gotta pick your own path." The two of them gazed down in unison upon the barely bulging stomach. "This isn't a matter of ten months. It's an entire lifetime we're talking about."

In the past, things might have ended a different way, back when Steely Bo was still leader of Kin Tek Hall under the imposing Toa Pek Kong Society. Yip Mong Sang would have been given a brutal beating by Steely Bo and his entourage before being forced to foot the bill, so to speak, and marry a heavily pregnant Lau Lin. It would have been what Lau Lin wished for fervently. On the other hand, Du Li An would have uttered prayers. That alternate reality led simply to a dead end of a different kind, where the progression of decay was more dragged out, more tortuous, and even more painful.

But now there were no options. She brought Lau Lin back to the doctor, who asked her to undress for an examination. This time around there was no hiding, no cover possible from Du Li An, who retreated to a corner. Lau Lin stood there with her bloated stomach, emaciated limbs, and a vacant stare. To Du Li An she looked like a starved refugee. After a careful exam, the doctor said it was too late. They had passed the point of no return.

"Late?" Upon hearing the sentencing, Lau Lin blinked as if wrestling awake from deep sleep. Alarmed, astonished, she mulled over the meaning of the word "late," bearing the look of someone drowning. It was as if Lau Lin had all along assumed that, as long as the child hadn't emerged from her, she could pluck it out of her stomach like picking fruit from a branch.

"It's too dangerous," the doctor said. "The fetus in you is far along enough to look like you and me. Even if you aren't afraid of dying, I can't afford to lose my license."

The two women received the same answer at each of the three different gynecology offices they visited that day. No Entry. Lau Lin, nearing collapse, covered her face and sobbed in front of the doctors. Finally she began to intuit the devastating consequences. A couple of older women at the factory seemed to have put two and two together. They teased her, remarked on her bloated cheeks, pointed out that the ends of her hair were split and yellowing. Those are signs of pregnancy, they said with a tone of having arrived at some truth, confidence glimmering in their eyes. This caused Lau Lin to panic. She suffered from severe insomnia. When she did sleep, she bolted awake from nightmares pervaded by wailing and a rotten stench. Eventually she became too fearful to leave the house. Every day she shook like a leaf, afraid of exposing herself.

She clung to the telephone as the proverbial drowning man did to a straw. After work each day she called the number Yip Mong Sang had left her. No one ever answered. The silence between the dial tone was as empty as his promise. Still she clung to hope, dialed the number whenever she awoke in the middle of the night. She kept it up until finally the number was disconnected.

A recorded message played, the terrible audio quality making the female Malay voice disjointed. "The num . . . ber you have dialed . . . is not . . . in service." Lau Lin docked the phone receiver. She suspected the recording was false, just another of Yip Mong Sang's tricks! Du Li An caught her slumped over for a good half an hour, doing nothing but compulsively picking and clawing at her skirt, as if yanking off the yellow flowers adorning it petal by petal.

Later, she woke up in the night to wash her hair and locked herself in the bathroom for a very long time. When she emerged she bumped into Steely Bo, who had gotten up to pee. He took in her dripping, wet hair and death-like pallor. She shivered a little, like a damp piece of clothing strung up to dry in the night breeze, or like a ghost who had just peeled off from a drowning victim. "Are you out of your fucking mind?" he roared. "Washing your hair in the middle of the night!" Lying in bed, Du Li An could hear only his voice. It felt to her like he was acting out a monologue in the little sitting area outside the door. Lau Lin greeted the outburst with her signature silence and cowering. Beads of water dripped off the ends of her hair onto the teak floorboards. Then Du Li An heard the sound of her softly closing her door.

The next morning Lau Lin said she wasn't going in to the factory, pleading dizziness and chills. Du Li An looked at her curled up under the covers, her face tinged green and her lips white. Her forehead felt slightly warm. "Who told you to wash your hair in the middle of the night? And with cold water too?" But once Du Li An got to Ping Le House she couldn't shake off a feeling of deep unease. Lau Lin's face under the covers kept floating up in her mind. The eyes in that gaunt face were as dull as two black plastic buttons. The more Du Li An tried to capture the message hidden behind them, the more her heart thumped irregularly. She felt as if a gecko was crawling up her spine. At noon she called home. No one picked up. Then she dialed the factory where Lau Lin worked, and was told Lau Lin never came in, nor had she asked for the day off. Sensing trouble, Du Li An immediately got in her car and headed home. Steely Bo's rusty old tank was gone from the yard. The house was so quiet the buzzing of flies could be heard. Even the neighbor's two watchdogs refrained from barking, but instead stared at her with sinister eyes. There was practically a scent of tragedy in the air. She went up the stairs and knocked on Lau Lin's door.

"Ah Lin, are you feeling better?"

No response from inside the room. Du Li An tried the handle and discovered it was locked. Unable to tamp down her anxiety, she broke out into shouts: Ah Lin! Ah Lin!

No response.

Du Li An slapped the door as hard as she could and gave it a couple of kicks. The door didn't budge, though a boom reverberated through the house, like an earthquake combined with a landslide, as if the world was about to come crashing down. Lau Lin, hiding in the room, could not withstand the shock to her senses. She was so flustered it took her a few moments to respond, her voice shaky. "I'm fine, Auntie Li. I'm fine."

"Open the door!" For some reason, hearing that sickly voice caused a geyser of rage to shoot straight up from Du Li An's heart to her brain. Waves of disgust overtook her. That was the voice of the weak and terrorized, the sound of useless sorrow.

"I said, open the door!"

She knew Lau Lin would never dare to disobey. If she had the guts, she'd already be dead without any of this fuss. And as expected, Lau Lin opened the door a slit without putting up a fight, trying to conceal herself behind it. With a hard shove Du Li An sent the door flying open. Lau Lin wore the sky-blue dress like a badge of honor. Du Li An caught hold of her wrists and dragged her out from the room as if scooping up water from a lake.

"You want to die, right? You think I don't know?" Du Li An was seeing red, her heart pounding hard to sustain her frenzied worry. Lau Lin's hot wrists seared her ice-cold palms. To her surprise, Lau Lin was smiling faintly, as if to say, "What can I possibly do?" Du Li An detested that face with its empty, shell-shocked expression and sunken black-button eyes. It made her think of a mask that was overly thick and stiff, or a Cabbage Patch Kid whose eyes had been scooped out by a naughty kid, utterly powerless to resist its fate.

That face tore at one's heart. Du Li An wanted to put Lau Lin through the wringer, but could manage only to suck in a long, chilly breath when confronted by the face, so like those drawn on corpses by morticians. "It's no use, Ah Lin." One of her wrists was still in Du Li An's grasp. Waves of melancholy crashed within her as she gazed into those bottomless eyes. For some reason she was the one to shed the first tears. "If you die just like that, who'd cry for you other than your poor old mother?"

Du Li An and Lau Lin spent the afternoon bawling into each other's arms. Lau Lin certainly had shored up a dam of repressed anguish. But in Du Li An's case there was nothing that made her sad; or at least there wasn't anything she could think of. She couldn't figure out the source of her torrential tears. It was as if a spring burbled somewhere within her body. Her crying seemingly originated from a strictly physical despondency, completely disconnected from her emotions and spirit. It reminded her of sex. What Yip Mong Sang gave her had a similar effect. But why was her bag of flesh so sad, so discontented? She couldn't say. Eventually the two women grew exhausted from crying. Each of their shirt fronts were soaked with the other's tears. Du Li An felt relieved, even satiated. A sense of well-being enveloped her as she washed her face and changed her clothes. Lau Lin, on the other hand, did not budge from her spot on the floor. Though the tears had dried on her face, her eyes still shimmered with wetness.

They slept in the same room that night. Steely Bo was away at the club playing mahjong till dawn. Worried that Lau Lin would drift toward dark thoughts if left alone, Du Li An insisted they share her bed. They lay fully dressed on the wide bed, both feeling awkward and reserved. Du Li An turned on the bedside radio and switched off the lights. In total darkness, they listened to the evening broadcast. The music chosen for this time of day was always especially gentle; the sounds of sunset flowed like water, like passing years, like spiral-shaped mosquito coils reciting a litany of incantations to insects. The radio host's rich alto murmured, luring them into the realm of sleep. Du Li An closed her eyes obediently, falling under the spell. In her dream she and Lau Lin were both stranded on a sandy beach, two mermaids desperate to morph into human form, yet simultaneously longing to swim back into the ocean.

Moonlight scattered countless pieces of silver film strips among the tides. Anita Mui's singing floated across the ocean's surface, her nasally voice warbling, "The years flow like water."

Du Li An turned over. The darkness in the room was diluted by moonlight and the street lamp outside. Lau Lin's eyes were still wide open. There was a transparency to her face, though her eyes were as deep as two wells reflecting the night sky.

Du Li An subconsciously lifted a hand to stroke Lau Lin's face, hoping to find the tears that moonlight could not detect. "In all my life I've never shared a bed with another woman except my ma, and I'm no spring chicken," she said, her fingers swimming across that face until she found the stream she'd intuited within the valley formed by the wing of Lau Lin's nose. Du Li An meant to wipe away the tears, but her strokes instead had the effect of stimulating the spring bubbling over within Lau Lin's body.

"Me too," Lau Lin choked out, tears running freely. Du Li An shifted closer and gathered Lau Lin's head into her bosom, letting her listen to the music spangling like water inside her body.

. . . Then again my heart is like a little wooden boat, forging ahead though the distant shore remains invisible.

Du Li An stroked Lau Lin's back softly, her throat pulsing as she hummed along to the melody as if coaxing a sobbing child to sleep. The music, the moonlight, they sparked a multitude of thoughts and emotions, transformed the room into its own little universe. Sky and earth were still a muddle, the line between them ambiguous. The moonlight carried with it the smell of limestone. She and the man were covered in sweat, their skin littered with dust and wood chips. Each sigh and pant contained the other's scent. Mong Sang. I'm here. Mong Sang. I'm here. Now she held tight another woman of his, comforting the barren field he'd abandoned. Ah, but no, his seed was nestled within this female body, the child forming tight little fists, an expression crumpled like paper spreading across their face. Protest! Protest!

. . . *Who masters me in fate. Struggling, every day, in a sea of humanity.*

Du Li An fervently wished to smooth out that ball of paper so she could get a look at the child's features. Would the child be a mini Yip Mong Sang? The child was so close to her, a mere distance of the skin separating two abdomens. She felt as if she could already feel them, know them. The doctor said the child was far along enough to look like him and her. Did they have their own will? If so, surely they would not abide with the burden of sin fate had dictated for them. Though they clung to their mother's body, they would never adore such a weak, timid mother. Du Li An tilted Lau Lin's tearful face toward her with a strong, forceful hand. She was so excited she could pop. Her eyes burned like hot coals as they stared straight into Lau Lin's, which retreated further inward. "Listen here. I have an idea." Du Li An lowered her voice until it was a whisper against an ear, as if she was divulging a secret.

. . . *Until all that's left is yearning, loop after loop of it forever clinging. In the fog rolling off the water's surface I stand, reminiscing years past, missing them.*

—

A few days later, Lau Lin resigned from her job at the factory. She received her last wages, then packed her bags and left the big house. She told Steely Bo there was no future for her at the factory, and so she and two girlfriends were going to look for jobs in the border city to the south. He concluded from the phrase "the south" that she was going to meet up with Yip Mong Sang, and so refrained from prodding. All he asked was that she leave her contact information and details about her whereabouts with her mother at the fishing village. Du Li An noted his carefree demeanor. This separation between father and daughter was so casual, so starkly different from the time he lost his hold on that boy Candlenut. When Lau Lin emerged lugging a huge, hefty suitcase, he simply looked on without once asking how she planned to get to the bus station. While she may have been used to this treatment, Du Li An was incensed on her behalf. Before leaving the house she glared conspicuously at Steely Bo, a dirty look of detestation that he failed to comprehend.

Du Li An was to drive Lau Lin and see her off. Together, they jostled the suitcase into the car. It was quite heavy, as if it contained yet another pregnant female body. But the car did not head to the bus depot. Instead, Du Li An parked the car before the old house, and the two women dragged and pushed the suitcase until they managed to maneuver it upstairs. The house had been empty for some time. Inside, it was so quiet one could hear every sound of a matchstick being struck. For some reason, Du Li An's first concern was to clean up the altar. She relit the oil lamps on the shrines. The four paraffin vessels, posed at varying levels, each exhaled a wispy lick of fire. She put her palms together in prayer, and generations of Du ancestors opened their ancient eyes.

"Do this for Auntie Li: tidy up the shrines every day and light some incense." She turned around. In one smooth motion she grabbed hold of Lau Lin's hand and deposited the matches and a bunch of keys into her palm.

"I'll bring whatever the house needs. TV, VCR, and your sewing machine."

Instead of replying, Lau Lin stared fixedly at the three unfamiliar keys in her hand. It seemed she was still undecided, or else scratching her head raw trying to clarify the meaning and symbolism of these keys. Or as if she gazed upon the few pieces of meat from all those years ago, stranded in her bowl. Du Li An held her hand and closed her fingers tight around the bunch of keys.

"Just stay here and let your worries go. I'll figure out everything else," Du Li An said. She knew Lau Lin could not struggle free of what would happen next. It was the only course of action left, fate's final mercy granting her a way out. Du Li An patted the back of Lau Lin's hand again, and still she made not a sound. She simply nodded feebly. Ever since entering this old building, she had become an actor without any lines.

Du Li An boiled water in the kitchen. Before leaving, she methodically latched the iron grille door and snapped shut the oversized lock hanging from the door. Lau Lin sat on her suitcase, unmoved, lost in thought. Du Li An glanced at her through the iron bars. This foreground, this depth of field, gave Du Li An the impression that Lau Lin was a lonesome prisoner. In that moment the name of a place abruptly floated to the top of her mind, like an island rising up from ocean waves. Jerejak Island. It was faraway because it was unfamiliar, like the paradise called Penglai.

She slipped an arm through the bars and gently pulled the inner wooden door closed. She took such care, like she was locking a safe deposit box holding grave secrets.

—2—

Your father is my husband;
your man is my lover;
your son will be my son;
your secret will be our secret.

You watch as Du Li An transforms into a deluge and swallows up the pregnant woman's place and sense of belonging, leaving her adrift on the water with nothing but a suitcase. You look upon Lau Lin's guileless, foolish face typical of the eighties. She thinks she occupies an entire island, but later she suspects it to be just a mound of jutting reef. Gradually, she realizes it is a mere suitcase. There is nowhere left for her to go. Though she understands her place in life has been reduced to no more than a butcher's block, she can only drift along amid the stink of carcasses.

The beast of a secret furrows its brow, grows fingernails and downy hair in her stomach. She is meant to give birth to this inflating secret in an old building, under the watchful eyes of someone else's generations of ancestors. You can see how dim the old house is. Newborn cries ring out in abandon, quaking the shrines until the lit fires undulate like snakes.

Because results for the national exams will be posted today, many of your coworkers asked for the day off. Not you. The manager even asked you to work a double shift. You work from noon until midnight closing. Afterward, Black Jack volunteers to give you a ride home. He no longer dares to pull any motorcycle stunts on you since what happened last time. You're the one who suggests cruising around, out of extreme boredom.

It's been two weeks without a single drop of rain. The night air is arid. The tarred road resembles the corpse of a giant black python that has been run over and dried to a crisp. Exposed to the merciless sun during the day, the road quietly disperses heat into the cool night. Black Jack's motorcycle runs along the reflective dotted line marking the center of the road. The bike goes faster and faster, until the line is continuous and you are on the highway with its wide lanes. As if approaching a race course, his bike speeds up, flics forward. You do not protest, your eyes on the neon needle gauging your speed. You're far over the speed limit. The bike charges against the wind, its growls and trembles swallowed whole into the wind's long throat. You raise your eyes to the road ahead. Every sharp bend erects a towering preview of death, but all this is not as fearsome as you'd imagined. At the time, you believe you're acquiring a misanthropic bend. Later on, recalling this scene, you pen a few lines of poetry in the novel:

> *I'm unclear whether death*
> *is a total exile of the soul, or*
> *the ultimate entrapment*

Black Jack is taken aback by your calm. He takes you on a pursuit of death's shadow along the nearly empty highway for at least twenty-some kilometers, then hugs the road's curves back into the city. The bike ascends an overpass. It's built far higher than you thought, drawing out a feeling of suspension and precarity in you. "What's this place?" you ask at the bridge's pinnacle. This is a unique spot, the only one of its kind in the entire world.

Where longitude, latitude, and that specific height come together, you see a strange, glowing object in the far-off distance, shaped like a green bronze goblet from ancient times. That's right—jue.

The blanket of night lies thick and heavy. Little remains of the lights on earth and the stars in the sky. Only that gigantic jue glitters like gold, looking for all the world like an illusion. You ask Black Jack what that is. He glances at it in the rearview mirror but doesn't seem to see what you saw, or perhaps he finds nothing incredible in the scene. "What?" he says.

"That big glowing jug just now." You point a finger backwards.

"Jug?" Black Jack does not turn around. He mulls it over. "The fountain that doesn't spout any water?"

"Fountain? You're saying that's a fountain?" You twist around to look, but suddenly there's no sight of the enormous jue.

"Yup. Older people call it The Luminous Jade Goblet."

You can't help turn but around once more. The dark night's curtains lower layer by layer. Indeed, the waterless goblet is no longer in your field of vision, though its shape and form linger in your mind. How exciting. The Luminous Jade Goblet, beneath which is the unwell man's bathing pool. The goblet connects the worlds of fiction and reality, like a gargantuan brass lock looped around both *The Age of Goodbyes* and your world of actual existence. You dwell on the goblet for the rest of your ride. It's like you're standing between two parallel mirrors and staring down an infinite tunnel, seeking an image that exists on its own independent level and interface. There you find the goblet, a portrait drawn to anticipate the future.

Black Jack shrugs when you probe him for the location of the goblet. "Feels like it can only be seen at night, and only from a distance. When you're too close it becomes unrecognizable."

You understand what he means. He's never been near that colossal creature. He describes it the way he would a mirage, posters plastered all over the walls at night by deities and gods. "It's like the goblet is on the other bank. You know what I mean? The opposite shore."

You both know very well that no body of water runs under the bridge. Instead there is inland soil on which rises a number of rocky hills. The dwellings beneath you look like tiny plastic Monopoly houses densely and neatly arranged on both sides of the road. And then the overpass delivers you back to flat land. "Almost like returning to the world of the living," you say.

The experiences of this night, the impressions it forms, are imprinted forever in the deepest recesses of your memory. So much so that many years after you lose *The Age of Goodbyes*, you remain convinced that "Notes from the Left Bank" is your creation. You truly did once see a fountain like that, just as you really did once witness a rough sleeper pushing a bicycle and behaving irrationally. Certainly you possess adequate potential and reasons to craft such a story, one that centers around a man who scrubs and bathes in the fountain under The Luminous Jade Goblet. Black Jack can be your witness. "About that night . . ." He narrows his eyes into slits and recalls the hint he gave you— it's like the goblet is on the other bank, the opposite shore.

—

Black Jack drives the bike to Mayflower. You take off your helmet and give it back to him. No goodbye kiss? he says teasingly. You ignore him and walk across the five-foot way to open the gate at Mayflower's entrance. He cackles loudly, like a drag queen who has just inventively and colorfully read someone for filth. Then he speeds away with a furious howl.

You push open the gate and discover a motorcycle, chained and leaning against a wall. It's a lightly used Honda 90 with an unfamiliar registration number. Apparently a rider is staying the night here, something that hasn't happened in Mayflower for quite some time. Over the past few years, Mana has been the one and only overnight guest from outside. She comes unbidden to your thoughts. Though you know it cannot be, you nevertheless pause on the second floor, your head cocked as you stare at room 204 in the middle of the hall.

Since Mana's departure, many of the rooms here have been reduced to nothing more than doors. Room 204 especially has become taboo, sealed away within your consciousness and placed under lock and key so that it is transformed into a flat drawing. But tonight, could it be that the motorcycle rider is staying in this very room? You tiptoe until you're up against the door. Conspiring with you, the floorboards do their best to repress their moans. You stand there for a while, sensing no sound other than your own breathing. If the room really did contain Mana, you imagine she is in the exact same position on the other side, both of you staring intently at your respective shadows cast onto the same door.

In that moment you dearly wish for Mana to be there behind the door. You have a powerful urge to tell her about how The Luminous Jade Goblet floated into view late at night. But Mana isn't here. Quietly, you head to your own room and sit on the bed, entering something like a meditative state. Having drained yourself of boredom on the roads just now, you've made space for more sorrow to surge in. Right before you fall asleep, Mana's devilish name seeps in like water, enveloping you until you are submerged. You dive into the dream in search of her, but she is not there.

Uncle Sai appears in the doorway while you are washing up at dawn. He asks if you'll be heading to the school for your exam results and offers to give you a ride. Mouth full of toothpaste bubbles, you first nod, then quickly shake your head. He understands what you mean. "If you don't have anything else going on, maybe come back earlier after you get your results," he says. "I told a few people downstairs we'd get dinner tonight." His voice is hoarse. There's phlegm in his throat, making him sound like he's stuttering or like his lungs have been ravaged.

"A few people downstairs" must mean the only remaining two old sex workers and the ancient doorman. The two sex workers depend on each other for everything, but the rest of you eat your daily meals alone except for annual Weiya celebrations at the end of the year. That Uncle Sai planned a dinner gives you the feeling it must be an extraordinary day. Is it really just because exam results are being announced? Although you're confident you scored well, you still feel he's making too much of a fuss. For some reason you remember the motorcycle at the bottom of the stairs. It remains there, parked and silent, more or less indicating that the unidentified owner is still hunkering down in Mayflower. You run your fingers along the bike's seat. Since the bike has been given permission to enter the premises, you deduce that it must belong to someone on good terms with Uncle Sai. Would they show up at dinner tonight?

It's the day after the initial announcements, and

so the rush is over. The school's offices are no longer crammed full of graduates back to receive their results. The reporters sent by various newspapers are gone too. You walk in quietly, receive your results, and wordlessly leave the office to saunter along the lane outside dappled with light and the shadows of trees. The secretary's eyes tracked you all the way out after she handed over your report. Sliding her glasses down the bridge of her nose, she squints as if she vaguely recognizes you, yet is unable to recall your name because of your reticence and aloofness.

You go next to that cave in the exurb to visit Mother. You brought neither incense nor flowers and instead spread open your report and read its contents to the woman smiling beatifically in her porcelain photo. She is as pleased as always. Since primary school, she delighted in you reading your exam scores to her one by one. Sometimes she also had you read the congratulatory phrases on the prizes you won. Afterward she'd softly stroke the top of your head, or the back of your neck. Then she'd sprawl across the desk and very carefully sign your report cards. She always applied too much pressure and performed the act with somber ceremony. Her name emerged crooked, as if penned by a kindergartner learning to write.

You criticized her. A whole life writing nothing but this name, and yet it never comes out right.

"Tsk! You're the smart one." She glared at you almost flirtatiously.

In the afternoon Uncle Sai calls your cell phone urging you to return, his voice shot through with anxiety. "No matter what the results look like, you should at least give me a call." But you find his concern hard to swallow. He, too, soon grows self-conscious at your hesitation, and so both of you turn to silence, hoping it will dissolve the awkwardness. But silence itself is another form of embarrassment that is even harder to resolve. The two of you wish the phones in your hands would come to life and supply the next lines of conversation.

"You at work?" Uncle Sai deepens his voice, tries to sound more casual.

"No, it's my day off." You lift your head to focus on the woman in the porcelain photo congratulating you with her smile. "I'm over at my ma's."

This is a very strange reply. It makes it seem like Mother never died but simply moved out of Mayflower and into a different residence one day. But Uncle Sai does not seem perturbed. He grunts in reply. "Well then, come right back and let's all go out for something to eat! Everyone's waiting for you."

Dinner is Thai cuisine. Everyone from Mayflower is present. The two old sex workers propping each other up wear loose blouses and cropped pants that look very similar in style and pattern. The ancient doorman brought his toddler grandson along. The clamor of crowds fills the bustling restaurant's tiny space. Glasses clink. Boisterous laughter. Some aunties' heedless screeching. The panicky wailing of children. Exaggerations pouring forth from people's lips: Do you remember, Way back when, That one time. The huge head of a grouper gasps in agony as it stews in a bubbling pot of curry soup.

You suspect you're tipsy from the several glasses of beer pushed on you. Why else do you feel so joyous and yet so despondent at the same time? Uncle Sai announces to the table that Mayflower is ending its run. The shopfront will be sold imminently. Everyone other than you and the doorman's grandson already knows all about it. Perhaps due to the alcohol's influence, you

barely react to the news. In fact, an urge to laugh hysterically begins to brew in your facial muscles. At the end
of dinner, you clutch your stomach and guffaw uncontrollably at a joke told by one of the old sex workers,
even though she hasn't even delivered the punch line.
You slump across the table, your laughter's vibrations
jostling a few tears out of your eyes.

Afterward, everyone walks back to Mayflower
together. Only two streets separate it from the restaurant. You're helped along by Uncle Sai, as your
movements have become slightly flailing and your
speech makes less and less sense. The doorman peels
away from the group, says he's taking a shortcut home
with his grandson. At the corner closest to Mayflower,
the sex workers bump into two of their mahjong buddies
sitting on the five-foot way in rattan chairs, cooling off
with cattail-leaf fans. The sex workers are reluctant to
leave once the conversation gets going. They squat and
stay to chat, leaving you and Uncle Sai to conclude the
last bit of the journey together. Both of you stay silent
until you're in front of Mayflower. You ask, burping,
"Whose bike is this?"

"Collateral from a friend who doesn't have the money
to pay me back." Uncle Sai opens the door and gives the
bike's handlebars a shove. "It's a little worn, but why
don't you make do with it?"

"I don't have a license." You intuit there's nothing
funny about this, but the muscles on your face float
lighter and lighter, the hint of a smile lifts your cheeks.

"Surely getting a license is child's play for someone
who got into university?" Spotting your lurching gait
as you navigate the stairs, Uncle Sai grabs one of your
arms and supports you as you go. The third floor is a bit
too far away. With every step you climb, you feel your
brains slowly curdle, the alcohol creating some kind of

acid-base reaction. You extricate your arm and curve it around Uncle Sai's neck to hook onto his shoulder, as if the two of you are old buddies. Uncle Sai, you say. Uncle Sai.

"Yes?"

You twist your neck to look at him. He's so close your eyes aren't able to focus. Uncle Sai splits into several identical layers, like a dispersed version of the Taoist theory of souls, three of which leave the body after death and seven of which do not. You shake your head forcefully to recombine the overlapping figures. Uncle Sai's images reinstate into a solid body, like a fan of poker cards shuffled into a neat stack. He's the only family you have left in this world.

"Have you ever seen a laser gun? The one my ma bought me?" As you let out a belch laced with alcohol, Uncle Sai blooms and dissipates.

—

It is a plastic rifle with a transparent blue body, a red trigger, and an opaque muzzle of yellow latex. When turned on, the blue body pulses with flashing red lights like the strobing beacons on top of cop cars. Mother's eyes lit up when she saw the gun. She rotated it in her hands, thinking about how happy you'd be when the prize was in your grasp. "Way cool! What do you think?" She showed the gun to Uncle Sai, who stood off to the side. Several times she lifted the gun overhead so that bright afternoon sunshine pierced its blue body, as if she was examining diamonds or precious gems for their clarity.

Uncle Sai could easily imagine the scene dreamed up by Mother. You were still young enough that she ran a comb under water and slicked your hair backward along your crown. Next, she patted clouds of baby powder on your cheeks, neck, back, and armpits, and dressed you in a stylish checkered button-down shirt paired with khaki shorts. Then she let you race down Mayflower's five-foot way, hot new toy in hand. You zoomed about the entrance and shot at the male pedestrians peering around sketchily. They watched as you hunkered down among the thick shadows, pretending to snipe. You in turn looked at their colorful shirts with targets drawn on, the innermost concentric rings right in the center of their torsos. Anyone who took so much as another step forward, anyone who dared say, "Hey, motherfucker!"— you took aim at their chests, one eye closed, and pulled the trigger!

Mother always turned away customers when your birthday rolled around each year. She'd fib about having her period to any man who knocked on the door. If they tried to force their way in or persuade her to carry on anyway, she'd lift her chin and slam the door shut with a bang. "Go home and fuck your mother!" she'd yell from behind the closed door.

On days like these the two of you hid in your room and ate egg tarts. You bought stationery and picture books in town. Mother even let you play games in the arcade. The sleazy man at the front counter was one of Mother's repeat customers. He looked the other way as you tunneled into that dim nest inundated with explosions, hollers, and the sounds of objects crashing into each other. You never got fully engrossed or stayed too long. At some point the arcade games' screens always flashed with scenes from your imagination: the man from the front counter placed a hand on Mother's waist or hip or thigh.

"Bang!"

He toppled with a low grunt, blood pulsing out of his chest. You cast a callous glance as he lay on the ground and clutched his wound, face full of torment. But on the horizon, never-ending enemies poured forth from every alley. Once your birthday was over, you had to wait more than 360 tomorrows before you could relive this day.

"Your ma did buy it." Uncle Sai says now. He remembers her being more excited than a child. Your birthday is approaching, she'd said, brandishing that gun in his face as if showing off.

He gazed intently at her smug expression. The sunlight reflected blue off the rifle's barrel.

You listen. Imagine her pleased with herself. Mother hugged the laser gun to her chest, examined it from time to time and pictured your excitement. You used it to execute every single man who pinched her thighs or arms. At the very least, the flashing red lights served to warn them, let them know: You're here.

You're here.

The third floor is really much too far away. You wake up in a room on the second floor. It's already dawn. The first streaks of sunshine blend with light from the streetlamp outside and pour into the room at a slant. The faint light, the direction in which the shadows stretch, the missing leaves from the Venetian blinds, the two bedside dressers mismatched in color and material, and the green soda bottle that used to house an African daisy—this is room 204, Mana's old room. You can just about hear the mosque's dawn call to prayers. You reminisce about how Mana always woke around this hour and slipped away from room 301. She'd return to this room and lie on this very bed. How magical, like opening a door within a labyrinthine dream to sneak into someone else's dream, then doubling back to your own lonesome dreamscape before the sun rises.

But right now the room feels warm and toasty, which pulls it closer to the waking world. Faint light and sheer shadows. A long litany of prayers that you still don't understand, despite having listened to it for many years, snakes in through a missing slat in the blinds. Next door, Uncle Sai tosses in bed coughing, lungs like an emptied-out beehive, phlegm fossilizing in his throat. The scent of mosquito coil is carried on each cough. All of these visuals and sounds make you nostalgic. You close your eyes once more and almost believe you can experience the dreams Mana once had here.

So it goes. Neither Mother nor Mana are at Mayflower anymore, and soon you and Uncle Sai will also leave. The dust has already settled on everything; what's left is just some seemingly unreal events that take place between dawn and early morning.

Those events are decidedly doors, multitudes of them. You pause in front of a peculiar red door in an open field, supported by no walls and sporting no handle. Standing there, you neither knock on the door nor cry out; you only listen silently to the various noises coming from the other side. Sounds from the world of the living: an overcapacity school bus driving by, a metal can leaking the cacophonous shouts of young children and teenagers; the neat slapping made by morning joggers as their rubber soles beat against the tarred road; the chirps and screeches of birds squabbling over puddles of vomit deposited on the side of the road by last night's drunks.

The door is pushed open. Outside, a fuzzy blur of sunlight. You blink open your dry eyes with some effort and see Uncle Sai is just outside the door. Astonishment stretches his face as he asks what you're doing in this room. "Didn't I help you to the third floor last night? You fell straight into bed."

Rubbing your eyes, you take in your surroundings. After a few moments you're still unclear where you are. This might very well be another dream, or a different level within an original dream. Between reality and dreamscape, between heaven and hell, between attic and cellar, there exists the difference of just one level, and so it is between the second and third floor. You feel dizzy, your brain swollen and muddled like the world when sky and earth first split apart. Out of this confusion, two lines of poetry bubble up.

> *Do not be afraid to love*
> *Though love is a dwarf,*
> *it casts a vast shadow*

"You were sleepwalking. Right?" Uncle Sai strides into the room, hands on his waist. He looks at you as if gazing upon a thousand-year-old jade burial suit.

—3—

Those two lines of poetry appear in "Last Words from Last Night." I'm talking about the short story you write late in your life. By then your eyesight has deteriorated, forcing you to craft only short little pieces by the scant light shining through your memories. This is when the unpublished poems of your youth come into play. Though you never wrote down those two lines of poetry, they remain in your heart's deepest recesses. The weak light of memory shimmers through and immediately projects an impression of that poem.

Among the output from your later illustrious writing career, "Last Words from Last Night" contains the most poetry, largely of a puerile flavor. Critics enthusiastically laud you for your success at capturing the mindset and language of young poets,[1] not knowing that all you've done is incorporate your juvenilia. Because of this you decide to burn all your notebooks before you die. "No sense leaving any clues behind for those presumptuous critics," you say.[2]

Compared to the rest of your work, "Last Words from Last Night" was undoubtedly more difficult to compose. There's the mist clouding your eyes that makes it hard to read, reducing you to relying on an assistant who types up your words on a computer. More importantly, there is simply too little information on "Last Words from Last Night" in that tome *The Age of Goodbyes*. All you know is that a newspaper unknowingly published that Shaozi story posthumously. Because its title contains the phrase "last words," it naturally attracted a giant wave of attention once the news broke about Shaozi's death. Unsurprisingly, many readers saw the story as the author's personal "last words." But that's all the book says. What little material that does exist is very fuzzy, not at all adequate to help you "restore" that piece of work.

You find a keyword, *sleepwalking*, within The Fourth Person's analysis. From it you get a vague feeling the story must be about romance, writing, and sleepwalking.

The Fourth Person's cold dismissal of the story is illogical and disproportionate in light of its market pull. "Last Words from Last Night" is dead last in his

1. Paraphrased from "Of Dreams, Books, and Dawn—A Short Analysis of the Literary Language and Rhetoric in 'Last Words from Last Night,'" published in volume 3 of "This Land: A Special Issue" produced by *Literary Plaza*.

2. See your biography, *The Person Blessed by Memory*, written after the author's death by his assistant, who worked with him in his twilight years.

"Rankings of Notable Work by Shaozi." He does not hold back from spelling out his disdain for the piece, even saying he feels "extremely disappointed." According to his close reading, the story is morbid and lowbrow, causing him to suspect Shaozi of intending to pivot from serious literary author to writer of potboilers.[3]

Because the local literary scene was still preoccupied with mourning Shaozi's untimely death, The Fourth Person's negative review, replete with such strong words, naturally drew intense ire from readers, some of whom wasted no time in penning rebuttals to condemn him.[4] The tome contains numerous documentary-style passages that record this minor controversy, mostly centered around the backlash against The Fourth Person and contentious debates comparing serious and lowbrow literature, which have very little to do with the actual content of "Last Words from Last Night."

The Fourth Person never defended himself against his literary peers' criticism. In truth, news of Shaozi's death dealt him a great blow. Not only did he suffer physically from paralysis caused by a stroke, he was also

3. See "The Next Beautiful Sojourner—On Shaozi's 'Last Words from Last Night.'" The Fourth Person writes, "In this story the author (Shaozi) expends much effort to approximate the mystery genre, amalgamating romance, poetry, dreams, and other such trendy elements, even blending certain deceptive techniques to intentionally nudge readers into linking the writer and her work, so as to encourage a variety of suppositions and suspicions. In addition, the story's plot relies too heavily on twists, greatly exposing the author's attempt to pander to the masses. Whether judged on intention or craft, the story fails to impress. Labelling it 'lowbrow' is no more than appropriate."

4. Those who published rebuttals included writers, scholars, psychologists, and researchers studying culture. The common charge was that The Fourth Person failed to fully appreciate "Last Words from Last Night" and was moreover too inflammatory with his word choices. The author's death further rendered his actions akin to "flogging a corpse," which was considered "inhumane and immoral." Suspicions were raised that he only sought attention by capitalizing on Shaozi's death.

emotionally stuck in a titanic wave of sorrow and self-pity. From that day on, he grew despondent and spent every day slumped at his desk, though he never worked on anything. He could no longer muster enough energy to pit himself against anyone.

"Last Words from Last Night" remains a blank spot in your heart. You are provided with one single keyword and a few scattered hints. Everything else is boundless white space and possibility. Late in your life you will sit at a south-facing window, savoring the last glimmers of light granted to you by the heavens above. Plunged deep into the past, you suddenly catch glimpses of the romance, poetry, and sleepwalking you've once experienced. You will close your eyes and say to the assistant beside you, "Get ready. I'm going to write the next story."

CHAPTER TWELVE

—1—

A relative from the fishing village said he once saw that boy Candlenut in the capital, though he sounded unsure about this claim. What he indisputably witnessed was a drug addict snatch a purse in broad daylight. The thief was caught by a crowd and marched to the police station amid shouts and jeers. Upon receiving this news, Steely Bo straight away collapsed in the living room, causing a loud crash like an old tree struck down by lightning during a raging storm.

By then Steely Bo was old and addled, his body full of faulty organs. He'd lost a lot of weight over the course of a few years. Aided by overeating and many other bad-lifestyle habits, his long-diagnosed diabetes worsened by the day until it began to wear down different parts of his body. His kidneys had completely shut down, which triggered blood poisoning and forced him to undergo dialysis treatment three times a week. Blood flowed from his body into a machine and flowed back after being filtered. It was like training qi to traverse his arteries and veins. The process took four hours, extending his life for a few days before he had to rinse and repeat. It was definitely a rich man's disease. Thanks to a connection, Du Li An had access to a nonprofit dialysis center under the umbrella of a Hindu religious organization. She falsified their income level to secure a low treatment rate meant to lessen the financial burden on impoverished patients. But over time the bills still piled up, and his medication wasn't free either.

Of course there was no way Du Li An would fork over the money. She put all her cards on the table and had it out with Steely Bo before registering at the dialysis center on his behalf. Not having much choice, he put a row house under his name on the market. That netted him around fifty thousand ringgit, cash he hoped would stretch to last what remained of his life.

He'd believed the rest of his days would go by in gentle passivity, carrying him on placid waves to the far shore. Yet he was struck down by a piece of shocking news out of the blue. Du Li An cradled the child in her lap, passing time before dinner with gossip and small talk. Half of her attention was on engaging her child with a plastic toy car; the other half was repeating the anecdote about the purse-snatcher who was possibly Candlenut getting beaten up. She didn't notice Steely Bo's face seize up. He sat silently for a while, then leaned on his cane to struggle up from his recliner's canvas seat. Slowly, he made his way to the dining room. When he reached the TV, he buckled without warning, like a wall disappearing into a sinkhole.

The child's nanny sat on the marble floor dealing with a stack of diapers fresh from the clothesline in the yard. She was so shocked by Steely Bo's suddenly topple that she shot straight up and started screaming nonsense. The child in Du Li An's arms was jolted by the commotion. After a half second, the child tossed the toy car and broke out into wailing screams. Du Li An too lost her cool. She and the nanny flailed about helplessly for a bit before finally calling out for help. Thanks to their neighbors, Steely Bo was delivered to the ER.

In that moment Du Li An had a premonition that he would not make it.

That night, Lau Lin received a call from Du Li An. By that point, Lau Lin was living above a sundry shop on the main street in Batu Gajah. When the shop owner summoned her from downstairs, she paused the sewing machine and clattered down the steps in flip-flops, child in her arms. Through the receiver, Du Li An listened to her reedy voice, full of uncertainty: "Hello." She was just as before, still perpetually afraid of changes knowable and unknowable. Ever since she left the fishing village and subsequently the tin mining town, the ringing of a telephone had posed an especially murky terror for her, a cajoling urgency that signified certain unavoidable bad omens.

Hearing her voice, Du Li An was momentarily stymied by both the passage of time and the sea change in their relationship. The words stopped up in her. Though her silence was brief, it seemed to elongate because of the corresponding silence on the other end. Then she heard the babbling of that faraway child. Clearing her throat, she said, "Ah Lin, it's me. Auntie Li."

The next morning, Lau Lin entrusted the child with her roommate and, after navigating three different bus routes, arrived at the hospital. Her mind was completely blank. She had some difficulty remembering her father's appearance and attitude when she saw him last. That must have been before the child was born. When she left the big house, right before she stepped into Du Li An's car, she'd cast a glance back. Steely Bo was bent over, fiddling with that new karaoke machine, his forehead shiny. She didn't have time to consider how aged he looked. Since then she hadn't seen him even once. When she visited the fishing village for a couple of days during Lunar New Year, her ma kept up a refrain: your ba hasn't been home for a few years now. Her wispy old country accent whistled through her toothless mouth and dissipated above the fishing village permeated with a fishy odor and the smell of fermented shrimp. In front of the house, ocean waves gently tapped out a rhythm.

Du Li An headed over from Ping Le House to find Lau Lin perched by the sick bed. Dressed in an old T-shirt and torn jeans, green-tinged bags puffed up under her eyes, she stared fixedly at Steely Bo on the bed. She was pale as a ghost, her arms wrapped around a bulging plastic bag. Steely Bo was truly ancient now. The air spluttered forth by his lungs was rotten and revolting. Liver spots punctuated his skin. On the whole he looked like a moldy, oversized bag of skin wrapped around coarse, ossified bones. A few thin plastic tubes snaked from his hands into his nostrils, completing the picture. It was a truly horrifying image of old age.

"He was suffering from lots of pain and illnesses, so I knew he didn't have much longer. But I really didn't expect to see him collapse just like that, with my own eyes." Du Li An stood behind Lau Lin. From that higher perspective, the horizontal person in view indeed seemed to be right at death's door. Du Li An had never witnessed the death of a family member. Sou Gei had passed quickly, a durian seed the size of a chicken egg lodged in her throat like an Adam's apple. She was already rigid and cold by the time she was discovered. She hadn't been there either when her old man swallowed his last. And now here was this person who qualified as her husband of twenty-one years. Though their relationship had morphed in the last ten years and they kept separate bedrooms, it was still twenty-one years. If nothing else, sharing a house and being in each other's proximity day and night made them family. As the saying went, those who leave drift further with each passing hour, while strangers near at hand grow more intimate as time goes by.

She was aware, too, that though marital bliss ceased to exist long ago between her and Steely Bo, feelings of gratitude and loyalty remained. In fact, there was no turning her back on those feelings. They were even harder to eradicate than love. They could not be rung up like a bill; there were no details to itemize. Impossible to pay it off. After all he was once a massive tree that shielded her from wind and rain, giving her breathing room from which she climbed higher, step by step. Though he never held this over her head, it was carved forever in her memory. Thus for the next ten years she treated him the same way she did the old man: She indulged Steely Bo's short-sighted spendthrift habits, his lotus-eating ways. Secretly she thought letting him while away his twilight years was pretty fair recompense.

And yet she was still extraordinarily shaken when he collapsed. She didn't sleep a wink that night, remembering their shared past, which she had not once thought of in many years. There was that ancient couplet about how, for two people to share a boat, they must have sustained a decade-long relationship in their past life; for them to be married took a hundred years of prior entanglement. So of course she felt her sadness keenly.

That was why, when Lau Lin turned around, she saw wretchedness written all over Du Li An's face. She pressed Lau Lin to call the fishing village with the news, while she got in touch with her brother at the capital, doing whatever she could to summon everyone to his bedside. A thought kept circling: *Steely Bo will die now and it will be a clean break; maybe it's for the best.*

Ah Sai and his wife, Helen, drove up in time. He was stirred by emotion when he saw Steely Bo all shriveled up on that bed. When Ah Sai got married last year and threw a banquet at the restaurant in the capital, Steely Bo had sat at the table of honor with Du Li An. They were joined there by Auntie Fong and Uncle Wah Zai, Ah Sai's mentor when he was a teenager. His sister's adopted child had just turned one. She asked for a high chair and placed the child into the tiny, barred seat. The child was particularly active, always twisting about to examine his surroundings with large blinking eyes. Occasionally he pummeled his chair with a little plastic gavel that looked like an air pump—bang, bang, bang— seeking attention at all times. The lively restlessness of Du Li An's child had contrasted sharply with the demeanor of Steely Bo, seated next to him. Steely Bo's face was the color of dead trees and ash, his posture off-kilter. Halfway through the banquet he shuffled to the bathroom and returned with splatters down one pant leg. Ah Sai recalled that his old man had passed away around this age. He also had difficulty walking with his swollen arthritic legs. Ah Sai felt a sudden wave of pity and misery. After the banquet, he had helped Steely Bo into the car. "Take care of yourself, Brother Bo," Ah Sai said as he closed the door after him. Even Du Li An was taken aback. In unison, she and Steely Bo looked Ah Sai up and down.

The last two years had been ones of ease and comfort for her. Since her son had come into her life, her heart had become especially full. Her body correspondingly grew plumper and her face was always radiant with smiles. She looked well off, more so than at any time in the past. The body fat she had piled on didn't bother her in the least. She was already forty-six or forty-seven, after all. In fact, she thought her new figure was well served by emerald green or scallion white jade accessories. Even Auntie Fong couldn't keep her eyes off

Du Li An at the banquet. Your sister is blessed with such aristocratic looks, Auntie Fong told Ah Sai. She looks just like a rich tai tai.

Everyone was on the up and up as they approached the prime of their lives. Through Auntie Fong's matchmaking, Ah Sai had married a teacher and settled down in the capital. His wife spoke no Chinese dialects, Mandarin or otherwise, and was unflatteringly nicknamed "Banana" by Du Li An. As for Auntie Fong, her family's paperwork had come through and they were all about to immigrate to Australia, and so the restaurant in the capital would soon be under new management. Ah Sai was to stay on as head chef. He was even a stakeholder in the new venture, partly thanks to Du Li An's behind-the-scenes investment. She considered it her way of supporting her younger brother. Seated amid this vibrant circle of flourishing people, Steely Bo was out of place, his hoary, withered figure thrown into the sharpest relief. Ah Sai involuntarily thought of the Kin Tek Hall leader of yesteryear, body rippling with muscles, face like a bloodthirsty demon. Compassion overcame Ah Sai at the memory. It made him behave generously toward Steely Bo, as if by cosseting him he'd be venerating all the old men in the world who found themselves abject and dismal as the sun set on their lives.

And now, despite the sick room's sterilized air, Ah Sai could pick up a scent of death. In his coma, Steely Bo's eyebrows were tightly furrowed, like he could hear Death whispering into his ear. Soon, a group from the fishing village arrived. Du Li An greeted them, then made some excuse about taking care of business at Ping Le House and hurriedly left. Lau Lin chased after her and the two spoke outside the room in low voices, pushing and nudging each other with their limbs. Ah

Sai caught sight of Lau Lin shoving a plastic bag into Du Li An's arms.

Du Li An spread open the bag. Inside was a brightly colored, exquisite little plastic windmill.

"I was thinking, since it's almost their birthday, I bought a pair so they can each have one." Lau Lin bit her lower lip, her hands still holding up the bag as if afraid Du Li An would push it back toward her. "That child . . . I've never once bought him anything."

Du Li An did mean to be firmer, but she couldn't escape Lau Lin's earnest eyes. Du Li An felt, too, the strength and determination radiating from those hands. "Don't you think I'd already have something like this? You think Auntie Li would mistreat him?" She sighed, accepting the item. "Ah Lin, that child is my son now."

Ah Sai couldn't make out any of those words, of course. Du Li An turned and walked away. Lau Lin returned to the room and gazed as if in a trance at her father on the sick bed. The fishing village was represented by an old woman who walked with a cane, her pair of sons and their wives, plus two teenagers. Every single one of them stared at Steely Bo with somber expressions, as if they almost looked forward to his last breath. Turns out none of those present had ever witnessed another soul depart this world. Even the fishing village crone who looked as ancient as a centenarian said she wasn't present at the deaths of her parents and siblings. And yet after twenty or thirty minutes of everyone standing around in anticipation, Steely Bo's brows smoothed out. He opened his eyes.

Lau Lin and Helen were the first to notice. They both sucked in their breath and exclaimed a soundless "Ah."

The visitors immediately crowded the bed; ten faces whose expressions were either nervous or lovingly concerned surrounded Steely Bo. His eyeballs performed a slow rotation before they paused on Lau Lin's face. "Where's your older brother? He didn't come?"

She was the only person in the room who truly understood the meaning of his questions. Immediately she burst into tears of misery. All she could do was shake her head hard in answer.

But rumors persisted that Candlenut was still alive. Someone was always saying how they saw a person who resembled him here or there. The descriptions always painted a picture of a disheveled drug addict, or else a homeless man who had lost his wits. Some said he had been tortured at the police station or was in jail. Others said for a period of time he was a pimp in one of the capital's red light districts. Steely Bo had just seen a teenage Candlenut in an exceedingly long dream. In the dream, Candlenut was on the main road of a sepia-toned small town, squatting in front of a bookstore reading serialized comics. He was completely engrossed until Steely Bo loomed over him, gray shadow blanketing him and his comics. Candlenut raised his head. As if caught red-handed in a crime, he suddenly leapt up and tore away at top speed. The dream then turned into an endless chase, as Candlenut transformed each time he rounded a corner. Sometimes he was as lean as an Indian monk and sported a bushy beard. Other times he was a boisterous child who shrieked and squealed, a kite in his hand. Steely Bo shouted at Candlenut to stop, even begged him to wait. But he merely turned around and spat on the ground. Steely Bo slipped on the thick wad of mucus and hit the ground hard. The road abruptly morphed into a slope, sending him tumbling downward.

And that was how he returned to life. Du Li An felt only astonishment when all this was recounted to her over the phone. Life and death coupled with dreams—it all seemed profound, even somewhat mystical. She hurried to the hospital even though it wasn't yet Ping Le House's closing hour. By the time she arrived, the room had emptied of the morning's visitors. She'd assumed Lau Lin would stick around, but the woman sitting by the bed was middle-aged and unfamiliar. Behind her stood a pair of teenagers, a boy and a girl.

A heavy silence had settled over the room. On the bed, Steely Bo seemed to be in deep sleep. Du Li An approached, asking, "And you are?"

She was certain she'd never seen these people before. They looked like a family, a mother with her children. The woman and the girl behind her had the same sallow faces, same high cheekbones, and nearly identical brows. The boy, solidly built, had monolid eyes and a flat, broad nose. His eyebrows flared with an air of aggression. Du Li An was of course thrown for a loop when she saw the boy's face. Meanwhile, the woman began to show signs of panic. She nodded at Du Li An and yanked at the teenagers beside her. They rushed out with barely a greeting.

The strange woman's embarrassment inflated Du Li An's suspicion like a balloon. Unable to stop herself, she shouted after them, "Hey, you!" But the woman quickened her steps and was soon out of sight, dragging the girl with her. Only the boy, lagging behind, twisted his neck for a final look. That one glance was more than enough. Du Li An made out from his eyes a teenage boy's restless agitation and disdain directed at the world of adults, plus an impatience toward middle-aged women like herself. That expression, those facial features, and his age all combined to form a facsimile of that boy Candlenut when he first stepped foot in the tin mining town all those years ago.

Du Li An felt her hands and feet turn ice-cold. The chill spread rapidly into her bloodstream, as if someone had thrust a giant block of ice into her heart chambers. For a moment her eyes could not process the world in front of them. Inside her brain bright lights flashed, clicked, and clacked. She saw only blinding blankness. As a wave of dizziness swept over her she clutched the railing at the foot of the sick bed. She spread wide the lobes of her lungs and breathed with all her might, so that jets of air flooded her body. Only then did the world gradually fade in before her eyes.

It was still the same sick room. Steely Bo remained on the bed, eyes shut, perhaps even dreaming that same dream from before in which he chased after his son. The bag suspended from the IV pole continued to drip. The monotonous beeping of some electronic device reverberated in the space, sounding like tinnitus. But the strange woman and her teenagers were not there. Du Li An saw Lau Lin standing in the door holding a thermos.

"Who were those people?" Du Li An heard a metallic ring in her own voice. "Who is that woman?"

—

There was a time when, every two or three days, Steely Bo would head out the door holding infant formula, many adorable baby outfits, and various shiny toys. For his grandkids at the fishing village, he claimed. Occasionally Du Li An noticed one or two bottles of Bénédictine peeking out of the plastic bags he held. That was good stuff, an herbal liqueur better known as DOM, used to promote recovery after childbirth. Du Li An had taken along a couple of bottles to the old house after Lau Lin delivered, leaving instructions with the postpartum doula to serve Lau Lin two small glasses daily. Now Du Li An turned it over in her head: Back then, why hadn't her suspicions been roused by bottle after bottle of DOM? They should have raised a red flag for her. Since when had Steely Bo been so thoughtful and caring? Even if he were the attentive type, he wouldn't have expended that level of effort on his daughter-in-law. At the time he was still leading Kin Tek Hall. There was an aura of power about him. He scoffed at the rural folk in his home town, and even once referred to his two daughters-in-law as "country bumpkins" in front of Du Li An.

That whole night she stayed up in the sick room, not sleeping a wink, her mind obsessively combing over the events of those few years. Lau Lin said the fishing village had long known about the woman and her two kids. She ran an herbal tea shop in a small town called Papan, where she'd grown up helping her father at his tea stall. The townspeople knew her by her nickname, "Twin Pigtails." Her son was born a year after she got together with Steely Bo, and he bought her a double-story shophouse near the town's wet market. The house's lower level was made into her herbal tea shop, while she lived upstairs. But business was dismal. Despite branching out to sell soy milk and grass jelly, and later on throwing in a couple of noodle stalls, she was still barely breaking even. Slowly, the place turned into a commonplace kopitiam, indistinguishable from all the others. And Twin Pigtails, who was once known for her innocent good looks and sweet demeanor, had at some point transformed into an auntie with a mournful long face. Though usually a woman of few words, she was a nag when it came to her children.

For a time Steely Bo was especially attentive toward Twin Pigtails and his new son, and often spent his days in Papan, which was situated smack between the tin mining town and the fishing village. He'd look after the kid while she sold herbal tea downstairs. The boy was, after all, his own blood. In contrast, he'd later complain incessantly about Du Li An's adopted child, calling him disruptive. Steely Bo was moreover bothered by that child's pretty looks, and as a result never wanted to spend much time with him. Du Li An did the math and worked out that Ping Le House was about the same age as the Papan son. Therefore, Steely Bo's claim about diverting funds to help finance the fish farm started by his fishing village sons was nothing but a big fat lie. That ice block in her heart refused to melt; frigid water kept on dribbling into her veins. She stared agape at the man in deep slumber. His brow was furrowed, his nostrils stuck with plastic tubes. His face was fixed in a censorious expression, as if he was holding out even in his dream, frowning and refusing to come clean.

"All right, Steely Bo, all right! Good on you!" She thought about how the man had holed up in the Papan shophouse for three whole days, then came home and embraced her from behind. How she responded with warm tears and slightly chilled hands. She'd almost believed that was what she wanted—a man and an apology. All that was missing was a child to complete their family.

—

From then on Steely Bo was dead to her. Du Li An didn't tell him that she'd murdered him in her mind again and again at the hospital that night. Several times she fought the urge to pluck out the IV tubes hooked to his body. Then his escape would be complete, and he'd be reunited with his beloved son in that dream from which he would never awaken. Leaving the sick room the next dawn, she caught a glimpse of herself in the elevator's stainless steel doors. She looked haggard, her eyes webbed with red capillaries, her posture deformed. Outside, the sunlight hurt her eyes. She raised a hand to block the glare, and for an instant felt as if she'd crawled out of a hole in the ground after much struggling, as if she'd narrowly escaped death.

The room was a field of stillness when Steely Bo woke up again that afternoon. Everyone who'd been at his side had left. He'd kept hollering after shape-shifting figures in his dream, not suspecting that the world beyond had also undergone a metamorphosis. A square of sunshine slanted onto his bed like a coverlet. He quietly observed the wind outside caress and mold these lights and shadows, his bad eyesight conjuring ripples of water where the sunshine was sheer as muslin.

Lau Lin and Steely Bo's eldest son and daughter-in-law from the fishing village showed up in the following days. Du Li An never appeared again. Steely Bo drifted in and out of sleep, but even so, he realized something was wrong. She didn't show up on the day he was discharged, either, though she did take care of the hospital bill. She also left behind an address and some keys, along with a message for the fishing village folks—every single one of Steely Bo's belongings from the big house had been moved elsewhere. "He can go back to his hometown if he wants, or there's always Papan. If he just can't bear to leave town, I'll set aside an old place for him."

The two sons from the fishing village butted heads with her over this matter, but nobody could hope to overcome Du Li An when her heart had hardened like iron. After a week of back-and-forth, the two salt-of-the-earth villagers still couldn't come up with a counter-strategy, and so had to give in. It was impossible for Steely Bo to leave the tin mining town due to his dialysis treatments. Therefore, the sons had no choice but to drive their father in his antique tank of a car to the address she'd specified. The house was easy to find, and moreover, Steely Bo recognized the route. It turned out to be Du Li An's old home. Hadn't he sat in this very Mercedes all those years ago, at the head of a seven-car delegation? All of them honking the entire way, putting on a flagrant display as they sped toward that very house to receive the bride?

The sons helped Steely Bo upstairs and settled him in the empty abode, that old dream shared by many. He saw that the altar had been cleared of shrines, making way for the karaoke machine he'd bought. The machine was an ancient hulk. It looked like an old engine torn from an abandoned car. In that moment he finally understood Du Li An's hatred and resolve. He walked unsteadily toward the TV and plopped into his beloved recliner. That canvas seat had long bore his burden and took measure of his weight; his familiar body odor lingered. There he lay, almost wishing he would never again wake up.

His second son stayed behind to keep an eye on him while his eldest went out for bread, condensed milk, Milo, crackers, and instant noodles. That afternoon, after filling up a thermos with boiled water, they left for the fishing village. It was a weekend day. Wind rattled trees outside, disrupting light and shadow. Occasionally street racers sped past downstairs with whistling howls. In the evening, an unexpected troupe of sorrowful clouds swam into the air above the tin mining town, bringing with them a long-lived rain that drizzled through the night.

And indeed Du Li An never set eyes on him again.

Sitting at the counter in Ping Le House, she'd sometimes see a similar old man walking by with the help of a rattan cane, or she'd glimpse a car resembling his antique tank crawling past at a snail's pace. At times she'd hear an update about him, such as how the Papan woman and her daughter once stayed over for a while to take care of him, though they left for their little town once school started.

Guen Hou was the one who delivered the updates. She preferred to appear in Du Li An's life during its darker periods, though Du Li An never exhibited any of the expected self-pity or spiteful rage. She maintained a faint smile no matter the topic of conversation, as if she couldn't care less, or then again as if everything was already in the bag. Probably it was because half her attention was always dedicated to the child in her arms. The boy was fair and plump, with handsome, delicate looks. He loved to suck his thumb while nuzzling against his mother's impressive bosom, blinking at people with wide, clear eyes that seemed to sneer and see through them.

"Ah, the kid has the look of a playboy," Guen Hou said. "Who knows how many hearts he's going to break."

"Will he?" Du Li An beamed as she lifted the child overhead. "Will he?" She asked again.

If he did, it'd be something that would happen much, much later.

—2—

As the novel nears its end, the author spills much ink on a fantastical dream that visits Du Li An. The dream scene takes place over twenty-three whole pages and is frankly a recap and an extension of the novel. After returning from Lau Lin's funeral, Du Li An takes a nap in the big house. The nap seems to last quite a while. In the dream, day and night succeed each other like rapidly spinning wheels; pages of a book flutter and fly. A young man hugging a tome to his chest stands beneath a window. In the dream, the child has grown up. She knows very well that she's in a dream, and realizes too the illusory nature of it. But its elements and environment are so enchanting, she's unwilling to wake up. When she finally does, the sky beyond the window is dim and murky. Hard to tell the hour and day, whether it's dawn or evening. The child who'd been lying by her side has gone downstairs to fuss with his many toys under the nanny's watch.

It is only after reading over twenty pages describing this dream that you sense the tome's hollowness. The characters either leave or die off one by one while the tin mining town's population booms. There's nowhere for the story to go except toward a gradual withering. Such a big chunk of the book is occupied by the dream, as if it is a huge and unavoidable mirror placed in the path of the characters' lives. Reality and dreams are the equivalent of life's days and nights; or maybe they are like doors that confound you as to which side faces in, and which out.

Lau Lin's death is handled with a light and careless touch. In truth, when you approach this section near the end, you have an eerie illusion that the tome has been vastly decimated by nibbling insects. In your hands it no longer feels as cumbersomely heavy as it once did. You flip the pages. All the words are still there . . . or, rather, every single page remains filled with words. They line up in neat rows, emanating a faint inky smell that sits somewhere indistinguishable, between bitterness and sweetness. The feeling given off is that of a new book produced just yesterday by the printing house.

After reading the tome, you develop a nostalgia toward this city that is hard to explain. You begin paying attention to those alleys developed and then gradually forgotten by the times. On bus rides, you keep your eyes on old buildings about to be left behind. You feel like you know them, just like you can recognize a wall from Mayflower or some specific graffiti on it. Like the perennial moon, they witnessed the lives and deaths of you and your ancestors, all your cumulative glories and defeats. Now they exchange cold stares with you on their own slide toward extinction.

This city's older district still teems with places like Du Li An's old home and Lau Lin's Batu Gajah dwelling from the novel, all prewar shophouses close to being abandoned. They predictably house old businesses downstairs with few customers and insufficient lighting, while the upstairs spaces, originally meant for residential living, are vacant. The wooden window frames and doors are mostly dilapidated, beyond repair. Under the eaves hang countless mud nests made by swallows. They come this season and depart the next, the same as they've done year after year. You imagine that if a person were to appear in that window, they could only be a rough sleeper with a drug problem.

Mayflower might well escape the fate of these old buildings. Uncle Sai tells you its next owner plans to spend money gut renovating it into a café with nostalgic nods to the past. You can just imagine its gaudy future. Its outer walls will be lacquered with lemon-yellow paint, and it will feature vermillion banister railings. The front entrance will sport cutting-edge patio sun shades. Stylish young people will perch on lightweight but poorly crafted chairs with aluminum frames and woven rattan seats. As the young people sip coffee they will stare at the sepia photos on the walls, trying to identify their ancestors' figures from those overexposed street views.

It takes you and Uncle Sai two weeks to pack up in Mayflower. Then on a weekend morning, you rent a truck and make three trips to move. Everything that should come with you gets put inside a newly purchased house. It's a small single-story row house that sits in a residential area. There's a tiny attic. Knowing you secretly admire it, Uncle Sai ceded the house to you without any heads-up. It's neat and sunny inside. A smell of assorted construction materials mixed together still lingers in the air. At night the stars, flitting in and out of visibility like fireflies, settle on the skylight that is propped partially open. You rest your head on your forearms and gaze into the void in the air. Mother—the eyes within her eyes—delight and sorrow sparkling like hints of tears.

You place the suitcase Mother left behind under the bed. That case still holds and protects her beloved objects, all of them worn and broken, most of them your things, though they conjure almost no meaning for you because the memories within the items belong only to her. At last you understand Mother will never return to claim her suitcase. That is the final thing she left you. It encapsulates a history, wishes, and the act of waiting.

As if she's still here. As if she will be back.

It's here in this clean, bright attic that you finish reading *The Age of Goodbyes*. Only a few days remain until university starts. You're still of the opinion that the dream in the closing chapter is described at too much length. Reading those endlessly rambling details makes you feel like you've fallen into a great river, neither deep nor shallow, rushing on at breakneck speed. Submerged in the river is Time, eras and ages of it, harder to tame than either water or air. And the dream, it is an ocean, a lake, a river; or maybe it is merely a fishbowl.

Lau Lin dies. It's mid-autumn festival, and she makes a stop on the way to visit her mother at the fishing village. During that stop she buys two pomelos and a box of mooncakes containing one each of the following fillings: salted egg yolk and lotus seed paste; bean paste; five nuts; nuts and ham. In addition, she purchases a goldfish-shaped paper lantern for her nephew along with three boxes of colorful candles and some arthritis medicine for her mother. Laden with these gifts, she squeezes onto a bus headed to her hometown. The bus that has seen better days zooms along at an unusually high speed. She feels a headache coming on from all the jostling, but she does want to make good time. Her plan is to take the evening bus back to Batu Gajah so she can also celebrate mid-autumn festival with her son.

When the bus crashes and flips, Lau Lin is tossed from an open window onto the road and dies on impact, her hands clutching a torn lantern of indeterminate shape. Because she wasn't carrying any identification, her body is parked in the General Hospital's morgue for nearly two months. Later, her eldest brother from the fishing village goes with Du Li An to identify the body. As soon as the black bag is parted, the fisherman bursts immediately into wild sobs. Du Li An, on the other hand, holds it together. She gives a nod to the middle-aged Indian man who parted the bag. Yes, it's Lau Lin. When she died, she did so with an expression of guile and purity on her face.

After taking care of affairs, Du Li An returns to the big house and takes her son from the nanny. That night, humming the child to sleep, she begins to cry out of the blue. She doesn't even realize she's thinking of Lau Lin, the woman who was once as close as a sister because of the man they shared. When she went into labor, Du Li An drove her to a birthing center and kept her company for eight hours, until the two boys were birthed, one after the other. The midwife lifted the infants by their legs, suspending them in the air like two chickens that had just been plucked and drained. When they let out their first cries, the two women were both moved to copious tears, yet they also turned to each other and smiled.

You imagine their intimacy. During Lau Lin's post-partum confinement, they each cradle a newborn on opposite ends of a sofa with a rattan frame. From the start, the Hokkien doula hired from out of state assumes they are sisters by blood. Du Li An knows there's an element of conspiracy in their closeness. What connects them is a secret, which snares and binds like a creeping vine that bears bunches of bitter fruit. They can no longer clearly comprehend the secret's contents. All they can manage is to share its burden, split its harvest.

Yet there are winners and losers even in a private, tightly woven relationship between co-conspirators. Real secrets should never be co-owned to begin with, much less with an unusually fragile person like Lau Lin. Du Li An is reluctant to split the secret into halves that the two of them would respectively safeguard. Before she leaves for the night, Lau Lin trails her to the door and murmurs timidly about wanting to keep a baby for herself. Du Li An's heart sinks. She lets out a long, slow sigh.

"Fine, then go somewhere far away." That is the last thing she says before leaving, after her many attempts at advice have failed, as have her various gentler or harsher tactics. "Talk about being a laughingstock if your ba ever finds out he's raising his grandkid as his son. Who could stand losing face like that?"

Since Lau Lin's body was completely frozen for a time, her innards are chilled through, from her heart and lungs to her bone marrow. In the end she is transported home to the fishing village and cremated in an incinerator that belongs to a countryside temple. It's then that Du Li An thinks of the son Lau Lin took with her, the other key to the lock that is their secret. Du Li An makes two trips to Batu Gajah, but the three women who lived above the sundry shop have moved away, taking with them the three-year-old child plus all of Lau Lin's possessions on the excuse of repatriation to her family. One of the items, her Singer sewing machine, was speedily acquired by the boss lady of the sundry shop downstairs for eighty ringgit, with needles, thread, measuring tape, and so on thrown in for free.

The novel pretty much ends here. The rest is just the usual clichés that wrap everything up neatly. After finishing the book, you lie on the bed for a catnap, overcome by tiredness. When you wake up in the afternoon, you tear out the page in the book that belongs to you. Then you ride your motorcycle in search of the oldest library in this city. Returning the book is easier than you thought. The librarian who's getting on in years has his attention laser-focused on a badminton match on the TV. Without raising his head, without even checking the book, he flutters his hands to indicate you should set the book on the desk next to him.

On the way home you feel like you're carrying around a deflated balloon on your back, your book bag now limp and floppy without the tome. The lightness of it dismays you. You ride to the recently developed residential area. It spans about four hundred acres and consists of several hundred houses built exactly to two models chosen by the developers. The houses are crowded so close together and adhere to such strict geometric lines that they look comical, like their tiny plastic counter-parts in Monopoly. The evening sun's rusty rays gild you as you ride between two rows of identical houses. The sounds of spatulas stir-frying in woks drift from various windows, accompanied by the fragrance of hissing oil and garlic. You slow down until you're almost at a bicycle's speed and start to play "spot the difference" like you used to as a child, trying through a clumsy method of elimination to pinpoint the house where you live with Uncle Sai.

—3—

About *The Age of Goodbyes*—the truth is, there are many parts you never did read. But those take place years after you've passed away. By then the local literary scene, which had been in a bit of a slump, is rocked by an extraordinary event. An emerging writer no one has ever heard of wins a major literary prize in Europe with a novel written in English. This not only makes waves in the local literary scene but even garners high interest from the federal government.

The overnight sensation is a young woman of Chinese descent named Mariana Du. Born into a well-heeled family in the capital, she was educated entirely in English and Malay. She knows no Mandarin as a result, though she is a fluent Cantonese speaker. The prime minister at the time arranges for a special luncheon with this award-winning writer, an event covered with ample buzz by various newspapers in the country and resulting in coverage splashed across the front pages of all the dailies. The political coalition in power also takes credit for what it sees as an illustrious victory. Speaking through the Ministry of Education, the coalition both loudly proclaims and also broadly hints that today's truly "global national writer" is the result of its implementing the correct educational initiatives within this multicultural society. The claim, as the idiom goes, is that it takes ten years to cultivate a tree and a hundred years to nurture a person.

Mariana's prizewinning work is her debut. Titled *Adieu*, it centers around a multigenerational family narrative. It is later translated as 告別的年月 (*The Bygone Era of Goodbyes*) and 辭別 (*Farewell*) by overseas Chinese publishers, appearing in both traditional and simplified formats. During an interview, the author reveals that she used her own family history as a foundation, and enhanced the story with research and her own imagination to produce this magnum opus.

Mariana opens the novel with a joyous dinner banquet. The scene takes place in the country's capital, in a new restaurant[1] jointly launched by her grandfather and grandaunt.[2] The occasion is the one-month birthday of her grandmother's firstborn girl, and they have spared no expenses.

The scene is only the beginning of a very long book. Is the novel any good? Because it bears the stamp of approval from a major European prize committee, the local literati shy away from publicly considering its qualities. Though later on *Adieu* does spark a heated and juicy debate; the phrases "literature by writers of Chinese descent" and "Sinophone literature" are bandied about. Luckily you're already dead, or you would have become the next Fourth Person.

---

1. Called "Wui Hoi Grand Restaurant" in the book. The author clarifies that its original name in Chinese encompasses the meaning of convergence and confluence. Translators into both traditional and simplified Chinese settle on "匯海大酒家" in their translations.

2. The grandfather's sister. In the author's memory, she is a businesswoman "who worships our entire lineage of ancestors in her home."